A Case full of Insects

Jack Everett

Published by Bamboo Books
First published 2014

ISBN-13: 978-1499754971
ISBN-10: 1499754973

This book is a work of fiction. All the characters in this book have no existence outside the imagination of the author, and have no relation whatsoever to anyone bearing the same name or names.

Many thanks go to all the fictionalised characters that appear in the book who in real life have inspired and changed so many lives for the better. Also, to my younger sons, Felix and Oscar, for initiating stories on the road which became, in time, written tales. Finally, to those people who encouraged me into and through the publishing process: Jacqui Stearn, Rob Gardiner, Alice Pantin, Scott Messenger, Alice Shepherd, Kate Ward, Ricardo Hunt, Andrew Floyd and Leisa Wakling.

for
Coe Oona
Lawrence Pax
Felix Hickory
and
Oscar Radcliff

CONTENTS

1
The Old Ship

Before he was fifteen Loïc had slit a goat's throat, skinned it and made a carrying bag for orphaned kids. He had also been working the gardens and helping Beatrice his mother prepare food since he could remember and was skilled with a sling shot and a bow. It was now time according to his father to learn how to build a house. His father was getting on and had said it was time he knew how to look out for himself. He was still not strong enough to say no, neither did he want to; life in their mountain home suited him well. For most young people the isolation was too difficult. What interested them were cars and shopping, leaving home was what they had done in droves since before he was born.

Loïc's world expanded on his fifteenth birthday when his father Bertrand 'the dour' as his mother called him, presented him with a transistor radio. He placed it on a small shelf by the window of his room. At night as he gazed out on a star peppered sky a world of tongues and tunes crackled and sang their way into his life, feeding his imagination and colouring his dreams. Life in the nearest city held no substance for him.

Loïc knew that once most of the grandparents had died, his parents would be the last generation to work and live on this rugged and beautiful land. Many of the roofs had collapsed, the houses fast becoming ruins. The old life was marked by rusting wheels, faded curtains and dried out leather shoes. Weeds grew in the living rooms and bushes bloomed on the chimneystacks. It was hard to have neighbours who were mere memories.

The hamlet backed in below a ridge and looked out over limestone cliffs to a sweep of plain and the eastern seaboard. It hunched there like the wife of an absent sailor, watching the distant surf waiting for an arrival. This was country untamed, both harsh and vivid. The ruins of cut stone redoubts protruded from defendable outcrops, the higher ground was the domain of rosemary and goats. His were a hardy people embedded in their landscape. When he was small, families had tumbled out of every door. Now most of the houses were boarded or broken. Occasionally a shutter hinge spoke in the wind or a barrow wheel would clack on the cobbles. Gradually, after centuries of vibrancy silence had become the voice of the place.

Squatting behind the houses a tiny church clung with its one bell to the steep slope. For three generations there had been a priest in the village. Christianity had been a long time coming this far up the mountain. Now all naming, marriages and deaths were either recorded on paper in the vestry recess or carved in stone in the graveyard. It looked like the records were straight, everyone had a father and a mother; brothers had sisters with the same name, the families were now ordered. Or so the men thought, and since they thought they were in charge of such matters the women said nothing and let them believe what they liked. It is easier that way.

Down in the mill house by the stream lived the miller's family. In the autumn for a while the stones would grumble and grind but the work was soon done, five families don't eat so much bread and few of the terraced fields were put out to wheat any more. Only the miller's youngest daughter was still at home. The same age as Loïc, Anna Cecille had grown up with the spirit of nature flowing in her veins. They both knew all the hiding places that village children do, the ones used by each successive generation. There they had discovered themselves and each other during a time of change and decline.

When Bertrand had announced house building, it had seemed a little contrary as everything was falling apart, but within two days they had packed bags with clothes, tools and money, strapped them to the backs of the lead goats and set off east in the direction of the sea, herding the flock. With the clonking of bells and laughter in their voices, they took off down the mountain with the unknown at their feet and the rumour of a wreck on the beach. They arrived one rainy night days later at Fitou a village set back from the coast. A noisy bar found Loïc and Bertrand deep in conversation about the hulk of a four masted schooner that lay listing on a strand a short way south. She had sailed the world for 130 years and now lay holed in the stern so badly that no modern shipwright would touch her. She would never float again.

This was music to Bertrand's ears, good seasoned hardwood, waiting to be dismantled and given a new life. With the salvage papers on the table, a deal was struck; work would be able to start the next day. That night all in the bar were well pleased; with the main timbers of the deck of the old ship being traded for a flock of goats and a few too many drinks.

At sun up Loïc and Bertrand, tools on their backs, travelled the few miles south on a sturdy four-wheeler mason's wagon drawn by two, solid, short-legged Pyrenean workhorses. From the coast road, they saw the ship from a long way off, listing badly, half buried in the beach sand, tired and broken. One mast remained, two others were broken half way up and the last had long gone. Pieces of ragged sail trailed in the water, seaweed like, slipping in and out of the huge opening in her stern.

They tethered the horses to a large boulder high above the watermark and climbed down the pebble bank to the long strand. From close up, her bare breasted bowsprit towered over them, the salted planking lifted from her frame. The layers of barnacles that covered her hull alone were enough to ground her on this lonely spit of sand. No longer buoyant, the sea was hastening her end.

They waded out and threw grapple ropes up the stern and climbed aboard. They found much of the deck missing and what remained was scorched, revealing the squared up oak timbers that made up the structure of the deck. These were the ones they were after. They knew that once they had been taken, the back of the craft would be broken and she would soon be battered by the tides, fall open, spring planking from her sides and leave a skeleton of ribs for the seagulls to perch on. They looked at each other as they stood there on the deck, aware that they would be the last to do so in a long line of men whose lives had been transformed by the ship's travels round the globe. Theirs was the job of bringing this vessel with a hundred tales to tell to her end.

"We'll give the timbers of this grand old ship a new beginning." Announced Loïc as Bertrand grunted and set about examining the construction of the deck. "Yes, we'll bring these trees back onto land where they used to be."

The heart of oak cross braces were themselves the girth of a man and a good twenty feet in length. These were once trees in the fullness of their youth and since cutting and squaring up for boat building, had sailed the world under many captains and many more flags, riding out storms and mountainous seas.

Father and son set about with brace and bit, mallet and gouge to take out the oak pegs that held the joints. Swollen by years at sea the cracking of the tenons was a long job. By tapping in soft wood wedges to the peg less joints, wetting them down for expansion and waiting for the crack as the joints gained air and the timbers jumped free of their junction with the stem beam. From there the landward list of the ship served them well; with block and tackle off the remaining mast they dropped each timber over board into the rising tide and floated them to the shore and the waiting horses.

One by one ten main timbers were hitched to the harness then dragged ashore and rollered onto the flat bed. By the time they were done five days had passed and the masons wagon creaked and groaned under the weight, but it was solidly built and held. On the last night, as they cooked a snared rabbit over the fire, there came a series of loud cracks as the dowel pins in the keel gave way and splayed the ship like an open hand. They looked at each other and laughed. That they were no longer on board was a relief, that part of their job was done.

Since long before the timbers had been found, Bertrand had talked of being gripped by the vision of a special kind of construction that had come to him twice, once in a dream and again for real in the evening of the same day. The village had been busy then and full of life. A stranger had sat at the bar, an empty glass in front of him.

"Ah", he says, "you want a drink? I'll pay if you can solve this little problem. Balance my empty glass on these four matches, the heads touching the glass and the tails touching the bar. If you can, I buy the drinks. If you can't, you buy the drinks."

After a pause, Bertrand agreed to try as the image from his dream came into his hands. They both watched his fingertips arrange the matches to meet in the middle in a square each one resting on the previous until the fourth knitted under the first and locked into place. There, it was a tiny frame, on top of which he proudly placed the stranger's empty glass. The bar hushed, but the glass stayed as a coin was dropped into it.

"First time I ever lost a drink on that one," said the stranger. "First time I ever tried it," replied Bertrand.

He had often referred to this event and the odd confidence of the stranger. Now it was his plan to do the same thing on a large scale. He planned to re-roof the barn next to the house and create one big room. For what purpose he never could say, all he would admit after mulling it over was that it was the newness of the thing that interested him. Then he added prophetically. "Dreams made manifest must have consequences."

These reminiscences had passed between them as they encouraged the weary horses up the final incline into the village. Shouts were heard and the few remaining villagers appeared from above to watch the arrival of the timbers from the old ship. By the time they had been unloaded at the barn everyone was excited but tired. It was the first time in the people's memory that any of the village buildings had been repaired let alone rebuilt. Anticipation was in the air.

Later that week when father and son had recovered, a big fire was built, the fiddle and the concertina came out and the wine flowed freely. Song and dance filled the little plaza in the centre of the village and, for that evening at least, spirits were high. As the fire burnt down and the 'crème de chataigne' started to lace the white wine, Bertrand told their story. The deal, the deconstruction at the tide's edge and the long journey home. It was when Bertrand came to the part about the missing bridge that the musicians stopped playing and children climbed onto their parents' laps.

"To the south of Quillan, where the road crosses the River Aude, there are many bridges, the gorge sides are steep, the river narrows and one of the arched stone bridges had dropped. There was no going back with such long timbers and now there was no going forward either. It was evening and we made ready for the night and consideration as to our next move.

"Just before dawn there was a storm. It started with roiling thunder chasing the already high waters down the narrow gorge, bouncing off the sheer rock walls and disappearing downstream. Everything calmed for a while, then ball lightening zigzagged between the towering cliff sides, reaching down to the river surface from high over our heads. Occasionally it struck the rock surfaces where there were iron deposits and loud explosions shook the gorge, as rock broke free and plunged into the torrent below. The horses were terrified but they could only stand and tremble while we sat under the wagon, waited, and watched in awe as the river roared below.

"Then came the rain, the sky opened and dropped its load, fast and heavy. Within the hour the water level was rising, and with it came boulders and broken branches. The remains of the bridge stood some ten meters above the main flow where the gorge narrowed. Now, a white spume, almost within reach, roared through the narrows, rocks cracking together deep in the flow.

"As the light of day tipped the mountains, the rain ceased. It was then that the water level really started to rise. The rain had drained into the valley and now it tore downstream as if pursued. We stretched our stiff bodies at the edge of the collapsed bridge, watching the waters, mesmerised. Then came an eerie sound that shook the rock we stood on. A deep knocking in the earth itself. First we thought it was an earthquake, what else could make such an enormous sound?

"It was Loïc that saw it first. As we stood and watched, a huge jumble of tree trunks and broken branches were being forced downstream, a whole barrier was on the move, hammering on the stone walls of the gorge. The waterpower was enormous, forcing the tangle of splitting and crushed vegetation further and further into the narrow gap where the bridge had once stood. As the flood brought more and more debris from the banks up stream, so the waters rose higher and higher forcing its way up and over the building barrage.

"Very soon the water reached up to the road level and untying the frightened horses we fled up the road to find higher ground, leaving the wagon loaded with the timbers from the old ship to its fate. From the hairpin bend on the road above, we could see down into the gorge. We watched as more and more trees pounded into the existing barricade, both strengthening it and forcing the waters to rise over the top. By midday the roar of the waters had diminished and timidly we returned to check on the state of the road and our prize.

"Rounding the bend we saw the wagon, still loaded, standing in a mass of branches that had gathered at its wheels. At road level where the bridge had been, there was now a tangle of skinned and splintered timber and lying across the top, two huge tree trunks with the floodwaters spuming through the interwoven mesh of vegetation beneath. Downstream of this natural dam the water was near its normal level, flattening out into a discoloured stream.

"We looked at each other and laughed, tears of relief and dismay rolling down our cheeks.

"It was time to take our chances. Loïc tentatively stepped off the road and onto one of the trees that spanned the gap. It didn't move, he jumped up and down, it held, he walked across, and it seemed strong. I walked across the other one, they were all but parallel, and the whole structure was firmly wedged into the narrow gorge. It would, in time take some serious sawing and axing to clear. As we sat looking down into the gorge, our heads came up together.

"If we can get the horses across the rest will follow. We said at the same time and laughed. I know a thing or two about horses. They don't like being separated and where the leader goes the others will follow. However, to get a horse to walk across a tree trunk over a foaming mass of water was not going to be easy but not impossible. If the horse can't see too much, just where its feet are, then it's possible.

"Knowing this we fitted them with blinkers leaving a narrow view in front and led them up and down the road. After a while, they became more confident; slow but steady. Loïc went first; we each lead a horse across the larger of the two trees. Step by step, the horses trusted us. With their ears swivelling and their nostrils flared they trembled their way across to solid ground on the far side.

"With the horses safe, our real work began. We had already moved these oak timbers from sea to the land using the tide and horse power, now there had to be some way to bring the wagon and wood across a chasm with an angry river churning through it. By using the levers and ropes, we unloaded and dropped the front end of the wagon onto the two trunks. Using ropes and the horses, we dragged the wagon across to the other side on its axle. It was gradual heavy work and many times we thought that the unevenness of the trees and the weight was against us but by evening light, we had hauled it up onto the road on the far side.

"The next day we used the two trees to guide our old ship's timbers across, hauling and levering, working the strength of the horses to bring the dense oak beams to the other side. We were almost done, with the last timber from the old ship roped up and the horses ready to bring it across, when a deep roar came from the gorge. The water level was rising again and more debris was floating downstream on a huge wave; a higher barrage must have broken. The power of the water was immense and the barricade that we were crossing began to look very frail. Taking our knives we cut the horses free as the tangled barrier began to shift and change shape.

"Suddenly a huge swell lifted everything including the last timber as if it were mere matchwood and swept it away. When the water level on the road began to rise as we goaded the horses away, leaving our prize to the whims of the flood, but before long we were cautiously making our way back down, and there stood the loaded wagon with more debris woven through its wheels."

For a moment there was a stunned silence as their audience held its breath; then a wild cheer went up. The account brought heart to them; it was time for good things to happen in the village again.

As the fire burned down and the fiddle and the tambour played, Loïc found Anna Cecille sitting at his side smiling. He felt that one day they would be together; now was their time of friendship.

"Later", he said, "this will be more."

"There's no hurry", she smiled, "I enjoy knowing that we matter to each other."

Fitting the timbers from the 'old ship' as a barn roof required some serious engineering. Scaling up from matchsticks to boat timbers involved some careful consideration of weight and how to lift things into place. Bertrand kept musing about skyhooks but settled in the end on a realistic scissor prop. They decided to follow the example of the 'drinks trick' and use four of the timbers coming in from the corners to meet one on top of the other in a central square hole. Using a block and tackle, they lifted the four timbers up onto the four walls leaving an overhang for the eaves, which served as a counter balance for the beam weight. Then using the scissor prop they walked the end of the first timber out to the centre of the barn so that it ran from the corner up to the prop in the middle. The next timber they levered one end along the first until it too ran from a corner of the building into the central space. The third timber, with one end at the corner they slid the other end up to the centre forming the third side of a square hole at the centre. The fourth, with enough clearance, slid up the length of the third and under the end of the first to form a square central hole. Carefully they knocked out the legs of the scissor prop and lowered the self-supporting roof frame into place, each timber taking the weight of the others.

As they worked on the barn so Loïc and Bertrand became very close. The dangers involved developed a deep trust between them. Loïc often spoke of his feelings about Anna Cecille, but Bertrand would brush her aside saying, "Oh, she's not the one for you."

Loïc felt this to be out of character; Bertrand was naturally a generous man.

When Loïc pressed him to say why, he would just say, "She's not your type."

As the building progressed, Loïc spent most of his evenings with Anna Cecille and he began to suspect that his father was wrong, she most definitely was his type. They became close and were open about it. The more they were seen around together, the more distant the adult men became towards both Loïc and his father. If they did talk they spoke as if she didn't exist. Only Loïc's mother said good things about her and then only when they were alone together.

With the completion of the floor, the job was all but finished. Not only had they achieved the unlikely, but also in practise they seemed to have hit on a new way of building. The finished slate roof allowed light to enter the centre of the room and, once a miniature of the same frame was built over the central hole, the rain was kept out. The entire heavy loading on the walls was downwards with gravity, not pushing the walls outwards as with other roofs and the eaves were good shelter for animals and firewood. They were pleased and many came to marvel at the barn which amongst the people had become known as the 'the old ship'.

One late spring morning they were repairing the outside steps that led to the door when again Bertrand made a comment about Anna Cecille being unsuitable for him. Suddenly a pent up rage swept over Loïc, he'd heard enough. He sprang at his father, pinned him down on the steps and put a two-inch chisel to his throat.

"Enough!" he shouted in his face. "The more you bad mouth her the less I like you. Why are you so against her?"

In his attempt to stay calm Bertrand slipped on the step, the chisel sliced into his throat. As the blood welled up around the bevelled edge Loïc backed off, shocked by its vivid colour.

"She's taboo."

The blood oozed between his fingers.

"She's your half sister."

"What? How?"

"Her father was away fighting when she was made."

"So, how then, you mean you're her father?"

"This is what her mother tells me and she should know. Everyone knows; even your mother knows. So, she's not for you, she's taboo. Now back off and give me that cloth, I need stitching up."

"This is your taboo not mine. I don't care who her parents are I love her."

This was the first time these words had come from his mouth.

"This may be so, but nothing must come of it, you're too close in blood, your children would be only part formed."

Loïc believed this to be true. There were two such children in the next village; they sat together all day by the water fountain dribbling. People always crossed themselves as they walked past. Loïc did the same. Everyone knew.

He looked down crest fallen, saw the cloth, screwed it up and went to throw it at his father. For a moment, her image came between them. Faltering he dropped it into the outstretched hand, turned and walked down the steps of the 'old ship', his father's pleading voice at his back.

2
Whistling Troglodytes

First light the next day found Loïc throwing a few things into a bag, and scrawling a note to Anna Cecille explaining his departure. He cut the palm of his hand and pressed it against the back of the paper, as if to say this is my blood and yours? The radio and the message he wrapped in a cloth and hid them between the stones of their meeting place, paused, took in what he was doing, and then in turmoil, walked away. No-one had shown him what to do with feelings.

He saw no-one and struck out to the east, up over the summer meadows and past the rock peak. His heart was in his throat and his mind struggled to account for his aliveness. He only knew that he could stay no longer. A few words had changed everything. He hurried on over the first two passes, then the mountains became less familiar and he slowed, knowing he had no destination, just the need to be away from his love and his hate. He felt as though teeth were eating him from the inside. It was this painful impulse that set Loïc on a journey that he'd never thought of taking. He'd wanted more than his father, yes, but he'd never imagined a bigger world. Now he felt tricked and lied to. He felt he had to step away from the secure and familiar to find what was true for him. He had stepped unknowingly onto his own path.

For three days he walked along animal tracks, lost in loss, deep in the mountains but always heading east. On the third night as he shivered under his blanket in the dry leaves beside a fallen tree, he woke to find nestled in with him what he thought must be a bear cub. At first he froze knowing the mother would be nearby, but as all stayed quiet he threw his arm round the sleeping bundle and fell asleep. Come the morning he woke thinking he must have dreamt the bear until he noticed the warm pressed hollow of leaves at his side. He felt trusted, the bear; the ' keeper of the dream' had restored some measure of faith in himself, at the same time he knew he dare not think of returning.

When Anna Cecille found Loïc's hidden note, something felt right about his decision to go. She knew that it wasn't going to be easy without him, but she also knew that as they had grown closer it had become harder to ignore the whispered conversations. Life would be easier without the talk. She trusted how they felt about each other. She could live with that knowing.

Very soon she began to spend time outside the curtilage of the village, a basket over her arm and a cape for weather changes. She walked and collected plants, fruit and seeds; the landscape became her friend and companion. During September of that year, four months after Loïc's departure, the berry harvest was at its height. The summer had been dry and hot and the mountain paths were a profusion of sapid fruits, which stained her hands and mouth. These she collected and bottled for the lean months. It had been her grandmother, swathed in layers of skirts that would return, pockets bulging with myriad plants, who had taught her about the gifts that waited each day on the mountain.

In this way the young lovers were directed apart, the wounds in their hearts became their companions and their guides. And so it was and so it is for all of us, our paths are put beneath our feet, we either take them or we do not grow.

After Loïc's night with the bear cub his confidence was a little restored. He took his bearings from the rising sun and set out for the northeast, the coast and the major port of Marseilles. From there he found work on a ship going to the Canaries in the eastern Atlantic. He had his doubts about the captain who was clearly fond of the bottle and even more partial to the contents. Despite his doubts he signed on anyway. He was keen to be on the move and put some distance behind him.

It was a full moon by the time the small wooden vessel reached the coast of La Gomera, one of the southerly Canary Islands. By late afternoon the captain was looking for landfall, by early evening a big swell had begun to build. The wind changed direction and a heavy rain beat down from the north driving the boat away from land.

As usual the captain was drunk and
situation was a string of curses that defame
and half of his family. Defiantly he dropped
and hung his backside over the edge of the
washed his rear clean he swore at the sky.
behind the clouds while the wind built the waves into white crested peaks. Rapidly the swell of greying sea became mountainous, and the small craft raced across the surface as if it would fly away. Instead it tore down massive moving gullies and slewed up foaming slopes, the bow pointing at the sky, water filling the hold. The whole crew felt the end was at hand. Each in his own way praying to a greater power to calm the sea and save their lives.

As the sea rose up in ever increasing size so the frail craft seemed to shrink. The sea monstrous and merciless, the tiny boat a cork in a giant's play pond. In reality a skiff in an Atlantic storm. As the rain beat down visibility dimmed, the moon slipped behind heavy cloud and with it went sight of land. At this point the enraged captain gave the order for the sail to be dropped completely, thrust a bucket into Loïc's hands and told him to climb off the stern and bale out the tender which was by now full of water and a drag on any progress the boat could make in the tempestuous wind. Forcing him over the back of the boat, the captain blocked his return with a mallet. Fearing the captain more than the storm Loïc baled bucket after bucket, seeing little progress, but baling anyway. The boat and its tender drifted at the mercy of the waves, rising and falling, a stillness within the huge motion of the storm. Before Loïc had finished, the sail was rising again and the pull of the wind gave them direction. As the captain pulled him aboard he roared a satanic laugh and took the wheel. The heart of the storm died away and a new wind drove them to the southern tip of La Gomera where they grounded on black sand.

They woke next morning to find the boat set at a sharp angle, dug into the volcanic sand that fringed the island. Casting out an anchor, they would have to wait for the next storm, or a high tide, to refloat. Loïc, delighted at being beached, took off inland, the terrain immediately rising at the p angle of a huge volcanic cone. Within two hours he was high above the shore deep in a steep ravine. The day was hot and he was exhausted from the night before, soon he was asleep in the sun. When he woke it was to the sound of whistling, it wasn't a tune as such, more a variety of trills and repeated notes, birdlike and nearby. As he lay there a long wooden pole was thrust down on to the rock next to him and a figure vaulted overhead. It was a long vault and done at speed to clear the wide ravine. The figure was dressed in a skin apron and evidently male. Then more whistling and another flew over head. Neither had seen him but his curiosity was aroused. He climbed out of the ravine to see two figures jumping ravine after ravine, long poles held high as they ran across the ridges between the ravines. One took off at an angle up the mountain towards a flock of goats with clonking bells at their necks. The men, whistling to each other, brought them down. It was a strange sight, the goats popping out of the ground then disappearing down the next ravine, the men flying up into the air dangling on the end of poles. They covered the rough terrain much faster than the goats that had four times as much footwork to do than the men, who stood around whistling to each other from a distance.

These were the Guanches, the natives of La Gomera. Some said they were descended from the Berber of the Atlas Mountains on the mainland, some said they were related to one of the twelve tribes of Israel. Whoever they were, they certainly knew how to get around using their vaulting poles and the Silbo. That was the name of this whistling which was a whole language of its own. Loïc was impressed. He caught up with them, and found that with sign-language they could talk, and when Loïc pointed down to the boat on the shore they understood where he had come from.

Pulling another pole out from a hiding place and throwing it to him, they showed him how to hold it for vaulting. Loïc was even more impressed, when after a few failed attempts he managed to clear a small gully. They all fell about whistling and then flew atop their poles down to the beach, the boat and the disgruntled looking crew.

The tide was coming in and the boat was knee deep in water, enough to refloat . Using the three poles they levered it round to point out to sea. Signing that there would be a high tide in three days, the Guanches left for the mountain and their goats. Loïc grabbed his bag and left with them. The captain belched and farted and the rest of the crew stood around looking glum. These were men tied down to their lives, conditioned and set. Loïc was not about to lose his freedom to their problems.

As soon as they were off the beach the Guanches set off at a diagonal to the slope, pitching themselves onto their poles and clearing the gullies and ravines. So long as you swung your legs through first there was a good chance of clearing the drop and touching down on the far side. Going up was more difficult, since more effort was needed. If you didn't swing the body weight just right it was easy to get perched on the pole in mid gully and then either drop or slide down into the depths. Either way Loïc was soon left behind while the shepherds dodged up and away. Eventually they stopped for him to catch up, and then they fell about laughing when Loïc's pole stuck in a hole and he was left stranded like a monkey clinging to a stick.

Halfway up the mountain the Guanches suddenly disappeared. Vaulting and whistling one moment, the next nothing, gone. He stood, pole in hand listening to the breeze in the scrub, scanning the mountainside for movement. How did they do that, the place was bare, no trees, nothing. Suddenly there was an explosion of laughter from nearby. He turned to see a closed door in the rock face. It looked so absurd that he almost chose not to believe that it was there. Then it burst open and the two laughing Guanches tumbled out and thrust a glass of clear liquid into his hand.

As he drank, it burned its way down his throat. They plied him with another as they showed him the inside of their troglodyte home. The wooden door had been built into a dry stonewall across the opening, otherwise it was all natural cave tapering back into mountain. A low shelf was organised like a bed with goatskins and an arrangement of worked stone formed the chimney with a cooking iron and a grate. Shafts of light came through chinks in the door wall, lighting the interior. Numerous goatskin items hung from pegs in the front wall; water bags, collars, straps, coats and boots. Dried meat and cheeses hung from the roof; their flock provided almost all of their needs. Outside they showed him a carefully constructed goat proof terrace with a fenced off overhang. Inside, squash, maize and beans were growing in profusion. Going inside for a refill they revealed their storeroom that was carved out of the soft tuffa rock at the back of the cave. "Guaycos" they said, holding up black obsidian cutting tools.

The deep recess was lined with stone shelves where they stored the produce from their tiny terrace, to see them through the winter. Above the cave a collection of ancient looking vines hung heavy with the year's crop. They touched their glasses to the swollen bunches, Loïc doing the same. They all laughed.

Finally they showed him their water supply, of which they were justifiably proud. Above and behind the cave there was a tiny seepage which oozed out from between two rocks, clear and cold. Most people would walk past it, but these two brothers had noticed that all year it was the same, never more, never less. They had run a stick from the crack in the rocks to the neck of a goatskin carafe, allowing the water to run down the stick. Two days later it was full. From there they made pantiles over their legs and fired them in the hearth. Laying them from the seepage to the back of the cave they formed a channel. Then with their obsidian chisels they had cut a cistern from the rock, which in turn flowed to a trough for the goats and then away to their vegetables. As Loïc clapped, they laughed and reached for that clear throat burning liquid, which made them all laugh even more.

Loïc liked their style; turning harshness into paradise was a good human trait. So often he'd seen hardship harden and break men in his village, but these two had their hearts and their heads working together. When asked, he stayed, mostly to master the vaulting, but the Silbo language also fascinated him. By way of exchange he put the reciprocal frame in front of them one evening.

He did it with six of their vaulting poles and then threw a

rope loop round where they met to stop the slip. They were delighted, jumping onto the central ring they bounced up and down to check it out, it held. That night there were a lot of difficult mimed questions, but they got there with the help of the burning liquid and loads of laughter.

A month later, the shepherd boys, with his help had built a big platform across a gully using the reciprocal system as a goat shed roof. They covered it with thick slabs of rock and the goats sat on top in the morning and underneath in the heat of the day. Much like their house, until you were right on top of it you couldn't see anything, just another part of the mountain. The boys loved it and with a safe outdoor fire and a smoke hole in the roof they moved their beds outside and sat watching the sun set out to the west while they cooked with all the goats bedded down in the back of the shelter.

One early morning, the boys, clean and sober took Loïc up and over the mountaintop. They passed through a fog forest, green tunnels of living fossils. Ancient laurel, holly, ferns and mosses formed an evergreen cap to the highland. Tertiary era plants, contemporaries of the dinosaurs, surviving remotely as an endemic evergreen forest. The emerging sun pierced the canopy, revealing smooth grey stemmed laurel trunks, some a metre across, forming an impenetrable mass of magical forms. Some way down the slope, out in the open between ravines, stood the reason for their early morning enthusiasm.

"El Draco, Dragon tree", they announced touching the stems with a delicate respect. This aged plant of the asparagus family stood five metres tall and had numerous trunks clinging together before separating into wriggling branches tipped with pointed leaves forming a huge mushroom shape. They had come to collect the fruit of this sacred tree, which was originally fertilised by its seeds passing through the gut of a turkey sized flightless pigeon, *Raffus cucullatus*. With the bygone biped now extinct, germination was the work of humans. This extraordinary tree reputedly had come into being from the blood spilt as Hercules battered the hundred-headed serpent, Ladon, guardian of the orchard of the Hesperides. As the serpent's blood spilt, it spread, and where it fell on these offshore islands, there sprouted into being tubular plants with a blood red sap. The Guanches valued this tree juice as a medicine and an embalming fluid. Once many moons past, weight for weight it was more valuable than gold; the red resin of the dragon tree became the favoured varnish of the world's violin makers.

They spent the day around the tree collecting the sweet orange seeds and bleeding stem and leaf sap into tumblers. Then, refreshed by their day of reverence they trudged up through the darkening green tunnels of 'bruma' mist to their troglodyte home laden with an annual harvest.

Soon Loïc felt it was time to move on and the shepherd boys found him a boat going south. She was a trader taking wine down to Senegal and the Cape Verde Islands. Loïc had never heard of these places but his taste for adventure had been aroused and in preparation he made a pair of goatskin air bags, because being a mountain boy he had never learnt to swim.

Since his first storm at sea, Loïc had realised that dying came at any time and to be one jump ahead might help to tell his tale for no one knew where he was or where he was going. It would be his wits that would keep him alive.

With a clear blue sky and a light breeze the 80 foot wooden hulled trade ship slipped her moorings from the Playa d'Inglesia and silently took a bearing of south-southwest. The steady breeze was hot and dry bringing a fine dust off the Sahara desert out to the east. If you didn't cover your face with a 'kerchief the grit was soon between your teeth. It filled the well-patched sails that gave the ship an impoverished look that belied the good trade she did up and down the coast. The captain, a Spaniard, was wise to the ways of the opportunists who plagued the trade in the region. He never flew a flag unless it was the same as the approaching ship and he was heavily armed. His ship looked as though she would soon sink, but it was all theatre, the patches were sewn onto good sails.

The Captain had agreed to take Loïc on the condition that he worked his passage and he was put to work from dawn to dusk, at the beck and call of the captain who made sure that he never had an idle moment. His job was all aspects of the ship's maintenance, from coiling ropes in perfect no slip towers, to slopping out the kitchen. Other chores included setting hooked lines with spinners at the stern, bringing in the catch and filleting them for the cook, sewing and patching the spare sails using old gunnysacks. These sacks were stencilled and stamped with the names and produce of exotic places that Loïc had never heard of. As he worked with them the smells and names conjured mystery in his imagination. All the hours of the day he and everyone else on board, was busy, the only looking at the horizon done by the captain and the bosun. As the days passed he was asked to do less and less, he knew what was needed and so just did it. Occasionally the captain would shoot him a passing scowl but never passed any comment.

On the fifteenth day they sighted land, an island out to the starboard, bare and grumbling with two smoking volcanoes. The word was that there were two others, both barren rocky sandbars, also deserted. It was Santiago the fourth and last island going south that was their port of call, for water from the Riberia Grande, best known best for being the last water stop before the Caribbean by slavers coming off the West African coast. The slave trade was supposed to have stopped 200 years ago but the captain said you could still buy slave stock that had never been granted freedom, and those he added, could be black or white.

3
Amazing Grace

These were the Cape Verde Islands, 600 miles off the Senegalese coast, first occupied by the Portuguese when slavery was at its height in the 1500s. Since then the slavers had established a small fortified garrison at Cidade Velha at the mouth of the river, the Riberia Grande.

This was a strange landscape of smoking volcanoes and barren plains littered with pancakes of rock that had cooled where they landed. These once molten stones made walking impossible unless they were cleared into pathways or piled into circular compounds to house trapped hairy boars, the only domesticated animal on the island.

When they docked at Cidade Velha late in the afternoon the tiny quay and town was in full swing,; it was market day and as in most hot countries the cool of the evening was the best time to do business. A few stalls sold fruit and vegetables, another some dry goods, rice, couscous and the like. Across the square, pieces of hanging meat attracted a swarm of flies. On the corner an enormous woman dressed in a petticoat shouted about the virtues of her plastic calabashes, no other sound penetrating the thick air.

In the centre of the square stood a barley twist marble column elevated on three octagonal stone steps. Four metal hooks protruded from its top. This Loïc was told was the Pelourinho, the pillory from which runaways were suspended, often upside down,.and whipped. He gave it a wide berth and walked down a small street of single storey stone buildings with palm thatch roofs, out to the dried up bed of the Riberia Grande. There came a terrible sound from the other side of the riverbed. In a motionless row sat the remains of men, eyes bright red, mouths slack with hardly a movement between them. Behind was the origin of the noise, a man and donkey operated a sugar cane press. Its groaning and squealing wooden cogs were punctuated by the braying of the balding donkey. The sickly smell from the vats drifted over to him and he recognised the smell of 'grog'. The row of faces that sat watching him did not respond to his greeting. Red eyes registered in dead brains, there was no recall left in these blank faces, their souls stolen by the alcohol; one spirit had replaced another. He turned back towards the ship. As he walked down the dry riverbed toward the beach he heard music. On the edge of the square a group of musicians serenaded the lethargic shoppers. The music was true to its name, 'la mourna', a mixture of the guitar, a singer of great sadness and a strange ribbed piece of metal stroked with a nail, for this was the rhythm section.

Out of Africa the slaves had been stopped from playing the drum, it was thought to quicken the blood and therefore be too dangerous by the Portuguese. A ship full of slaves outnumbered the slavers fifteen to one and it was only the shackles worn by their captives that kept control. Now that slavery was illegal, the flattened, then crimped iron ankle strap was still there, but now it was in the music. It was the missing drum, rasping and ringing, holding the beat. There was a longing in the songs that made Loïc think of his own rugged mountain homeland and the girl he'd left behind. The thoughts brought a tightness to his chest and salt to his eyes.

The arrival of the 'wine ship', was evidently a welcome occasion in Cidade Velha, and the captain was soon opening a bottle or two with the mayor and the only policeman in town. The music became more rhythmic and soon feet were finding steps that they thought long forgotten. By nightfall half the cargo of casked wine had been swung ashore by the yardarm and sold. The Captain ordered three days shore leave and went in search of new cargo and personal pleasure.

For Loïc it was an opportunity to explore. Next morning with a few provisions in a gunny sack over his shoulder he took to the dry riverbed and walked inland looking for the water that once made this island so essential to the slave trade. The riverbed was forty metres wide where it met the beach, giving good reason for the founding of port.The riverbed swung through a broad swathe of palm trees before coming to the bend where the hellish sounds of the sugar cane crusher stood. The blank faces still sat in a row watching the waterless river flow past. He hurried on, avoiding contact. Tiny fields of maize contained by drystone walls lined the river sides. Small paths led to more stone houses with wilted thatch pitched up on the banks. A slavelaid stone path wove its way between the fields, he took it. The path turned into steps that led up the steep bank to the plateau above, but he passed them by and followed the dry riverbed. Soon all signs of human settlement dropped away, but there was still no sign of water.

Curious about the river's disappearance he wandered inland. Soon he was in a canyon with steep sides and no way of climbing the cliffs. The palms along the banks gave way to a massive trunk, the girth of which he'd never seen before. It would take twenty people holding hands to ring its trunk. But more remarkable was its appearance. Squat and broad, it was not so high before it divided into seven parts that looked more like tapering roots than branches. Occasionally it sprouted solitary flowers or pairs of waxy leaves. Even the tips of the long tendril-like arms of the tree carried very few leaves, making the whole tree look like an enormous turnip, 'the upside down tree' as it is known.

This was Loïc's first encounter with a baobab tree. Pitched up on a bank next to the river's course the tree's size was only visible from a distance. Huge buttress roots, folded and tapering grew down from the many divisions of the trunk. These curves snaked into earthing roots, a family could be hidden in the folds of just one of the many buttresses. The size and number of these roots made it hard to experience the tree as a single growth, simply walking around the tree was a challenge. It sat on a steep bank next to where the river had once flowed, buttresses bracing the down side, forming huge curtains, blocking the way and folding him into dark dead ends. The upper side of the trunk was just as convoluted, snaking roots anchored the enormous growth to the bank above. At one time it would have known a profusion of water, when wildness and volcanoes were the only inhabitants of these islands.

'This tree,' thought Loïc, 'must surely be two thousand

years old.' The bark was textured like an elephant's skin and had the memory of many centuries deep within its smooth exterior. 'How can this mammoth survive unless its roots reach down to the water' he thought as he moved up stream, still curious to know the river's story.

Gradually the foliage either side of the riverbed became lush and at last Loïc arrived at a slimy green puddle. In the distance he heard the laughing singsong of women's voices. Drawn by the sound he walked on until he came to a huge cliff face raised across the riverbed. From half way up the smooth surface trickled a flow forming a pool at its base. Here it was that the women washed their clothes and themselves.

So there was still water, but not enough to feed a river. The seepage in the cliff face was some eight metres below the lip. From its smooth curves this was once a forceful waterfall. As he climbed the steep bank of rocks to gain the higher riverbed the women shouted at him wagging their fingers, warning him off. Loïc took the warning wrongly, he laughed and they threw their hands up in despair.

Above, the landscape was very different, the heat rebounded off the sharp rocks. The canyon soon tapered into a narrow cut which abruptly ended in another wall of rock, this time enclosing him apart from the narrow entrance gap. He looked up to get a sense of the missing water flow. There sat a large male monkey armed with a rock sitting above the way back. It bared its teeth. Suddenly the rock crashed at his feet; it had come from directly overhead. So there were at least two monkeys onto him. He flattened himself against the overhang as another rock shattered in front of him gashing his leg. It was time to be out of there but the big male was still armed and waiting for him to make a move. He was trapped. He tried edging round and another rock smacked down into the dead waterfall basin. His interest in water suddenly evaporated. If he had a future he would listen to women's warnings.

A primordial energy froze him to the spot, his body changed, fear took over. Now it was fight or flight. He felt a strength take hold of him, but there was nothing to grapple with and nowhere to run. Another intelligence moved inside him and he began to sing, a child's song about goats climbing mountains. As he sang he watched the expression of the alpha male change, as with a perplexed tilt of the head it moved from aggression to curiosity. A deep inner loss spread across its face, followed by a loss of intention, which had been to get a look in Loïc's gunnysack. Shoulders hunched the rock dropped from its hand; the fingers became limp, as if over taken by a great tiredness.

The monkey cannot sing and would dearly love to because then it would have its own story to tell.

With aggression turned to confusion it shambled out of view without looking back. Loïc made for the undefended gap; he glanced up, no monkeys. Once he was clear of the gully he looked back; the three monkeys sat together, flea picking as if nothing had happened.

His heart was still racing when he got back to the now deserted women's washing pool. He sat for a while regaining his breath and his heartbeat. That was his first monkey encounter; they were scary with a quick penetrating force. As he sat with his feet in the water washing the cut, his fingers trailing across the surface, he realised again how alone he was in this uncertain world. He had put himself in the path of danger and drawn it towards himself. There was no other reason, he had created the situation. 'Surely,' he thought 'if I can make that happen then I can make anything happen.'

With these reflections and fear draining from his body he saw his face clearly in the pool. His experiences away from the mountain village had changed him. The laughter lines round his eyes had increased and the query on his brow had appeared as a knotted line. He had become distanced from innocence and closer to doubt. His intelligence had moved from his heart to his head.

The light began to leave the canyon walls, purple shadows appeared between the orange rocks. It was time to move. His return would take too long along the riverbed. When he reached the slave built stone stairway, he took its uneven twisting steps up onto the plateau above and into the setting sun. There on the leafless plain, peppered by beads of rock he found himself being watched from a distance by a familiar pair of eyes. The alpha male had trailed him to make sure that he left the canyon territory. Occasionally he barked just so that his position was quite clear. Outriding Loïc all the way to the town, he then silently dropped over the canyon's edge and out of sight.

As Loïc climbed down towards the town he came to the crumbling church of Nossa Senhora do Rosario. There he was stopped in his tracks by the sound of singing. As he stood beside the tombstone of a wealthy Portuguese sailor, a priest appeared at the heavy wooden doors and beckoned him in.

"What is this song? I know it well."

"This song, said the priest, "is a hymn with a history."

"Ah yes, It's Amazing Grace."

"Indeed it is and do you want hear its story? Everyone knows the words but no-one knows the story."

They took their seats on either side of the porch, and as the choir sang, the priest told Loïc the story.

* * * * *

"John Newton was the captain of a slaver out of West Africa heading for the New World with a full cargo of chained men, women and children in the hold of his ship. His was one of many trading ships working the 'triangle' as it was known. He had recently unloaded printed cotton, copper pans, iron bars and gunpowder at the cantonments and garrisons in Senegambia on the West African coast. It was there he had bought slaves for delivery to the West Indies. From there he planned to ship sugar, indigo and raw cotton to the English West country. This was the triangle. His trade was considered to be quite legal and his ship's papers were underwritten in the port of Bristol. He was a rich man with a hard heart.

Having filled his water barrels from the Riberia Grande and stocked up on salted pig, at Cidade Velha, he set sail, hoping to cross the Atlantic in four or five weeks. Reaching mid ocean they ran into rough weather and for three days and nights they could only use one sail to give them any headway, the wind was that strong. The ship was tossed about with little chance of survival. However survive it did and once the storm was over and the sea quiet again Captain Newton checked his ship. There was little damage and all the crew were safe except the ship's bosun who had been swept overboard just after relieving the captain at the helm. Being from a good Christian family, he grudgingly thanked God for his safe keeping from the storm. It was as he did this, standing at the helm cutting through the calming sea in the evening light, that the voice of the now drowned bosun came to his shoulder and told him that it might be wise if he checked his cargo. Alarmed by the familiarity of the voice he turned to find no one there.

"Why is that?" he found himself asking.

"Because Captain," came the bosun's voice, "I fear that their value may be much reduced."

"By fever?" he inquired.

"By severe chain injuries and overcrowding." came the reply.

This was a captain proud of being able to carry twelve more slaves than his competitors by stowing the children on improvised racks above the adults who were laid head to toe unable to stand sit or even turn over. Chained by one ankle only he had further saved money, reasoning that if their arms were free then they could look after each other thus saving on the extra expense of a surgeon's assistant. He thought through these matters with a degree of pride as he stood there on the deck.

"Sir, the hold, the cargo," the bosun's voice reminded him.

"Yes, yes, I will attend to this myself."

As he went down the steep wooden steps into the hold, he realised that it was a long time since he had inspected this part of the ship. Ahead of him the ship's surgeon began to wretch as a foul stench billowed out of the lower hold as the hatch was lifted. Both men gagged with horror as the smell of vomit and urine, faeces and blood, reached down into their stomachs.

Carrying lanterns to give them some idea of the mayhem at their feet they crouched their way down the 'slops run'. It was hard to move, mangled legs, torn and tangled were everywhere. Blood and bones in equal measure. In some places heaps of bodies were so crushed between the layers of shelving that no movement or sound could they detect. In other places there was a disturbing low groan that came from the dim stench. Still Captain Newton could only think of the money he was going to lose. It was not until he heard a feeble female cry that he thought about lives.

"Unlock the fetters, wash this place down and pump out the bilges then bring me a head count of the living." With that he left, a 'kerchief pressed over his mouth. As he reached the hold ladder, about to step up onto the first rung he noticed a figure huddled beneath. The bloody stump of a leg stuck out, the flesh torn; blood oozed on to the floor.

The colours red on red on red on drying red.

'Like the insides of my own men', he thought as he climbed out of the carnage.

In the air on deck the thought persisted.

'Like the insides of my own men.'

Captain Newton was one of a large breed of men that did not believe that humanity could come with a black skin.

'Like the insides of my own men.' Persisted. This notion that there were human beings in the hold of his ship was beginning to get a grip on his thinking. This he did not like, it made for a very uncomfortable realisation, but realise it he did.

He ordered that the loose slave underneath the hold ladder be cleaned and brought to his cabin at once. He needed to be rid of this nagging sentimentality. He needed to be sure.

He poured himself a glass of port and prepared himself for being wrong. Of course they weren't the same as his own men, because that would mean that they were the same as him on the inside. He called for the ship's surgeon; he needed confirmation.

There was a knock at the door and the surgeon presented himself. There was another knock at the door and the first mate stood there with a black man leaning on an improvised crutch. Clearing a carpet from the floor the captain told him to lie down. They looked at each other, the slave being seen for the first time by his captor; the white man looking for signs of pain in the black man's face. Everything froze. Shocked that the slave had the nerve to look back at him, Captain Newton ordered the surgeon to examine the stump where he stood. As he did so the surgeon described the fractured remains.

"The fibula, broken. The tibia, broken. Longus tendon, detached. The brevis tendon, detached. Soleus muscle, detached. Achilles tendon, frayed and detached. Remains of detached skin, veins, arteries. You want me to continue?"

"And, said the captain, you would expect to find the same if the bosun were to lose a foot?"

"Yes I believe so, said the surgeon, with the exception of skin pigmentation, exactly the same."

"All right, you can leave us now." he said, pushing his chair toward the Negro. The surgeon and the first mate backed out the door.

Captain Newton walked round the seated figure. His mind was in turmoil. His usual blustering confidence was very disturbed. Images of the bosun smiling rose up in front of him. What his feelings were he was no longer sure, but they were certainly strong. He believed he could re-establish the inhumanity of the slave in some other way.

"I am Captain Newton," he started, uncertain as to where this was going.

"I am Chief Mapfumo," A gentle voice came from the man in front of him.

"You speak English!"

"Reasonably well."

Newton needed a seat now and his body temperature was rising.

"How?" he said in disbelief.

"My father was English speaking, he helped an English missionary to understand the Koran."

"The Koran?" Newton was already out of his depth.

"Yes, we used to learn nursery rhymes, it was a novelty. I still don't understand what they mean, but as children we were told English might be useful one day."

For the next hour they talked openly and personally until Mapfumo's wincing brought Newton to his new senses. Not only did he give Mapfumo water from his own carafe, he put into operation a whole new agenda for his ship. First he called the whole crew up on deck and told them that from now on all slaves were to be treated as humans and not animals and anyone found doing otherwise would be kept in the hold. He ordered all slaves to be brought up on deck. He also ordered that the dead should be wrapped in old sailcloth and prepared for burial.

One hundred and eight living souls came out of the hold that day; only twelve of those could stand. Eighty-four dead were brought up including all the children. The racks in the hold were removed and the walls and floor scrubbed clean. All shackles were removed from the slaves and their wounds dressed with pitch and kerosene. Many would die from infection but measures were taken as best they could. When boats full of slaves were lowered over the side to wash in the sea, many of the slaves became fearful that they would be cut loose or worse be expected to swim. Chief Mapfumo, leaning over the gunwales did his best to reassure them that the sooner they washed the sooner they would be back on deck.

By the time Newton and Mapfumo had slid the last body overboard with prayers in two languages it was dark. The slaves returned below to the hold and arranged themselves as best they could, to grieve their lost people. That night the ship was becalmed, not a whisper of wind came from anywhere. All night the beginnings of 'la mourna' and weeping came from below decks. All night Captain Newton tossed in his bunk. At dawn he fell asleep. Within the hour he was awake again as wind from the west gathered in the limp sails. He gave orders to turn the ship and set a new course for Dakar on the West African coast.

The crew were now convinced that Newton had become insane and the talk of mutiny was on their breath. Sensing this Captain Newton set the men extra duties, mending sails, caulking leaks, re-lashing ropes, anything to keep the men apart so that gossip did not develop. Those that he did trust were sent below to tend to the needs of the slaves. He said nothing of release; he was not that clear in his thinking. He was following an impulse that was not backed by logic. That day the wind was with them. Newton stood on the bridge at the helm, commanding the ship. It was here that he was overcome with grace. It was then that words came to him. It was a song that took the form of his epiphany. It came in the form of the seven verses of a hymn."

* * * * * *

As the priest came to the end of his story, candlelight and the last rehearsed verse seeped from the interior of the church.

Amazing grace has set me free
to touch to taste to feel.
The wonders of accepting love
have made me whole and real.

"Once they reached land," the priest added, "Newton released all the slaves, returned to England and in time became a rector and preacher at the church of St Mary Woolnoth, in the City of London. Through his preaching he became the mentor of one of his parishioners, one William Wilberforce and hence the anti-slavery campaign. He described himself as being, ' haunted by the ghosts of twenty thousand slaves.'

By the time Loïc left the church porch it was dark. Tears stained his cheeks and his heart was in turmoil. His ship was silently rising and falling on the port swell, the cook was asleep, the crew on land. Loïc took to his canvas hammock.

4
The Hunter Plant

After leaving the Cape Verde Islands they sailed south in search of new cargo; men in chains filled Loïc's dreams. Without cargo, the atmosphere on board soured. The Captain turned his troubles on his crew, cutting rations and banning music. Many talked of leaving the ship at first landfall. There was trouble brewing and Loïc too wanted out. By the time they reached San Tome in the Bight of Bonney he had seen enough of the sea and decided to take his chances travelling over land as soon as they docked.

When the boat docked at Port Gentil on the West Gabon coast half of the crew, desperate to leave, accepted half wages and took their bags. Loïc agreed to stay on board as anchor-man and was fully paid. Soon after docking, the captain, who during the voyage from the Cape Verde islands, had become daily more mean and nightly more isolated from his men went ashore in search of cargo, knowing he had saved himself a good pocketful in wages.

Loïc waited until the following evening, still there was no sign of the captain. With his gunnysack on his shoulder he walked down the gangplank for the last time. He knew that it was asking for trouble to stay in the town so under cover of darkness he took off inland as a dawn sky woke up a whole new continent and a new chorus of birdsong.

Seconds after he woke slumped on his gunnysack Loïc knew he was being watched. It wasn't as if there were eyes on him; it was like having someone exploring his insides. He was on the outskirts of town and there was no one about. He looked around again, was that someone over there sitting in the shade? He was being scrutinised by a very old and very small man, the same colour as the tree he sat next to; the same tree that shaded Loïc. If the feeling hadn't been so strong he would never have noticed him. His skin was the colour and texture of tanned leather. His teeth were black or missing and his eyes were a deep green. He sat at a respectful distance, his body relaxed and waiting, his face moving between amused and blank. Under the gaze of this small man, Loïc, instead of feeling uncomfortable, began to breathe deeply. Soon he was as still as his watcher. Time drained away. There was no urgency to fill the space. For Loïc just being on land that didn't sway was a relief. At this moment waking did not appeal to him. He went back to sleep.

Not for long. Yhis time he was wide awake as if something had woken him. Soon the small man and the young man were talking without words.By quickly turning the wrist with the palm up and raising the eyebrows at the same time, asked a question.

All the fingertips of the right hand touching the lips of an open mouth, asked for food. A hand on a tilted cheek, talked of sleep. Shrugs, grimaces and smiles gave replies.

They exchanged names and Loïc explored the back of his nose as he repeated the name, N'zingu, while the old man from the Babongo tribe laughed at his attempts. By nightfall they knew things about each other that no one else did. A closeness had rapidly grown between them and they fell asleep that night in good company.

Next morning Loïc followed the diminutive man away from the shanty at the edge of town and into the rainforest. Immediately a thick greenery heavy with the scent of decay, coloured by flourishes of exotic flowers interwoven with dangling creepers, enveloped him.

Everywhere a voracious mass of different insects were eating vegetation. Brightly coloured flocks of screeching birds stooped between the treetops. Overhead was a dense mixture of greens. Occasionally a huge fallen tree lay across their path where shafts of sunlight revealed a moving mass of floating and flying insects that gave the air the thickness of water.

With the swing of his machete N'zingu kept the shoulder-wide path open. All day they walked, stopping only to take drinks from Loïc's goatskins, which N'zingu stroked with approving puckered lips and a nod. He gathered the occasional ripe fruit as they went but did not eat. By evening they came into a settlement of palm roofed huts.

"Ngola," N'zingu announced as he led him to an outlying hut by the river. Here there were other Babongo people all diminutive and dark skinned. Together they ate fresh fish, exchanged news and marvelled at the 'white man' N'zingu had found, touching his skin and staring into his blue eyes with expressions of wonder and disbelief. Eventually the hammocks came down from the roof and everyone slept. As he lay there Loïc realised that this was his first onland night off the ground. At sea he found it difficult to sleep without a hammock. Here the ground was teeming with life, including snakes and scorpions. He noticed that a whole family of four fitted diagonally into a hammock. Then he fell asleep.

For the next two days they travelled in a pirogue with a long necked outboard motor slapping the muddy waters of the River G'uango. Staying close to the bank they nosed their way against the current. Occasionally they passed small bamboo and palm leaf river shanties. Some with white painted, cross topped mission churches. Occasionally they hailed fishermen out with nets and harpoons. But mostly they cut through the brown water and watched the dense rainforest slide past in an ever unfolding curtain of green.

When wildlife appeared N'zingu became very animated and chattered enthusiastically in Creole which, once his ear was tuned in, Loïc could understand. He pointed out a sloth, hanging immobile and staring as they passed. Crocodiles lurked in the shallows, just blinking eyes and flared nostrils. What lay below the water Loïc had no idea, N'zingu just shook his finger. Birds and fish were everywhere and when they disturbed a group of hippos on the bank Loïc couldn't believe his eyes. Gradually the smells of the forest and the river washed over everything, leaving him hot, humid and raw.

Towards the second afternoon Apari was reached. This was a town of some size, reaching away from the river bank into a large forest clearing. This was a trading post, everything was for sale; either it was coming out of the forest or it was going in.

Boats, all variations of the canoe, were tied up at the small jetties that clung to the bank. There was a mixture of people milling round the market place. The taller coastal Mitsogo people, dressed in various ways of tying a coloured cloth around one shoulder, and amongst them the many Bantu people strutted about as if they were very important.

Loïc noticed their attitude toward N'zingu; they treated him with pride and fear.

"They know they need us." N'zingu said. "We have knowledge of the medicine plants. They never know whether to hate us or not. Their pride stops them from learning, so now they are dependent on us but they treat us badly. They are a lost people without a home in their hearts."

Loïc himself created even more confusion for the haughty Bantu. If he was travelling with a pygmy, for that's what N'zingu was, why was he carrying a gunnysack and why if he was white, was he up river in the forest? Since there was no answer to these questions it was just as well that no one asked. But many people looked very perplexed when they saw him.

It did bring Loïc to the very same question, why was he travelling with N'zingu away from the margins of his known world with no ship to retreat to and no company of the same tongue? He had no answer that explained his actions but the feeling was that N'zingu was going to show him something, bring him to another place in himself. They had talked in their broken kind of way, Loïc understanding a few of the words but not really clear about where they were going. So they had left it alone.

N'zingu saying "I take you to the N'ganga. Prenz tu N'ganga."

So that's how it was, they were going to N'ganga. Now nearly everything with a name started with N', so Loïc had decided to just wait, N'ganga was going to be revealed to him; his journey was a lesson in patience and trust.

N'zingu, after buying some beeswax, was ready to leave. They stopped at a small stall for some hot and spicy garbanzo soup and then returned to the river and the pirogue. By the end of the day the river had opened out into a huge lake and on the far side they docked at a tiny traditional village called Youngodoulongo. This was N'zingu's home and they were greeted by his whole extended family, some forty people. Old and young and very small, these were Babongo people, forest dwellers with ancestors going back five thousand years. These were a people living in harmony with the deep forest. As they said. "We were grown by the forest to be a small people so that we would always know our place."

So it was Loïc remained in the village with the Babongo, in the house of N'zingu, as an honoured guest and a source of endless amusement to the whole village. The forest is many things to the Babongo people. It is in fact everything. It is the living Bwiti, the maker, the creator and destroyer, their god, their place. In the forest there is everything needed for life and death. At one time not so long ago most of the inhabited planet was forest of one kind or another. The Bwiti for the Babongo is everything in their world, which is the forest. The Bwiti is the spirit of everything, it is the spirit of the forest and it is spirit that connects everything to you.

N'zingu took Loïc deep into the forest every day. He taught him how to use a blowpipe and gather the anaesthetic from the vines for numbing the prey. How to charge the thorn and beeswax darts and chew the fibrous flights into shape. Finally, how to master that explosive blast of air that came from deep down in the body and carried the dart with deadly accuracy to the bird or beast which had been called on to be hunted that day. For the Babongo taking anything from the forest came as a request for it to come to them and for them to be ready to receive it. 'If you don't catch you're not ready.'

When they went out on to the lake or into the backwaters, N'zingu showed Loïc how to attach thorn barbed points to the harpoon, the release loop knots and the line that turned the harpoon into a rod when your catch was large. Then he taught Loïc about the trick that water plays on the hunter. How the fish is not where you see it. How the surface of everything tells you lies about what is really there. How the hunter will always be hungry if he is eating the fish with his mind before the fish has given itself up.

"See the story in the water," he would say, "then fish will come to listen, because the fish is very vain."

Many things were special about the forest for Loïc. One was the noise in the gloom of the shade which was at first very loud, and then as he became more familiar with it, he noticed the changes. At dawn, sounds were louder and carried further because the air was cooler. By midday the same sounds had become muffled by the humidity. Everything was done by listening; the foliage was so thick that in five paces you could disappear. The bongos were the masters of this, they were brown deer with white vertical stripes. A whole herd could pass within five metres and unless a twig snapped there was no knowing. At night the birds and insects stopped and the tree frogs started, a deafening chorus of different rhythms and pitches filling the darkness.

When Loïc started using the Silbo whistle the Babongo became very excited and wanted to learn. They crowded round him keen to see his mouth and finger positions. Often they couldn't make the right mouth shapes because a lot of their language is on the tongue and in the mouth, not the lips. When they got it right everyone laughed. But they learnt quickly and came back to the village to impress the women, who got it right away.

By now he understood many of the Babongo words. Talk was usually about daily events and needs, hunting and gathering. At the same time there was an endless string of jokes peppering the days. Most of these went over his head. Sometimes he would try one of his own, and as he laughed they looked blank, until they winked at each other, then everyone laughed at him laughing.

Soon Loïc was one of a group of young men, mostly younger than him, that spent their time with the older men. First they went to meet with their brothers who lived alongside them. These 'brothers' were so called because they too ate the 'iboga plant'. They came in different shapes and sizes; the largest was the path maker. This was the elephant that had old track ways through the forest wide enough for the herd to pass along between mud hole clearings where they went for clay to clean their stomachs. The small group of Babongo stood on the clearing edge and watched as the elephants sucked up the clay from below the water. Pale grey in colour, it was good for balancing the many plant toxins that the elephants ate and the Babongo used. Another visit was paid to the 'black brother'. The elders warned the boys to be respectful, for when angry the gorilla is no longer the friend that you need. The chimpanzee, the scorpion and the black mamba were all visited, as were the warthogs and the porcupines, all eaters of the medicine plant. All were invited to the Iboga ground.

The Iboga ground was obviously very important. One morning a group of elders, men and women, announced that they were going into the forest to ask the Macoi to come to the Iboga ground. The Macoi, when it did appear at the long pole house, was one scary dancing bush. One moment it was jerking about like an injured creature the next it was just another standing tree. Where it would be next no one knew. The small children clung to their mother's legs with round staring eyes. The Macoi is a forest spirit. It is enticed out by the N'ganga to be present when the boys take the medicine plant, iboga. Now was the time for the boys to become men.

Now that the Macoi had shown itself, Loïc and the group of boys were led out of the village to the compound where the ceremonies took place. As they were led into the longhouse they were each given a bunch of ferns and told to hold them at all times, they were told that the ferns were an ally, a helper. They were shown mats at one end of the longhouse and told to choose one and lie on it. Already they had been fasting all day and had been given enough water to make them vomit. They were empty.

As they lay on their mats, the Bwiti was being made at the other end of the longhouse. The Bwiti, in ceremony, is their world in miniature. The forest was represented by different plants, trees, vines and flowers. The medicines made from these plants stood in bottles next to them. The animal world was there in pelt and horn, bones and feathers. Tied in bundles of coloured cloth were minerals and earth colours. The hunting weapons, bows, pipes and spears were all there but scaled down. All this was the sacred Bwiti in faith and form.

Also in miniature were the sounds of the forest in the

form of musical instruments. The 'mongongo' mouth bow, that makes the melody and tells the story. Next to that sat the 'soke' the seed rattle and next to that the 'tseghe' a female rattle that puts you into trance. With them sat a hank of dried peccary hooves, whose rattle chases thoughts from your head. Next to the 'balafon', made from strike plates over tiny dried gourds was a narrow percussion board that when played made the blood race. Hidden in the forest of the Bwiti were the spirits of the ancestors who came to help take that step between the two worlds.

As the evening light pierced the roof thatch the N'ganga arrived wrapped in red and white chequered cloths, the women on the left and the men on the right, they took their seats behind the Bwiti altar. Sounds started, delicate and small as if the forest itself had begun to enter the longhouse.

In turn 'the boys' came up to the Bwiti, and as the N'ganga listened, each spoke of his intentions; what he wanted to happen in his life, what he needed from the grandfather plant, what he needed to heal and what kind of man he wanted to become. When they had finished they were told to return in the morning with news of the vision that Iboga had brought them. When Loïc's turn came he told the N'ganga of his broken heart; how he wanted to find a new way of being himself; how he looked for love and happiness and accuracy with the blowpipe.

When all the boys were back on their mats the assistants, those males who had been through the ceremony before, took their places and a mass of rattles and drums began playing. The sound was deafening, the whole forest could hear. The wall of sound was right inside Loïc's body, it moved him and the fresh fern bundle waved like riverweed in his hand.

One of the N'ganga came round with ground up iboga root. Each 'curist' took as much as they wanted. As Loïc started to chew his, a vile bitterness leapt into his mouth, and his whole body became alert as he swallowed it and lay back on his mat. The music became lighter and more distinct as a wave of uncertainty swept over him. He was really in this, there was no leaving. He chewed and swallowed many times, and then the nausea came upon him. Deep inside his body he could feel the plant hunting, first in his feet and ankles, hunting, looking for something, something unneeded. Stopping around old wounds and injuries. Then it tracked up the inside of his legs, searched his genitals collecting wounds as it went. Then moved on to circle his kidneys, checking, cleaning, it was like an entity alive inside him. Then it circled his waist, searching all the time, looking for knots and blocks, dissolving them and moving on.

His hands cramped into claws and his arms ached as if overworked. His neck and shoulders crept and cringed and the skin of his scalp felt as if a thousand termites crawled just below the surface. Then it dived into his lungs, riding his breath. The sickness came rising up from all over his body towards his throat, and then he vomited. What he produced was no larger than a bean. Quickly it was taken away. A great heaviness descended on him, he clutched at his fern bundle; already limp it somehow reassured him.

He lay on his mat watching feelings come up and go. He watched what was happening to himself from a distance. Yes he thought from here I can see who I am, not what I think I am. A wave of joy swept through him like a gust of wind in open grassland. He smiled as thoughts came and went. For an age he lay there watching the workings of his mind. How it worked in such a habitual way. The same thoughts over and over again. How he made such an effort to work things out, trying to find their meaning instead of letting things rest and allowing their resolution to emerge. His head began to ache with the strain of its use. As he watched his confused mind he called for help. The polyrhythmic music divided into two distinct beats, one in each ear; his head had become a sound box of jarring noise that span round and round.

One of the female N'ganga came to his mat. She sat cross-legged at his head with her hands close to his temples. As she worked, never touching him, the two rhythms dovetailed together and the pain eased. Then she started moving her hands with quick twitching moves as if knotting threads. There seemed to be many repairs to do for she sat at his head untying and tying many connections. Gradually his mind calmed. His attention shifted to the harmonies in the music, his eyes closed and he sank back into the texture of the earth and the rhythm of his heartbeat. He felt her pushing the fern bundle into his hand and lifting him to his feet. Lights continued to move as he stood still. She urged him forward, his feet leaden, the air like syrup.

In front of the Bwiti some of the boys were dancing, he tried to join them but his feet felt they were growing roots. Swaying to the music, his head cleared. Now there was no pain, no nausea, just the waves of heaviness and the feeling that each breath was an enormous wind blowing through his insides. Dancing soon made him weak with the effort, and he shuffled back to his mat.

The movement had activated the medicine plant. He could now clearly see two parts of himself, one watching the other. His dream mind watched all the details of his thinking mind. One could question the other, point things out, remark on stupidities, habits and obsessions. It also revealed other ways of seeing. The causes and results of his behaviour patterns were clearly and simply put in front of him. Every step along his way he had chosen.

Often he stood up, and dragged his body to join the others dancing at the Bwiti. Clutching his wilting frond he let the music move him, but he tired easily and returned to his mat. Each time he lay down another one of his voices came to him.

'You see, you make yourself up, you are your own creation, be what you can imagine.'

As the night wore on his mind became less and less active. He felt unclear about where he stopped and started. He seemed to bleed into everything around him. The music drew him back onto his feet. When he danced with the others, there were many magical spirits helping them to be in a new way, encouraging them to be less self conscious just part of the movement of it all. As shreds of moonlight seeped through the wall of the longhouse, he saw his father there dead, but dancing. Stranger still was that he felt no connection with him. This surprised him, he loved his father, he had taught him many things but now there was a feeling that Bertrand was a trickster. At first he felt a pang of disappointment then it seemed so natural that he let it go.

He noticed a group of chimpanzees sitting, watching from the edge of the longhouse. Their heads slightly tilted, giving curiosity to their attentiveness. An infant chimpanzee sat on the lap of one of the N'ganga They were familiar with vibration of the plant and the mixture of sounds that mirrored the forest. All this Loïc read as quite normal.

A part of the N'ganga broke away and came towards him, its painted face no longer human. As he moved to the music it took him by the elbows and started to bounce him up and down violently, the medicine became activated and then he moved on to another of the tiring boys. Loïc felt as though he continued to bounce, like getting off a boat, the movement was still inside him. He could feel the plant inside him again searching for blocks and injuries. It was as if his body was no longer his. Hours passed unnoticed. When dawn showed its signs, the long house started to shrink back into size.

Searching out his mat he went to lie down but his attention was drawn up to the sky hole in the roof. There, in the sky, clearly detailed by the first rays of the sun hung a large bird. In the eye of the bird he saw the reflection of a star with complete clarity. Fascinated he sat and watched; the bird turned its head to look at him and told him to tell the N'ganga what he had seen. Then for the first time that night he fell asleep, his mat now soft as an embrace.

When he woke it was to a high sun and a crystal clear mind. One of the boys sat at the Bwiti in front of the N'ganga. He spoke and they listened intently. Occasionally there was a pause then he would pick up the thread; he was reporting back from the spirit world. He was a messenger from the Macoi. When it came to Loïc stepping up, his body was light and full of energy. He looked down at the dry fern frond in his hand and the night before came flooding back. He took his place on the ground by the Bwiti and told of his encounters, his meeting with his mind, his awful heaviness. The N'ganga nodded and hummed, they had heard this all before. He described one of his dreams with lots of mime because he had few words, everyone laughed as he acted out travelling very fast down a tunnel of fire. No one understood, but everyone enjoyed the drama. Finally they asked if there was a message for them and he remembered.

"The star in the eye of the bird in the sky."

"Ah! Aha!" went round as they touched the backs of each other's hands. "More?"

"No just that."

They nodded appreciatively and Loïc returned to his mat.

Once all the boys had spoken with the N'ganga the familiar driving sounds of the ceremony started again and they all danced. Now, the music Loïc could hear was a mirror of the rainforest, punctuated by alarm calls, insect sounds and that driving rattle, all riding on the narrative of the mouth harp. More iboga was taken but by now the heaviness had cleared from his body and Loïc danced through the whole day, copying the style of the other boys. Quick hip and wrist movements captured the counterpoint of the music and sparked his mind. All day, on and on they danced without weight, without tiring. Only at dusk did they put down the remains of their ferns and take to their mats as water and smiles were shared. As the sun set N'zingu came to his side and laid his hand on his shoulder.

"Soon you will go on with your journey to the east. We will give you Mbe' as a guide for the first part, after that a bird will come and be your guide, this is what your vision tells N'ganga. The grandfather Iboga will work with your healing for some time. Open mind and good attention, this is your work. Now you have met N'ganga, now you are family."

The next day N'zingu told Loïc about the warthogs and the porcupine that also like iboga. They dig up the roots and chew on them. They too like to dance, usually in circles until they fall down. It brings out inner smiles. Rarely do they get sick. Sickness is the price that men pay; they are the ones that kill their own kin in the name of power. Man's healing is deep soul healing. They talked of the other animals that shared the grandfather plant, the Bonobos that got very giggly, then did what Bonobos do all the time, couple. How gentle the elephants and gorillas were, letting the Babongo women hold their babies.

"We are all sharing the forest" he said, "we are the movement and the plants are the stillness. They too move and we sometimes put down roots."

For the next two days Loïc was prepared for his ongoing journey. He was taught how to collect, prepare and cook a variety of plants from the forest. Some he would carry as dry, others he would find along the way. N'zingu had noticed how Loïc had trouble with the insects, especially the mosquitoes. His arms and shoulders were covered with bites that he had scratched. They were now open and weeping wounds that would soon become septic. When N'zingu pointed to them, Loïc shrugged and scratched. He then took him to an unusual place. The ground was a little higher than the river plain. At the top of the mound stood a strange tree with spiky branches like anteater tails. There was something familiar about it and Loïc recognised the resinous pine smell. N'zingu collected the seeds from the branch cones, peeled them and stone-crushed them into a paste, then smeared it over Loïc's body.

"This is the medicine of this tree. No more insect bites. When you want it, it's is never there, take seeds with you."

At one point as they gathered fallen seeds they both reached for the same one. Looking up they saw into each other, they smiled, there had grown a deep connection of trust between them.

"We leave that seed here." they said and laughed.

5
Breathing under Water

Mbe' Bounaka was a year younger than Loïc and had been one of the other boys at the Iboga ceremony. His girl was Minanga, well not quite his girl yet. Their parents wanted them to be joined but so far they were friends. It had been decided by the N'ganga that they would both go with Loïc. Minanga was loud and quick with an infectious smile. Mbe' was quiet and stealthy. In Babongo culture it was normal for a boy and girl to spend time together before joining as a couple and usually an excuse was found for them to go on some kind of errand. They were the perfect couple, young, naked and beautiful. Babongo clothes don't really exist, just a string round the waist for carrying things. Often Loïc would watch them and try to imagine Anna Cecille naked.

The night before they left, N'zingu called him to his hut, where he found gathered most of the tribe including Mbe' and Minanga. Loïc was placed in the centre of the space and everyone closed round him. Those close to him put their hands on him, the others touched them, they all connected with him in a web. They sat like this for a long time. Loïc felt held, loved and connected to them all. N'zingu told the people that they would not be alone when Loïc had gone because they would all be in the same forest. They hummed in agreement. These were N'zingu's last words to Loïc. Quietly he had shared his ways, taught him how to be in the teeming rainforest and the waterways and now how to be with himself.

Early the next morning he silently took Loïc down to the water's edge where a group of the Babongo were waiting holding curved stick hoops joined into a frame, a vesica. Through this Loïc was passed three times. Then he was given a small pouch of Iboga, a hunting bow and arrows and some dried fish.

With his Guanche water bags on one shoulder and the

bow and quiver on the other he set off with Mbe' and Minanga towards the east. The sun was still low and the day young, the land in front of him unseen and enormous. His heart sang as he tried to keep up with his feet.

For twelve days they moved along wide elephant paths, that cut from one clay bath to the next, often days apart. Many different species used these routes, but it was the elephant that kept them clear, snapping off intruding branches and scuffing the earth. At nightfall they made leaf canopies and strung hammocks to avoid some of the insect activity. From his hammock Loïc marvelled at the way his footprints glowed in the dark. This was where he had crushed the tiny fungi that covered the forest floor. It was these fungi that consumed all the decaying leaf mould and sometimes the insects leaving husks of moths and ants occupied and covered in spore, these too glowed in the dark like jewellery.

At first the forest seemed endless, but as each day passed he became more familiar with the detail of this immense greenness. It felt like breathing under water. The light filtered through so many different plants that the air was in layers. Where there was a tree fall, rays of sunlight pierced down through these layers to the ground, reminding him that there was still another world out there.

Immersed in the deep green light Loïc witnessed the subtle interplay between his two guides grow into an intimacy that was both tender and practical. Living in a place that they shared with so many animals and plants gave them a special kind of awareness. It was almost impossible not to be in contact with some other life form, how you moved through this world of variety was always being considered. When not on the elephant paths some plants needed to be avoided, others you could brush through. Mbe' led the way carrying a machete. As he walked he moved around the poisonous ones and held back the thorny ones. Minanga behind imitated his movements with a flowing grace. Mbe' did the thinking, leaving her to watch for fruit and small prey. Loïc, his clothes dripping with sweat, followed in their steps learning how to be at one with it all.

One mid morning Mbe' stopped, Minanga stopped close

behind him and rested her hand on his shoulder, they both turned to looked at Loïc. The air had changed, a dryness had entered his nose; ahead seemed to be a lighter green.

"Congo." Mbe' stated as he moved forward.

A few moments later they stood looking out over the huge Congo River. Suddenly there was sunlight, water and air. They had arrived at the edge of another world, one of immense heat, a river so wide that only the flow told you it wasn't a sea.

That night they pitched camp on the sloping bank, hoisting their hammocks high in the trees to avoid the watering animals. The next day they would reach up stream to Liranga a settlement on the west bank. From here Loïc would be on his own. He wrapped himself into his hammock to avoid the swarms of insects and dropped into a fitful sleep.

His dream came to him in fragments as he woke at dawn.

'A row of huge metal boxes on wheels pulled by exhausted oxen and pushed by whipped men, rolled along freshly cut paths through the forest. These riveted boxes looked like slices of a cut up boat hull.'

The image evaporated with the mist that the sunrise peeled off the forest canopy, leaving him feeling uneasy, with a tang in his mouth. The day was different to others; they followed a path along the bank, at the forest edge keeping the river on their right. Loïc realised that soon he would miss this playful loving couple that had led him so far east. He would miss their unity with the forest, each other and their respect for the balance and sacredness of their world. He also saw how N'zingu had constructed the situation, so that he would see how to be. He rummaged in his pockets; somewhere he was bound to have a shell. Not only were they a beautiful picture of energy but a good calcium source, or so his father had told him.

"For N'zingu," he said presenting one to Mbe' "and one for you," he said pressing another into Mbe's hand.

When they reached the outskirts of Liranga they placed their hands on each other's hearts. Then Mbe' and Minanga melted back into the forest.

6

Leopold's Legacy

Left standing there alone between town and compound, between river and forest, time stood still for Loïc. There was no before, that was in the deep green of the forest, and the after, that was unformed. As he stood there, a slight breeze at his back, a 'tush, tush, tush', came from down river. It was approaching so Loïc made his way to the riverbank and the path that led into the town. After the earthen houses with palm leaf roofs came the more conspicuous wooden houses up on low stilts; they attempted to imitate a western architecture but were full of termite holes. He automatically made his way to the dock and then he saw it coming up stream. It was a boat with no sails, instead it had a chimney with smoke pouring forth. As it approached it let fly a piercing whistle that put all the river birds into the sky. Its 'tush, tush, tush' sound was insistent and everyone who saw it stood and stared.

The images from his dream suddenly came to mind, although he could make no connection between this bizarre thing and the fallen oxen and the bleeding men. The metal boxes of his dream sprang together as if by magnets and assembled into the smoking form in front of him. He sat down on the jetty and shook his head as the puffing slowed, and the boat docked there in the middle of Mbandaba.

It didn't take Loïc long to strike up a conversation with the Captain of the 'Le Stanley' as the steamship was called, brought in parts across Africa by the English explorer Stanley on his quest to find the mysterious Doctor Livingstone. Now rusted and re-riveted it was running the newly named Zaire river passage from Mbandaba to Kisangari further east on the grand curve of the waterway.

The captain, surprised to find a French boy carrying a bow and quiver, assumed that they were souvenirs and noted the intelligence of Loïc's questions about the steam powered sternwheeler. He asked whether he was looking for work. Fresh from the forest and his experiences with Iboga, Loïc's answer was no, but a qualified no. He was prepared to work his passage but he didn't want a job.

The captain was impressed by his honesty.

"You're on, we leave in two days. Be here in one and I'll show you the ropes before we sail."

"Sail? "

"Ok, steam," laughed the captain.

When Loïc arrived at the quay a day later the Le Stanley was being loaded with heavy sacks of a gritty brown powder. It looked like an ore and large wads of money were changing hands, hands shouldering guns.

"What is that stuff?" he asked once the hold was battened down.

"That's coltan son. Good business, we take it to Kisangari, unload and it pays for everything."

"What's it good for if it's so expensive?"

"I don't ask." said the captain." Where there's guns that are loaded, I do the job and keep my eyes down. I suggest you do the same if living is what you like."

"How long have you been working the river?" Loïc asked, curious to know more about the sacks in the hold.

"Since she was welded up and re-riveted, must be five years now."

"Do people round here remember her on the river from before?"

"Yeah, sure they do. There was four steamers once when King Leopold was in charge."

"Who's he?" said Loïc imagining leopard skin throne and drums.

"He", said the captain. "He was the murdering monarch who first brought this beautiful country to its knees. He," the captain said again with distaste in his voice, "managed to kill many millions of people of this place. He, King Leopold the Belgian, in twenty three years organised the deaths of the Congo people just for rubber. Rubber my boy, for fan belts and wheels. People round here have learnt that it's not so easy to stay alive. They keep their eyes down and don't ask so many questions. Once it was rubber, then it was diamonds, now it's coltan. It's all the same, lives are cheap."

"But what do they do with this coltan?" Loïc insisted, his curiosity becoming dangerously aroused.

"I'm told," said the captain looking towards the quay as if alert ears were hidden amongst the cargo on the dockside, "it's traded directly for arms to continue the war." He paused, "the struggle, I mean." as if he had made the mistake before.

"The struggle, yes this I understand, but what use is this coltan, how come it's worth so much?"

"As I say," he went on in hushed tones, "I'm told it's what's called a combined element."

"An element?"

"Yes like lead is an element."

"Oh yes, is that right, and what's this Coltan element good for?"

"I'm told, said the captain cautiously. "capacitors."

"What?"

"Pinhead capacitors, mostly, in mobile phones, lap tops, air bags, high tech toys that sort of thing."

Loïc was now out of his depth; these things were outside his experience.

"I'll just watch and listen." He said to the captain.

"That's right you do that, but out of the corner of your eye. Life round here is cheap as pommes frites. Round here you are of no consequence to anyone."

With a pull on the whistle chain and the opening of a valve the only working steamboat on the Zaire River eased out into the deep trench and puffed its way upstream. By the time the birds had settled, Mbandaba was a memory and the size of the river dominated everything. The flow was sluggish and brown. Loïc leaned on the rail. The sensation was of stillness, the bow wave hardly evident.

By mid-morning the next day Loïc had realised that he was entering a period of madness. The temperature was that of a blacksmith's shop on a busy day and the awning under which he sat gave shade for maybe an hour and that hour was yet to come. The ship being metal, had become impossible to touch and he now understood why the captain wore shoes made of canvas with thick canvas soles and not plimsolls. At first he thought he was just mean, but rubber soles were not a sensible option. Loïc sat marooned on an island of empty gunnysacks. Added to the sun was the heat that rose up from the boiler room; there was no hiding place. A plume of smoke listlessly drifted from the ship's funnel as they bore up river.

By midday he sat in a fragment of shade on deck, his body dripping, his goatskins nearly empty. He had engaged his mind and left his body to stew in its own juices. He turned to the 'hunter plant'. The bitterness on his tongue awoke an inner conversation. N'zingu had told him to work with the plant and it would work with him. He had also told him that nothing was what it first appeared to be and that most of life was a contradiction. Death was an old friend not something to fear. He also warned that Iboga would bring him visitations of the consequences of past actions, not only his own actions. 'Just sit and watch them come and go,' N'zingu had said.

For many days it was the same. The same steam power. The same heat. The hot metal, the pool of shade and the medicine plant. Many thoughts came to him. What the captain had said about rubber and diamonds, King Leopold and Coltan, death and money. For a while they all span around his head as if chasing each other into a new order, attempting to form a clearer picture of the present. He was well aware that these things and events were from different times. But for him they were all happening now, he could see their connections with each other. How conflict attracted more value than peace. How love and fear had become such enemies. How mining for diamonds or Coltan gave miners terrible diseases, but those same materials gave others such pleasure and saved people's lives. How when something occurred in one place it became part of the future in another place. How being worked to death bleeding latex sap from a rubber tree gave someone else in another place and time a smooth air cushioned ride. All these consequences came to him as the river slipped beneath.

Another day he was just full of doubts. For the first time on his travels he doubted his sanity. What was this urge to move on? Where was he going? What was he leaving behind?

By the time they reached Kisangari his head was empty and he felt clear about just being in the now. Just breathing in the now, for what seemed to be new,, was just another forgotten old coming round again. The river had narrowed a little and at night the orchestra of the forest could be heard beyond the churning of the screw propeller. By now the madness that Loïc thought was his, he knew was just the madness of the place. For some it became them and they acted it out. For him it was a place that put him in touch with old truths. Truths that fed on fear and greed.

The Babongo always told him, 'If a place feels like metal in your teeth and sour in your stomach, don't dig there, walk on.'

Docking in Kisangari looked simple enough to start with but once they had tied up and before any paperwork had been completed the game had begun. The pecking order was clear. The captain told him that if he wanted to know the value of coltan, he should watch wait and listen and that's all.

As soon as the painters were hitched to the capstans on the quay, four soldiers boarded the boat. They wanted cash. They knew the value of the load and had stung the captain many times before. The amount they wanted varied with the successes and failures of the 'struggle'. Today it was a quarter of the value of the load; things were going badly for the army. The captain, for his part, had ways of adjusting his load.

The soldiers looked down into the hold to count the sacks. Whereas the harbour master looked at the Plimsoll line that told him how low in the water the ship lay, the soldiers didn't know there was a false bottom to the hold. The harbour master who was next in line for payment could read it all from the painted white load line. Or so he thought, the captain himself had seen to the painting of the Plimsoll line while he was renovating the boat. As usual nothing was quite as it appeared to be. Once the soldiers and the harbour master had been paid off, the chief of police paid a visit, very nice, very dangerous, like a large snake constricting its prey for a bottle of whisky. Finally it was the turn of the customs officers, by now it was a formality, 'nothing to declare', and the docking form was stamped and another bottle of whisky left the ship. The whole process was completed by nightfall; greed moves fast. There were warehouses at the dock full of food aid that had begun to rot before permission had been given to get it to the starving. As Loïc watched and waited he began to feel a lot older; the ways of this world had the suction of wet clay and a fatal fascination for the unwary. He found himself in this situation without place or favour.

"You go with the truck to the airport and I'll pay you with a ticket out of here."

Loïc unsure of what the captain expected of him agreed to take the Coltan to the 'other port'.

"This stuff is going to Rwanda," he said. "In the last eighteen months they have made $500 million for the army and killed over five million people. That's $100 a death. That's expensive for round here. It's the death run for you, but with a ticket and no cash on you to steal you'll be safe. Make sure you get the first plane out of here. Hook up with Aussie Joe."

Once again Loïc felt a strong compressed sensation. Time and events were not making any sense to him. He was in new territory. He was in a war zone. He grabbed his bag and bow from the cabin of the 'Le Stanley' and jumped into the passenger seat of the truck. There was a rapping on the window. The captain thrust papers into his hand.

"One's for the shipment. Show the other to the pilot, he's the one that does the flying jungle boy. Good luck."

The driver slammed the lever into first gear and as Loïc stared blankly ahead they lurched out onto the gravel road. All buildings were blacked out. They travelled by moonlight. Occasionally flashes lit the horizon followed by distant gunfire. The taste of death gathered in the forming dew. They drove for twenty kilometres and pulled off at a picture sign that was not familiar. Soon after the truck stopped, out of the darkness stepped armed men, faces numbed by confused emotions.

Loïc produced the assignment document and they were waived through onto a wide tarmac area that stretched away from a corrugated metal building. Two flying boats, as he saw them, were standing up on wheels. The truck was waived through to the second. It pulled up and more soldiers started unloading it onto the plane.

"Yes, plane," said the driver, looking at Loïc with suspicion.

"That other one's yours, the pilot is already aboard."

Loïc was struggling with reality. Ever since getting a ride on the 'Le Stanley' things had started to take on a strange shape. First there had been the airport, then there was the flying pilot, and guns that just carried on firing. Then the motorised truck with the rubber wheels, corrugated iron and now tarmac. All this mixed up with 'onboard pilots' and 'shipments' and Loïc began to feel as if he was either making it all up - or was it the medicine of the Iboga plant showing him the consequences of human actions.

He jumped down from the truck, bag and bow in hand, aware of a wave of suspicious eyes on him. He slowly walked the short distance to the steps of the other plane and climbed them without looking back. At the top a gun was jabbed into his ribs and he held out the second piece of paper. Before long a tall white man brushed aside the gun and asked Loïc for his papers.

"That's it in your hand."

"Your passport I mean."

"Only the paper."

The pilot, for that's who he was looked him over.

"You won't get far without me. Grab a seat, we'll talk later."

There were two rows of seats; the rest of the interior was stripped down for cargo. Loïc took a seat next to a porthole and watched the activity outside. Everyone was on edge. The loading of the Coltan onto the other plane was particularly tense. The soldiers doing the work would not put down their guns, which continually got in their way as they tried to move the heavy sacks. As the sun rose Loïc could see that they were boys not men, boys his age and younger. They were scared and acting tough. Occasionally gunfire was heard and they all hit the ground sighting up their guns from behind the sacks. Then once it was all quiet again they got back to work.

Loïc was surprised when he was not frightened by the gunfire; to him it was not a threat, to him it was still unreal. It was true there was nothing he could do to change it, but at the same time he felt calm, no panic. He waited and watched, noticing the details. The sun raked the ground, the rising light revealing the distressed appearance of the other plane. The paintwork was barely evident, most of the body was covered in riveted metal patches, and the curved window panels of the bridge were cracked with a filigree of splits enclosing the pilot behind a veil. He too was agitated and wanting to leave. Throwing back a sliding panel he shouted down to the toiling troops as they manhandled the awkward cargo up a ramp and into the belly of the metal hull.

Loïc had never thought about flying, it wasn't real to him. He'd only experienced planes as remote metal birds that trailed a pair of disappearing white feathers across the sky. Now that he was sitting in one and looking at another he was filled with a sense of disappointment; they seemed so far from the beauty of flight, cumbersome and earthbound.

A wave of the place washed over him and he felt the presence of many dead. He felt the fear and pain of many voices trapped in the habit of revenge and self-importance. He felt the boys with their guns and their fear had no expression for love. Long ago the simplicity of their love had been eaten by pain.

A door opened behind him and a ladder was pressed against the threshold. A man in a dirty tired shirt and trousers climbed aboard. Cardboard boxes were passed in to him and he arranged them behind the two rows of seats. All the boxes were old and taped together, printed on their sides was the company name Marck. The bases of the boxes were stained and had been dried out. They were placed in two lines. Loïc had a strong feeling that there was something odd about them. He stayed in his seat and counted thirty. The pilot appeared from the bridge and looked at them, they seemed to affect him too. He became agitated and he too started to count them. He acknowledged the man and then saw him down the ladder and closed the door. He sat down next to Loïc, his mind elsewhere.

"Where is it you're trying to get to?"

In that moment Loïc realised that he had no idea. All he knew was that he needed to be out of this place.

"I'm going east." he blurted.

"Yes I can take you east, but where east? East is big. Everywhere is big here, the country is big, how far are you going? I'm going to Madagascar and that's a big jump from here, but I do have stops to make along the way. If you're coming there's work to do."

"Okay," said Loïc relieved, "what's the job?"

"You have to take care of the cargo, these boxes."

"Okay. What's in them?" the feeling came back to him.

"Take a look, any box they're all the same."

Loïc got up and slowly opened one of the boxes. Lying on an old woollen jersey there was a sleeping child, a small child, an infant. He stared horrified at the pilot. The pilot shrugged.

"Now you know."

Loïc opened three more boxes. It was true, each box held a sleeping baby.

"They're all the same?"

"Yes they're all the same, they're all asleep, but for how long I don't know, two hours maybe, it's meant to be two but if not you're in charge. There's some food and drink in that ammo box and there's no co-pilot, so you're on your own."

"And what if they all wake up?"

"They will, then you deal with it. Oh! and when you've fed and watered them give them one of these." He handed Loïc a bottle of pills.

There had been children in Loïc's village, not many, but enough for him to have carried a few when they had grazed their knees, but feeding babies was a whole other world again. He had a choice, ride the plane with the children or, with no papers, walk off into a civil war and open gunfire.

"Okay I'll do it. What are the pills for?"

"They're on the pills now. Quiet eh? They last for a couple of hours and then they wake. It's not so bad. Many of them are so used to starvation that any food sends them back to sleep but give them a pill anyway, we don't want a plane load of screaming babies."

The boxes were all repaired with tape and were obviously home to these orphans of war. The pilot ran a strap around them for fastening and then pulled the plane round onto the pot-holed runway. The back of the pilots head held Loïc's gaze as his mind slipped into measuring this new world that had seized hold of his reality and shaken it. There were now many loose ends.

Since leaving the company of Mbe' and Minanga, metal seemed to be everywhere. Trucks, boats, guns, planes and this mysterious coltan ore that seemed to be at the heart of all this darkness, and now babies in industrial cardboard boxes. His world had in a few days contracted into being sharp and angular leaving him little room for movement.

The sudden roar of the engines brought him into the present. He was being pushed back into his seat. The whole plane shook as if it would fall to pieces as they took a course down the side of the runway where there were fewer potholes. It was a narrow strip and a splatter of gunfire missed them as the ship laboured into the sky. The fear that gripped Loïc was not balanced by any belief that it was even possible to fly. As the ground slipped away beneath him, he was amazed to see the river snake out beneath the plane's wing. Fascinated he watched the world shrink and become a growing curve at the same time.

As the sun rose rapidly into the sky he had a clear picture from the Iboga ceremony; he was now in 'the eye of the bird in the sky,' he was in 'the reflection of a star.' So what was this star, what did he reflect?

Very soon the roar of the engines settled into a dull whine. The river that had had such width was now a mere track of brown weaving through a surface of green. Loïc was in awe as the clouds passed beneath him. The pilot shouted for him to join him up in the cabin and sat him down in the co-pilot's seat.

"It's better up here huh?"

"Couldn't be much worse down there."

"Oh yes it can, much worse, but yes you're better off up here than down there, that's for sure. We have three hours before landing so do you want to learn to fly?"

"Sure." His resistance to everything gone, lost in a mass of newness that was everywhere he looked. "Sure, why not?"

"What's your name son?"

"Loïc."

"What kind of name's that?"

"Old Breton."

"Is that so. I'm Joe Blusher, that's new Aussie."

7
A Bird in the Sky

"How long you been buying children Joe?"

"We trade them, we don't buy them. We collect them from the hospitals and get them out of the war zone into fostering, that's what we do. Their parents are dead, families shot to pieces, they have nothing 'cept us. We don't pay for them, what we do is use them as currency for medical supplies. We trade them and it seems to work, seven out of ten survive."

"But why are they drugged and in cardboard boxes?"

"We can't be seen to be carrying children, that's why they're in industrial boxing, we have a licence for carrying parts and products not people. Once they're out of here things can begin to change for them."

They fell silent and Joe began checking the instrument panel.

"Now about flying one of these, it's fairly basic. One you always take off with a full tank, whenever you can. Two you make sure all the controls are working before you take off. Three you know where you're going and how far it is. Can you read the stars?"

"I know some." Loïc said with hesitation. He knew the Big Dipper, Venus, Orion's belt and the Dog star. There were others but he didn't know very many. He decided on "No!"

"Well that's a good start. In the day you can fly by the sun if it's clear, otherwise you've got a compass here and an altimeter, that's for height; always good to give it a tap." Which he did. "It tends to get stuck. Always fly high if you can't see, mountains have a habit of popping up out of the ground. This is the stick. In one of these it's more of a wheel, but we call it a stick, turn for left and right and push for down and pull for up, the rest is in the hands of the gods. Take a hold of it; get a feeling for it, it's there right in front of you. Dual controls in one of these. She's old but she flies like a bird, an old goose, a big fat old goose." He laughed and let go of his stick.

The plane started to dip and Loïc took the stick as his stomach started to lurch. He pulled the three quarter helm wheel and the craft started to level out, taking his stomach with it, the vibration of the plane in his palms. He pulled slightly and the horizon disappeared as they rose into the blue. Pushing away, it reappeared and the feeling of nausea began to leave him. Left, right, he played with 'the stick', she moved with a rattling strain but the feeling of flying was a wonder to him.

"Now level her out and keep on course, fly on the altimeter and the horizon. The art lies in riding the air and using as little fuel as possible."

Loïc looked down at the curved aluminium instrument panel, a few lights, switches and dials screwed down on a board. Black letters announced an instruction.

'Feathering motor not fused.

No feathering action within ninety seconds.

Open switch by pulling.'

As he read this he again realised that he was in foreign territory. There were big gaps in his understanding of what was right in front of him. What was a 'feathering action' in a metal plane? In a bird yes, he knew, he had spent hours watching raptors riding the thermals over the ridge. It was all done with slight movements of their flight and tail feathers, but how did that translate to a plane?'

"What's feathering?"

"Ah that's the flaps son, you can't see them from here. From back there you can, it's the back edge of the wing, it goes up and down, gives us rise and fall. There's one on the tail too, that's the one that gives us left and right. Like a rudder in a boat. Don't think of air as a space with nothing in it. It's got substance - eddies and currents just like water. Sometimes it lifts you up other times it presses you down."

Air like water. Loïc could relate to that easily, exchanging one element for another gave him a clearer picture. Suddenly the whole plane started to judder, the noise and vibration was intense, everything appeared to be coming loose.

"Turbulence." shouted Joe over the noise. "Hold on, it could get worse-and buckle that belt."

They were flying over a series of ridged hills. Joe tipped the planes black snub nose up into the clouds and lost the waves of airflow.

"Plays hell with the rivets." He laughed.

"See what you mean," said Loïc, "you get the same thing on a shallow fast incoming tide. Takes the caulking out of boats."

For the next two hours they flew the plane together, Joe correcting with Loïc flying. He learnt fast.

"Take-off and landing are the ones, those take practise, one's never like another, especially on the runways around here, they keep blowing holes in them."

A tiny high-pitched cry cut through the drone of the twin engines.

"Time to go to work." Joe said catching the alarm written on Loïc's face.

Back in the hold boxes were stirring. The loudest got Loïc's attention. The ammunition box held an ancient collection of full feeder bottles with gnawed plastic nipples and taped-on lids. He held one up to the loudest infant, it was too young to hold the bottle and was frantically hungry. He sat the child up and balanced the bottle on the edge of the box. That only worked until the child took a breath, then it dropped out of the box and rolled away. Three of the boxes were now wide awake and others were stirring.

"Must have all had the pill at the same time," he muttered.

As more boxes awoke he realised that the situation would soon be out of his grasp. Then it came to him. Most of the boxes still had their tops folded in to disguise the contents. He folded out two of the sides and with a knife made a cut in each side where they met. Into this he wedged a full bottle and propped an infant at the nipple end. It seemed to work, at least the bottle fell in instead of out. Before long all thirty boxes were awake and hungry.

Before long Loïc had cut and propped and was now dealing with slipped bottles. He sat pushing them into reluctant mouths until a sense of sucking calm descended on the hold and bottles slipped from sagging mouths. He sat and watched, occasionally making adjustments to bottles. These children were part of a trade in pain and distress that reached back a long way. They were the legacy of a foreign king who had built the city of Brussels from the blood money of rubber. The world was full of bizarre contradictions that had become normalities. N'zingu was right, nothing was what it first appeared to be. He slipped sleeping pills into sated mouths and folded down the box lids.

There was a shout from Joe. Loïc put his head in through the door of the cockpit, as he was told it was called. Cockpit? What was a cockpit doing in the front of a flying boat? Surely that makes no sense, he thought, then checked himself.

"We'll be coming into Kigali in a while and it won't be pleasant, so make sure they're in their boxes and strapped down. The airstrip's a mess and the squatters are camped right up to the edge. Oh yes and don't open the back door till I tell you. We'll lose the lot otherwise. We'll have to taxi into a hanger before we unload."

"Okay?"

"Okay. "

Why were the words so scrambled? Squatters, taxis and hangers. What did it all mean? He decided to wait, watch and guess.

Loïc's stomach slipped into his mouth as the descent began. His ears felt as though they were crushing his head, however much he gnawed the air. Before he had knotted the ropes the whole frame of the plane was shaking. The pressed metal oval of the hold moved like a tired basket, rivets were popping and the chances of completing a landing seemed unlikely. The boxes bounced on the floor, a couple slipped under the rope, but none of the contents woke up.

It was dark before Joe brought the plane into a huge corrugated curved structure peppered with gunshot holes and enclosed by rolling doors.

This must be 'taxiing into a hanger', thought Loïc.

"I didn't see the squatters." He shouted over the propeller noise.

"You were busy baby watching. The squatters are on half of the runway, soon this airport will close."

"What do they look like? " He shouted not expecting to be heard.

"They're like you and me, but in rags and tatters," Joe shouted back. "They're not all sitting on their haunches as you might think. Theirs is a city made of garbage that grows by the day and looks like what it is, a mess. It's where the people and the waste have become mixed together."

The image this formed in Loïc's mind made for discomfort. People and waste becoming one, people like him joined to the garbage thrown away by others. He put the image to one side as the engines spluttered to a stop and the back door was thrown open from the outside. A face appeared at the threshold, it was tanned, green eyed and with an infectious smile.

"Where are those babies of mine?"

"Not so fast." He came back. "They've been mine for some time now and I can't let them go to just anyone."

Joe Blusher came back into the hold, tired and smiling.

"This is an anxious moment," he began, his eyes flicking between the two faces. "This will be either war or love. Loïc, this is feisty Fran McNulty, the winner of the Many Hearts Award. You have to hand over your charges to her. She's the one who sees to the rest of their journey. You did well, they're still asleep."

The boxes were loaded into a waiting truck and, as Loïc watched from the plane door, the sun bleached curls and deliberate movements of the winner of many hearts award began to reach him as if by some unknown magical current and, before reason or understanding had entered his head, he had once again grabbed his bag and his bow and began loading the sleeping boxes into the back of the truck. She took one look at him, smiled the winning smile and that was it, whatever she asked he would do.

"Be back in two and we'll go further east." Joe shouted as the truck pulled out of the hangar.

8
The Many Hearts Award

For the next two days and nights he never left her side. They drove from village to village talking to the nursing mothers that had lost children; there were many. Some at childbirth, some to warfare, but many to the cholera that had swept through the country leaving some areas without any children at all. The women came to the truck and simply chose a box. Fran then opened the lid and handed her the drugged child. The box itself the women couldn't have, though many wanted them. Then they were encouraged to sit in the shade and wait for the child to stir and see if it would take to the breast. Usually they were so hungry they did, but some were so weak that Fran would give them a wild honey tonic to give them the energy to feed.

There was a great naturalness about the way Fran turned the trauma of the grieving mothers into a practical happiness. Their gratitude was expressed by their gifts, which Fran carried in a small box. They were now her treasure trove, items of incalculable value, given from the heart; buttons, small pieces of coloured cloth, minute bundles of black hair, tooth picks, hairpins, three yellow beads on an animal hair, half a comb. Items of worth, born out of such hardship that they were tokens from another dimension. Fragments to remind her that the world is easier to value through less, rather than the extravagance of more.

The truck did its rounds and Loïc and Fran sat in the tool box on top of the cab. They watched the boxes in the back, the landscape around them, and didn't stop talking and touching. She was twice his age, and radiant. In her he found wisdom, beauty and a higher self. In him she rediscovered innocence and enthusiasm. Apart from that, a chemistry fuelled their nights of lovemaking in small straw huts lit by tiny wooden cages filled with trapped fireflies.

Wherever they went they were greeted with; 'Ah Fran.'

They loved her, she asked for nothing and was without need. She was beyond the material world. Which everyone around her was striving to achieve in some humble measure. In things she found no value and as a result she was surrounded by an abundance, which she gave away with grace and with great care so that she didn't create jealousy amongst the people.

One of the things that Fran attracted was food. In a place where there was so little it was the greatest gift. As a consequence gatherings and celebrations followed in her wake. As the food accumulated, so too did the urge to party. Evidently she had been finding orphans for years and now she was finding children for her own orphans who were now bereft mothers. Wherever she went in the villages a posse of infants surrounded her, happy just to be in her presence. Sometimes the women would chuckle behind their hands when they saw her with a young man at her side but she took it with a smile and a tilt of her head.

They arranged for Loïc to have a change of clothes. He looked like a walking pile of rags; boats, forests and the sea had seen to that.

When Loïc stepped out of the hut that evening to join Fran at the fireside, she had to look twice to be sure. With his hair tied back and the growth of his soft beard defining his good looks, dressed in a traditional cut of loose drawstring pull ups and a long sleeved and pocketed shirt, made from broad stripes of yellow, red and green covered with repeating maps of Africa, he looked resplendent. The drums increased in volume as he joined the throng.

That evening the village came alive. All the food that had accumulated had been chopped and cooked. The women strutted in their best, dancing in long weaving patterns and responding to the changes called by the master drum. The men sitting in a huge curve with a family of drums gripped between their knees played the complex patterns into the feet of the dancers. Wide eyed children stayed up for the night. Dogs patrolling the perimeter of firelight.

With laughter from the women, Fran was cajoled into joining them in the dances. She made her way into the midst of sweating bodies that milled around the fire. Suddenly with a tack, tack, tack from the master drummer's stick, they all came straight in together. High energy, synchronised, high stepping, back arching, polyrhythmic, drum and dance. Beauty in the personality of each dancer; how they moved differently within the same steps. Dignity in the way the drummers listened to the whole and the parts at the same time.

Everyone's attention was held as feet and hands stepped and slapped together. Then came the song, tightly woven into the beat bringing the story to the actions. Fran was up there with the others, she knew exactly what was going down; she'd been there many times before and dance with passion she could. In this way the evening progressed, wave upon wave, until it was time to eat. As quiet descended the dogs closed in on the circle scavenging for scraps.

When Joe Blusher had said 'see you in two', Loïc had taken it to mean days, but Fran assured him that 'things don't happen in days round here. Weeks, maybe months, but days no. So if you want to pick up a ride with Joe best you leave it for a while, Africa is not a hurry place'.

The shadow of war that Loïc had steamed into on 'Le Stanley' had moved on from these parts, digging deeper into the towns and cities. Leaving in its wake more complicated ways of dying than a bullet or a machete wound. On the heels of war comes sickness. Great swathes of the country had been scourged by 'the Cholera'; some still wore the 'cholera belt' for protection. Now dysentery took the people down in days, everyone knew what 'lost family' meant. Every week someone else became an ancestor.

Soon two days had turned into two weeks, and for a short while Loïc learned what the love of a woman meant in the fullest sense. All his needs were attended to in ways that he had never imagined. For him part of his grief at leaving Anna Cecille was refreshed by the attention, but at the same time being appreciated gave birth to a new happiness and confidence.

Each day he was able to see Fran differently; age seemed to dissolve around her. Light, time of day, even slight movements, gave him pictures of her in her past and future. Loïc could see how beauty had become written in timeless rhythms all over her body, face and eyes. At once she was girl, woman and crone, never losing the essential beauty of herself that radiated out into her every day.

He realised that it was not her doing that allowed him to see her like this, it was an inner change; an arriving at loving his own life that revealed the beauty of it all. He had begun to read the meaning within the story. He could now acknowledge the consequences of his actions. Each act of kindness drew to itself the same if not a greater gift to receive. Delivering babies in boxes had brought him into a circle of influence, the thrall of love.

As he sat gazing into the fire, a voice spoke in his head. N'Zingu's voice from the Iboga ground. 'Listen.' He listened through his bones.

'First there is stillness
Then movement brings the mind awake
Then comes action
Between the mind and the action, place your intentions, make them good and clear.
Then the nature of everything will know it can trust you.
From this trust comes the love that is like ripe fruit in the mouth.
Now nothing stands in your way, everything moves in support.'

Loïc felt these words as if spoken by the fire.

From his bag he took out a bundle and unwrapped it. Inside was his now dried out fern frond from the ceremony in the forest. Carefully he tipped the spore off the cloth into his hand. The grains he poured like sand into the fire. As a huge sheet of flame leapt up into the sky he realised that he was watching himself again as he had whilst taking the Iboga. He had no idea that the spores were volatile and fell back in surprise and delight at the discovery. He felt that N'Zingu was somehow playing with him remotely and he laughed at the possibility.

The next day Loïc discovered a bowerbird clearing it's mating ground and making the bower at one end. It was a long and particular process. Every twig was placed for both structural and aesthetic reasons. Each stone arranged according to size. Piles of flowers arranged by colour were placed at the sides of the cleared compound. All insects either eaten or removed. Every now and again he would freeze, cock his head to one side and consider the results so far.

"Attention to detail, huh," Fran whispered as she embraced him from behind.

"Tantra," she said in a low growl.

What she meant he had no idea, but was destined to find out.

'All the time he clears and cleans, he thinks only of the female. Will she like it this way or is it that way that will work? The female meanwhile remains quiet and watching. He is not the only one, there are others busy trying to please her. When she is through with waiting she will make her inspection. It pleases him but does it please her? If so he will do his best. In truth she only has eggs in mind; the best eggs.'

"Tantra." Fran whispered again, "the art of bringing ecstasy to the female and healing the creativity of the male. It's time to go if we're going to hook up with Joe."

The prospect of flying was not one Loïc relished, especially in that box of rivets that Joe insisted on calling a plane. Being a passenger left him feeling dislocated and since he didn't really have a destination, why arrive dislocated?

"If you're thinking of staying here you won't be able to. My work is finished for now, I'm going east. Perhaps Joe has another trick up his sleeve, you never can tell with Joe. Just when you think you've got the measure of the man he comes up with the unexpected. We'll check him out, let's go."

It took all morning to say goodbye to everyone and no one could be left out. Then it was into the truck and back to the city and the airstrip. The journey weighed heavy on Loïc. There was about it a sense of loss as if something was being taken from him. He knew this was not so, and that all he owned was himself. He was now unsure about the truth of his feelings and how to manage his grief. He sank into a deep silence as the truck wound its way through waving villages and along rutted tracks. By mid-afternoon Fran could resist no longer.

"You shame yourself with this silence, I don't recognise this grumpy little boy that now sits at my side. Let me tell you something that will stand you in good stead for the future. When you have a feeling about something and it feels like a hurt, stop. Make sure that the feeling is really about what's happening now and not a triggered old pain, loose from its truth. The child pain body feeds on any doubts you have, twisting them into those feelings of separation. If this mood you're in has something to do with loneliness and me then I suggest you get with the moment. There's no injury intended here, and while we are talking plainly, don't take this wrongly because I, for one, have enjoyed every minute of our time together. When you want something, ask yourself the question, what do I have to bring to the situation?" She paused and smiled at him.

"If it's a woman you want, don't show her this wanting part of yourself. Women know all about wanting, they don't need more. Show her something different, show her how open and prepared you are, how ready you are to bring her beauty to the surface. Behind every frown there's a smile waiting for an opportunity. Show your teeth. Showing each other our teeth is very ancient. It separates us from the animals. They show theirs as a warning, we show ours as an invitation to come closer. If you can make a woman smile then show her what you bring to the meeting. When we met I smiled at you, right? And how's it been since then? Don't lose your grace in the face of an unknown future. Get with the beat baggy."

Loïc couldn't resist this last part; a huge smile spread across his face and his mood lifted.

"Next time, do it for yourself, Okay? Anyone who wants to carry that poor me stuff, you don't want to know, believe me."

"Yes, yes, I'm with the beat." He kissed her "I'm a bit new to all this."

"That's OK, you learn quickly, it makes it worth my

while."

They looked at each other and laughed.

At dusk they pulled onto the airstrip. The light was eaten in a couple of mouthfuls. Joe was there, spannering up his plane, and replacing rivets. It was true the runway didn't look so wide. What looked like a thick layer of garbage spread down either side of the narrowed tarmac strip. Joe was his usual cheerful self.

"I see she taught you how to matter." He laughed. "Two means all numbers except two, this I like. I've got a proposition for you both."

Fran gave him a wide berth, crept up behind and held him round the waist.

"Sounds good to me," she said as his hands covered hers, "where, when and how?"

"There's a group of young people working out of the forest on mainland Madagascar. They're gathering seed stock, periwinkles; they want to get them into Europe to explore treating Hodgkin's disease and diabetes. Sounds interesting and they can pay. I need assistance. What's your plan?"

"Do you really think this bucket of yours is going to get into Europe?"

"That's not on the cards. I couldn't use it anywhere but Africa. They have a plane they just don't have a pilot. I'm going in the morning. If you want to work that's fine. If you want a ride that's fine too. Either way it's leave at dawn. Now I need to get her into shape, the rivet and bullet holes are competing for space these days."

He fired up a kerosene lamp and got back to the hand drill and the rivet gun.

"See you first thing."

Before dawn Fran and Loïc were at the hangar, ready to ride. Joe was bleary, he'd been up half the night getting her airworthy. Once they had cleared the flapping plastic and flattened oilcans that was the squatters camp and gained some altitude, Joe handed the controls to Loïc and the navigation to Fran.

"We need to re-fuel in Mombassa. Wake me in three hours and I'll take her down."

Within minutes Fran and Loïc had slipped into team mode, both of them had a way with flight.

N'zingu had said he would be led east by a bird. He had never thought of a metal bird. As they rose into the sky light burst into the cockpit. It was late June and early morning temperatures were in the high thirties, shade didn't make much difference; water was always tepid and if there was no breeze the air thickened like boiled soup. It was one of those days, the fact that they were in the air made for better lift but nothing else, the plane was a magnet for heat.

As he shaded his eyes Loïc could see, above the rising sun, another point of piercing light heralding the day. He didn't know then that it was the Dog Star, Sirius. He just felt a great surge of happiness spread through his body, like the penetrating warmth of a hot spring. Loïc wasn't to know, but he was feeling the strong magnetic downstream energy from Sirius, the body of the great bird Manu. He looked down at the landscape slipping beneath them, colours moving in unfolding forms. The reality of size merely an idea. From here he had the eyes of a hawk and the view of a star.

It was then that Loïc had a clear image of his home village, pitched up under the ridge; the smell of rosemary and thyme seemed to invade the cockpit. The texture of the rock seemed to be on his hands as he gripped the stick. He knew the place was in his blood wherever he went. The bands of outcrop rocks, the caves deep in the mountains, the sanctuary of the springs.

Then it was gone, just the engine drone, the sun and Fran pointing down at a vast expanse of water.

"Lake Victoria," she announced, "you're right on course."

9
Nosy Boraha

He was pleased to be out of the sky and on land again. Fran and Joe had offered to fly the small periwinkle plane up into Egypt and then on to Greece. The northerly direction had crossed his mind, but this was far too sudden for Loïc, as there was much more for him to find out before going north,, so he stayed with his feet firmly in Madagascar. Within days he met a stout bearded man called Trumpet Dan who was building a boat out of bamboo on Nosy Boraha an island off the north-east coast. They hit it off and he invited Loïc to visit him.

The first morning on the island Loïc woke to a growing light. He'd slept outside under a wrap and now, as dawn persuaded him into the day, he realised that newness had awoken with him. He was covered with small white moths, dying moths. They had settled on him as a cloud finding a final resting place and moved feebly if he touched them otherwise they feebly died. By the time he had sat up considering how to move, the ants were already collecting their dead carcases, hauling away small white sails with determination .

The second morning, TD as he preferred to be called, took Loïc over to the beach where there was a large pile of bamboo.

"These have been soaking in flowing water for a whole season. It washes out the starch and it's the starch that the 'boogies' like. Damn things can leave you with a pile of dust in a month."

"What are boogies?"

"Powder beetles, the scourge of bamboo, they multiply faster than bamboo can grow and that's fast. In the growing season I've measured seven feet in ten days, but these little suckers munch like there's no tomorrow. Just when you think you've done a good job. Say you made a beautifully jointed bamboo table, you eat off it for a few months then one day you move the table and there they are, four piles of dust with just the outside of the legs left. You can hear them gnawing at night, drives me crazy."

"Not only that, I met a man once, Cesar an Indian bamboo basket maker. He's splitting culms to make himself a basket or two and he gets bitten by one of these boogies and thinks nothing of it. That night he is struck with a fever that puts him into his bed and burning up. A week later he's still in bed. At the end of the month he's weakly tottering around on his feet and feeling somewhat better. Everyone who knows him says he's looking different and he is, every hair on his body has fallen out even his eyelashes. When I met him he was more naked than a new-born and still making baskets. He shrugged, " For sure can't happen twice."

Loïc winced and studied the hairs on his arms and legs.

"Nose, nuts and navel," laughed TD. "Don't worry, it's a rare reaction that's all. More important is how we are going to construct this boat using the bamboo that we have washed the starch out of. The Chinese have been making everything out of bamboo for millennia. They were the ones who figured out that if you made boats in sections and then if you got a hole in the bow it would only flood that section and you wouldn't sink. That came from looking at bamboo and its enclosed internodes. This boat's going to be a bit different, I don't know if it's been done before, probably most things have even if they've been forgotten, but I'm going for a ten meter catamaran using full bamboo culms over a frame. You want to help build her?"

"Tell me more." said Loïc intrigued by the impossibility of the plan.

"I have ideas but nothing's fixed as yet. The buoyancy isn't going to be a problem, it's how to hold the whole thing together without making holes in the bamboo."

By now Loïc had seen the construction of many things in many places and had always enjoyed the ingenuity of humans. They not only adapted well to their environments, but also in turn adapted their surroundings to work in their favour. He saw the possibilities of the bamboo boat and how to construct it, by strapping each bamboo culm to the one below and staggering the joints. Caulking the joints was a mystery, but the boat would certainly ride high in the water. TD agreed and disagreed and between them they came up with a basic working plan. For caulking between the hull culms they tried kelp, though it continued to grow in the water, the job of keeping the water out it didn't do.

One day TD was lying under a palm, taking a little shade while he ate. The locals had been wagging their finger at him but he stayed put and fell asleep. Suddenly there was a mighty smack on the ground next to his head; a big green coconut had made a sizeable dent in the ground. It was a big wake up for him. Deaths from falling nuts are very high, everywhere they grow skulls get cracked. However the tree fibres of these palms, especially the fibres of the black palm, are so special that their use is considered sacred. The matted layers of the trunk, unlike everything else in the tropics, doesn't rot and to find a natural fibre that's rotproof is an exception to the rule; with its oddity comes new possibilities.

So they tried it. First it was twisted into a string and then woven into narrow straps and used to join the bamboos one to the next. With the blessings of the locals who supplied the fibres, the boat began to grow between the shady but deadly palms.

As the hull took shape, strap by strap, culm by culm, so they grew more familiar with the beach and the sound that lay between them and the mainland of Madagascar out to the west. Each morning before work TD, Loïc and two of the local boys went out into the waters to line fish. Towards the end of the second week the boys took the skiff further out into the waters of the sound. Here the water was deep and the island formed good protection from the currents of the ocean out to the east.

"There! Look there," was the shout that went up that particular morning.

"Look, look," the boys said, pointing down into the water. They all craned over the edge of the small skiff, rocking it precariously. Below them the sea had changed colour, to a grey black. It seemed to move as a mass, hard to see the edges but definitely not water.

"Humpa," whispered one of the boys. "Humpa whale."

Loïc had seen whales from a distance before, but this was huge and almost within reach. As they watched, a fin broke the surface followed by a smooth enormous back. Then there were others, slowly emerging from the deep. They formed a ring around the small craft and blew vapourising sprays from their double blowholes and gradually sank down again. Loïc noticed how different their dorsal fins were from each other; one had a distinct notch, bitten out perhaps, another flopped to one side, another small and ribbed. Their fins were like fingerprints in humans, singular to each whale. They sank and swam unhurried just below the surface. Fishing was soon forgotten as the feelings of fear melted into wonder.

"Humpbacks." said TD.

"Yes Humpa," said the boys, "they come to make their babies and to birth them. They come every year, they stay all season, make babies and play."

Loïc was in awe, they were so graceful and calm, their enormous mass gliding through the water, hardly disturbing the surface. It was then that Loïc saw a calf swimming close to its mother's side. It was very young but still twice the size of their boat. Every movement from the mother was echoed in the calf. The pod again rose to the surface blowing jets of spray in the air. On their heads and jaws they had lumps with stiff hairs growing from them, and Loïc was reminded that they too were mammals like himself and these hairs would be as sensitive as whiskers, able to detect changes in the water currents and temperatures. The boys kept the boat moving and the humpbacks seemed to enjoy their company, opening their giant jaws and waving their flukes in the air.

It was at that point that they all leant to one side of the boat to look down to see the calf as the mother nosed it up to see them. As they looked at each other the boat went over and slid all four boys into the water. Instead of panic it seemed quite natural, the mother continued to encourage her calf and there they were swimming with whales off the coast of Madagascar. They ducked and dived down into the warm water. Protectively the mother edged her way between them and her calf. The situation changed, now an eye the size of a saucer and surrounded by folds of skin regarded him without curiosity, without fear, just impassively looking. The unblinking enormous eye saw deep inside him and he felt he was being truly seen for the first time in his life. They hung there in the clear water, eyes to eye a few feet apart, lost in the moment, found in their hearts. If whales can smile then Loïc was certain he saw one flicker across that enormous eye. She gently rolled over showing her 'fanons', long ventral pleats of skin that stretched from her chin down to her navel like a huge pleated curtain, mottled black and white. As she rolled, so the calf appeared and the four of them touched and stroked the new-born while the mother looked on. The other whales surrounded them, sunlight playing patterns on their black backs. Huge, passive, watching. Then there was an unseen signal and off they drifted. With a lazy tail movement they were gone and the sea felt empty. These mighty swimmers, in just fifty years of their lives, swim the oceans from equator to the Arctic so many times that by the time they sink down into their watery graves they have swum the distance to the Moon.

The skiff had drifted away and the boys swam after it before the current swept it away. TD and Loïc lay floating on their backs.

"Wow," was about all they could say."Wow,"and laugh.

For the next four mornings the four of them sailed out and dropped the sail. Then one by one they dropped over the side and swam with the pod. Sometimes they knew when the whales were coming because they sang long continuous chants. Long cycles of varying pitches. When Loïc listened to them coming it was loud and clear underwater, but when he came up for air it was slower and muffled, because sound travels four and a half times faster through water than air. He noticed that it was only the male humpbacks that did the singing. They say that you can hear them from hundreds of miles away. They also say that their songs are sound maps that they sing, to remember their way from the tropics to the ice fields where they go in winter to eat. And do they eat, sometimes as much as four tons of krill each day, so that they can build up their coats of blubber. When they swim the 3000 miles back down to the warm waters they're good and fat their bodies able to cope with not eating at all for months.

"How do they do that? said Loïc while they were working in the palm shade.

"Well," said TD, who seemed to know everything about humpbacks, "they use those sound songs to navigate. Not only are they long distance songs, they can hear the echoes off the land and especially the islands. That's how they know where they are. Smart or what?"

"Smart." Loïc had to agree.

"They're really smart when it comes to fishing too. How do think this huge creature with the most massive mouth in the world can live on krill which are about the size of your little finger at best?"

Loïc thought about this for a while as he carried on tying the ijuk knots. The big mouth and the little fish.

"Four tons a day did you say? That's how much they eat?"

"You know nobody really knows, but yeah, let's say on average four tons a day. Let's put it another way, they eat so much krill when they're fishing that they only have to eat for about half of their lives."

"What do they do for the other half?" said Loïc. "Sleep?"

"They don't really sleep, they switch off and doze near the surface. No we're not counting sleep time, this is waking time."

"Okay, I don't know, tell me how do big mouths catch little fish?"

"Well," said TD, settling down to whittle another bamboo cleat. "Firstly they hunt the krill together as a pod. As they herd the krill they start to swarm and once that starts, the pod circles up beneath the swarm, driving them up into the warmer surface water where it's light. Then, staying in their circle, they start to blow bubbles, yeah, streams of bubbles. They form a rising ring of bubbles. As they rise to the surface round the krill, the krill believe they are surrounded, which they are of course, but it's only air. They don't know that because they're just behaving in a frightened mass; the more fear, the more they press together. Then up comes a Humpa with that massive maw wide open and sucks in, thousands and thousands in one mouthful. Krill and water, all goes into that gaping mouth. Then they sieve out the water through a curtain of baleen ribs and swallow the krill. That's how. One mouthful - half a ton, something like that, smart eh?"

There was a loud crack as another coconut bounced off the bamboo boat frame. They looked at each other and raised their eyebrows.

"Best get on with it and out of here, before there's no one left to sail her."

They laughed and called to one of the fishermen's boys and flipped a coin in the air. He shinned up the tree overhanging the boat with bare feet and a machete in his teeth and started dropping down the ripe coconuts. He was back down again in moments, brushing ants off his legs. Loïc flipped him the coin. He caught it, punched the air and stomped off in the direction of the Fanta stall with his hand flapping around in his shorts.

By laying the bamboo culms with the tapering ends at the bow the hull emerged. They worked with the boat hulls upside down, lashing each length to the next and then, with the palm rope lashed them to the ribbed skeleton frame. It seemed to be strong enough, but it left narrow gaps between each course of bamboo.

"They'll float for sure," announced TD one morning, "but like this it's going to be full of water and that'll create a lot of drag - too much drag. What to do Loïc, got any good ideas?"

"It'll come," came from Loïc.

He was surprised he'd said this with such confidence, but that was how he felt. Outside his rational self grew a belief that everything was possible if you persevered and stayed open to the signs around you.

"Maybe this comes from the Humpas?" slipped into his mind and out of his mouth.

"What's that you said?" came from TD.

"Let's just stay in the zone, we haven't come this far to

turn back now. If this is the right thing to be doing then it'll come, I'm sure."

"Okay," said TD, giving him a perplexed look.

"There's something I forgot to tell you about the big mouths these Humpas have."

"Tell me."

"It's not just the krill they catch in the sea water."

"What?"

"It's the plastic now, in the seawater, there's plastic."

"Plastic, come on."

"Plastic breaking down into fragments, it's everywhere, not just where it's thrown into the sea. Everywhere, all over the globe, It's like a snow globe of multi coloured flakes in suspension it gets into everything in the sea that has a mouth. Humpa as well, it gets in and doesn't come out."

"Everywhere?"

" It's found everywhere they've trawled with fine nets. It's killing everything. We are choking the seas but because we don't see it we keep on using plastic bags, just once and then throw. We've laid waste to the forests of the world now its the oceans. There'll be no plastic used on this boat."

"Okay."

That evening the women who had been twisting the palm fibre into ropes for the boat, called them away from the grove, indicating their mouths and their stomachs. They were hungry so they followed as men do where food is concerned.

A hundred metres down the beach was a small settlement of stilted bamboo houses. Here in the whispering bamboo grove where there was no danger of falling nuts, the tiny fishing village bathed in the cool evening air. Feather footed fowl and spotted pigs occupied the dry sand underneath the houses while they sat up on the decking drinking a black chai. Cooking smells drifting from the charcoal burners. On the deck of the house next door sat a stove with a steamer on top pumping out a white trail into the slight breeze. Loïc climbed down the ladder and walked over. The woman of the house appeared and he pointed to the stove, flicking his other hand over in the gesture of a question.

She laughed and beckoned him up. As she lifted the lid a

cloud of stem enveloped them, as it cleared he made the question gesture again as he peered into the pot.

"Agar agar."

"Agar agar," he repeated, enjoying the repetition.

Fingers together, he put them to his mouth, she nodded. He spread his hands in a large gesture and she nodded again touching her lips and pointing to a hollow in the ground below the roof eaves and making a smoothing gesture with both hands. A furrow appeared on Loïc's brow and she replaced the lid and tugged at his sleeve. A split bamboo was hung from the trimmed roof edge, the end directed over the hollow below. They climbed down and she showed him how she was smearing the steamed agar agar around the surface of the shape. A line of ducks waddled into view and headed in their direction.

She made an egg shape with both hands, "Atody, atody."

Loïc too said, "atody atody."

The roof, the bamboo gutter, the hollow and the ducks. At that moment something fell into place. He got it. He had the answer to the boat-building problem. Turning he called to TD.

"Hey where's agar agar from?"

"Agar agar is red algae, there's loads of it out there," he said gesturing vaguely in the direction of the sea. "It's prehistoric, one of earth's first life forms, without it we wouldn't be here. Why so interested?"

"It might just be the answer."

"Answer to what, the meaning of life?"

"Who knows, but it is the answer to watertight."

"What are you on about," mocked TD, "this is only black chai you know."

"No, no come and take a look at this," Loïc shouted.

He shambled down the steps certain that Loïc was joking.

"Look what she's making."

"Yes a pond for the ducks."

"That's right, a pond, and what do ponds do?"

"Hold wa…"

They looked at each other as smiles broke across their faces and they leapt into each other's arms, jumping about wildly as the tepid black chai slopped all over them. This brought disapproving looks from the women, not for their behaviour; their men folk were forever in each other's arms, jumping up and down wildly. No, it was the chai, their men folk never spilt their chai, the women made sure of that.

The next time it rained they rushed round to see if the pond worked and much to the ducks' delight it held water.

"Entonces, donde esta el algae rojo?" Loïc was practising his Spanish as TD was Spanish speaking.

"Esta en el mar," he replied uncharacteristically vague.

"Pero donde? The sea's very big."

"Yes that's true," he said leaning back from tying another knot. "To be honest I've never seen it grow but I'm told it shoots six to seven metres down, you have to dive for it."

"How do the locals get at it?"

"Guess they do just that, dive and bring it up somehow. I'll leave that to you. Deep water I'd prefer not to get into."

Loïc got a strong feeling that TD was not fond of the water. This was followed by the shock that TD was afraid of water.

"You can't swim, can you TD? How come you were in with the whales and not scrambling about for the skiff?"

"I hold my breath, that way I don't sink so far but I can't do it for long."

"So you're telling me that we're going to sail this bamboo experiment across the Indian Ocean and you can't swim!"

"That's right, you don't need to swim if you've got a boat, most sailors can't swim, otherwise they would be swimmers not sailors."

"Oh come on that's just defensive."

"I don't want to."

"Why not? I'll teach you."

"I don't want you or anyone else to teach me. I've got this far without swimming and that's good enough for me."

"Come on it's easy, I couldn't swim until I was sixteen. It used to scare the hell out of me, but working on boats, well, there wasn't anything else to do off the boat most of the time."

"Look that's all very interesting but I don't want to know,

I steer clear of deep water."

"You're frightened of water aren't you?" said Loïc amazed.

"That's right I'm a sailor, I like being up on the surface where the wind is. Down there is where old sailors go; I'm not ready for anyone's locker especially not Davy Jones's, whoever he was. That's why red algae is your department. It's a good idea but we could use cow dung, only it smells so strong, so I'm up for the agar agar treatment but sourcing is up to you."

Loïc went back to tying knots and thought about 'deep water'. He too was not keen on going down deep; it was cold and seemed to suck you down further into the darkness. There must be a method the locals used. His thoughts turned to the pond and the ducks again.

"How does it grow?"

"Look I don't know about red algae, if you can get it we'll use it. For my part I'll live with the smell of smeared cow dung in preference to scratching around on the sea bottom."

The discussion was over. It was up to Loïc to see this part of the boatbuilding through.

It was two weeks later and the boat was beginning to look distinctly different. The hulls were beautiful curves tapering up at the ends and bowed like long slices of melon. They had saved four of the longest culms to finish the gunwales, which would receive all the rope cleats, which were also made from the split bamboo nodes and strapped on with greased ijuk lashings. Emergency paddles, fishing rods, fish traps, baskets, an awning and sun hats were all made from split and worked bamboo. They devised a detachable brace with two poles that locked across the two hulls. Once an old waxed sail was stretched between the hulls it also served as a rainwater collector. Things were taking shape and there was an imminence to their departure.

Although they had little money their boatbuilding had brought some well-needed changes to the local economy and the women in particular wanted to show their appreciation. For days Loïc had been gesturing 'armfuls' to the village women and smiling while he repeated 'agar agar, agar agar,' like some kind of mantra that would bring an abundance of the stuff.

"Yes, yes, agar agar, barabosy agar agar." The women sang, making big gestures with their arms.

"Agar agar barabosy," Loïc repeated, smiling holding his arms wide. They replied with their hands patting down the air as if to say, 'wait a little, wait a little.'

10
A Living Fossil

The day was bright and cool when it came. The full moon of the night before had left a bank of mist hanging over the sea. Five of them arrived with nets, knives and a bullock cart loaded with cooking kit and bags.

"Agar agar," they smiled as Loïc fell in with the chattering group. To his surprise they started off inland leaving the sea behind them.

All morning they walked through the bizarre landscape of the tiny island. Madagascar itself had broken away from mainland Africa after a massive earthquake 165 million years ago and floated into the Indian Ocean coming to rest 260 miles off the coast but Nosy Boraha had broken away from Madagascar and had evolved even more remotely off the east coast.

Stranded out in the Indian Ocean, development had been particular. At the top of the pecking order for thousands of years had sat and often strutted, the Vorompatra. *Aepyornis maximus*. This ten foot tall, thousand pound, flightless bird, with a beak tough enough to crack a coconut, was the ruling two legged. They were big and fearless because nothing preyed upon them. Then, one thousand years ago man arrived, and man being man with his usual desire to eat everything, clubbed them, cooked them and ate them. Then he stepped out again and again until he had clubbed every last one to death. Now it was the aye ayes and the bug eyed lemurs that ruled the roost in their numerous varieties, from giant to miniature; mostly nocturnal, they had avoided men who knew them more for their singing than their taste.

As they approached the other coast all the trees except the baobabs had gone. Tall bottlenecked columns stood dotted through the underbrush. They tapered at their tops and then sprouted a few unlikely looking branches and even fewer leaves. There was no shade along this part of the journey and the heat was intense. The women patted their smooth barks as they passed.

"Sacre sacre," they announced.

"And the others?" He gestured at the empty landscape.

They made chopping movements with flat hands and mimed huge machinery. It was then that Loïc read the pain on their faces. To the people the baobabs were sacred, all the other types had been cut and taken away by people from another country. Now it was the tears of the people and the skinny baobabs that told of the crying shame that this bizarre landscape could not explain. They walked on in silence until the shore was reached, where they set up awnings and made an evening meal.

The next day the women showed Loïc their method for harvesting the algae, which grew offshore, some five or six metres below the waves. By tying ropes to large stones they jumped from rocks into the sea. They were naked and greased to avoid becoming entangled with the plants and to deal with the deeper, colder water. With knives in their mouths and nets at their waists they sank down to the algae beds. Slow motion was the character of the harvesting of this water plant. To Loïc it all looked like fishing with mermaids. Their shiny bodies gliding through the fractured light gave them scales and liquid forms.

The sunlight filtered down to give the sea bottom a clear but green tint. He soon found that you had to work hard and fast. The stalks proved to be rubbery, only a slicing cut would get through the stems. Loïc was up and down like a cork, but the women stayed down long enough to fill a whole net. Once full they floated up to the surface and shouted.

"mariaria, mariaria. net, net." To the others waiting in the surf.

They exchanged nets; one being hauled on shore the other taken for the next dive. They worked in pairs, Loïc taking the place of the sixth woman. By the end of the day a cartload of agar agar lay drying above the high tide mark. At dawn the next day they spread it out to dry, occasionally turning piles as the sun baked it into huge pancakes. By nightfall the wagon was loaded and another fire built and a soup of algae was bubbling in the cooking pot. They were pleased with their work; by leaving roots in the sea bottom it ensured that the algae would grow back on this particular spot where their ancestors had been harvesting the plant for years. They were also pleased because there had been no injuries, which had been a worry for the women. Usually this was women's work and taking a man along had been risky. Now they were calling him. "Lucky Loïc."

By dawn the next day they were already on the return journey back to the village on the other side of this sliver of an island. Shortly after leaving the coast the heavens opened and rain fell in a torrent. The earth pathways turned to slurry and the Brahma bull simply stopped and stood there in the shafts and decided to wait it out. Temptation and persuasion made no difference and the women made a fire underneath the wagon, and brewed up one of their bitter black chais avoiding the drips as best they could.

Sitting there, waiting and watching the landscape through a veil of rain, the nature explained itself to Loïc very rapidly. Since there were few trees, there was little ground cover and hence few roots to hold the soil. As the water rose filling the track way, large sections of the sides, sodden with rain, just fell away and sank into the spreading water. Small plants started to drift past on a building current.

Once not so long ago there had been a Queen of Madagascar and its islands, She was known as Queen Ranavalona, the people knew her as 'Ma Dieu' which of course, is creole for 'Mother God'. She ruled with a cruel hand. She reasoned that no roads should be built because without roads it is very hard to capture a country when the enemy is using wheels. So, ever since then there were no roads with hard surfaces. Like swollen rivers the track ways would change course, taking the path of least resistance. She also kept her people in the grip of fear, declaring that should she dream of anyone, they would be executed.

Where they sat under the wagon was fast becoming part of a maze of waterfilled trenches that no longer spoke of the numerous routes that people had taken to the coast. Now a widening red lake was finding its own way to the ocean. The slurry rushed past, carrying ancient soils to pollute the algae beds that they had just been collecting from.

The bull stood drenched and resigned in the shafts, he too was part of the same story. After the trees had been taken off to become laminated sheets for the building trade, so his ancestors had been shipped onto the island to graze the remains of the forest. So that they in turn could become beef burgers for people who had either drunk too much or couldn't be bothered to cook any more. As he stood there, torrential rain pouring off him in curtains, the tragedy of man's behaviour was clearly reflected in the earth rich waters that swirled around his legs. By now they were all soaked to the skin and the women had taken to the wagon bed to sit it out, which in turn was so wet that the pats of algae had reabsorbed the water and were in danger of slithering off the sides of the flat bed.

"Famogena, Famogena Loïc." They shouted to him as they struggled to slip the algae into the nets before it joined the swirling mud.

"Help, help. Loïc before it all goes." They eyed him as he clambered up onto the wagon.

"Yes yes, not so lucky now."

"Yes yes, not so lucky Loïc now."

They laughed at their predicament, rain rushing into their mouths until their laughter turned to tears and they all wept for the piteous state of their island and how so much can be undone by so few. They sat like this for a long time, pulling swelling algae nets back onto the wagon bed until the sun broke through and the rain clouds drifted west to douse the Madagascan mainland.

Rainwater was soon being converted into vapour by the extreme heat of the sun. Thick clouds rose in layers from the ground and the humidity made it hard to breathe. The lack of trees made it clear that life without their oxygen supply was near impossible. When they did decide to move on, walking was heavy going. The loosened soil, now so saturated that it too was starved of oxygen had become a viscous slip. Each step seemed to suck feet down into a soupy mass and refuse to let go. They edged the wagon forward, pushing from behind and leading the fearful bull by the nose.

Progress was laboriously slow, the wheels became clogged with spuds of mud and the hooves of the beast sank so far into the morass that its belly became caked with a thick red layer, making each step a struggle. A slight breeze from the east eased the blanket of water vapour off the ground, revealing in the near distance three enormous baobab trees. They must have lost the path because Loïc hadn't noticed them on the outward journey. The women became very animated and goaded the exhausted bull towards the trees. It took an hour or so to cover the short distance, the mud becoming claggier with each step as the sun drove out the water and thickened it into a caking mix. Beyond the three baobabs, which formed an open triangle, flowed a swollen torrent of slurry, more earth than water, ploughing its way back towards the sea.

The women were soon making camp in the huge folded buttress roots of the central tree, cheerful and pleased to have found sacred shelter. The baobabs reminded Loïc of the ones he had found on the Cape Verde islands, huge with many branches, quite unlike the tall thin bottlenecks they had passed a few days before. These three were ancient and spoke of a forest not long forgotten. A place within memory where humans had made their mark. He sat in the folds of the trunk and distractedly watched the red river ooze past. At times large sections of the bank just broke away and slumped down into the lava like flow. As he sat mesmerised by the slow motion his thoughts wandered back up the mountain of his origin. He wondered if his parents were still alive. Who was still in the village? Was it now deserted and falling down? Was Anna Cecille with someone? Did she have any children? What shape was his past in? He was unsure how long he had been away. It wasn't possible to tell from the seasons here because they no longer had any characteristic differences. He guessed he must have been away for two winters by now. As he tried to recall some details of recent events that might mark periods of time, he realised that something was happening before his very eyes, and he had no idea what it could be.

A large section of the bank loosened and slipped away

into the flow and a large creamy coloured curve was revealed. It didn't look like a stone for it was very regular and it could hardly be a mushroom that size and that deep in the earth. As more of the bank escaped from the thick bed of soil, so more of the curved shape was revealed. Loïc slithered over to it, for it was about to break away and join the general flow. He reached out to touch it and as he did an egg came into his mind. An enormous egg. He dug his hand into the sodden soil beneath it and tried to lift it up onto the bloated bank. Struggling, his added weight threatened to collapse more of the bank. He started to slide into the moving mass of mud. Dangerous he thought, I could easily slip below the surface and that would be it; disappeared in Madagascar.

"Famojena famojena." He shouted.

"Famojena barabosy atody. Famojena mariaria, Famojena Famojena."

Where this spontaneous outburst of Malagasy had come from he wasn't sure but he had evidently remembered something because the women came running with one of the algae nets and scooped him and the egg out of the thick red flow and deposited him at the roots of the nearest tree.

There he sat, between his feet an egg the size of what? He was lost for words. The egg of what? He couldn't imagine. He had seen ostrich eggs for sale in markets and they were impressive, but next to this egg they were ordinary. He sat and marvelled at the impossibility of his find. How was it that it had been revealed to him from deep in the earth? Of all the things that had happened since he had left home, they had just been eclipsed. This surely was the most extraordinary. It was surely an egg from another dimension. The women brought him some food. Their chatter had ceased and a sombre awe had spread over them. They too had never seen the like of it. But unlike Loïc they had heard stories about rare but occasional finds of egg fragments of the legendary 'elephant bird' that once ruled Madagascar and her islands, but never a whole egg. This flightless creature had stood twice the height of a man and before his arrival had been the dominant two legged over all the land with the occasional unwary loss to a crocodile.

For now the women said nothing. They were impressed and some of that awe passed over to Loïc. They became respectful towards him and from then on gave him special consideration. After all he had just unearthed an egg that could be a thousand years old, and they were unsure about who he might be. They blessed the baobabs, the hungry and unhappy Brahma bull, the river, its banks and finally Loïc and the egg, and then turned in for the night beneath the trees.

Huddled in the folds of the baobab Loïc sat embracing the egg as if he could hatch out this ancient bird. A behemoth from a time beyond imagination. A slot in the evolution of this planet after the dinosaurs had died in the aftermath of the meteorite hit in the Yucatan and the ascendancy of the burrowing mammals, the survivors of that holocaust of blackened skies and fireball winds. Between the giant reptiles and the hairless mammals lay a short period of millions of years when the winged and flightless 'Ornios' were top of the pecking order. Some with beaks and claws, others with leathery wings and still more with feathered flight they escaped to obscure land pockets and isolated islands where they flourished until humans came and saw to their demise.

It brought tears to Loïc's eyes as he thought of all the wonders of nature that men had hastened on their way. What was this egg destined to hatch into? It was so enormous that his cradling arms could just touch on the other side. Its texture was that of polished stone, the pores the size of pinholes, its creamy colour shot through with traces of azure. Even the dinosaurs had never laid an egg like this, their diets lacking the calcium to form such a shell, making their leathery clutches more akin to the crocodile and the turtle. No this was a mega egg, a symbol of the unpredictability of life.

The morning sun rose full and hot, soon clearing the ground of water in drifts of wispy vapour, drying the surface into its altered form. The few remaining plants stood dazed at the prospect of recovery.

The women, ready to leave, found Loïc slumped over the egg. They had arranged the slimy algae nets on the wagon to form a nest for the egg and helped his bleary self to lift it into place. The rest of the journey was uneventful. Keeping to the higher ground they wound their way through the remains of the forest. There was however a revived atmosphere to their muddied trudge. The delivery of the algae and the egg was like the delivery of a giant's breakfast.

TD was watching out for them, knowing that the heavy rains would do for them what the old Queen had intended for the voracious colonising French and British, get them stuck in it. This part of her plan to keep the Christians off her island stronghold, and matching their weaponry had fought off two of the superpowers of the day. She had killed encroaching Christians, giving the Welsh missionary chapter led by one David Jones the colder than cold shoulder.

Was there, he mused a connection between Dafydd Jones and Davy Jones? He knew from his own travels that the West Indian for ghost was 'duffy' and that Jones was easily understood as Jonah, the prophet who had spent some time roaming a fishes abdomen, which was of course a mammals abdomen. Was he somehow mixed up in this, could that be the locker he really feared, Duffy Jonah's coffin? He let go of the train of thought; the origins of things was one of those mysteries in life.

It was then that he saw them, covered in mud, slowly heading towards him with a laden wagon and singing loudly. When they stopped by the hull of the boat he understood their high spirits. He had seen fragments of shells before but this was something else.

"Loïc, he smiled, you go for one thing and you return with two. How is this?"

Loïc could offer nothing but a weak smile in return. The women unhitched the weary bull and set off towards their village promising to return the next day with their steamers. The combination of Loïc's outburst in Malagasy and finding the egg had given them more than enough to discuss away from his presence. Tomorrow would be clearer after a night to dream and see it all from another place in themselves. That and the three old sacred baobabs they had found was enough to last them a month of discussion. Exhausted by the return journey Loïc took to his bed early that night, the egg nestled in next to him. He was having some difficulty knowing what to do with it, but for now he was keeping it close. He knew from its size that it was important, but what to do was another matter.

'Sleep on it,' his mother always used to say, when things weren't clear. It would have to be sleep with it on this occasion. He wrapped himself around the orb and dreamt.

'Women sat in a circle seeming to wet nurse large eggs and telling stories in Malagasy. He didn't understand, recognising only one word, 'atody'; egg. The image left him feeling isolated. He knew the egg wasn't his but whose was it? Perhaps the best thing to do was just bury it again before too many people got it hear about it.' He was about to do this when he woke from the dream with the wind rattling through his shelter, threatening to blow it away down the beach.

The women arrived early and fired up the steamers. By now the catamaran was up on chocks and a path of rollers were placed ready to launch it for its maiden voyage. All day was about pressing hot agar agar into the small gaps without burning their hands. It was agreed that a hot folded banana leaf and a large scallop shell was the least painful way. By nightfall the job was complete. The boat lay there, a sticky mess of red algae and bamboo but when she rolled down into the sea the next day she took to the water like an otter, hung in the water with a good draught, and not a leak did they find.

Out in the Humpa sound she took the wind with urgency, the sail full bellied and the bamboo mast flexing in the gusts. The removable mat canopy worked well and with everything stashed away and tied down, left plenty of room for sailing. They decided she was ready and could wait no longer. That evening was one of exchanging gifts and clinking glasses.

11
Maiden Voyage

As the sun turned the overnight damp into a drifting ground mist, they eased the new craft out of the Humpa sound heading north, past the old pirate town, and tracing out to the northeast leaving Madagascar and Nosy Boraha behind. The egg went with Loïc, wrapped with palm fibres in a bamboo basket.

There was a stiff westerly and they trapped the wind giving the craft a strong test of her abilities. She rose to the occasion skipping through the waves, rising up onto one hull, with them both hanging out on ijuk trapeze straps.

Now every boat needs a name and TD and Loïc had launched theirs without one. This they knew they had to change and fast. That night with sail down and the wind abated they cracked open three of their precious coconut supply. One on each hull and one at the base of the central mast. They named her Elephanta because of her cargo. And so it was that a bamboo boat carrying an ancient egg took to the ocean with India as her destination.

For a long time they attended only to the sailing of the boat, eating and sleeping. It wasn't until the seventh day out that there seemed any time for conversation.

TD was a mariner and a man of theories. When there was time to talk he revealed a little more of himself and these theories; life to him was an opportunity to prove them. He had many that he would agree were in the proving process and his favourite was related to eggs. When Loïc had appeared with the algae and the egg, TD had decided that it was a sign that this mammoth of all eggs had arrived in his life to prove his ovoid theory. But before he got on to that he told Loïc about the planet being overpopulated four times already. Each time, he said it was the plants that suffered first; being cut down because people thought that plants couldn't speak, which was, of course, a convenient way of saying that they didn't have to listen to their hearts. Just cut them down and use them up because they never complain and they just grow back. So it was and TD reckoned that this had happened four times to shake off those pesky people who didn't listen for very long.

First time it had become very hot, volcanoes and earthquakes had shaken everyone out of their dreams. The second time there was a great darkness and the people could see nothing and nothing grew. The third time came the great cold and the world was covered in ice and the cold drove the remaining people into caves where they learned to use their other senses. The fourth time T.D. said had only happened 30,000 years ago and on that occasion it was the water that changed everything; the oceans became drawn up into the clouds in such volume that it rained whole new rivers down onto the mountains and the land itself floated and broke into pieces and spread all over the planet.

Every time over hundreds of thousands of years some of the people had survived. According to TD it was the plants that had saved the people and every time the people praised the plants but they soon forgot. Once again they became self-important and once again started cutting them down, for doors, boats and houses, that sort of thing and before long there was no respect. Every time the people forgot how to remember they always wanted more. Now it was time for the fifth world, again the people had turned the forests into deserts, filled the skies with smoke, blotting out the sun and changed the seasons into one great jumble of hot and wet one day then dry and cold the next. The plants could no longer relax and grow and so according to TD's theory something big was about to happen and if it was coming soon then the best place to be was at sea.

Loïc made it clear that he thought TD's theory a bit woolly but in general he agreed it was always the plants, the animals and everything else that got the sharp end of the stick. Whilst the people seemed to spend a lot of time and effort thinking up ways and means of killing each other off, it never quite worked, they always came back in far greater numbers and took it out on the trees.

"So!" Said Loïc, "Why India?"

"It's a long way."

"I know it is."

"That's why we go - because it's a long way. It's a maiden voyage; we have to give her a good run, all weathers, all conditions, see how she shapes up. Remember this boat is only one move away from the pile of culms we started off with, let's see what we have done. India was one of those floating broken pieces of the earth's crust that went from here to there, so we're going to follow it."

"OK", said Loïc "India's good with me."

It transpired that TD was full of theories, some more convincing than others, however his favourite and most unproven was all about numbers, the helix and eggs. TD had amongst many other things been studying all three for many years and was just now putting together his theory. The numbers he worked with were those named after an Italian mathematician Fibonacci. Which of course was not his real name. In his time, the Middle Ages he was known as Leonardo of Pisa. The Fibonacci sequence described the population growth of rabbits which in turn he didn't discover, but has forever after been credited with in the western world. In truth the Indians had known about it since the sixth century.

"Despite all that," said TD, "Fibonacci noticed that if you start with the number 1 and add 1 you get 2, most creatures can do that you might say but if you add 1 plus 2 = 3."

"Yes 3 is usually the result of 1+1+1 getting together.", said Loïc.

"But hold on it's not that, its 1+2, not 1+1+1 that's different, it's adding one number to the next in the sequence, and that number happens to be 2. To continue, you then add 2+3 to get 5. Then add 3+5 to get 8. Then 5+8 to get 13 and so on. 8+13=21, 13+21=34, 21+34=55, 34+55=89."

"That's what mathematicians do; they spend their time playing with numbers trying to make sequences that make sense of something else. As you add the numbers this way and then draw them out in a geometrical curve, the same curve found in a sunflower or a fir cone. You'll see this ever-expanding curve. If we were to draw out that kind of curve in space, then reverse the sequence; do we get an egg shape, that's my question? The growth spiral it's called." said TD watching Loïc as the information sank in.

"Yes, yes," muttered Loïc after a short while, he was having difficulty visualising how the numbers translated into a spiral, let alone drawing lines in mid air.

"And, TD announced. I want to see how this relates to the egg."

"Which egg?"

"The egg."

"But they're all different aren't they?"

"Sure they are. In shape they're different, to deal with different situations. If you're a bird that lays eggs on cliff ledges then you need to lay an egg that rolls round in tight circles or you're a dead species. What I'm interested in is, do all eggs have something in common?"

"I'd say yes, they're all about to become birds."

"This is true, but are they all mathematically true to each other, even if some are pointed and others are almost balls? What is it that says an egg is an egg?"

"The bird that laid it," said Loïc.

"Yes, yes, what of the egg that we have on board? No living person has seen the bird that laid that."

"As far as I'm concerned, said Loïc, this is the egg that does not become the bird. It does not reveal itself, it is a mystery best left in the shell. For now if you want to test your theory by measuring the Elephanta egg, go ahead. Theories lead to truths isn't that right?"

"Possibly, but the more we know the less we understand. Life's a contradiction. What we are here to do becomes clearer for each person the more we lose. The less attached we are to being alive, the less we have to fear, the easier it is to step into the unknown. Then the more alive we become. For me the purpose to all this living is to find the geometry that underlies everything. I'm sure it can all be boiled down to a few numbers."

"Well, you can measure the egg but you can't boil it okay?"

They laughed at their refusal to join with each other's point of view and agreed to differ.

However much in agreement they were it was not possible to measure anything. For the next four days the wind took over. It was a moderate, westerly warm wind that made for perfect sailing weather. Though they had little to measure their progress the wind was constant day and night. They rode the waves, cutting a strong course east. Elephanta proved to be a craft worthy of a sleeker name, she moved in the water with grace and speed.

The algae seemed to grease her way through the water, giving her glide and good handling. At all times a shoal of tiny fish rode her bow and fed on the agar agar in the eddies off her leading edge. Loïc sat and watched them, fascinated by their ability to swim, eat and stay on course all at the same time. Eventually TD told him they were 'cleaner fish' and that they were living off the mould that was growing on the algae. Same as the cleaner fish on whales or the birds on buffalo's backs, they clean off the parasites.

"So Elephanta is more like a living creature than a boat?"

"That's right, and we hope she doesn't get eaten before we get there, otherwise we'll be full of water and going nowhere."

By the end of the twenty-fifth day they were down to the last coconut and water was low. A few flying fish had landed on board but fishing with a line had yielded little. The sun rose and set, the midday heat scoured every surface of every trace of sweat, the sea was a calm fast blue. They measured the egg in all dimensions and TD sat in the stern absorbed in the calculations. Loïc scanned the horizon. They appeared to be right off any shipping lanes, for they had seen no other craft since leaving Nosy Boraha. The slack sail furled and flapped; there was no consistent breeze to capture. The cleaner fish were now all around the craft busily eating the mould and the agar agar. Without wind they would be in trouble on both counts.

When Loïc first heard it, he dismissed it as an impossibility and continued watching the fish eating the boat. What he did hear, when it was so loud he could no longer ignore it, was a motor. It was so long since he had heard a machine; he had at first filtered it out, denied its existence. Then suddenly there it was, off the port bow heading directly towards them, a rifle trained on him and no words necessary.

They pulled up alongside and boarded the Elephanta, five men in ragged western clothes, guns at the ready and not a civil tongue between them. They wanted to know the cargo and destination, 'none and India' were not good replies for these men, they were not looking to trade, they wanted whatever they could get and take it they would. They searched the small craft for evidence of wealth and found nothing.

They became angry and demanded money, but neither Loïc nor TD had anything but a few coins. Next they wanted passports, then credit cards and their final disappointment was no mobile phones or G.P.S. Device. Things weren't looking good. Apart from Loïc's bow and arrows, a few of TDs tools and his maps, there was nothing apart from a little food, very little water and then finally they found the 'egg'.

On finding the elephant bird egg the atmosphere changed. The pirates, for that is what they were, stood back. Then the one with the rifle called back to his boat. Another man emerged. He walked with the necessary swagger of a captain, a hat of sorts shaded his eyes and his clothes were intact.

"What do you mean nothing?" he shouted in creole.

"Nothing but an egg Captain."

"An egg!"

"Aye Captain, a compass and a very large egg."

"That I'll see," he said, boarding the Elephanta and eyeing Loïc and TD as if they were some kind of subspecies. He peered into the basket and separated the ruffled nest of fibres. He stiffened and pulled back, then peered in again. Sliding his hand round the egg, he decided it was whole and carefully recovered it, as if it was incubating.

"Rukh," he said, looking at Loïc.

This was no time to disagree.

Loïc nodded," Rukh," he repeated.

The captain smiled then checked himself and scowled for the benefit of his crew.

"You carry Rukh egg in bamboo boat to where, India?"

Put that way, the answer was yes.

"Yes," Loïc spluttered, aware that all the guns were now pointed at him.

"This is very good. I hope you are not too late."

"I hope we will be in good time." improvised Loïc. If timing was so important, and good was what they were doing, then now was a good time to be agreeable.

"We are waiting for the wind." He said in French, the captain raised an eyebrow.

"Indeed, of course you will be knowing all there is to know about the Rukh I suppose, I think not. So to pass the time, while you wait for this wind of yours to arrive I will tell you what I have come to know of the bird that laid this egg."

At this point all guns were lowered and the resigned crew shuffled about then sat down to hear yet another story from their learned leader. Loïc and TD exchanged glances and suppressed smiles. They were baffled. How could such a dangerous situation suddenly turn into a bedtime story? Far be it for them to complain, they indulged the captain by relaxing and paying attention to his flowery language.

12
Solomon and Queenie

"Back in the 16th century," the Captain announced with a dramatic hand gesture, "When storytellers had mastered the art of double meanings and hidden messages in their tales, back then fabulous birds darkened the sky and people had good reason to quake and cower. Back then there was a huge bird, bigger than all the others. It was the Rukh, also known as the elephant bird; not because it was the size of an elephant as you may imagine. No, its name was such because it was in the habit of picking up elephants in its talons and dashing them to death on the rocks before eating them. Such was its size and strength. We know the bird of old and that is the story you need to hear."

The captain paused for effect. Checking the faces around him and finding he had their attention, he continued with an expression of triumph spreading across his salted face.

"As you have no doubt noticed," he glanced at Loïc and TD. "Unlike you my skin is adapted to the sun. This is not because I spend months at sea without an umbrella for shade. No! It is because I come from an ancient and honourable lineage stretching back over 3000 years. This I know because of a sacred book, the Kebra Negast. This is the holy book of my people, the people of Ethiopia one of the older peoples of this world of ours.

Now in the Kebra Negast is the story of the 'Rukh', the elephant bird of old. It tells how Solomon, the main man of the Jews, the son of David, was building the temple, the very one that his father had promised God but never got round to making. Well Solomon was wisely tying up the loose ends that his father had left hanging. The temple had come down to him to clean up the family reputation. He had just put the whole project together when he found to his chagrin that he was short of one piece of wood to finish the job.

'How this happen?' he says to the head carpenter.

'It don't add up boss,' says the carpenter, 'I check the invoice, I check the delivery and everything in order 'cept one piece of wood.'

'Hmm', says the main man Solomon,' without this one piece of wood, there is no temple.'

'Hey boss that's a wee bit radical,' says the head carpenter, 'I mean, one piece missing ain't that serious. I mean who's going to notice anyway?'

'I gonna notice,' says Solomon,' I gonna know and I ain't gonna sleep none with that piece missing.'

Now you have to understand what this piece of wood was. It wasn't some little twig for starting up fires; it wasn't some kind of board for putting your jam and your chutney on. No sir, this was a whole mean tree size piece of wood for holding up a temple. That size piece of wood isn't just an order in triplicate type piece of wood. No, this has to be the best of the best - cedar of Lebanon, you know slow grown hard wood all the way from the slopes of the mountain.

'Okay.' Says the head carpenter seeing how steamed up the main man was getting.' Okay, let's call in the Rukh for a special one off delivery, if anyone can, he can. He's got the talons for it.'

So that's what happened, Solomon summoned up the Rukh. Now the Rukh was big, not like anything you see flying around these days, except for those metal birds with the two long white tail feathers you see way up high. Because the Rukh was so big everyone was scared and ran away except the main man Solomon. He was big on wisdom and baby problems and he wasn't afraid, he just sat and waited on the temple site. Soon the Rukh arrived and the Rukh agreed to do this one big favour for the main man. One tree, no branches, and flew off up country.

Now it was around this time that Solomon was making special noises in the direction of the south. When you're a big cheese like Solomon everything you do is special. The man had no privacy. Anyway the reason he's making special noises this time, is 'cos he's heard of a big female cheese with special status, she's just called 'Queenie'. Solomon kinda likes that, he thinks that's kinda cool kinda contemporary. Anyhow

Queenie comes from this place down south called Sheba and the story goes that she's not only loaded but she's cute, like she's gorgeous! Anyhows, Solomon's got ears out every place and he likes what he's hearing 'bout this Queenie broad from down south. So Solomon, being so wise and all, figures he has to stay real cool on this one and sends a messenger with some courier pigeons down to Sheba saying,' I hear you're ready for conversion to my way of believing.' He thinks this spiritual approach is the right way to go.

Nothing, he hears nothing. Days pass, nothing. Weeks of nothing. He's checking his pigeons every day but nothing. Finally his messenger returns, with the pigeons but without 'Queenie from Sheba' but instead with one massive delivery of gold, four and a half tons of the stuff, enough gold to make a rich man weep. But this doesn't do it for Solomon, no sir he's full of wisdom, he figures if she can send him that much gold she must be saying ' I am worth much more than four and a half tons of saffron nuggets. I don't come cheap. I don't just come because you say I gotta listen to your jive about believin', you just got me all wrong so back off.'

The messenger hands the main man a cage with a pair of Queenies turtle doves, you know those ones with big puffed up chests that walk round in circles doing funky things with their little beaky beaks. Well Solomon, he's thinking fast and taking one of those doves out the cage, he tapes a message to its leg saying, 'Hey Queenie come to tea, see you soon'. Then throws the bird into the sky, after a couple of turns round the temple it disappears direction south.

It's about this time that the Rukh flies in with one huge tree trunk in its talons and makes a delivery in the temple compound. Solomon is well pleased and gives the Rukh a couple of tuskers for dinner. The Rukh is well made up knowing that the tree is top quality seasoned cedar of Lebanon. Master mason Hiram Abiff gives him a nod and wink, which as you know means you're well in with the main honcho.

Several months later, let's call it nine, 'cos the tree trunk is still lying around, Queenie arrives from Sheba with her entourage. Canopied horses, parasols and a magnitude of luggage bearers. They've been through the insignificant villages of Mecca and Medina on the way and trekked through the heat all along the edge of the Red Sea longing for that cuppa tea.

Solomon, he's standing on the steps of the unfinished temple checking his measurements when he sees Queenie for the first time. All the reports are true, she really is big, black and beautiful, and his eyes are all over her but she does seem to have the feet of a goat. No she's not wearing high heels; she has the feet of a goat. Solomon at this moment finds Queenies cloven hooves to be a bit of an affront to his sensibilities. After all, things like cloven hooves run in the family, and he's thinking of breeding stock. Cloven hooves, they're a bit too satanic for me he thinks.

What about all those strange gifts she had bought with her. Dice, playing cards, asafoetida (what a smell that has), then there are those dark scarab beetles, and puff balls and all those attendants with those fancy tricks on their diabolos. All work of the devil, his soothsayer whispers in his ear.

These were not the usual gifts of a visiting head cheese. He prefers to think of the four and a half tons of gold she had sent, which he had impulsively refused. He would have to reconsider the gift; after all he had planned on covering the inside of his temple with cedar and then covering all the cedar with gold leaf. He was going to need all the gold he could get and four and a half tons was a goodly amount. Flattened it could go a long way. Yes it would be good to accept such a gift if he could access the 3,000 outer calf intestines needed by his beaters to laminate it all into gold leaf. But that was another problem for another day.

Solomon, he was in a quandary. He was gawking, rudely she thought, at her cloven hooves.

Then there was all the pomp and ceremony that happens when two big honchos meet for the first time, lots of smiling and some bowing to equal degrees, questions about the journey, the weather that sort of thing. Then as they turn to check that Queenie is going to be happy with her accommodation, she stubs her hoof on that cedar trunk that the Rukh flew in.

Well it's all very embarrassing for Solomon because he's the one that's responsible for it lying around outside the temple in the first place. He could blame Hiram Abiff, but he's wiser than that. For Queenie it's even more embarrassing, because amazingly her hooves have now been transformed into ordinary rather plump human feet. She has just lost her uniqueness, she's not nearly so nimble and sure footed as before.

When Solomon notices the change he's hugely pleased and decides to give the Rukh special mythical status when he next sees him. As for the tree trunk he assigns it to an honoured place in the temple and orders the head carpenter to get to work on carving it into shape, immediately. He then commands the silversmiths to inlay the hallowed timber with silver rings. No one is quite sure why he orders the silver rings but it's well paid work so nobody questions the idea. Solomon too is only following the Lord's orders in his dreams.

Up to this point in the construction of the Temple, Master mason Abiff has had 30,000 men cutting and transporting stone in the mountains. He has had all the squaring and preparing of stone and wood done away from the temple grounds. This is to be the first fully pre-fabricated temple ever made. But when the Rukh makes his one off tree delivery Solomon's pre-fab plans have become sabotaged. In the heat of the moment he had forgotten to give the Rukh another delivery address and the whole unprepared tree had arrived at the temple site. Could he show his displeasure? Of course he couldn't, so he praised the bird and wisely said nothing.

When, with one tap of the toe those feet were transformed from hoof to human, Queenie became Solomon's fatal attraction. The final tree inlaid with all its silver rings was the only one never to be covered with boards or gold leaf.

Well, so the story goes, Solomon and Queenie of Sheba tried very hard to stay with the agenda and keep their relationship strictly business. But it seems that Solomon had a ferocious attraction for her. Knowing this, Queenie tried her best to protect herself from his advances. She told him that he must never take her by force. To this he was obliged to agree because that would be an unmanly thing to be doing anyway. That was easy, thought Queenie, it seems I hit the right spot there.

Well things aren't ever that simple, especially when it comes to a big wise honcho like Solomon. Okay, says he, I agree not to take you by force but you have to agree not to take anything of mine. Well Makeda, for that was Queenie's real name. Makeda agrees to that. Easy, she's got everything she wants already, and anyway if she hasn't she can send any of a hundred runners to do her bidding.

That night Solomon makes sure his servants attend to all her bedroom needs. They check the curtains; fold down the bed; place water on the bedside table; shake out her slippers, for you don't need snakes to be biting your visitors. Meanwhile the two of them are tucking into an especially prepared spicy supper. Taking her leave Makeda heads off to the guest accommodation. Just before settling down, feeling a little thirsty she has a drink from the bedside glass. Half way through the night in walks Solomon unannounced.

Of course Makeda is mad with him.

'Get out, Get out,' she shouts.
He picks up the now empty glass.
'Water,' says he,' you have taken my water.'
'Aaarrraaagghh,' groans she, 'Get in, Get in.'

They say with Solomon that his wisdom was as abundant as grains of sand. That night, after he'd had his way with Queenie of Sheba, he is said to have had a vision of the sun going down over Ethiopia, her place of origin. Nine months later as she approached the great capital city of Axum, she stopped for she was heavy with child and there almost home she gave birth to a son, Menelik, meaning 'wise man's son', and so began the Solomonic line of the Emperors of Ethiopia.

"I come from that union, I am Ethiopian," said the captain adjusting his hat. "The Rukh it was that brought King

Solomon round to liking the lady from down south, so this here Rukh egg is the symbol of life to us Ethiopians. And that, my merry sailors, is why it's coming with me. I shall take it right away to the main man in Addis Ababa, just so that the story is complete and I can't be accused of leaving things out,

"Later, much later, when Jesus Christ, you know the biblical Jew, was making waves and upsetting some people and transforming others, the cedar tree, the one with the silver rings comes into its own. It's said that the hewn and decorated beam was taken from the temple of Solomon and the silver rings taken off and given to Judas for betraying Jesus with that garden kiss at Gethsemane. Then the wood of the very same beam was used to make the cross for his crucifixion.

"As we storytellers say everything is joined up, and in time everything comes apart at the seams. So I'll be the keeper of this egg from now on, but I will cross your palm with silver just to show there are no ill feelings."

He adjusted his headpiece and passed Loïc a pouch, a small heavy pouch which clinked in a convincing way. Suddenly all the guns were raised again as if everyone had just woken from a spell, which is exactly the purpose of the storyteller's art. Scratching their heads and adjusting their testicles, the pirates once again became ferocious. Stomping around as if they were doing something manly and meaningful.

Loïc was not ready to hand over his precious find even if it was the only thing they had to barter against their lives. He had become very attached to the possibility of it's hatching, now that it was out of the ground and warmed by the sun. What would an egg that size grow into? He tossed the pouch back to the pirate captain. The atmosphere changed, what had been amusing and friendly suddenly went sour and guns were cocked and aimed at TD, Loïc and the egg.

Once again the pouch was thrown to Loïc this time a gun was raised to his head, just to make the point. TD groaned at the possible outcome of the impasse and Loïc held up the money.

"Atody egg," he said, then he pointed at his mouth.

"Food, water," he said pointing at TD and then himself, gesturing a drink.

The captain laughed and directed one of his men into the bowels of his boat. Another he directed to the stern of the Elephanta where he dismantled TD's compass from its bamboo plinth. He threw the brass instrument to the captain. The other pirate soon emerged from their boat with a sack full of something and reluctantly threw it across.

TD and Loïc exchanged glances, the compass was a serious loss but they had nothing else to trade with. They gently handed over the egg packed in the basket of palm fibres. The pirates, however comic they seemed, were armed and an exchange was far better than a robbery. As the last pirate stepped off the Elephanta, TD gave him a loud shipmates growl. The pirate was so surprised he nearly slipped between the boats, and so frightened that gave a spontaneous growl back.

Both Loïc and TD fell into uncontrollable laughter of relief as the boats drifted apart and the pirate adjusted his composure. The egg was gone, the compass gone and instead they had a sack of dried offal and the essential first whiff of a breeze from the west crinkling the skin and crimping a fresh texture to the sea. They set their sail, nosing away toward the northeast as the fading sound of the pirate engine took a course for the Yemen and Ethiopia.

"Do you think it would have made any difference if that crazy captain had known that was the egg of a flightless bird?"

"Not really, said TD, people like to believe whatever suits them. To him it had to be a Rukh egg, to us it had to be an elephant bird egg. Either way it's a mystery. Whether his story is true I don't know but for sure he wanted the egg so he can sell it to the highest bidder."

"Who's going to want an ancient egg apart from a museum?"

"Loïc my boy that egg is worth a fortune in the right hands, I've seen reconstructed shells of the elephant bird sell before, but the one you found has the foetus of the bird inside, that's what they want, they want its DNA."

"What's DNA?"

"DNA is a type of acid, to be precise it is deoxyribonucleic acid. Ever heard of it?"

"Never, it means nothing to me."

"That my friend is obvious, otherwise you would have struck a harder bargain. Anyway the deoxy part means that the oxygen has been reduced in the situation and the ribonucleic part contains sugars that have complex molecules which are in the chromosomes that make up all animals and plants. The DNA carries the instructions for passing on the genetic characteristics of all living matter. It's like the kernel in the shell, the nucleus, the important part of anything. It's the seed that the next one grows from."

"How do you know that? Anyway what's that got to do with the value of an ancient egg?"

"I'm not sure how I know that, but it is so. As to the egg, well those sneaky scientists have now found a way of taking a slice of DNA and reproducing the creature from the slice. Which means your egg may indeed become the bird if it gets into the wrong hands."

"And you think that crazy pirate knows that?"

"Never think that a crazy isn't sane, he's a pirate as well and to survive you have to know the value of things. I think he told his story to fool his crew, with boredom. He told us because he wanted to appear honourable. His story may well be true from the Ethiopian viewpoint so that's fine, we have our lives and he has the problem, it's good that way. As for the compass that's different."

"What do we do now without a compass Master mariner?"

"It's a setback, but it could be just the opportunity that we've been waiting for."

"How's that? It always helps to know where we're going."

"It's essential to know where we are. That much we do know. Where we're going is less important. We're going to have to use Wayfinder techniques of doing things from now on."

13
Wayfinding

Again TD had Loïc in the dark, there seemed to be so much he knew and so little that he revealed.

"Wayfinding is the way the Polynesians got around and still do. Thousands of years without a compass and living in an area with thousands of islands spread out over it."

"Thousands of square miles. That's it isn't it, lost without a compass in a big place." Cut in an alarmed Loïc.

"When have I let you down?"

"You can't swim and now you want to sail the ocean without a compass."

"Have you heard of the Lapita people? Have you heard of Irian Jaya? Have you heard of New Guinea?"

Loïc looked blank.

"Okay tell me what is Lapita Jaya or whatever it is you said?"

"First calm down. A lot of these things I will show you and I can only do that at the right time. For now I'll give you a bit of an outline, the rest will come out as we go along."

Loïc had no idea what he was talking about, but that happened with TD quite often, usually it came clear in time and usually it was interesting.

"When you're ready I'm ready Ok."

Loïc busied himself with some hook lines and bait, they'd been reduced to using small slithers of coconut, but it worked, anything that was put in the sea seemed to get eaten. Often before they could haul it aboard.

Over the next few hours they strapped a couple of short bamboo uprights across the stern and then fixed two horizontals, making a long bench. Then they set the inverted triangular sail, took their seats with Loïc on the paddle rudder and set a course for the estimated northeast.

"I'm not able to tell you all this, but what I know will come out as I see it and read it." TD then told Loïc what he knew about navigation 'wayfinder' style.

"This is a tradition that goes back thousands of years, handed down through families, island families living in the Great Pacific Ocean. The Lapita of the island of Irian Jaya are credited with wayfinding but there are many who used to know how to travel the sea without a sextant, a compass or a depth gauge, these are all new inventions. Before, these sailors could read everything that was around them. They were tuned in.

Before they could walk the children of the 'wayfinder' families would be put in rock pools and left there so that they could embody the nature of the ocean, so its essence was inside them. Most people lived on islands so their surroundings were waves and water, they knew how and why the water changed, same as the humpas they could read the echoes off islands not just by reading the wave ripples but by hanging over the edge of the boat and getting those supersensitive testicles in the water they could feel the changes in water temperature which happens as water gets shallower then they could feel the rhythm of the waves. The waves tell you about the land."

"Testicles in the water," exploded Loïc.

"Everything has more than one use. Life is very economical like that. So long as you have not become stuck with some stupid social viewpoint. Anyway that's an aside. What the Polynesians did was look and listen to everything out here, and they didn't just use their eyes and heads like people these days. It may just look like water and little else."

He stopped and pointed out off the port bow.

"Look, see that white tern skimming the surface, that tells me that at maximum we're no more than 120 miles from land. If it was a booby said TD, not only is it very easy to catch but never goes further than 25 miles from land."

"What about an albatross," chipped in Loïc.

"Albatross tells you nothing and leads you nowhere, they can fly for weeks and rarely go on land, so they're not any help at all.

But the brown tern rarely goes 40 miles out so you can tell when you're getting closer."

TD now had Loïc's attention.

"When you see dolphins and porpoises swimming for sheltered water it means there's a storm brewing. Same with swordfish they change their swimming patterns with the weather. But it's not always possible to see what's happening under the water, but the sky, yes. If you're standing on the deck on a clear day you can only ever see thirty miles because the earth is round, but the clouds will tell you more than you can see. Shape, colour, character and place in the sky can tell you loads. Like brown clouds bring strong wind. High clouds no wind but lots of rain. Then there's the obvious, movement tells you about strength of wind direction, storm fronts that sort of thing. But they also gather over land, then they are much higher, you can see the island long before going thirty miles, maybe double. The tone of the sky colour is always darker over an island as well. No island and the clouds just sweep across the sea. Then there's the light."

"Red sky at night shepherds delight, red sky in the morning shepherds warning." Loïc chanted.

"Well that's all right for you mountain boy, but at sea it's different. Red sky at sunrise and sunset tells you that humidity levels are high. And if you see rainbow colours round the stars or they twinkle and dim, then there's a storm on the way. At night if you see a halo round the moon, which you often do especially at full moon, then that's caused by clouds of ice crystals which reflect sun light shining through them, it tells you that rain is on the way. When you do get a moon halo with less than ten stars in it, expect trouble, high winds and torrential rain. But if you get a double halo it forecasts that the weather will move on the wings of a gale."

"Sounds like we're going to be busy."

"The art is to stay awake, day and night and conjure up your destination in your mind."

"How do we know what kind of progress we're making?"

"With Elephanta we're about 30 feet long, so if there's some flotsam or seaweed or even a bubble, and we pass it in 1.5 seconds we're travelling at 8.5 knots. If it takes 7 seconds then were doing only 1.5 knots."

"How do you know that?" spluttered Loïc. "How do you

know the bubble isn't moving at the same speed as the boat?"

"Loïc my friend, you know that when there's no wind and the boat just sits there going nowhere, you must have noticed that if something goes overboard then it just floats there next to the boat, this is true, huh?"

It was true, but Loïc found it very difficult to accept that the sea wasn't going anywhere, just those bold enough to cross it.

"When the real navigating takes place is at night.", continued TD. "As the earth rotates so every star comes up on the eastern horizon, it then describes its arc across the sky and sets on the western horizon. These two points, east rise, west set remain the same throughout the year. However the time each star appears in the east changes by four minutes every night. So if the 'wayfinder' can memorise some 220 stars, their trajectories, their positions, the time they appear and their east west bearings, then the 'wayfinder' can envisage a 360 degree compass. What happens is the boat becomes the needle, and the compass is the night sky."

"Can you do that? Do you know that many stars? Are we going to be able to imagine our way to India?"

"We can but try," said TD laconically, "what else to do?"

"Let's do it." Said Loïc, "I'll keep you fed and watered and anything else you ask. Let's do it."

So it was, TD took up his position on the bamboo bench with the rudder paddle at hand and entered into a new place in himself. Deep, silent and trance like. For ten days he hardly slept and when he did it was for moments only. When they did see the odd cloud on the horizon out to the north, TD dismissed them as the Seychelles and took a course further east. For those ten days and nights Loïc's experience of sail was transformed into a deep bonding with everything. His belief in TD and what he could do it made every bird he saw, every fish he caught, every floating piece of flotsam of enormous significance. The colours of the waves and the sky, the smell on the wind and the movement of it all brought him to a new awareness of life. TD just sat and sat and smiled and sailed. For the next 1300 miles that was what they did, they found their way through the huge, but not so empty expanse of the Indian Ocean without a compass.

If it were not for the increase in bird activity, the fringe of palms weeping into the shallow silver sand that are the Maldives would have evaded their attention. There was little enough change in profile and no resident cloud to show them that the patch of green was any more than seaweed. They tacked towards it thinking it might just vary their diet a little. As they approached, a fringe of white coral slowed the tide and broke up the waveforms. The islets appeared like a sea mirage, floating just above the surface. They had no height and if it were not for the coral the sea would have eaten them long ago. What was familiar about them were the algae beds that swirled beneath the boat as they edged up a narrow channel on to the beach.

It was down in the waving plants that Loïc, equipped with rock and rope first saw a shank shell. He imagined that it would be occupied until a spume of glistening sand drifted out of it as he turned it round and round. He brought it up to the surface with the algae.

They had beached the boat and ventured inland in search of fresh water, but there was none. When they returned to the boat on the shallow shore the state of the bows became clear, the cleaner fish had eaten the agar agar at water level all around the boat. Repairs were necessary and a session of diving brought up a large bundle of algae and two further shank shells, which Loïc lined up on the sand. Two spiralled one way, to the left, and the third to the right. He liked them and they were completely undamaged. Wrapping them in palm leaves he stowed them away in the boat. Next he started devising a way of steaming the algae into workable pats. With the little equipment they had on board, Loïc decided to make a split bamboo basket and set it over boiling water using the many dry palm husks as both fuel and container.

Within a couple of hours they were smearing the sticky mass into the water line of the hulls of the Elephanta. They worked fast and by dusk she was waterproof again. The agar agar below the waterline had formed a thick rubbery gel; it was only where air and water met that the feeding fish had done the damage.

At first light they moved inland again in search of food, but there was nothing except coconut-laden palms, mangroves and banyan trees. Small flowering shrubs were the only ground cover and there was no high ground. Wherever they went they were only a few feet above sea level. They tried digging; if the plants could survive there must be water.

Beneath a thin layer of soil they came to soft sandstone. This they broke through to a bed of sand, and digging into the sand, water started to collect. It was fresh, this they couldn't explain, fresh water at the same level as the surrounding sea. The seepage was slow and it took all day to filter each coconut-full through a cloth to clean the sabulous liquid and fill their on-board tank. They re-stocked with coconuts and fish and had stowed it all away by the close of the next day. They paddled out of the narrow channel and took to the open sea again. For the next few days they passed hundreds of tiny tufts of palm islands all low in the water and surrounded by coral. When the wind picked up they struck out to the east.

It was while they sat there running on a stiff breeze that TD started to teach Loïc about cloud formations: the various layers were of differing types and behaved differently. The lower white cumulus clouds were slow and held no rain. Above, higher wispy stratus clouds raced across the sky at a much faster speed. TD went below deck and reappeared with a small bulging bag. He had spoken little about his reasons for going to India, except that it was a good run for a maiden voyage. In fact he had other reasons for going. The southeast trade winds swept up the east coast of Africa and then swung northeast into the Arabian Sea and the coast of India at this time of year. The slight breeze dropped the belly out of the triangular sail and they made little headway.

"Check out those high clouds."

Loïc looked up to see long lines of cloud shredding across a bleached-out blue.

Out of the bag TD took a mass of cloth and strings and started to stretch out the lines on the deck between the two hulls, he tied them off to the mast and started blowing up a valve in the red coloured cloth. Soon the edge of the cloth was inflated in a longbow shape and the rest of the material stretched out into a sail behind it. Strapping on a harness that he hooked onto the base of the mainsail TD eased the inflated wing over the bow of the Elephanta.

As soon as slight breeze came through the kite, it lifted off the sea and climbed rapidly up into the sky. TDs back strap tautened and his twin stick lines fanned the kite into a perfect wing that hung there above the boat.

"That's great," remarked Loïc," won't it cramp our style with the sail?"

"You can drop the sail, replied TD, we haven't started with this thing yet."

He played out more line and the kite climbed high above the craft, snatching the fast edge of the stratus cloud current. He played out some more line. Now it was more like a strange bird than a kite. For a while he made some adjustments to his lines then tightened the belt on the harness and slipped on a pair of shades.

"I need your weight up front," he called to Loïc, "leave the rudder to itself, we can steer with the kite."

Loïc had no idea what he was saying but could see that TD was ready for something to happen. TD glanced up then dropped the kite down in front of the Elephanta. For a moment the lines tensioned and then the whole boat lurched forward, lifting the bows high in the water and stretching the anchor line attached to the mast base. The boat became alive, straining with the energy of the high wind. The lines sung with the increased tension and the whole craft lifted high in the water and surged forward.

TD with legs apart lent back into the strong drag of the kite, the harness strap tightened on the mast base, and they were away. TD dropped the kite a little more into the power window and their speed increased. They were now moving far faster than being driven by any surface winds that they had encountered so far. Both of them were stunned by the kite's power. All day they ran with the stratus wind and by evening with weary arms TD slowly wound in the kite and landed it on the deck.

"Your turn tomorrow mountain boy," he said as Loïc

prepared a meal of fish on their suspended brazier.

"It's easier to tell you about the clouds when you can be up there and feel what they're like through your hands. Just so you know, ok."

"Sure thing Maestro", said Loïc and they laughed as TD shook out his aching arms.

"There is one cloud type we haven't seen today, they're rare but becoming more frequent. It's called 'Undulatus asperatus', I'm not sure about its properties. It looks like upside down water. The others like cirrus we'll see soon, they're a little like beach sand formations."

For the next few days they travelled northeast by kite power and read the clouds and the night sky for direction. Loïc taking the kite sticks eagerly and taking to the flying wing as naturally as flying the bag of rivets that Joe Blusher had insisted on calling a plane. The kite gave him a truly connected feeling; an entire sensory world was felt in his hands and rooted him through the harness to the boat, which anchored him to the sea. The wind took on a substance with quirky stills and changes of temperature and lift; it ran through his fingers as a blind man reads Braille. He learnt how to ease slightly off full power and in so doing lift the boat slightly and reduce its drag on the water.

Staying just above the equator they followed an easterly course riding the monsoon winds that drove them along the coast of Sri Lanka and up into the Bay of Bengal. The strain on the bamboo hulls had been heavy and the constant movement of the journey had stretched the ijuk straps and lashings. Despite hammering in bamboo wedges, everything needed tightening. By the time they sighted the long strand of the Coromandel coast they went for a high tide landing using the onshore wind and the kite to drag them onto the beach. Exhausted they hauled the Elephanta up to the tide line and collapsed on the sand. They had been at sea in this small craft for six weeks and the land swayed beneath them.

A small knot of fishermen left their net mending to come and inspect this curious bamboo craft. Meanwhile Loïc, loose kneed and wobble legged, had gone to look at the lashed three-log raft boats that littered the upper beach. When the fishermen saw him walking they couldn't contain their laughter and started to imitate his gangly gait. Loïc played to the crowd and soon a group of grown men were laughing and flapping madly around the bamboo boat as if solid ground no longer existed. Drawn by the raucous howling of their husbands the women appeared from their palm leafed shacks with wide-eyed children on their hips. With their saris pulled across their faces they too doubled up with laughter as hoots and cackles spread like wild fire from one person to the next. Everyone was infected with the pleasure and pain of laughter and tears.

Once they had their breath back and a fragile calm had descended, the Elephanta was hauled further up the beach. It was then that TD, for the first time, took out his trumpet from its hiding place on board and played the sweetest tune that Loïc had heard in a long time. Right there on the beach with fishermen and their families under the spell of his horn he expressed his joy of crossing that huge ocean and being at last, in the land of India.

He gave his soul to the moment and the people loved it; their day had been changed by the arrival of the bamboo boat and her crew. Who were these exuberant and exhausted sailors who had kited in on a bundle of grass? No one along this interminable coast made boats out of bamboo. Outrigger poles, yes, but complete boats, never, and yet there they were making people laugh and cry and dance as if they were drunk.

TD and Loïc stayed on the beach for a few days. TD said that their voyage from Madagascar had proved one of his theories. He claimed that before, long before boats were made of cut wood and before rafts of logs like the local Coromandel fishing boats existed; boats were made out of bundles of bamboo. Two bundles with a deck between, like the Elephanta, a kind of primitive catamaran. Not only that, his theory was that there had been a global bamboo culture, when everything the people used was made from bamboo. Houses, food, drainage, clothes, transport, weapons, even their thoughts would have been like the whisper of bamboo leaves in the wind, their behaviour borrowed from the forces of nature. He had numerous examples to prove his theory and now he had another. Together they had shown how this bamboo culture had spread. His theory was connected to his other theories about how the plants always saved the people as the world went through its changes and how the best place to be was at sea, even if you couldn't swim.

Again he took up his trumpet and played to the setting sun.

14
In the Land of the Tamils

It was soon time for Loïc to get some earth beneath his feet. He split the pirate purse with TD, gave him one of the left spiralling shells, said his farewells and with his bag on his shoulder took off down the beach one morning, heading south towards the small town of Mamalipuram. Here, he was told by the fishermen, stone carvings of great beauty were made. Not only were there Krishnas but modern works of Ganesh playing the saxophone and reading the Times of India. The prospect amused him, and he set off with a fine windblown sand cutting into his ankles as he tramped barefoot along the beach, relieved only by walking in the sea as it snatched at the shore. His journey took him through tiny fishing villages that clung to the higher beach. Every few kilometres there was another huddle of buffeted bamboo shelters covered with the huge faces of film stars on perishing plastic from the hoardings of movie theatres. The onshore winds and the rip tide created a habitable narrow margin before rising to the cultivated soil. Each village stop he made, they knew of him. They had seen the Elephanta and her kite heading up coast. Word of their landing had come down the coast before him, they even knew his name.

By the time Loïc reached Mamalipuram, the sea had eaten six of its seven famous pagodas, the last had survived a recent tsunami, but there were remains and carvings dating back over two thousand years. The Buddhists had been here and the Pallava kings, in fact the town had gained its name from the great wrestling king Marmalla, you don't wrestle against a king and expect to win if you want to live. There were temples cut out of the stone and animated carvings dotted all around the area of the town. It's fame dated back thousands of years, not only for the giant 'butterball' that sat and did not roll off the enormous rock slope facing out to sea.

On arrival he was pointed in the direction of Anna Nagar

the stone carvers quarter, a little out of town. It was a single street running parallel to the coast that rang with the sound of metal chisels striking granitic stone. Rows of finely detailed figures, resplendent with flowing robes and hair, waited for a temple to inhabit. Stone elephants the size of elephants stood with sleeping live goats on their backs. Small braziers oxygenated by goatskin bellows tempered chisels while artisans blunted others on the carved silk saris of lusty busty temple dancers. The fragments that fell at the feet of these courtesans were gathered by small boys who in turn filed them into pendants, suns and moons and scary faces. Everyone was busy in the stone carving trade.

Behind Anna Nagar lay the village. A few rows of humble compounds with wells and families and chickens. Here lived the widow, Idly Padma. She was known near and not so far for her idlys, which if you don't know are a steamed rice cakes shaped like flying saucers, especially good when dipped in samba sauce. Every morning Padma was up steaming idlys, getting her children to school full of idlys and making ends meet. One of those ends was supplying the district with child collected steaming idly breakfasts. Another was renting out two small rooms, swept clean with a twig brush and lit by single dangling 40 watt bulbs. The shower was a bowl of water over the head, the toilet a hole between two concrete footprints open to the sky.

It was here that Loïc stayed and it was in this way that Idly Padma taught her children the meaning of work. Life was hard but there was still time to smile and share. Loïc thought a lot more of Padma than her idlys. Sure he ate them, they were good, but to him she was a temple goddess in the flesh, not carved in stone like the ones out on the main street. They just stood there looking beautiful but, Idly Padma moved with grace, so that each thing she did, each way she turned, captivated Loïc. As yet he didn't know that India was full of beauties, he had only just floated ashore; but he was certain that he had arrived in the right place.

Once she had found out the value of the coin from the pirate purse she treated Loïc like royalty. Nothing was too much trouble; she liked the colour of his money. She fed him with much more than idlys and returned each morning from the market with an array of exotic vegetables to add to the evenings curry. With the vegetables, she returned with a series of invitations for Loïc to visit many people and places around the town.

In this way he saw many ancient carvings and temples and had their significance explained to him. He got a real feeling for the importance of the tiny enclave and the carvings that left it to embellish temples near and far. It was a place with an ancient tradition; skills passed through the hands of generations of stone carvers, refined unquestioningly through the blood. Even the humble tourist was assured of a souvenir worth having. People from all over India and beyond came to the town in bus loads, ate thalis at the bus station canteen, trawled the temples, and then paid their respects at all the sacred places before boarding again and disappearing into the twilight. All this was new to Loïc, these were a people that put religion and family first. Old and young, rich and poor came to pray, though some of the rich paid someone else to do their pujas for them.

He soon decided that he was getting fat watching the beautiful Padma and his feet told him they needed to move and explore. In turn Padma told him of a temple a day's journey away where priests fed the eagles that flew in from the north each day. With his few possessions over his shoulder the hot and dusty roads of Tamil Nadu opened up beneath his hardening feet.

The highways of India are ruled by the largest not the fastest, the trucks and the buses. All else scatters to the rough and dusty roadside as they thunder through missing all by a whisker. Before, everything had travelled at the pace of an animal. The Brahma bull was as fast as it all got. Loïc was drawn to the slowness of these narrow, high, two wheeled bullock carts that carried everything out into the landscape along the dusty arteries of the south.

Loïc went old style and took rides on the back of anything without an engine. He wanted to take it all in, not just pass through. Long lines of ragged palms lined the irrigation channels that fed mile after mile of paddy fields, rice in all its stages of growth. Fields ploughed by taut skinned wading buffalo. Seeded by brightly clad sari hoisted women. Reaped into balanced green bundles set in rows awaiting collection. Everywhere white egrets picked clean leathery buffalo backs while their noses and horns protruded from muddy wayside pools. Everything moved at a lazy pace, dusted with a thin film of earth red grace. Smells amplified his immersion in the land. Frangipani dripped heavy with scent. Saliva wept into his mouth as papaya and jackfruits passed within reach. Those sweet smells and foetid human waste competed for his attention.

They passed through numerous bicycle stand villages, where the bicycles became buried under their uses. One parked on its stand carried thirty full trays of eggs balanced on the back rack, with thirty to a tray that's six hundred eggs poised in the sun. Another nearby was so covered in airy calabashes, plastic and primary in colour that the wheels no longer showed.

Bicycles as hay ricks, bicycles as family transport, bicycles fitted with pedal powered grindstones, bicycles sporting disco sound systems, even bicycles carrying a flock of live chickens dangling from the handlebars. All was moving at the pace of a well-loaded bike looking for a parking slot. By midday shade had become a necessity. The driver of his current ride pulled in to lose the heat and sip fresh coconut milk.

Loïc found a little thali house, one table two benches and a charpoy out the back. There was little else apart from a calendar advertising nuts and bolts and displaying an early printed image of the Taj Mahal. From this faded and curled calendar he discovered that he was still only fourteen and that it was already August. He ordered a thali because there was no choice and drank the tepid water that arrived in a battered aluminium jug. Both were very welcome. He then lay back on the knotty charpoy and dozed through the heat of the day.

By nightfall he had arrived at Kazhugu Koil and found a room in a guesthouse overlooking the mound on which the eagle temple sat. There was nothing else of significance in the area and he took to his bed after watching the sun sink into the palms and the paddies. For a moment the plain was a patchwork of orange and purple diamonds as mosquitoes screamed in his ears and flocks of green parrots streaked across the near sky.

His was a troubled sleep, slipping between dreams and a distant memory that persisted each time he woke in the stuffy room, soon to drift off to sleep again.

'A soft knock came at the front door of his village home. He and his mother were in, his father as usual out somewhere. A man stood at the threshold, he wore a raincoat and a felt hat, a suitcase in hand. This image he saw from the level of his mother's waist. There was a friendly tone to his mother's voice but what was said he could not recall. The man entered and putting down the case, hung his coat and hat on the back of the now closed door. Loïc remembered his hand on his shoulder, it was reassuring. Some time must have passed. Loïc saw the man lift the case onto his bed, he could still hear the double click as the clasps sprang open.

The man opened the brown lid, inside were Players Medium Cut tobacco tins tightly packed together with sky blue lids. An air of mystery pervaded the scene. The man reached into the suitcase and randomly took out a tin and opened it. Loïc was at his elbow. Inside was an iridescent blue-black horned beetle pierced by a dressmakers pin onto a piece of cardboard. Written in a tiny neat script it said 'dung beetle', *Scarabaeus sacer*, beneath a date 1946 and a place Kanpur U.P. Loïc and the man made eye contact, he smiled, Loïc smiled back and carefully touched the shiny carapace. The man opened all the tins one at a time. Man and child sat side by side on the bed and explored the universe of insects in all their myriad forms and colours through a small magnifying glass. The tins were then replaced in the case and he put on his hat and coat. The memory closed with the man placing a parting pat on the head and a kiss on the lips of his mother and then the door closed.'

This flash of clarity had rushed back to him as he lay on his pallet in the half-light of the room. Again he drifted off and woke to the image of the man in the doorway with his case. Finally dawn brought him to diurnal consciousness. A deep unrecognised knowing brought tears to his eyes and a familiar trouble to his heart. He knew this was an event in his life not a fragment of a dream, with it came a certainty, a confidence. He felt assured that he was in the right place at the right time. Whatever took place he was on his path and trust would be his compass.

Once again N'zingu's voice came to him.

'All the parts of you are scattered by the winds of knowing. These fragments can only be caught and put together in your quiver. When you have mastered the power of the breath, then your blowpipe will be accurate and your targets close by.'

A sigh gathered deep in Loïc's belly and came out of him in a shudder. He sat for a while gazing at the monkeys on the tin roof opposite arguing over an orange one of them had stolen from a vendor in the street below. Meanwhile the vendor was arming himself with stones from the putrid drain at the roadside muttering curses.

As Loïc sat there a fine glitter of minute light particles fell upon him. Both extraordinary and normal at the same time. In some way he was changed by the brilliance of the shower, but the feeling that arose in him was that he was here merely to do good.

Then that laugh of his bubbled up and out of him, across the street to the rock throwing vendor who saw the folly of his ways and got back to hawking his pyramids of water sprayed fruit. Meanwhile the winning monkey dropped orange peelings on his head.

A hot breeze brought Loïc to realise the lateness of the morning. He grabbed his possessions and paid for his room. Waving to the fruit vendor and catching an orange in return, he hurried across the street to the temple gate. Here he was told to leave his shoes in the rack provided and proceed barefoot and bareheaded. Reaching steeply upwards was a long flight of stone steps, which initially he took two at a time. He was soon out of breath and clinging to the narrow strip of shade cast by the low balustrade.

The steps were hot and many, the shade slipping away.

After two hundred and eighty the stone temple appeared atop the final flight. From inside came a musical cacophony as he cooled his soles in the doorway, before being led up onto a higher level. Initially the interior was black and foreboding but as his eyes opened he could make out carved murals, an altar bedecked with incense and flowers, smeared with milk and honey and littered with small coins and clay votives. He put down a small coin and followed the sound to the topmost chamber. Here sitting in two window openings were two priests, one beating a frame drum, the other, balloon cheeked, playing a shenai. The drummer kept breaking into different rhythms and the wind player screeched painfully at the sky. Loïc took a seat in a niche, enjoying the cold almost chill of the stone and the madness of the noise. It wasn't long before he saw a pair of birds soaring towards the temple. The booming stopped but the shenai continued to creel in conversation with the raptors. He was led back down to the temple door while the priest/musicians offered up small chunks of meat, which the birds stooped on and ate from outstretched hands. It was amazing to see these large birds with sharp talons and razor beaks carefully receive their daily meal and the priests' undamaged hands.

The sun was now directly overhead, only the unwary and the well shaded stirred. Inverted fruit bats jostled in a banyan tree near his shoes below. The demonic hee-haw bray of a donkey drifted up to the temple from a sunburnt compound outside town. Occasionally the tuneless shriek of a peacock pierced the heat, otherwise all was still. Loïc lay on the cool terrace next to the temple wall and bathed in the peace. A solitary cloud adrift in a bleached out blue heralded afternoon. It edged imperceptibly over Loïc, its grey underside chilling the air and shading the stone stairway. Moving with the moment he descended to his shoes with the feeling that this climate suited him, he felt at home within his homelessness. He delighted in the way events connected with each other yet never failed to surprise him.

The vendor was dozing on his wheeled fruit stall but sprang to life and offered to juice up some limes.

"With shinni?"

"Yes yes."

"Good for the heat sir."

"Yes." Loïc agreed as the sharp sweetness woke his tongue.

"Another sir?"

Loïc was already studying the dusty road out to the west.

"Arunachala in that direction sir, Shiva fire mountain, very special, very good place for sir to go."

"How far?"

"Far is not important sir. How is the question sir needs to be asking. How to go is the best place to start, far is always getting a little less that way."

The vendor ducked into a doorway and returned with a burly looking Sikh driver who indicated a Tata truck parked on the other side of the road.

"Arunachala?" he asked.

Nodding Loïc picked up his bag.

"Chello chello," said the driver.

The truck was completely full of cashew nuts, even the passenger seat had sacks of them piled high. The driver pointed to the toolbox above the cab.

"Arunachala?" He said again.

"Yes yes," said Loïc.

"Okay," smiled the Sikh, his beard twisted up to his ears and his long hair contained in a hair net with a topknot. Loïc noticed the fringe of black hair that followed the rim of his ears, then he swung up onto the cab roof and they were off. Another orange flew into his hands and Loïc waved, the vendor taking up his sleeping position once more as the shade temperature increased.

This was the other side of road riding, the truck took the crown of the road and ran on its air horns, blasting everything but buses and other trucks right off the road and into the dirt. Many of the trucks seemed to crab towards them, their chassis out of line from overloading. Everything just squeezed through, everything happened just in time. All traffic was an accident barely avoided. Loïc gripped the edge of the toolbox, the hot air bruising his body and driving a fine dust into his eyes and hair. By the time the truck ground to a stop in the town of Tiruvanamalai below Arunachala his hair stood on end, his eyes wept and night had fallen like a brief blackout. An hour later the moon grew almost full from the palm dotted horizon.

Again Loïc found the ever available cheap hotel room, each with some kind of singular disadvantage. If it wasn't lack of windows it was the stench of the toilet. That or some invasion of cockroaches or monkeys. This room was nice enough but sleeping on the silent roof was one of those numerous screeching peacocks. This of course he didn't know until dawn when murder leapt into his waking mind, only to find waves of avian call and response cries rippling through the towns vegetation.

15
Sri Pukka Baba

There had been a shower in the night and the mountain seemed to glimmer in the morning light as Loïc explored the lower reaches and took a narrow path that formed a circuit of the whole mound. The path was timeless, the feet that walked this way were endless in supply and were not concerned with arrival. Thorns of various types kept it to a single file. Weaving with the uneven ground took Loïc past ancient animistic totems; feathered and bound. Small stone temples occupied by gangly grimacing monkeys. At one point off the path, huge decorated horses stood elaborately harnessed and saddled, all cut from now crumbling stone. At another place two lines of pantomime-like horses, brightly painted, stood side by side, made of biscuit fired clay, waiting, life size on a bouldered knoll. He stopped, explored each and moved on. At another place just off the path a variety of stone animals was grouped in front of a ferocious black figure in a sumo wrestlers stance. Flanked by attendants and girls bearing bowls of fruit, all cleaned and cared for, he rested for a while in a tiny thatched hut, empty and devoid of traces of ownership. A ragged shirt hung from the roof, a fire pit outside. Further around the circuit there was simply a patch of swept earth. Small items, sticks and stones were placed in arrangements of lines, circles and squares. Everything was painted in black and yellow stripes, he felt a great respect for the simplicity and beauty of the place, even if he didn't know its meaning.

He walked this timeless path until there wasn't a thought, a memory or even a question in his mind. He became stilled each step along the way. There was nothing, but being in the place, the heat and the clear blue over this mighty mound that sat squarely on his right all day. Occasionally he found a drink, a spring or a seepage, mostly he just walked, soil beneath his feet, breath in his body and a love of being alive.

Come evening he passed through the business hour of Tiruvanamalai, aware but not distracted by the crowded streets, noisy blaring traffic and the odd cry of 'hey mister' and 'very nice you want to buy'.

The sky had changed and low cloud was catching the setting light on its underside giving it the appearance of the sea. A mauve roiling surface shot through with golden troughs now passed above him. It was new to him, fascinating and threatening and with it came that heavy feeling of compression. This must be 'undulatus' the one TD had spoken of 'undulatus asperatus' he thought as he turned down the lane to his room. I wonder what 'asperatus' means he thought as he turned the key in the lock but the door was already open.

Sitting on the floor was a shaven headed man wearing a red and yellow applique vest, and otherwise swathed in maroon cloth. His feet were bare and his laceless black shoes were placed neatly beside the door. For a moment Loïc thought he had the wrong room until he saw his bag on the bed.

"Come, come in, said the man, yes this is your room. I have come to see you."

"How did you get in?" said Loïc.

"The lady of the house knows me and meditation is best done out of the sun."

"How long have you been here?"

"Since an hour ago."

"An hour," thought Loïc, that's when he had first seen the cloud, towards the end of his walk round the mountain. "What do you want?"

"My name is Chogrum Tenshe, he said standing and proffering his hand. I've been sent by my Rimpoche to ask you a few questions.

"That's fine," said Loïc "but now is not a good time, I'm tired and hungry and unsure about your intentions."

Ignoring Loïc's resistance Tenshe leant forward.

"Firstly, blessings on you." For he was a Buddhist monk. "Secondly I am instructed to ask you whether you know what a sankhar is?"

"No I don't," said Loïc, "you tell me."

"A sankhar is a shell in the language of the Bon."

"The Bon?" said Loïc.

"The Bon are the original animist priesthood of my country Tibet. Before Padmasambhava managed to bring Buddhism in, there was an animistic culture called Bon Po. However things changed and they became part of Buddhism only on the condition that they could do everything the Buddhists did, but in reverse. Padmasambhava tricked them, saying they could be the protectors of the new faith. But that's another story."

"Okay, but what this got to do with shells and what has any of this got to do with me?" Loïc felt intruded on. If nothing else apart from his bow and quiver of darts he had two large shells. How could that be known? He must have gone through his bag.

"I haven't looked inside your bag, as you may think, we don't operate on that level. Our information comes through signs and divination. It's rarely incorrect. I am here only to ask whether the sankhar shells are the same as each other, we understand they are not."

"How did he know what I was thinking?" Loïc had to pass on that. How does he know I have two shank shells, or sanhkar shells or whatever they are called? He had to pass on that too. As to the difference between them, that was a precise detail to know or even want to know. TD and he were the only ones there when he pulled them up from the algae beds, how was it possible that these people knew and what else did they know? His hunger and tiredness had melted away completely; he was now on full alert.

"Tell me more about this sanhkar shell," he said.

"Naturally," said Tenseh, adjusting the folds of his robe in a relaxed way as he sat on the floor. Loïc sat on the bed next to his bag.

"We have in our tradition the eight Ashtamangala. These are symbols but they are also actual things. They represent qualities, aspects of humanity, they also relate to parts of the body. They are precious qualities and have been used for keeping peace and clarity in place for aeons. We, the people of the roof of the world know of their importance and use them to bring balance and truth into the lives of the people.

Loïc's attention was complete.

"Tell me, what are the other seven symbols?"

"These I can tell you, but at present I am here to talk about the shell. Do you have such a shell or know of its whereabouts? It is large and white and is sometimes known as a shank shell."

By now Loïc was convinced that he was dealing with a genuine monk, who despite entering his room without invitation was there on a mission of some importance.

"Yes, he said, I know of these shells they are in the ocean."

"And it is correct that you carry two, one that turns left and one that turns right?"

"What's so important about left and right?"

Loïc was playing for time and was curious to know all he could before revealing anything. Tenseh could see that this boy was not just some naive traveller stumbling from place to place taking photographs and expecting everyone to speak his language. No he genuinely wanted to know.

"These shells, he began, these sanhka, are not all sanhka, only the ones that spiral to the right are Sanhka. I'll tell you why. The Buddha."

Loïc stopped him there.

"Buddha, I know a little about Buddha. There was a lying down stone Buddha I saw once, not that long ago but that's all I know."

"Yes, said Tenseh, you sat at his feet in Mamalipuram a few days ago, this much we know."

"I was resting," said Loïc defensively.

He had realised that nothing in this place went unnoticed. It had been the same coming to land in the Elephanta; every fishing village knew how he had arrived.

"Yes" the monk said, "resting at the feet of the Buddha is a sign of respect. It is also a way of taking refuge in the Buddha, and the Buddha is the great teacher, the teacher of non-attachment and compassion in this mad world of human folly. These, I see, are matters of importance to you. But I digress. The shells. The one that turns to the right, is the sankhar shell, not the other. In its spiralling right it mirrors the movement of the sun and moon, the stars and the planets.

Loïc could see the connection, having just spent weeks at sea navigating with TD.

"What's more, he went on, this right hand spiral is reminiscent of the Buddha himself. The hair whorls of the Buddha's body, his head, his body hair, the curl between his eyebrows and around his navel, they all spiralled to the right. This is unusual and so is the shell."

Loïc glanced around his body but resisted the temptation to pull up his shirt and look at his navel. So it was hairs again, the bogey bamboo man, the humpback whales and now the Buddha, hair seemed to be rather important in the scheme of things.

"There's more?" he asked.

"Yes," said Tenseh, "I can tell you why they are so important to us."

"I'm listening."

"Yes this I can see. The Buddha shell is used to bathe a phenomenon that is so ancient that it connects us with our origins. We use the shell to pour a right hand spiral of blessed water over an ammonite cut by worms, Vajra Kita worms. This ammonite is called a Gandaki and is over 140 million years old. For both the Hindus and ourselves use these sankhar. They are sacred tools."

"I see," said Loïc, more to himself but out loud. Sacred, rare, important, ancient. "Yes, I do carry one."

Although Tenseh's face didn't show it his body relaxed. He nodded and stood up, rooting around for his shoe with his toe.

"Someone will come and see you again, here are some momos." He reached inside the folds of his robe and handed Loïc a small, slightly greasy package with his right hand.

"You should sleep now." He turned and as he let himself out his feet searched for his incongruous shoes.

Loïc looked at the tepid package in his hand, not sure whether to explore further or not. Distracted by it, he had forgotten to ask what the sankhar shell symbolised. He pulled open the door but there was no sign of the monk. Now he couldn't resist. Inside were three round dough balls, obviously fried. Another kind of idly! He thought of Padma as he sunk his teeth into the first. It wasn't an idly and he realised how hungry he was as he wiped his lips and screwed up the paper. It was then that he noticed something on the packaging. He flattened it out. There was a pattern of eight lines, exactly the same as the reciprocal roof he had made with Bertrand, underneath was the single word 'mandala'. He laid it by his bed, put his bag under his pillow, 'not that that was going to make any difference to anything' was his final thought before falling into sleep.

He woke from his reverie with a start, a peacock's kreel inside his head. The incident with the Tibetan monk preoccupied him during his breakfast at the small crowded dubba where the choice was idlys or samba idlys. While he ate he decided to climb Arunachala as the streets were crowded with pilgrims attending the huge Arunachaleswara temple in the middle of town. Tomorrow would be full moon and the main focus of the month was making the connection between the temple fire and setting fire to the Shiva mountaintop. He had decided to keep his bag with him, as his room was an open house. Once he'd crossed the road, which was a constant flow of people making the circuit of the mountain he cut up a side street, through a small metal gate and onto the base of the mountain. As he started the gentle climb he wondered how it was that he kept finding things that other people wanted, not just small things but things of some cultural importance, first the egg then the shells.

"Would sir be interested in some precious stones?" A gravelly voice cut through his musing.

Standing next to the path behind a box covered with a soiled cloth sat a middle-aged man smiling sweetly at him. Loïc looked at his display. A row of six oily slivers of stone sat on the cloth.

"These sir are fragments from the top of Arunachala, very precious, very nice."

Everywhere Loïc looked there were fragments of the same kind of stone. He picked up a stone from the path and offered it to the vendor.

"Oh sir is having a practical joke." "I'll trade you," said Loïc blowing off the dust." Mine is cleaner and bigger than yours, it's a good deal."

The man smiled and wobbled his head from side to side in a gesture of condescending amusement.

"Sir is not understanding, these are from the Shiva flame, from the top of the mountain. Last year's stones very rare, very long way, very good price."

Loïc threw both hands up in the air and walked on up the path. People here, he thought, wanted to sell anything and everything.

As he climbed through the increasing heat he realised that the mound was indeed a mountain. What had been a path was merely a gap between thorny brittle shrubs not nearly as clear as the tour he had taken round the base the day before. Soon he was stepping over small rocks and within minutes he was lost in a barren maze of jagged boulders and ferocious heat. His notion of a quick stroll to the top, while he considered the significance of his visitor of the night before, had now had become eclipsed by a predicament. He was ill equipped, his small bottle of water was already half empty and he had no head cover. With the heat building and no tree shade he assessed his situation as somewhat precarious unless things changed within the hour. He kept moving, trying to get his bearings from the peak, but each time he lost sight of high ground it seemed to appear again in an unlikely direction. After half an hour he knew he was lost. He had thought of Arunachala as yet another mountain, after all the mountains was where he was from, you went up them and down again. Not so here, of all the mountains to take lightly he had chosen a Shiva mountain that stood at the centre of the universe and he was being tripped up by his arrogance. Within thirty-six hours there would be a cone of flame leaping from its summit attended by thousands of pilgrims and the quality of transformation would be emanating out into the world from a full moon ceremony.

As he said these things to himself he realised he wasn't even prepared to be out for the night. It certainly wasn't obvious from the heat of the day, but at night, he had been warned the temperature dropped to a severe chill, burning peak or not.

He found a pitiful patch of shade in the lee of a leafy bush and assessed his situation again. From where he sat he could see nothing of the lower slopes or the surrounding landscape. Not only that but the mountain above was hidden by jagged outcrops of rock. His small bottle now had little water remaining. Two shells, one bow, a quiver, another layer of clothing and the sack itself.

Water first, it's easy to lose body fluid when you go searching for water in the heat. He moved to a vantage point and wrapped a shirt round his head. From here he could take in a large area without moving. Initially it all looked much the same. Dusty grey green thorn everywhere. It left black thorn tips buried in the skin. Usefully it described the norm of the place, any other colours were unusual and worthy of note. Down the slope something was different, the green had changed to a bluish green. Tenaciously something else was growing there, probably a plant that needed more water than the thorn bushes. As he sat there keeping the sun off his skin he noticed that his parched nose was picking up familiar smells on the breeze. There was a faint stream of eucalyptus, dispersed and from some distance. The same with jasmine, faint and tired, then there was a brief rush, a sweetness, a sticky taste that he couldn't quite place. Then as another waft skimmed over the mountainside, he got the sticky sweet; date palm. Now the date, you may think, grows in the sand, but wherever it manages to grow, water is not far away, it's a thirsty tree, anxious that a drought could happen any moment. It locks up all the water it can get in a fibrous trunk and then feeds it out to its fruit. With eyes closed and all his attention on the wind in his nose he identified the tree's direction, though there was nothing the height of a palm anywhere to be seen.

N'Zingu had come to him again. This tiny man with so many sayings that just put you back on track.

'When you become part of a place, then you remember how to recognise yourself.'

Loïc remembered his mouth salivating before the last time he had eaten a date. This time he drank down the saliva with a relish that relieved his dry throat. He moved off slowly, looking for signs of anything greener or fruiting. He followed a rock outcrop of granite that dropped diagonally across the slope. The sweet odour drew him down to the lowest point of the seam. There above where the thin crust of soil sat was a damp patch, below, more so, and further down stood a very squat stumpy date palm, twice as tall as a man and heavy with small ripe dates. From here the landscape below was revealed, the town the temple and markets, all from a bird's eye view.

It was then as Loïc was being choosy about the ripest date that a man appeared leaning on a bamboo stick and wearing very little but a kind of nappy in brilliant white cotton. He said nothing, his body twisted slightly to one side. He had difficulty walking but his progress was good. When Loïc offered him his choicest date he took it, smiled with his eyes and kept going. Loïc felt deeply disturbed once he was out of sight, thinking that he should have done more, maybe given him all his dates. He couldn't explain it; he felt that he'd missed an opportunity.

He found a tiny seepage and thinking of the Guanches brothers, he fed a stem into the dripping moss and directed the drips into his bottle, but still the feeling lingered. A while later the man returned, approaching from another direction. Loïc watched him. When he got abreast of Loïc he signalled for him to follow. Slowly and deliberately they descended the path, for there was one that led to a long low cave furnished with a floor mat and little else. They entered the shade and just sat for an eternity and said nothing. Occasionally the old man, for he was old, adjusted the hem of his white nappy but nothing else. Loïc was happy with the situation; his anxious moment on the mountain had passed. Being quiet and cool was just what he needed.

"I feel that you don't know who I am," he eventually said to Loïc, more of a statement than as a question.

"That's not important to me," said Loïc." I don't know who anyone is. Sometimes people show me things, and sometimes people tell things that they think I want to know.

It's all the same to me, I live in a world full of people I don't know, and they all interest me. Why, who are you?"

There was a pause filled by a lizard making its way across the cave roof.

"That is the question I ask myself every day. Who am I?"

"Have you come to the answer yet?" Loïc said leaning forward and making eye contact with the greying face.

"I'm afraid the question remains, however I ask all those that come to see me to ask the same question of themselves."

"What do they answer?"

"They are all waiting for me to find the answer." Loïc felt there was a degree of disappointment in the old man's tone.

"How long have you been asking this question?"

"It must be many years now, the people believe that I am very wise for asking it of them and myself."

"Many years is a long time to get no answer, is it not?" Loïc said as he noticed the sadness that came to the old man's eyes.

"Yes indeed."

"Perhaps." Loïc hesitated, for he had realised that he was now sitting at the feet of a guru. "Perhaps you are asking the wrong question, could that be the problem?"

A silence ate their words. He closed his eyes and reflected on the possibility of his life revolving around the wrong question.

Meanwhile Loïc sat enjoying the cool of the cave and marvelled at the few possessions of this aged gentle soul. A bowl, a spoon, a stick, a pair of chapals, a sleeping mat a cover and his lily-white nappy. He turned away and moved to the shaded entrance that looked out over the eternal pastoral scene of paddies, palms, rocks and the busy temple town. As he sat he reflected on the old man's question.

Did he ever ask 'Who am I?' of himself? He didn't, his questions of himself were much bigger and more complicated. A hand rested on his shoulder, with it came some weight. Propping himself between Loïc and his bamboo stick the old man took in the view.

"I believe you may well be right. What question is it that you ask yourself?"

"Well," Loïc began, not sure whether he could tell him, but risking it anyway. "The only question like that that I sometimes ask myself is what am I not?"

A flock of green parrots shot past heading for a water filled tank outside the enormous Arunachaleswara temple. Nothing else moved.

"What am I not? What a question that is! That's brilliant." He muttered. An excitement seemed to course through him. His features became revitalised and a beatific smile spread across his face.

"Would you like some water?" Loïc said, holding out the half full plastic bottle that he had recovered from the rubbish bin in his room.

"Thank you young man." He said, distractedly taking the bottle and pouring it straight down his throat. "Thank you for the date, the water and this new question. I think you may have given many people a new dimension to their quest. Pray what is your name?"

"Loïc," said Loïc.

"Loweek," he tried to repeat. "This new question. What am I not? Will be known as Loweek's question. Do you have an answer to this mysterious question?"

"So far and this is only so far." Loïc began. "I am just part of it all. Everything and everyone makes me who and what I am. For me that answer feels good. Tomorrow I might have another answer for you. As for, 'what I am not?' I'm not separate. I'm not alone. I'm not fearful and I'm not unable. All those things are not part of my story. Those things I have thrown away. They don't work and I can no longer use them or be used by them. As a result I feel a lot lighter, and it seems that all I need comes to me. If it doesn't come then I don't need it. I don't really need or want anything, for surely wanting leads to more wanting and that sounds to me like one big disappointment. So there it is, that's where I sit with the question. What am I not?"

The old guru, somehow immaculate in his dazzling white nappy pondered the landscape and the miraculous coloured clouds as the sunset between the two. Eventually he spoke.

"You don't have any more of those dates do you?"

As it happened Loïc had tucked a few of the firmer ones in his pocket, just in case.

"Here's one."

"They're very good, where did you get them from?"

"You must walk past them every day." Loïc informed him cautiously. "Perhaps you should do a little less thinking and a little more seeing."

"Yes indeed," said Sri Pukka Baba, for that was his name, as he looked more than a little shamefaced.

"Would you like to stay the night, then we can talk more in the morning?"

Loïc could hardly refuse since only an hour before he was readying himself for sleeping out amongst the rocks and the thorns. Now the offer of a cave for the night was very attractive, even if his host didn't know who he was after years of searching. Also in a funny kind of way he liked the simplicity of the old guru, even if he was an old fool.

"I'd be delighted," he said.

"That's perfect then." Sri Pukka Baba turned leaning on his stick.

"I expected you to say that so I'm off to my bed. I have to be up early to meditate on your question and its full moon so the place will be very busy." With that he entered his cave.

Loïc watched the blackness of night descend between sunset and moonrise. Only the parping sound of moped horns and the moving lights of candles being lit in the temple below punctuated the stillness. When he did enter the cave it was lit from above. There tucked up in a comfortable bed with his glasses on sat the guru reading a comic. A tiger skin rug hung casually over the edge of his raised shelf boudoir. He turned and nodded to the mat on the floor.

"Do you need a blanket?"

Never one to suffer unnecessarily, Loïc thanked him. To his surprise he unfolded a top quality unused four point woollen trade blanket, made by Earlys of Witney.

"There." He said, tossing it onto the floor. "Nothing but the best. After being here for so long I decided it was time to get a little more comfortable. Oh, and since no one was wanting to build me an ashram, the mattress and the bedside light makes the reading of these very good comics so enjoyable, and I sleep so much better. Those split bamboo mats are such a miserable concept."

Loïc laughed, then they both laughed, then their thoughts made it bubble up again. That night they slept like babies rarely do.

Break of day came all of a sudden. One moment Loïc was dreaming of water buffaloes with their tongues up their noses, the next Sri Pukka Baba was shaking him by the shoulder saying 'quickly quickly I am needing to be sitting on the bamboo mat'.

For a moment Loïc was uncertain which of the two images was dreamt. Then as a steaming cup of chai was thrust into his hand he realised that it was urgency that was the waking reality. Sri Pukka Baba was standing there in a fresh white nappy being quietly agitated, while he could hear voices at the cave mouth. Clutching his things in one hand and chai in the other he hurried out through a growing crowd of white clad acolytes all pressing to enter the cave. He wrapped himself in the blanket and went to take in the sunlit view of the night before, as the crowd entered the cave like sluiced water. Within minutes music and singing began to issue forth and Loïc wrapped in the four point, enjoyed both the sung repetition and his chai, as a blanket of mist burnt off from the paddies below.

"Very nice view, sir, exceptionally important day for carrying Shiva stone."

Loïc recognised the gravelly voice, turned and at first didn't recognise the face. The figure before him was immaculately turned out in a new cream coloured Nehru suit. He palmed Loïc one of his greasy stones, as if it were a secret.

"No charge sir, this one is especially for you. I am thinking you are having very good audience with Guru Pukka Baba. Most admirable for one of such few years. Very important Shiva holy man, always waiting for the right answer. Perhaps young sir would be giving Guru special Shiva stone from me as special favour."

"No promises." Said Loïc. The balding stone seller bowed and shuffled his way off muttering: 'a thousand boons upon your mortal soul'.

Loïc finished his cooling chai.

'They are as strange as.....' the singing stopped and he never completed the thought. The sonorous voice of Sri Pukka Baba announced to the assembled crowd his new question.

"What am I not?"

All was hushed for some time until people started to leave in ones twos and small knots. They all seemed to be very animated and pleased, like children who have been given an extra day off. There were a few who expressed their disapproval at having to change direction so late in life, but even they looked a little relieved.

Once the chai wallah, the biscuit peddler and the stone hawker had left trailing the crowd like puppies after teats, a peace fell back into place. Sri Pukka Baba emerged some time later, nappy around groin, stick in one hand, and comic in the other. Sitting down next to Loïc as the bustling pilgrim town rubbed its bleary eyes, and milk was drawn down from sacred cows, he showed him his current reading material.

They were stories from the Mahabharata, the old Indian classic, but these were in comic form for the instruction of children. However they were a cheap and cheerful edition, both colourful and misprinted. All the speech bubbles the printer had omitted to print; the characters in the stories said nothing and it was Sri Pukka Baba's favourite pastime to fill in these bubbles with his own version of events in a neat Cyrillic script. Of course Loïc couldn't read what was written but the empty bubble comic told him more about the guru than anything he said. Loïc laughed as Sri Pukka Baba chuckled to himself pen poised over an empty bubble which came from the mouth of a ferocious looking warrior clasping a severed head in one hand and a bloody dripping sword in the other.

"I am thinking," he said with a soft south Indian ripple to his English. "This one says, 'there goes another one who is going to miss his idlys today.' What do you think?"

Loïc's laughter rapidly dissolved into something more painful, soon he was busy clutching his stomach thinking that he was going to be sick. Sri Pukka Baba filled in a whole page while Loïc mused upon the meaning of the spiritual life. If all saintly people had the humour of Sri Pukka Baba then it looked quite appealing. His experience to date had been all rather too serious and precious. This old man in his luminous nappy had thrown a new light on it all. Loïc's affection for him increased and his heart cracked opened a little more. He took a deep breath, glad to be alive and no longer laughing.

"Pukka Baba," started Loïc. "I have a question for you."

"Tell me, tell me, questions I like."

Loïc opened his bag and pulled out two bundles and unwrapped them, laying the two Shankar shells on the spread out cloth.

"Hummmm," intoned Pukka Baba as he turned each one round and round in opposite directions. They were translucent in the strong sunlight, with inviting entrances, smoother than any baby's bottom. The outsides undamaged and encrusting over a crenulated spiral.

"Where in the sea are these specimens from, or did you buy them?"

"The atolls of the Maldive Islands, far west of here, and no I didn't buy them I dived for them."

"This is good, very good, said the Baba, I am liking what I see more and more, pray tell me what is your question?"

"Well as you might say. What to do?"

"Indeed what to do. What do you want to do?"

Loïc decided not to mention the evening with Chogrum Tenseh.

"Tell me about these shells. Tell me what you know."

"Certainly Loweek," for he still found it hard to say Loïc,,"this one, in our Hindu tradition is many things, firstly it's a Lakshmi conch, it is a manifestation of the supreme goddess. Very rare, very sacred. She is the goddess of big money, property, you know very wealthy making lady god. She is the one in bed with the great god Vishnu. He's the great preserver of course. She's the one goddess big on water, fluidity that sort of thing. Oh yes, and fertility, she is making that happen. And of course the nagas, the snakes are her familiars, all that kundalini energy that's so good for your beauty and your strength. Then there's the ayurveda medicine that's made from the ground up shankar shell, that's very effective with those stomach complaints. What more do you want to know?"

"There's more?"

"There's always more."

"The trumpet, the first trumpet was the shankar shell, sometimes called the horn of war. They are also said to give fame and long life. Really the shankar shell is a calling card for the goddess Lakshmi who brings blessing on you sorrows, intelligence to your mind and success and worldly freedom to your life. Shall I continue?"

"No, no that's good for now, so much for just one shell."

The day's sun soon had the stone of the mountain heated beyond walking. Chapals were essential for the path, past the date palm, where they collected a few more dates, the guru tucking some away in his pristine folds. With one hand on his bendy stick and the other on Loïc's shoulder they took the rising path away from the plain up Mount Arunachala. Sri Pukka Baba was pleased to be with this young man who had come out of the sea with the goddess shell and its companion, one being the ordinary and the other, right spiralling shell, the extraordinary. He was also pleased that Loweek was not one of his acolytes; they all had so much wanting all the time. Wanting to be someone that they weren't mostly. That and wanting to know things that they couldn't quite understand. Always thinking they weren't enough. If only they would stop thinking they could just be happy with being themselves; all this self-inquiry went round and round. Loweek, now, he seemed to be different, not the sort of person he usually met. He seemed so light hearted and in the flow. It really was such a relief for Pukka Baba, he could be his true self with all its oddities and contradictions in the presence of this young man.

As they gained the flatter ground near the summit a white robed figure came running towards them beneath a black umbrella, breathless and panting something about ghee. He fell to his knees and put his hands on the old gurus feet. Others broke away from the long file of people climbing an adjacent path, steadying their bowls they hurriedly thronged around the old guru and the young man. They fell in behind them as others greeted the guru in the same manner. Slowly, en masse, they made their way to the burning ground. There on a huge flat rock stood an enormous pyre of wood. It was evident from the general atmosphere that something was wrong, or shall we say some detail was not quite right. The spiritual world is known for its futile craving for exactitude. On this occasion it was the quality of the ghee. Now ghee is clarified buffalo butter and is used amongst other things for cooking in these parts, also it is used for anointing the many stone lingams in the many stone temples, but here on the top of Arunachala used in huge volumes for lighting the Shiva fire on top of the mountain. There was, a heated discussion going on about using the ghee for the Joythir Lingam, which is the whole mountain.

"What to do?" said Sri Pukka Baba. "No one is happy."

"Just bless it," whispered Loïc in Sri Pukka Baba's ear. "Then it will be the best ghee of all, yes no?"

Sri Pukka Baba looked at him with his eyebrows as far from his chin as they would reach.

"Indeed." He said with his head wobbling from side to side. "Blessing is a good idea."

"I'm told it changes everything. I'm told it especially energises liquids. But what that means hasn't been explained to me, perhaps you can help with that?"

"Later, later, now we'll do it and see what happens, this is very good thinking."

Sri Pukka Baba set about blessing all the cans of ghee that stood around the base of the pyre that had been hauled by hand to the top of the mountain. Then he blessed all the pots of ghee that pilgrims had carried in bowls up the rough paths so that no one would be left out.

By now Sri Pukka Baba's acolytes were muttering amongst themselves about this boy that seemed to have the ear of their guru. Where had he come from? Who was he? Why him?. Because he certainly seemed to be rather influential.

Once Sri Pukka Baba had finished waving his hands

about and saying his sayings, anxiety dissolved and the anointing of the pyre with copious amounts of improved ghee, looked like it would now go ahead. Everyone seemed satisfied, the carriers, the pilgrims, the buyers, they all felt good about the outcome. The dispute had been simmering all month. How was it that the guru was so wise? At one stroke he could pour blessings on troubled ghee. It was a marvel. But it was not so.

Word had travelled fast, mouth to mouth, from phone to phone to sending a runner up the mountain. He arrived breathless as the first can of ghee was being opened. All the young man could do was wave his hands as he gasped for breath. The run up Arunachala in the midday heat certainly suggested that someone somewhere felt this was still a serious matter. The open ghee can was lowered to the ground and a small knot of those concerned was surrounded by a large crowd of those interested. After standing with his head between his knees and then gulping down a spun steel tumbler of tepid water the messenger announced that he was a representative of the bulk ghee providers who now required full and fair payment for the newly blessed and now rare ghee. Because the ghee in its original state had not been fully paid for, it was not, as yet, the pilgrims to use. Extra money was being demanded before the accounts on this particular batch of ghee could be completed.

As the flushed young messenger stopped talking uproar broke out. Everyone seemed to have an opinion and everyone thought they should be heard first. In Malayam this meant everything and nothing to Loïc, he didn't understand a word but he understood every gesture. His suggestion of blessing the ghee seemed to have opened a can of greedy worms. He felt a tap on the shoulder, and turned half expecting an enraged pilgrim to shout in his face. There stood Sri Pukka Baba, his lily-white nappy somewhat askew, a confused mask spread across his usually impassive face.

"What to do?" they said simultaneously, and then broke into laughter hidden behind their hands.

"Loweek I am finding myself greatly without a paddle. Not only am I without the paddle but I am facing up the stream. Everyone is always wanting more, no one is ever saying they have enough."

"Very true Shri Pukka Baba, but what to do here and now? The oil is blessed, the price has risen and the moon is full. These people cannot wait to know 'who they are or who they are not'. They want action not deep meaningful thoughts."

"Indeed young Loweek, your wisdom must be ready to find a quick and easy solution to this very delicate situation, must you not?"

So according to Sri Pukka Baba it was up to Loïc to resolve this sticky problem. And since it was at a time when everyone was saying, problem, opportunity. What was the outcome that was most needed?

By now the crowd was very loud, shirt grabbing arguments and scuffs of dust were breaking out. The ghee merchants runner had indeed made a run for it, with a posse of irate white pyjama clad pilgrims hot on his tail. Loïc could see it was the moment for a heroic distraction. Grabbing a bottle of water from the hand of a distracted bystander he climbed to the top of the huge would be beacon. As he climbed the volume of voices lowered and by the time he had reached the top he had their attention.

"This," he proclaimed, pulling a Shankar shell from his bag.

"This shell is a gift from Sri Pukka Baba to the people of the Shiva mountain."

"This," he said, holding the shell high in the air. "Is a gift from Vishnu to Lakshmi." Where this had come from Loïc was not sure, glancing down he saw Sri Pukka Baba staring intently at him.

"This, he went on, is the preserver of prosperity and the giver of fame. This is the giver of long lives. This shankar shell will wash away all sins."

Still mystified Loïc filled the shell from the bottle of water and turned it round and round until the water had reached right inside. Then glancing down at Sri Pukka Baba who nodded, he slowly poured the contents onto the pyre beneath his feet. The crowd cheered and started throwing down money.

"This," Loïc started up again. He now had their full attention.

"This manifestation of the great goddess Lakshmi will sit at the centre of the ashram you will build for the great Sri Pukka Baba, the guru of Arunachala."

As these words came out of his mouth Loïc looked down at Sri Pukkabuba. What was this, some kind of mind control? Was he a spiritual leader or some old trickster crook? Sri Pukka Baba was nowhere to be seen below the pyre. In the distance an old white nappy wearing man with a bendy bamboo stick made his way unnoticed back towards the date palms and his cave.

"This," Loïc shouted. His hand no longer his own as it shot up into the air clutching the shell. "This will bring great fertility and beauty to your women folk and a very great strength to their greatly improved bodies."

Now everybody should be happy. Thought Sri Pukka Baba as he entered his cave, but what to do about young Loweek?

Loïc somewhat stunned by the turn of events, clambered down onto the greasy rock that had seen many thousands of full moon infernos and beat a troubled retreat down the path to the town below.

By the time he had reached the base of the mountain a huge sheet of flame leapt from its top into the darkening sky diminishing the light of the rising full moon. The flame lit the underbelly of a layer of purple rain cloud, which appeared to want to settle on the mountain to rest from its interminable floating. Loïc sat, drinking yet more chai on the rooftop of his lodging house. Tomorrow would be 'two days later' and at any moment he expected the monk, Chogrum Tenseh to appear with some kind of proposition about the shankar shells. He was beginning to dread the subject, each time he found something it led to complications, which he had to admit, also brought a healthy dose of laughter material. The incident with Sri Pukka Baba on the mountain, especially the business with the gurus words coming out of his mouth, he had found disturbing, but more so the way the old man had just walked off. That stuff about building an ashram? Loïc wasn't even sure what an ashram was, except that it must be some kind of building that Sri Pukka Baba thought he should have. Then there was the conch shell being the centre piece of the ashram, it was in his bag, it had never even been discussed, none of it had. Was all this just going to happen, was there some mysterious force at work in this place, anyway who were these people? He was a fish out of water.

The next morning Loïc made his way back up the mountain, found his way to the date palm and then Sri Pukka Baba's cave. There was no one there. No guru, no acolytes just the mat on the floor, the bed on the shelf and a neat pile of those favourite comics full of empty bubbles. He slipped the left turning shell down the side of Sri Pukka Baba's bed. As he did so he was sure he felt some weight lift from his shoulders.

16

Painted Wagon

Loïc decided to ignore all recent events related to the shankar shells and revive a plan which had been taking shape in his mind as he had been travelling the dusty roads of Tamil Nadu. He would buy a cart, hitch up a water buffalo, and wander on in this ancient and sedate style. Loïc's way out of the confusion was to rearrange some of the detail of recent events into some other form. The moony-eyed water buffalo that stood looking at him from the farm compound next door he would name Lakshmi and the cart that was having its wheel fixed as he watched he would offer to buy. Walking over to the neighbours he did just that.

"I'd like to buy the buffalo and the cart if I may?"

"This is a real possibility, the farmer replied. And is there something else young sir requires?"

This is very quick and easy thought Loïc, what else do I need for a buffalo?

"A nose bag and a bucket would be useful."

"Very wise, anything else for young Sir?"

"The price?" said Loïc." How much for all these things?"

"There is no charge young Sir, everything is taken care of."

"Taken care of by who?"

"By Mr Nowragee, he has been instructed to see to all your needs during your stay."

"Instructed? Who instructs him?"

"Young Sir doesn't need to worry his head about such matters, all is in place. I too am instructed. My instructions are to tell you that wherever you go on this fair continent of ours that you need only check in with an outlet of Lakshmi Travels and your needs will be immediately attended to."

"Lakshmi Travels!" blurted Loïc, somewhat alarmed by the swiftness of events. It was only yesterday that the Goddess Lakshmi had spilled from his mouth. It had only been minutes ago that he had had the thought of naming the water buffalo and already there was a travel agent with the same name waiting to be instructed about his needs.

The moony-eyed Lakshmi watched and waited while she scratched her rear end on the cart shafts. It appeared that rearranging his reality did little to make more sense of it; things just had a life of their own. The farmer, who was now obviously much more, handed him a business card with an illustration of a buffalo sitting in front of an aeroplane. Lakshmi Travels it announced with a phone number. Loïc checked to see if the ink was still wet. It wasn't.

"Oh yes about the shankar shells," he said." Please keep them safe, we'll be in touch. Happy travels."

He turned the card round between his fingers. If he had been of a different temperament he would have been alarmed by the course of events, but he had learned that all things must pass and going with the flow was becoming his forte. He turned the card over. 'As I thought,' he thought, 'the reciprocal frame image printed in red.'

There was nothing for it, he hitched up Lakshmi to the cart with the farmers help, took a trial turn, leading Lakshmi by the nose rope round the temple compound, jumped onto the flat bed as he'd seen others do, and set off down the road heading north. Before long he was travelling down a long avenue of trees singing as he went. He found the words came to him, as did the hooves of Lakshmi on the road, the rhythm and the rhyme together. The landscape changed into a huge dried out marsh pan; reed clumps and sedum rimmed the watercourses lined with layers of brown and grey mud. The road cut a straight path through the duck infested waters.

The atmosphere of a lost tidal flow made for desolation, a place devoid of people, unpredictable and in the grip of the elements. Solitary waders and black headed storks punctuated the interminable quacking ducks. For a long time the narrow strip of road ploughed on through the acrid misery until at last the ground rose and lifted them clear of the estuarine rind. As the tufts of reed were left behind so the vegetation grew in height, small songbirds emerged from the scrubland and the familiar tablecloth of tilled land outlined by water channels became the norm again.

Loïc now knew that there was some other agency at work, something that had steered him in the direction he had taken. It was not that his decisions were not his own, more that whatever he choose to do or say had a shadow, an accomplice that gave everything another dimension. An overseer that didn't guide, just continuously adapted to his each and every action and thought.

They were on the road for many days and Loïc took to wearing a rather scraggy moustache, there were barbers and moustaches everywhere so its upkeep and the disguise were compatible. If he didn't speak he could pass through heavily populated areas without attracting any attention. He found this anonymity very pleasing. It led to the notion that with practise and a few more adjustments, he could become invisible, completely unnoticeable. The reality was that he was being watched continuously. Soon he ceased to care either way, there was little he could do.

Lakshmi was a slow and consistent form of transport, but she was unused to such distances and her cloven hooves on the hard road surface began to suffer. Loïc pulled into a small town one day, found a room off the main square, with some banyan shade for Lakshmi and just stopped. He realised he had been on the road for too long. There had become something compulsive about it, always leaving, always arriving. Not really being anywhere long enough to arrive at a new place in himself. He needed to know how he would behave if he were to stay in just one place, to know what would surface if he became still.

His room faced north and overlooked the junction with the main market. It was here he put the faded wagon and tethered Lakshmi to a shaded wheel. On the second day in town Loïc was out exploring, he had found the covered market tucked against the temple wall. He followed his nose in the direction of the sweet smell of jasmine, there amongst the piles of white blossoms sat the garland girls with thread and nimble knots stringing flowers into strands. The aroma was intoxicating and Loïc soon lost his logical mind. The girls were busy and beautiful and as always with Loïc it was female movements that held his attention. They laughed and joked as white mounds turned into endless coils, the scent of the heady jasmine increased by light handling. He sat down slightly overcome and within earshot. They had noticed him and exchanged remarks to which he had raised an eyebrow. They were amused thinking he had understood and turned towards each other with muffled giggles. Being around the jasmine and the girls was intoxicating for Loïc but it was also a frustration. Continuously men on mopeds, with their wives and daughters on the back would stop, buy a length that measured from hand to elbow, doubled it over and pinned into the long black tresses of the female. For Loïc the absence of someone to adorn was a poignant fact, he bought a strand for Lakshmi and left unsure whether it was the girls or the jasmine he liked most.

Down the same street there were rows of banana sellers. Large, small, green, yellow all types and sizes, some good for cooking, some good for diarrhoea, all good for potassium and the thyroid gland. He bought a hand of one-bite yellows and walked along eating, throwing the skins to various seated cows chewing the cud. These cows weren't tethered and were free to go wherever they pleased, but often they preferred to be with the people, parked outside the newsagent or dozing amongst the vegetable stalls, mid market. Loïc enjoyed this intimate trust between the people and the cows, there was something re-defined about it, a lack of separation, goodness for them both.

Behind the temple tank that stepped down and down to emerald green water, a series of narrow streets, maze like and crowded formed the main bazaar. It was here that Loïc looked for paint. He had woken with an impulse to paint his wagon. Re-paint would be more accurate as it had at one time been a splendid affair, with decorations around the edge and even up the shafts. There was evidence of flowers, vines, stalks and fruit. Parked in the right landscape it must have been able to disappear completely.

His decision to buy paint wasn't based on having seen a paint shop, unlike most other things in his life which just seemed to present themselves to him. This was something that had come out of wanting to make his mark in some way. The other thing he had decided was that Lakshmi needed a cobbler, not something he had seen in India, an ox cobbler. Back home in his mountains there was a tradition of shoeing the oxen if they were going to be worked. He knew this wasn't going to be easy here, as things seemed to be just allowed to happen, there was no culture of improvement. Everything looked like it had been done the same way for generations. Not only that but everything was falling apart even before it was finished. New paintwork grew mould before it had even dried.

Putting the idea of shoeing a buffalo in front of a cobbler was going to be a challenge. Not only that but the technique for getting boots sewn onto Lakshmi was going to be another matter. He paid a visit to the only cobbler he could find. He ran a shaded outfit that largely repaired run down sandals, cheap plastic shoes and anything that needed a few stitches with a thick greased thread. He was parked at the roadside, which was both a territorial claim and a refuge from the torrent of aggressive traffic that dominated the street. When Loïc tried to describe his needs to the gnarly hunched shoe mender, nothing got through, and he pointed Loïc towards a crate of worn footwear. Loïc found what he was looking for, two odd pairs of old army boots with hobnails covering the soles. These he gave to the gnarly stitcher with a sketch on a piece of cardboard of a lace up sock and an impression of Lakshmi's hoof, to get the sizes right. He gave Loïc a look of tolerant dismissal as Loïc pointed across the square to where Lakshmi sat in the shade chewing the cud.

"There, there, the one sitting down next to the chariot."

The cobbler was confused, not only was there no-one there and 'chariot' was not how he would describe Loïc's cart. He'd seen far too many historical movies. Loïc crossed the square and sat down next to Lakshmi and the cobbler's face dropped. However over the next two days he fashioned two pairs of lace-ups for cloven hooves, not from the old boots but from some thick leather that he produced from under his seat.

Meanwhile Loïc had moved his painting plan forward. He

searched the streets for evidence of paint. Eventually there was only one darkened alleyway left unexplored. At the end was a door and through this door he went. Inside in the half-light of a tiny cubicle sat one Mr Murali, the final tenant in the large empty building. Mr Murali was the third generation of Mr Muralis to sell powered paints and dyes. The living Mr Murali had sat in the gloom for most of his sixty-seven years, if not on his grandfather's knee, at his father's side, now alone. Thirteen years before he had been given notice to quit the property, there had been the rumour of a new road. Now thirteen years later his tiny ground floor shop was the only occupied part of the building, and his case was still going through the courts, it had been going through the courts for twelve of those thirteen years and the lawyers on both sides saw it as a 'rubber case.'

Both Mr Murali and his landlord got poorer as the lawyers got richer. Time passes quickly and both were now in the autumn of their lives and no longer talking to each other.

Loïc's first thought was. How can colour come out of this black hole in the wall?

"Namaste," they said to each other, a polite and common greeting.

"Colour is what I'm looking for, announced Loïc.

"If colour is what you're looking for, colour is what we have." Came the reply.

"Do you have some paint, some red or some yellow?"

"What kind of red would sir be requiring?" Mr Murali replied.

"Ah so I have a choice."

"Choice is the one certainty we have in life."

From then on a riot of bright colours spilt from tins boxes and bags. Dusting hands, shoes and out into the turgid street air where powders mixed in a thin film on the passers-by. Mr Murali showed Loïc colour after colour and it wasn't until the chai wallah started up with his 'garam chai, garam chai' and stopped his bicycle with its precarious urn on the back, that they were in the least distracted. He insisted that chai needed to be drunk before such important decisions were made.

Loïc left with eight small plastic bags tied with a twist of cotton. Three reds, tomato, blood and rhubarb. Two yellows, saffron and lemon, a leafy green, and two blues, sky and lapis.

"And lastly you'll be needing this." A tin of varnish was thrust into his hand "and these of course." A pair of brushes were slipped behind his ears. Mr Murali waved Loïc off as he gave the chai wallah an extra coin.

For the next thirteen days that's what he did, painted flowers and greenery from dawn to dusk with a long siesta in the shade of Lakshmi's tree. By the time he had finished, his chariot looked like a garden in bloom, ready for a carnival. While Loïc worked on the wagon a festive air developed. Stooks of sugar cane became available at impromptu corner stalls, leafy green and tall, it seemed that everyone was buying at least two, and they were flying off the corners aboard bicycles, scooters and bullock carts. There was also a brisk trade in rice flour, being bought mainly by the women.

He was soon told it was Pongal.

"Pongal what is Pongal?" He asked Mr Murali.

"Pongal my friend is many things spread over four days."

And it was. The first day, Bhogi, ran from dawn onwards. There was a flurry of activity in every household as more and more items of furniture, clothing and bedding in their most faded forms were heaped in the streets outside the houses. By midday a pall of blue smoke gripped the town, clinging to the buildings and awaiting a hint of a breeze to release the town from this year's burning debris. It was the day of spring-cleaning that contradicted the filthy scorched remains that littered the next day's streets.

That following day, Perum, brought the women out into the streets very early. Before any signs of traffic they stepped out in their new saris and with ground white rice and fine red clay dust sprinkled a multitude of patterns and symbols on their doorsteps and beyond. Many of these 'kolams' represented the sun and white bulls. Lord Suryas and his bull Nandi. Nandi had tricked Lord Suryas, telling the people to eat every day and wash once a week, instead of the other way round which was the message he was meant to relay. Hence the people loved Nandi so when it came to the third day of

Pongal it was Mata Pongal.

To Loïc's delight Mata Pongal was a day he too could be a part of, Mata Pongal was cow appreciation day, the sacred cow, the cousin of the people. The cow had another cousin on the other side of the family, the buffalo, that included the water buffalo. Firstly all the bovines were cleaned. With brushes rags and even sponges. With great diligence all their parts were scrubbed and rubbed with scented water, they were cosseted into an immaculate condition. Then they were taken to the temples where their hooves were clipped, trimmed and filed. Then their horns were painted with blue and yellow stripes, and bunches of tiny tinkling brass bells were fitted to their horn tips.

Lastly it was time for their tails to be teased out, and their eyelashes combed, for cows have the longest of lashes. This was surely the day of the cow's inner smile, for every bovine was made to feel appreciated. Some said it was the least you could do for a near relative. Some said it boosted their immune systems, others just saw it as yet another reason for a festival. But no, the cow was elevated at Mata Pongal.

Once they had finished in the temple Loïc took Lakshmi with the other cows to be garlanded and paraded down the streets behind the Bangra bands. Drums beating, horns bleating, crowds cheering as tiny bananas and jasmine flowers rained down. The cows loved all the attention and the crunchy sugar cane they were given for the next day's sweet milk if they were in calf.

The Bangra bands were always for hire whatever the occasion. They turned out in bright red and blue military style clothes with white spats and belts, feathered turbans, none of which quite fitted the wearers as if they were so hurried that they were wearing each other's uniforms, which was probably true. They played loud, very loud, loud screechy versions of marching music. Mostly they played battered and bent old military instruments. French horns, tubas and bugles and because they were so out of shape they were out of tune. They usually had a shennai in there somewhere, making a noise that would terrify a rat. The loud mixed with screechy, that was the bangra sound. They were loud and that was the thing that mattered. When the bangra band comes down the street all else stops. It was way into the evening before Loïc got back to the square and Lakshmi's parking spot. He was tired and felt good about being in the land of the Indians. They struck him as being still a little untamed and he liked the edge that they brought to everything.

Kanum Pongal came next and last. This was the day of the family, or so they said. Everyone left home and set off with bags, baskets and hampers filled with prepared food snacks and sticky sweet treats. Picnics were the order of the day. The town and his wife left their homes and for one day of the year they braved the midday heat armed with umbrellas and lightweight tentage while thieves ransacked their immaculately cleaned homes that were by now devoid of everything worth stealing. Loïc was both amused and amazed at this strange tradition that even allowed for the freedom of the dishonest.

First light the next day Loïc went out to check his cart. A light mist clung between the trees and the scent of oleander mingled with the lifting dust from a solitary sweepers broom. A cockerel struggled repeatedly to put the last note to its dawn phrase. An undercurrent scent of fresh faeces drifted across the square. Lakshmi's lower jaw ground cud into more green juice. The cart itself looked like the missing parts to a floral jigsaw puzzle.

Now that Pongal was over it was time to sew those new shoes on Lakshmi's trimmed hooves.

"Where I come from this is how we do it."

The cobbler looked sceptical.

"You pull and I push. OK?"

The cobbler's expression was fixed.

"You put your feet up here. Loïc indicated both sides of Lakshmi's rump. Pull very hard on her tail until I say hold, then I push here." He put his hands on Lakshmi's ribs." I push very hard and you pull very hard, and boom she is lying down and then we sew them on."

All along Lakshmi is sitting at their feet chewing the cud, with eyes half closed. The cobbler sat down on his old cloth, the one thing that kept him from the dirt that he had spent a lifetime trying to avoid. He had only got involved with 'shoes' in the first place so that he didn't have to go barefoot. Sitting on his cloth he gently fitted one of the new cow boots onto a hoof and laced it up. Loïc's eyes lifted to the heavens and the cobbler had all the boots in place in a matter of moments. Lakshmi still chewed as if nothing had happened. 'Yes', thought Loïc, 'let's do it your way.'

She was ready for the road. With the chariot in all its new finery hitched up behind, they were ready. Loïc grabbed his bag, his bow and the shell and paid his room bill. As he climbed onto the rig the guesthouse owner came running across the street, money in hand, his corpulent self heaving with each breath.

"No charge, Mr Loïc, no charge, everything settled, not a rupee out of place. Have a good journey and mind the trucks sir, very dangerous drivers." He bowed breathlessly and panted back across the empty street.

'How can they know, rather who are they to know?'

He let it go and took the road north heading for the banks of the Cauvery River that wound its way back to its source in the north. For days they followed the river bank, seeing few people but many watering animals. Loïc had hit on an ancient corridor of peace. Occasionally shepherds looked twice, unsure, but by now Loïc was swathed in white cotton and sported a full moustache. He had gone native in all but language. At night he took the cart back from the water's edge. From the safety of the flat bed he would lie in wait for elephant. Small groups of them came to wash and water in the moonlight. Tigers too would crouch at the bank, lapping, eyeing up gazelle and roebuck that also drank just out of reach. He saw mongoose arrive and leave with long loping strides carrying their bushy tails like banners.

When he did come into a village, it was always the same story. Constructions up on huge wooden wheels were either having bamboo towers built on top of them, or they were coming out of corrugated iron wraps. Some were elaborately carved with huge metal rings attached both front and back. Some were simpler, all were robust, ancient and with wheels twice the height of a cow. The next festival was in the making, he could feel it in the air, but what it was about he couldn't guess.

The river ran in large loops with the occasional waterfall to avoid. Mainly he stayed alongside the tranquillity of the wide shallows. Eventually he struck off across country, cutting through the tribal country, mixing with the Banjara people. The forgotten people as they now sometimes call themselves; not because they are, but in the hurly burly and hype that is India, they have become dispossessed of their land, their rights and their historical place inside this vast nation. They are so outside the caste system that they are referred to as 'unscheduled'. They are the countless hill tribes without any status at all living in the central forestland of the nation, the original peoples of this land.

Loïc found their villages quite timeless, with strong social structures in place. The old were respected and listened to; the young were encouraged and courageous. The men wore their hair long and their lungis short. Their women dressed in long multi coloured skirts and tight bodices covered with sewn- in mirror fragments and dripping with white silver jewellery and electric smiles. Loïc felt at home with them right away, they liked each other's styles and they appeared to be a long way outside the money culture that obsessed their lowland cousins.

Loïc found a well in the shade and pulled in to water Lakshmi. Sitting on a low wall was a young man reading a book. He didn't look up.

"Good story?" said Loïc.

The young man continued reading his paragraph.

"Very bad, very sad and very wrong." He replied.

"What's it about?" said Loïc.

"It's about economic occupation, you understand?"

"No not really, is that like being colonised?"

Yes, first we were colonised by the Brits, because we had things they wanted. Now they have gone away, thanks be to Gandhiji. Thanks, but no thanks because they haven't really gone anywhere.

They are still here, their thinking is still here and now they have decided that we have something else they want and again they will do anything to get it."

"You'll have to slow down I've no idea what you're talking about."

They looked at each other; they were about the same age. Loïc smiled and sat down.

"Tell me," he said, "tell me."

"Ok. In brief, this book is about the immoral British, who say one thing and do another. This time they are hiding their mining operations behind a nice Indian name, Vedanta, which means. 'complete knowledge of the Vedas,' in Sanskrit. They probably don't even know what the Vedas are, which shows their duplicity. Once again they are burning our villages and trying to clear us off our ancestral lands. This time they want to steal our mountain and kill our trees."

"Why do they want to do that?"

"So that they can make aluminium. Simply put that's why. Just when you think you can sleep easy in your bed they are tunnelling underneath it. That's economic occupation."

"Hang on, said Loïc. What are they mining for?"

"Bauxite, my friend, bauxite is under our hills and they want it desperately."

The Adivasi, as these people were called, were politically naive and stronger for it. They could see that big business was after the minerals in their territory and they knew that they could be easily sucked into radical politics but they also knew that their ancestors had been on this land forever. 400 years of occupation by the Brits had affected them badly.

"Now is the time to chase them out. They largely make weapons from the stuff anyway, and what good is that? They always did like killing people who didn't agree with them. It's about time they were stopped."

Loïc agreed, he'd seen what coltan was doing in the Congo; 'fuelling the struggle.' the captain of the Le Stanley had called it. 'Fuelling death', would be a better way of putting it. So this was the connection; bauxite for making weapons. Pinhead capacitors made from coltan to steer these lightweight weapons into wars.

"It's not just weapons and 'kill power' as they call it. By mining the mountain they destroy the water table and all the trees die. Without the trees we die. So first they try to kill us to get to the mountain, then when they leave there's nothing left of the mountain for us to live on."

"All this is in this book you're reading is it?"

"Yes, they have an obsession with death, but not in a sacred way. Not one good thing comes from stealing our land and chasing our people into the cities; so we stay and we fight and the newspapers report nothing because they are frightened of losing their jobs. We find we are fighting for ourselves and those people somewhere else that are about to die. This helps us, it tells us we are not alone. This tells us that the prayers for the dying people are also prayers for our dying mountain. This helps thinking people to see straight. We the Adivasi are here on mother earth to show the people the connection between mining and remote controlled killing."

Loïc had pulled up half an hour before to water his buffalo and now he was being overwhelmed by this torrent of passion. He looked up to the nearest peak. He had been thinking what a beautiful part of the country, so quiet, so peaceful, so untouched, and now all this.

"What's your name?" he said.

"Oopie, like rupee. What's yours?"

"Loïc, like oik."

"That's cool," they said together and laughed. They raised their hands and slapped each other's palms.

"High five." they exclaimed and laughed again. They were immediate friends.

"You want to see my house" Oopie said.

"Sure thing." Loïc got to his feet.

Oopie took the cloth from his lap and slung it round his shoulders.

"It's some distance, in the next village, Okay?"

"Sure, meet Lakshmi and my chariot; jump up."

"I don't do jump up," he said swinging his body between his hands. His withered legs stayed crossed and he hopped on his hands.

"Do you need some help?" said Loïc.

"You could give me a shoulder."

With one hand on the shaft and the other on Loïc's

shoulder he swung up with ease. He was, thought Loïc, immensely strong, well one half of him was. Side by side they took off down another dusty track through a grove of cashews and up an incline to the higher ground. A series of ridges folded in the landscape as a prelude to some low mountains, which Oopie pointed to with enthusiasm.

"That's home up there."

"How do you usually get around?"

"Oh, I'm usually down on the Tunga, I work as a ferryman, but they've sunk my coracle. I know who did it. They think because my legs don't work that I'm some kind of idiot and that I'm an easy target; I can't chase them. But in truth they are the stupid ones because I have many friends."

"Why do they want to get at you?"

"Because we talk to the foreigners about what's happening here, you know westerners. They've woken up to the evils of the world, they're more organised, not so frightened to say what they think. Didn't you know that Greenpeace has just celebrated its 46th birthday. It's come of age, Greenpeace advises governments now, it doesn't just flout international law. Where have you been? Asleep?"

"Okay, slow down, no, I haven't been asleep. I've been wide awake to other things, not all so far from bauxite mining as it happens. What can you do to stop a big company from mining, I mean they're motivated by money, what do they care about a few people living in thatched huts miles from the road? Nothing. That much I do know, so where have you got to? Realistically what can you do?"

"Alone you can do nothing, maybe get killed. Together you can attract attention, not the press, maybe some sympathisers, maybe one of them is well known, you know, wrote a book or made a movie that sort of well known. They give the campaign a little popularity. Then the press get interested. Then of course there's the other approach, 'sleeping with the enemy'."

"Sounds unpleasant, how does that work?"

"Well if you've got some money you buy a few shares in the mining company."

"What, you support them?"

"Hardly. A couple of shares is nothing, but it does mean that you are a shareholder and that gives you the right to go to the company meeting and find out their trading record. It means you can go to the AGM."

"What's the AGM when it's at home?"

"The AGM my friend is when the company puts the year's trade records in front of the people who have invested in the company. It's when you find out what they're doing with your money."

"So what's the point?"

"The point is that with your two shares you can get up during the meeting and say what you think about them tearing down mountains, displacing people and leaving an ecological mess wherever they go."

"What, in front of the other investors, they must be ready to lynch you."

"Exactly but they can't, you're one of the shareholders, so they have to be polite in front of all their big shareholders. You can shame them in public. They don't like that because you're probably better informed about their activities than they are."

"Does it help the cause or do they just put a tail on you and give you and your family a hard time?"

"Both, but they do know that they can't hide. Slowly more and more people buy shares, which they cannot refuse to sell, until they have all the protesters from the mountain at the AGM. What can they do? At some time they must listen. As soon as they do, it's the beginning of their end because they bought into needing more money than they had in the first place. That's why they sold shares to get other people's money to do their mining. They hate having shareholders and could now exist very happily without them. But they're stuck with them- it's in the company constitution, the interests of the shareholder are paramount. As soon as they listen- and they will- they will have shot themselves in the foot."

"How do you know all this?" said Loïc.

"I listen, I can't play cricket so I listen, and I listen good. There are some very smart people who ride in my coracle."

"So how many shares have you got?"

"I don't have shares, but many of my customers have, especially the English ones, it's a British company remember, Vedanta, sounds Indian doesn't it? but it's just them up to their usual tricks. So it's easy for the English ones to get to the AGM each year. We keep each other informed. You know some of those smart people from England know if their district councils are investing their money in Vedanta. What about that? They tax the ordinary people in England then invest it in mining for bauxite in our hills, to make weapons to kill off people somewhere else that don't agree with them. That way they fatten up their pension funds in England. Wandsworth Council, that's what one is called. Ever heard of them?"

"Never," said Loïc.

"The Church of England, heard of them? They have just pulled out £3.8 million."

"Wow, big bucks mining company."

"That's nothing the Norwegian government pulled out £13 million a couple of years ago. There's a big bad smell that goes with Vedanta."

"They laughed, relieving the situation a little."

"Seriously, Oopie began again. Some of these smart campaigners know which fizzy drink makers use the aluminium from our hills for their drinks cans. What they do is take cans of these drinks to the AGMs of Vedanta and pour them on the steps outside in front of the press cameras and explain why. They 'shame and blame', that's what they call it. The drinks companies get angry with Vedanta and take their business elsewhere. After making weapons from the aluminium the drinks companies use a lot for making cans."

"Seems you've got the measure of this mining company, Oopie."

"Not yet we haven't, there's big money in 'kill power', that's what they call weaponry these days. Weapons so light that they'll follow you down the street, turn in through your front door before you even know you're part of a war. Aluminium is that light that it makes it very valuable. You don't stop mining companies just like that. They have whole governments of many countries in their pockets. They have another company Balco that supplies aluminium for making the all India nuclear missile. The Agni warhead. Agni is the god of fire, it's all getting mixed together into a confusion, but that's just tactics."

"We're almost there, can you see the smoke over the trees?" Oopie gestured up ahead. "Don't take any notice of my mother, she won't stop feeding you. To her it's the most important thing in the world. She never had enough when she was a kid so everyone must be hungry to her."

They pulled into an almost treeless area. Two long single storey thatched buildings faced each other across a bare soil plaza with a well and trough at one end under a banyan tree. Both buildings were earth brick, bamboo and palm roofed. Ochre hand print decorations round doorways differed down the length. A collection of rock and poles was centrally placed in the plaza. A few people sat in the shade under the fringed eaves busy with domestic chores. All was quiet, even the fly-blown dogs continued to sleep. They watered Lakshmi and entered one of the doorways.

After the sunlight, the interior was an intense black, broken only by glowing chars in an earthen hearth. Nothing moved, the place smelt of cardamom and wood smoke. Oopie poked the fire and put a pot on to boil. Chinks of light appeared through the thatch. A charpoy stacked with bedding emerged. Insects patrolled the floor as his pupils expanded.

Oopie said nothing. He just put a milk chai in front of him and swung out of the door.

The silence became enormous. Beetles ate the roof. A piece of wood in the fire released a pod of gas in a blue flame and a high-pitched whine. An unseen dog whimpered in its hunting dream. Gradually the minutiae of life became apparent. The non-human world erupted in all its busyness. Time evaporated in the falling crepuscular light of the doorway as the chai boiled in the pan. The same doorway suddenly darkened as a hubbub of people crammed into the house.

"They have been to a meeting." Oopie explained.

"There is a man here, two men, one is a writer, a journalist, the other is Dr Padel, and he's an anthropologist.

They are working with the people, getting details about Vedanta, details about what they are doing in the mountains. Now the big boys are using dirty tricks. They are paying local people to spy for them. They think that after 400 years of divide and rule that we can't read the signs. Everyone is worried about a man in the village, he is a little simple but he knows the value of money, they are trying to tempt him, but he is so simple that he wants to tell everyone about his new found wealth. We must be careful, because if they kill him then the Naxalites or the Maoists will move in, saying that they are coming to protect us, that will make things worse. So far we have been okay in this village, we are still autonomous, we don't want this kind of problem. It will set us against each other. Then we are doomed, that's just what they want. It happened to our neighbours; the paramilitary boys came in looking for a showdown."

The house was now full of very animated people, hotly discussing the meeting.

"Dr Padel is a good man," they agreed. "And his friend, yes, but we don't know what he will write, it's all in Hindi."

"Oopie speaks Hindi, he will find out, won't you Oopie?"

"There's no need to worry-I will let you know everything in a few days, I want you all to meet Loïc. It's his fancy cart and buffalo out by the well. Please I must introduce you."

Loïc stood. He was a tall man in this company. Everyone shook his hand and touched their hearts and said Namaste.

"He is going to help us as well, yes Loïc?"

"Yes," said Loïc, taken off guard." I have no other reason for being here."

They exchanged big smiles followed by big laughter. Then the whole family laughed and then it was time to get the chapattis ready for the evening meal.

Over the next few days Loïc met the whole village. Ran errands with heavy loads using Lakshmi and his cart. Played games with the children. Listened to their music and loved every minute of it. Nothing was said about anything to do with bauxite mining. Oopie spent most of his time reading pamphlets, articles and books. A week later there was another meeting. Oopie explained what he had read. How there were new people, environmentalists interested in their situation and they were putting pressure on politicians by showing how they were making cynical and unpleasant investments to boost their pension portfolios. No one really understood what Oopie was explaining but they trusted that he knew what was good or bad. Oopie then talked about Dr Padel.

"He is the great, great grandson of a very famous man, known all over the world for his 'theory of evolution'."

This they liked, famous people were always impressive, like Bollywood stars, and if anyone liked masala movies it's the farmers and the country people.

"How famous is the great, great grandfather?" They asked," does he have a Mercedes?"

"No he has no need of a Mercedes now, he is with his maker seeing if his famous theory is right."

"Ah blessings on his soul," they said.

"And his great, great grandson, Dr Padel, what is his theory?"

"He doesn't have a theory, said Oopie, he is a musician and a man of conscience. A man like Gandhiji, who thought that the British quit India fifty years ago. No, Dr Padel knows that they didn't really leave, he knows they just changed their names and tricked the people. Dr Padel is British himself, he knows how they think, he believes that he and others can beat the mining company at their own game, or should I say that he thinks that making weapons from our mountains is an evil thing to do and so he is standing up and saying so in public. He is every day in great danger and his wife wishes he would stay at home and play his music. Dr Padel says that it's too late for that. The Vedanta goondas follow him everywhere he goes. Every day he says no to bauxite mining. It is up to us to pray for him and be with him in spirit every step along the way."

Everyone was very quiet and respectful.

"Dr Padel", said Oopie raising his fist in the air.

"Dr Padel", they all shouted together.

The mountain was shrouded in cloud as Oopie and Loïc hitched up Lakshmi and set off down the dirt track going north. At a leisurely pace they took the road north to find the

Tunga river and the scuppering place of Oopie's coracle, Hampi.

Oopie could arm wrestle Loïc onto the table with his thumb, his upper body was immensely strong and developed. They guessed that if he could stand they would be about the same height. They talked about running and Loïc described the exhilaration of crossing rough ground at speed. How, he never even thought about what his feet were doing, they just did it, adjusting to the terrain automatically. Oopie loved his descriptions of just breathing and moving.

Oopie persuaded Loïc to lend him his legs. He was able to open his feet wide enough to get them round Loïc's waist, and with his hands pressing down on Loïc's shoulders, they ran. They ran along a riverbed, jumped from rock to rock, climbed a slope at speed and leapt off dunes into soft sand. They were two with one pair of legs. Oopie was over the moon.

"You truly are my brother," he said as they disentangled themselves, laughing and exhausted. "When you go away, I will never forget today."

As they approached Hampi they passed through a vast area of ruins in various stages of collapse. Carved temple columns lay next to huge water rounded rocks. Isolated buildings crumbled in the searing light. Traces of pavement wove between mounds of architectural fragments. All was scattered, a civilization slipping beneath the surface of the present. At one point they came across a long oblong building; huge stables for elephants, arched doorways led into lofty domed stalls. At another waterside site were the remaining columns of a stone aqueduct, that took water across the river. Ambitious architectural remains were everywhere. In a huge compound stood a stone Ratha drawn by stone oxen. At one time, evidently, this had been the centre of a ruling culture that had been overcome. They pulled up in the shadow of a tiered and carved temple under repair. This was Hampi, a new town emerging from the ruins of Vijayanagar city. A few hotels and teashops had started doing business in the main bazaar. Some even occupied the remains of temples and collapsed buildings. Unlike most places, it was on the road to nowhere else. The ruined city spread out over 45 square miles around the temple and the plaza.

"Does Dr Padel have shares in Vedanta?" Loïc asked.

"Yes, he's the one who told me about sleeping with the enemy. He's brave, but, 'life is cheap as pomme frite' in India and I don't know if his great, great grandfather's reputation is enough to protect him."

Once they had settled into Oopie's tiny room off the Hampi Temple tank complex, they sat in silence listening to the bahjans being sung outside the temple.

"Tomorrow," Loïc announced," we will build you a new coracle. It is important that you have smart customers."

"Yes, yes." Oopie smiled," can you do this with me, can you work with bamboo?"

"That's how I got from Africa to India. We built a bamboo boat and sailed it here."

"Oh my goodness is that possible, you are joking me."

"No it's true. A coracle is no problem."

That night Oopie listened spellbound to Loïc's story about the Elephanta, the egg, the pirates and the shells. He left nothing out.

When he finished all Oopie could say was.

"Loïc, my friend, you are from another dimension."

17
Vijayanagara

There was an air of tension on the few streets of Hampi the next day. Outside the scaffolded tiered temple two enormous bamboo constructions were being built on top of a pair of Rathas. These highly carved, immensely heavy four wheeled juggernauts, which Loïc had noticed all along his travels were having their annual makeover, ready for the festival in two days time. A seven storey bamboo tower was being lashed together on the one with the wheels three times the height of a man. The other Ratha was only five stories of teetering bamboo tower. A frenzy of activity was taking place while everyday life continued in the eating houses and market that lined the main street. Inside, the temple was crowded with families bringing garlands of flowers to bless a huge black bull that stood tethered in the depths of the interior. It was tended by priests and passively enjoyed all the attention and tasty treats. Although it was very powerful, small children petted it and an atmosphere of peace mixed with the smoke of nag champa incense, the resin valued for triggering memories.

"Just look at it all for now." said Oopie, "later I will explain."

They joined the bhajan singers outside. These sacred songs were long repetitions with occasional variations in the instrumental parts changing the pace. Many people came and went, offering a bhajan or just joining in and clapping. Loïc noticed that even an on duty policeman, with his lathi, took off his hat, sat down and sang with the others for a while and then went back on his beat. Most of the musicians looked like people from Oopie's village and seemed to be without tiredness after singing all night. The music seemed to enter his body and he was soon singing and learning to play the finger cymbals. He felt included without question. Oopie smiled, Loïc nodded, both sang.

Later they checked out Lakshmi, who was tethered to her cart down by the river. She was eating melon rinds from the bathers at the ghat, tail flicking the flies, wearing the moony expression that attracts the esteem that cows are held in. They left her surrounded by fruits and went down to where the other ferrymen were plying their trade across the wide torrent, their saucer-like coracles skimming the water surface.

"You can paddle those things and get them to go where you want?' Loïc looked doubtful.

"Sure I've taken four people often, even took a motor bike once."

"So that's what you're after. Where's the bamboo?"

"Downstream a way, we can get there by road."

The next day they did. They hitched up Lakshmi, borrowed a couple of cuttees, the wide bladed curved chopping knives used by workers for everything and went to hunt the bamboo.

"Bamboo comes in many different shapes and sizes, hundreds in fact," said Oopie," but in these parts the most useful is very aggressive. We call it 'moongil' Its' a prickly character living in clumps, well defended. It sprouts its branches from low down on the culm and continues to sprout at each node way up the length. The branches are long and whip like, not designed to carry many leaves but instead are covered with hooked thorns and long spikes. The branches don't just grow out of the culms, they weave themselves back into the clump making an impenetrable barrier. However the prize is good. Its' a very thick walled, flexible version of the super grass.'

They looked at each other as they pulled up next to a clump that overhung the track.

"We need the man," said Oopie, "the man that owns the land. He will cut it then we can work it."

After a few questions the farmer arrived with his cuttee tied to the end of a long bamboo pole. They selected three curved and three straight culms. First the farmer had to cut off all the branches before cutting the base. Dressed only in a lungi and with bare feet he carefully extracted the six culms from the thorny clump. Again Loïc was impressed by how he worked with no damage to himself or the rest of the stand of bamboo. His economy of movement and effort were a delight to watch.

While he worked the boys cut the base off the first culm, long enough to split into four and hammer as pegs into the ground, a square meter and a half apart. Then they split the rest of the long culm into flexible strips, which they then twisted together into a circle around the pegs. Weaving the ends together they formed the top ring of the coracle. As the other culms were cut, they removed the almost solid base section and split the rest. Weaving it into a mesh to form a shallow basket. The ends of the mesh they forced in between the twists of the ring. Within two hours they had trimmed the protruding ends and made the thick butt ends into seats across the simple craft.

Oopie was delighted to find that Loïc's skill with the material matched his own and they rolled the coracle frame on its edge over to the waiting Lakshmi chewing the cud in the shafts. They loaded up, paid the farmer and headed back into town. By nightfall they had sewn plastic aid sacks all over the bottom and up over the circular edges and smeared the underside with a mixture of sand and bitumen. It stood on its edge glistening in the evening light awaiting its maiden voyage.

There was a fresh chill to the air at the riverside as they slipped Oopie's new coracle into the water next morning. Oopie equipped with his paddle, swung himself aboard. The river was wide and shallow and his skill at manoeuvring was consummate. His strength certainly helped, but he knew how water behaved, riding the eddies formed by the bank, managing to slip up stream on the far side. What he didn't have in his legs he had in his skill . He listed his coracle like a surfer uses a board. It wasn't just a form of transport it was a sport. When he had dropped Loïc on the bank he went back into the full force of the midflow. With an effortless few strokes he jumped up small waterfalls and skimmed up stream on shallow rapids. Waiting at points where water gushed down between large rocks, Oopie sat without paddling, tilting the bowl up on its leading edge, the torrent plunging down in front of his shallow craft.

Opie waited as a salmon waits, feeling the thrust and direction of the curling current deep within the water's energy. Then as he shifted onto thc back curl beneath him, Oopie, like the salmon, added his own full body power, to the water's force and flipped himself up the cascading torrent,, clearing the surface, sparkling in the spray, and paddling out of the flow as the coracle touched down on the deep green coolness of the upper reach of the river. Loïc stood on the bank, shouting and laughing as the remaining riverside mist swirled around his legs. Oopie was back in business. Loïc left him ferrying people from the small mud brick settlement across to the main town.

In the main temple plaza the towering bamboo frames on the Rathas were now being covered with coloured cloth. A sturdy platform had been constructed halfway up and hemp ropes as thick as an arm were being fixed to the metal rings, front and back of the carved chassis. People were everywhere. A long line of stalls had been erected down either side of the plaza leaving a wide passageway in front of the buildings.

A freak show had been erected. Poles and a windbreak obscured the unfortunates who formed the attraction. A long line of country people waited to see 'The girl with three legs and the human cow.'

Stacks of tiny yellow bananas were being broken off thick stalks into piles of singles, careful not to tear their skins. Large shallow aluminium dishes contained cones of coloured powders that made Mr Murali's supply look minimal. These were bold primaries and lacked the subtlety of his range. On the same stall ground minerals and ayurvedic remedies were displayed in compartmented trays. Everything was emerging from bright red tin trunks and being carefully arranged by the whole family. Across the street was a small white mound of the best night jasmine flowers being strung in hanks, their pungency competing with the hundreds of nag champa incense sticks that spread clouds of smoke from the temple door. The few restaurants and eating-houses were packed with people, locals and foreign tourists. Meals were flying out of the kitchen and trade was swift enough for indigestion. No sitting around after eating. It was: 'Here's the bill and there's the door!'

The throb of an engine cut through the bustle and a large man riding a motor bike eased his way down the plaza, turned at the temple and disappeared round a corner. For some reason, unclear to Loïc, this held some significance for him. He walked in the direction of the still audible bike, an Enfield being parked outside a shop hidden behind layers of clothes and handicrafts. The driver cut the engine and went inside.

Loïc walked in, uninterested in the items for sale. The back of the shop was dark and more like a living room. A family were about to start a meal.

"Come, come," said the man he'd seen riding past." Eat with us, this my wife and these are my children. Please take off your shoes and join us, we would be most honoured."

Loïc could hardly refuse. As they ate they exchanged pleasantries about the forthcoming festival, the weather and such like. When it came to transport Loïc idly asked about the motorbike.

"I have another shop in Goa, the man said. I use it for getting from a to b. All my goods go by train to Hospet, and I travel from a to b by bike. Out in the open air. Beautiful as the journey is this way, I don't like to do it anymore. There is little need, everything is organised these days. Only the goods from Hospet to here need taking care of. The season is almost over. The heat is coming in, soon the tourists will have left India or travelled north. There are so many places to go in India, but they only go to a few, thank goodness. Otherwise everyone would be infected by this tourism and we'd all die of inflated prices and poor English. Perhaps, I am a little forward, perhaps you are a tourist yourself."

"I'm not even sure what a tourist is," admitted Loïc.

"That my friend is music to my ears. A tourist is someone from somewhere else, who wants everything to be the same as where they came from, at half the price with twice the sunshine."

"They like a picture postcard world," Loïc offered.

"Yes, tourists love their photophones and their postcards,

they're pretty picture people. I am thinking that it is time for the 'scratch and sniff' postcard so that their friends can get the real India up their noses with their breakfast cereal. Tourists are part timers. Part of the year they blindly spread like a virus over the surface of the planet, spreading their television culture and mutating viral language. They have no idea what integration means. They're either loud and leary or lost in a layer of sun cream. They are a kind of photo trophy colonist who thinks that only they are right."

"Why is it that you run this shop selling to tourists then?"

"Because, my friend, I am a victim of their insatiable arrogance. They provide me with the good life. But as with any compromise there is a price to pay. For me the price is high. My wife says I'm gutless and should do what feels right for me and not be buttering up these people who have more money than sense."

"But you seem to like their money as much as they do."

"It's true I have sold my soul to the rupee and now I have fallen into the trap of wanting more."

"Surely," said Loïc, "money cheats people of their imagination. Without money everyone is of value and everyone has something to offer. Money just buys you stuff, most of which is badly made, tasteless and expensive. It leaves you with just one skill, making money. Without money people are much more open with each other and ready to exchange. I meet so many kind and friendly people and money never comes into it."

"Young man, your words are both wise and true but what do you have to exchange?"

"What I have, is simple but at the same time means sharing and helping a friend."

"Who would that be?" the rounded Goan asked.

"Oopie the ferryman."

"That cripple. Who could help him? His mother broke his hips at birth and he's been begging ever since."

"That's the story you choose to hear, I'm told different. Anyway whatever the truth, if you want to exchange my Lakshmi and cart for your tired motorbike then that's who you will be sharing with and occasionally employing. For that to be possible, I believe you will have to drop your judgements of Oopie and start seeing him for who he really is underneath this prejudice of yours."

The Goan looked round at his family. They were all nodding in agreement with their dinner guest.

"Let me think about that." He eventually said.

"I'd be pleased to, and now I must be on my way." He bowed to each member of the family. "My thanks for the meal, I trust I will see you all again soon."

He left a silence behind him and brushed through the hanging garments out into the bright light of the street. It was time to check on Lakshmi by the river. As usual she was surrounded by small children and a diet of soft fruit. Complacent and satisfied her lower jaw automatically moving from left to right. He sat down and scratched her behind the ear. Smoothing her neck and twisting with an anticlockwise movement the ticks that were gorged fat on her blood. He burst them between his thumb nails and flicked them away as he idly watched the bathers and the dhobi wallahs at the ghat.

It would be hard to let Lakshmi go; but if the deal were struck Oopie would make sure that she was cared for and he would be able to get around easily off the river. He refilled her water bucket and went back into town.

The atmosphere had changed again; there was agitation and perfume everywhere. Policemen with split bamboo lathis were holding back dense crowds. Tiny bananas and jasmine flowers filled the air and drummers with double skin stick drums played a frenzy of rhythms. The many directors of events shouted conflicting instructions to a deafening crowd. Beside the two towering juggernauts were men charged with thick wooden poles sharpened into wedges. These were for levering the wheels into position. People in the crowd were throwing clouds of coloured powder paint into the air. Holding the thigh thick ropes that were now stretched out front and back of the wheeled structures, were lines of bare chested young men jostling for a handhold. Everyone was shouting, sweating and excited.

Loïc realised that his trouser leg was being pulled.

"Come, come." said Oopie as he scuttled through the legs

of the crowd. They made their way down the side of the temple.

"But I want to see." Shouted Loïc as Oopie swung himself up onto the bamboo scaffolding that encased the temple.

"Then come, come," Oopie beckoned, "up is a better view."

To Loïc's amazement, Oopie swung himself up the horizontal bars without effort.

"Come, come." He shouted down.

Loïc began to climb.

The temple was thirteen stories high, repairs and painting were being done all over the outside. Halfway up Oopie swung along one of the bars to the temples front face, which overlooked the plaza. From here they could see all the way down its length and into the distance. Beneath, the towers were juddering as more hands grabbed the taut ropes. The first tower was being levered round to line up with the narrow plaza, which was thick with animated people. The signal to start had come from somewhere, nowhere apparent; danger hung in the air with the various coloured powders. The taut ropes held the quivering tower in tension as the huge iron rings strained to stay attached to the ornate hardwood chassis. Then the emphasis changed, the brakemen slackened and the wavering tower lurched forward slewing off the centre line.

From their bird's eye view it was obvious that the first and smaller tower was going to career into one of the many makeshift restaurants. It teetered and swayed as the occupant priests tried to keep a footing on their curtained platform. At the last moment with the levers wedged beneath the wheels, there was a slight change of direction and the swaying tower with hundreds of shouting people swept off down the compacted earth plaza.

Loïc's attention was drawn to a large rock at the far end of the plaza. There a group of men with flailing axes were hacking the black bull to pieces. It was hard to distinguish from such a distance but from his viewpoint high on the temple face, he was sure that the sacrifice was timed to happen with the moving of the towers.

Oopie nodded. "It didn't used to be like this." Then shook his head. "This is what the British and the Hindus have done to our festival. Now the towers carry statues of Shiva and Parvarti and they say it is their annual re-marriage that is being celebrated. Before when it was in the tribal people's hands, it was the celebration of our god, Jaggarnath, the Lord of the Universe. He takes the form of a huge black tree trunk with a big smiling face. His brother and sister always accompany him. Then it was that our warriors would sacrifice themselves under those huge wooden wheels. Not so many warriors, just enough for the many to know that their beliefs were real. In that way everyone took part in the turning of the year. It was an honour to die for our god. Then in the 1860s when the British were ruling India and trying to control everything, they said it wasn't right. They said it wasn't civilised and put a stop to the warriors' honourable deaths.

They said that a black bull was enough to sacrifice. They are a strange people. They go around selling arms to people so that they can kill each other. We know they have double standards. Really they are a bloodthirsty people who then moralise about their actions. In truth they are afraid of death, so they deal in it instead of embracing it. They have turned our god Jaggarnath into the huge truck 'juggernaut', which is the warhorse of pollution. Anyway they have gone, thanks to the fasting of Gandhiji and his allies. Now we have the Hindus in charge which is far worse. They have taken it as theirs."

The second tower lurched forward, almost toppled, and then careered off down the plaza pursued by an incensed, running, whooping crowd, detached from danger.

"The bull in the temple, is that the one?"

"Was the one, it's now in pieces, you can be sure of that. The other thing you can be sure of is that there's some human blood mixed in there. The hatchet men are all a little crazy when then the time comes."

The large now red rock lay near the resting place of the two towers. The focus had gone, the meaning already absent. From above, where they clung to the scaffold poles it was clear, people wandered in out of each other, looking to put their attention into something else. Blood had been spilt, fruit and flowers had been thrown and dyes had splattered bright random streaks of colour over buildings and moving people alike. There were no more heroes. A meaningless calm descended unworthy of the anticipation that had been building for weeks.

"It's just drama now, said Oopie, the spirit has gone from it. The connection has gone. The connection with Penu Tari, the giver and taker of everything has got lost in the fear of death. Now it's another event for the cameras. What was there before could not be described, it was unspeakable. Come," he said," it's more difficult going down but there's a way inside half way."

They edged their way around the side of the tiered temple. Briefly they perched over the narrow street. There were a few scary moments reaching from one vertical bamboo to the next until they crawled in through a vent between two full-breasted stone-dancing girls. Loïc cupped a passing breast in his hand and Padma sprang to mind. Most likely the carvings were from Anna Nagar. Inside led to a corridor and then a balcony looking down into the main chamber of the temple. Incense smoke rose to greet them. Pilgrims and priests went about their business. Where the black bull had stood garlands of flowers lay wilting. The only trace of his being was a neat pat of bullshit. It no longer steamed, the cold stone floor had seen to that.

They followed steps and corridors then more of the same and finally came out at the entrance arch. Closing the heavy wooden door behind them they attracted no attention.

"Chai?" they said together and laughed.

They perched on a bench opposite the Goan's shop and sipped the sweet thick drink.

"Look my friend, Loïc started. Will you help me make my next move?"

"Of course brother, tell me."

"You know the Goan across the way."

"Yes, he's a crook"

"Not you as well."

"Look he overcharges for everything. I know, my sister

makes his clothes, the Banjara ones with the mirrors."

"I'm sure you're right, but can you put that aside for a moment?"

"This I will do, but only for you."

"Okay I need his Enfield Bullet and he doesn't know yet but he wants someone to collect his stock from Hospet station and bring them here in the season."

"Yes, and..." said Oopie.

"And," said Loïc," if I give you Lakshmi and the painted wagon, will you do that for free when he needs it?"

"And," said Oopie.

"And nothing," said Loïc,"he gets his goods delivered, so he doesn't have to go to Goa and back every week, you get Lakshmi and I get the bike."

"And," said Oopie.

"That's it." said Loïc.

"Has he agreed to this plan of yours?"

"He doesn't know yet, but he will because he's lazy."

"But he's not stupid."

"No but he thinks I am. Meaning his bike needs a new piston and exhaust at least. I have an ear for it. He thinks the bike is dying and will cost lots of money to fix."

"Yes."

"Well it won't and he's tired of riding it. He can't get his wife and kids on it and I'm sure he thinks it's time to get a car and become a modern middle class Indian businessman."

"Well," said Oopie, "I will lovingly look after Lakshmi, and when you come back she will be waiting for you. Yes, to the free deliveries. Oh, and where do you plan to go on this Bullet with a new piston?"

"North," said Loïc, "I have a delivery of my own to make."

They sat and watched the sun go down and the Tilley lamps light up on the remaining festival stalls.

"Everything changes, everything is the same." said Oopie as he slipped off the bench and swung himself across the street towards his room by the temple tank. He turned his smiling face.

"Namaste."

"Namaste."

By mid morning they were sitting in the same places drinking fresh chai from probably the same glasses. The Goan arrived on his loud Enfield, glanced at them and didn't open his shop.

"Chai?," said Loïc "I don't touch that stuff." He grumbled.

"It's that or coffee." said Loïc.

"That I'll take," he said nodding at the chai wallah. He sat on the opposite bench.

"I have a proposition for you," said Loïc.

"That I know, and what does this man have to say?" He said gesturing towards Oopie.

"This man, has a name, it's Oopie. We don't know your name."

"I am the Goan around here."

"And other places?"

"Other places I am Basco."

"Good, at least that's straight."

"Okay what does Oopie have to say?"

"He agrees. Free delivery from Hospet station once a week."

Loïc studied this Basco who was slightly ruffled by Loïc's intense blue stare.

"Nothing is for free round here." He said.

"You don't have to pay him, but yes, nothing worth having is without its value. In this case it's your tired Enfield with a big bill coming that you give to me in exchange."

"That's a valuable machine my friend. Worth at least 16,000 rupees." He shifted uncomfortably on the seat as if his lie was trapped in his trousers.

"There's not a mechanic who would touch it for less than 15,000 and you know it", replied Loïc. "I can save you the headache, that must be worth the other 1,000 rupees."

"If that's the case, which it's not, why would you want it?"

"That's for me to know and maybe for you to accept that it doesn't matter. Think about it."

Loïc turned to Oopie.

"What was that you were going to tell me about the Enfield Company, cartridges and animal fat?"

"That story, cut in Basco, you don't want to believe any of that, it was just an excuse." He put his empty glass down on the table with a thwack and stood up.

"Just think about it." Loïc said. He left the table to angrily open his shop as his wife and children arrived on foot.

They smiled and greeted Loïc.

"Listen to your wife." Loïc called. She was Banjara, about Oopie's age. Small brightly dressed, smiley, the friend of his sister.

"We'll see," said Oopie. " But not now. Now I want to show you the Hampi that the tourists have been frightened off. The word 'dacoit' still seems to have a magical effect on some people."

"What's dacoit?"

"A bandit, usually with a gang, even the police are frightened to face them. Anyway they like the Hampi area because there are lots of ruined temples to hide out in. Usually they just steal your money but on a bad day they do worse. They are a slice of living history, they give the place a bit of an edge."

They took Lakshmi and the cart down the empty plaza heading out of town. The Towers were all but dismantled. Corrugated sheets awaited reaffixing over the carved chassis. The workers were lethargic and dismal. Beyond a balustraded compound housed the Vitthala temple that consisted of elaborately carved columns that rang at differing pitches when struck by hand. A single track wound between thorny mesquite and huge perched boulders with nothing to stop them rolling away. They dominated the sage green scarcity of vegetation. An atmosphere of stasis pervaded the place. Each ruin or monumental building they encountered spoke of a past glory and fading beauty. As they idled along Oopie asked Loïc what he knew about Enfield motorcycles that made him think that he was getting a good deal and an easy mend.

"Not much," was his initial confession, "but that's not new to me, the feeling around it is that the bike will bring me to some kind of understanding."

"They're not hard to fix, in fact that's what's going on all the time in India, everything is being fixed. Jugaad we call it, adapt and devise, we're good at keeping things on the road. The Enfield Bullet is at the end of a long line of business events that are really tied into our history with the British in India. Enfield is a district around north London where they've been making weapons since swords were in use. It was from this same armaments factory that the P 53 Enfield rifled musket was produced. Have you ever heard of the Indian Mutiny?"

Loïc looked blank. Where was this line of talk going now? How could Oopie know so much? Then he did do a lot of reading.

"Well it was this gun that had the new kind of cartridge that you asked about. The troops thought it had either pig or cow fat in it and they were expected 'to bite the bullet', pour the powder down the barrel and charge it. This was the final insult to the vegetarian sepoys and they rebelled. Blood everywhere, both sides did the unspeakable. It was the beginning of the end of an old love affair. Later the same English company made the Enfield motorbike, 'built like a gun, goes like a bullet' written on each one. That's just a part of the huge commercial empire the British had going here. Which, if you think about it, was a trading company that took over a whole nation. They gained so much profit that they could indulge their evenings on their bungalow verandas with a gin and tonic, with ice. The gin to loosen up that constricted formal behaviour of the British type. The tonic largely for the quinine that helped to keep the malaria at bay. The lemon from the tree in the garden, and the ice, yes the ice. Where in the hugeness of India do you get ice? The Himalayas would have been a good shot, but no, there was another plan. For quite some time the industrially wealthy English had been building icehouses down in the garden near their orangeries. So that meant they knew how to store it. It was decided in Madras, the East India Company HQ, that they would send a boat round Africa, across the Atlantic up the east coast of America to the Great Lakes and collect blocks of ice from where the water was good. Then with it packed in the ships hold, sail back for two months and pack it into the Ice Kings new icehouse here in the Triplicane district of Madras. So in the evenings, with clinking glasses and the mosquitoes flying by, libidos were aroused as the chunks of melting lake from the other side of the world confirmed the illusion that the Company could do anything."

"Okay", said Loïc, "I get the picture, everything is inter-connected, one thing leading to the next. I'm not just looking at a motorbike."

They fell into a silence as the bizarre boulder perched landscape stood depicted before a sky strewn with chasing rain clouds. No rain fell. The short periods of cloud shade were soon gone.

"What did happen to your legs?" Loïc eventually asked.

"Yes, my legs. When I was a boy I was strong and healthy and mother said I was clever and so they wanted me to go to school. That way I would be an educated person. She thought I would then have a better life than her. She was sold on the idea that I would become a civil servant. In India that's what educated people do they have a regular job, a wage and a mountain of paperwork to process. She was also told that poliomyelitis was spreading through the area and many children were getting sick and deformed. The government were rolling out a vaccination programme against the disease. You know what that is?"

"No, no idea," admitted Loïc.

"In a word it's a way of teaching the body to fight off a disease by giving it a taste. Next time it comes around for real the body knows what to do. For me it was an Oral Polio Vaccine, usually really effective, worked for thousands, well, ninety nine times out of a hundred. I was the one. Instead I got 'polio'. For many years my legs hardly grew. Most people get a withered leg or a limp, I am an extreme case."

"So," said Loïc, "to save you from a disease and to send you to school you lost your legs."

"That's right, life is a cruel master, I never did get to school."

"How come you are so knowledgeable?"

"Well I taught myself to read and I learnt English. What

does a sitting man do? Read. I read everything I could find. Then people started bringing me things that they couldn't read, now I have a place amongst the people. I'm civil but I'm no ones servant."

They laughed.

"What about you, what about your legs, do you want to run again?"

"Okay."

Loïc climbed off the chariot and Oopie fitted himself onto his back and they ran, two of them on one pair of legs. What a strange sight two grown boys, one panting the other laughing. Kicking up puffs of dust with a trotting water buffalo trying to keep up. Loïc stopped, exhausted, at the remains of a ruined building and fell onto the gritty ground. Oopie fell on top of him. They disentangled laughing.

"We'll have to call this Oopie's polo. You're the rider and I'm the horse," panted Loïc.

They lay there regaining their breath until a shadow fell across their closed eyes. She was small with a mass of tangled black hair. In her hand was a pistol and it was pointed at Loïc's head. There had been a time when he would have frozen but he'd had guns pointed in his direction before. He sat up.

"Careful," warned Oopie," this one is known, she's unpredictable."

She swung the gun onto Oopie and told him 'chup', be quiet.

Loïc stayed sitting and patted the ground next to him, as in an invitation to sit. Carefully he removed all the small stones from the area and placed them round the edge. The bowerbird was talking through him. She watched, distracted from her intention.

As Loïc fussed and re-arranged the scraps of foliage, sticks and stones, he hummed in a preoccupied way. Satisfied, he looked at her and patted the earth again.

She was charmed and disarmed. She sat. They all sat in a row as Lakshmi ambled into view pulling the absurdly floral chariot and stopped next to them and started chewing the scant vegetation. It took a while for one reality to slip into another. They all sat listening to their heartbeats slow down and birdsong fill their ears.

"Chai?" Said Loïc.

She looked at him from way back in her memory. Her father had said the same word always as a request instead of the usual male demand. Loïc's tone was far too familiar for her to refuse.

She stood and disappeared into the remains of the building.

"How do you do that?" said Oopie with emphasis.

"I was once told everyone needs love, and I believe it to be true, you, me, her. So why not love instead of fear."

"But she had a gun at you head."

"Yes, yours actually, but it was up to me what she did with it. She had it in her hand but not in her heart. Didn't you see the sadness in her eyes? I felt for her that's all."

Oopie adjusted his legs and sat up. He was in no position to run away.

"You told me there were dacoits out here, that's why we came wasn't it? I just didn't think they would be female for some reason. Better be on our best behaviour. Eh ?"

When she returned it was with three chais on a battered tray. The tiny glasses were chipped and dirty but the chai was with cardamom. As they took their drinks off the tray, which had obviously been used for target practise, the figures of Queen Elizabeth 11 and her Greek consort, the newly arranged Duke, stood side by side above the date 1952. Somehow this souvenir of a pro-British Indian administrator had fallen, probably accidentally stolen, into the hands of a wayward group of rebels. The duke had received severe ballistic injuries to both his right shoulder and foot. The queen however had had her reign cut short by two direct hits to the head, which from any medical point of view would be fatal.

From her breast pocket 'the dacoit' pulled out a packet of bidees and a box of matches and still in a daze offered them round. This was not a time to break the magic with a refusal, far from it. The boys with attempts to suppress coughing, both tried to smoke with the same distracted expression as their host. Wreathed in the blue smoke, she seemed to have entered an inner world that bore no reference to her present persona of violence threat and fear. She was deep in recall of another time. Some pastel reminiscence infused with morning light. A light playfulness erased her scruffy desperation and they all three were enveloped by an untroubled pleasantness. Once this had passed Oopie asked her if there was something she needed from town. She told him her gang; as if they were children, would be back soon, and they would bring everything. Seizing the moment they thanked her for the chai, climbed onto the chariot and waved goodbye.

Her hand rose as if by some other means, and as she watched, it waved them off. They sat silently watching Lakshmi's rump. The bones moving beneath the taut grey membrane of skin, until they were out of earshot. A glance between them and they collapsed in uncontrollable laughter.

"What was all that about?" spluttered Loïc, gasping for breath.

"You ask me, it was you that did it."

"Come on, I did what I did, but there must be magic in moving stones."

They rode on, making a huge loop through the remains of the vast city. Every mound of earth hid another architectural gem. Doorways and pillars of stone littered their route. Eventually they arrived back at the Vitthala temple where they knocked the slim granite pillars with their knuckles and played tuneless tunes while their laughter echoed amongst the exquisite carvings.

"That," Oopie said, pointing to a tall slim free- standing portal, "is called the Kings Balance. It is said the king would come here to be weighed on suspended scales, either against grain, gems or gold. Whatever he weighed, the same amount was given in gold to the needy."

"How often was he weighed? I bet it wasn't every day!"

"Just at Dashehera festival time. It's also said that the cooks in the kings kitchen would make his favourite foods to fatten him up and wherever he was carried there was always fatty food within reach. Everyone enjoyed the joke and the poor got some perks."

They saw no other people. The cloudy sky sheltered them from the seasonal heat. They spoke little and were themselves mesmerised by their brief encounter with the dacoit.

As soon as they were sitting in the chai shop opposite the Goan's shop, he pounced.

"Yes," he said. "Your proposition I will agree to on one condition."

"Why the condition, when this arrangement is unconditional."

"Unconditional, this is a business arrangement my friend."

"Not only but also, we make this arrangement as you call it, because it suits all of us, and is a solution to some aspects of our lives. Is that not so? However you have a condition, that may change everything."

"Simply this, if it is possible and when you have finished with the Bullet, you put it on a train back to Hospet and Oopie. He nodded in new recognition of Oopie. Oopie can collect it and bring it to my shop."

"This I like, if at all possible, I will do just that. Bearing in mind that motorbikes go where trains don't."

They all shook hands.

"The keys." Basco said, slapping down the documents. He waved his hand in the direction of the Enfield. "Good luck."

Next day, everything in the small dead end town was back to normal. Most of the country people had taken their carts and families and spread out through the landscape to their crops and villages. A calm descended, punctuated by the noisy temple workers hauling things up and down the temple facade. With the help of passersby the motorbike was lifted onto Lakshmi's chariot and the boys left for Hospet, to see a 'mistry', as Oopie called him, a mechanic. Hospet, though old and established, seemed to have little to recommend it. The streets were busy but the preoccupation of the people was expressed as the usual desperate scramble to make ends meet. The relaxed exception was the 'mistry', an ageing grease monkey with an assortment of ancient spanners and a smile that reduced his face to a sprocket of teeth and a pair of polished eyes.

He knew the bike and had it off the chariot and was checking it over immediately. After a brief word, his boy's were stripping it down rapidly. Bolts and nuts were dropped in to a halved petrol can, as were parts for cleaning. Within no time the engine was clear of its frame and exhaust and mounted on a large block of wood. It was split open, cleared of gaskets and cleaned. Loïc's attention was complete. He said nothing, but nothing passed him by. He needed to know the workings of the machine if he was to ride it. By midday it was being re-assembled with a new piston and rings, new cables, fuel pipe, new carburettor float, cleaned jets and a new air filter. The exhaust flange was replaced and a new chromium exhaust and silencer fitted. The battery was now new and all the wiring and bulbs had been checked. His intuitive diagnosis had been right.

The old 'mistry' then stepped in to check the boy's work. He kicked it over a couple of times and adjusted the knurled tighteners on the clutch cable. The oil chamber was filled and fresh fuel was put in the tank. Then with his thumb on the compression lever the 'mistry' primed the optimum thrust for the kick-start and kicked. It fired but didn't run. He leant over and adjusted the air intake on the carburettor and kicked it over again. It fired and ran this time. He adjusted the fuel intake a touch and it stood on its stand ticking over with a familiar throaty pulse. The blue smoke settling into a clear sound recognised all over the Subcontinent as the arrival of a Bullet.

"Now," said the 'mistry', switching the engine off, "you can go anywhere in this country of ours and beyond. Slowly and surely you will arrive. All you need to do is change the sprocket on the back wheel from 22 to 17 if you want to go over the mountains, and remember the art of riding this heavy machine is balance at low speeds."

"Thank you, thank you." said Loïc pressing two large coins into the mistry's hand.

"There's no charge, all is taken care of I'm told."

"This is not payment," said Loïc, "this is an entertainment fee. Oopie will tell you the story of these coins one night."

The 'mistry' opened his hand and a smile spread across his face as he examined the strange and rare coins from a pirate horde, another place and another time.

"Namaste," they said to each other.

Back in Hampi that evening Oopie cooked.

"You have a delivery to make?"

"I'm not sure to who, but I'm sure it will become clear once I'm nearer my destination."

"What is it you have to deliver or is that a secret?" Oopie's voice hungry for danger.

"It's only a secret because people will think I'm a little crazy, but from you it is not, because you know that I am." He laughed. They both laughed." It's a shell I found, which apparently has great importance in the right hands. A conch shell from the ocean. Remember, I told you, I was diving for algae in the Maldives."

Loïc opened his bag, took out the remaining sankhar shell and laid it on the bed. It glistened in the candlelight.

"Where will you take it? When you say north, how far?"

"To the Buddhists, is all I know."

"Since they were chased out of Tibet they've spread all the way across the north. How will you know?"

"I don't know, I will be shown, this much I have learnt from my travels. Always keep the faith, that's what you do. Nothing's just for your benefit-it's for the benefit of the whole. Along the way I've always met the right people, like you." They smiled, a deep bond of love in their eyes. "Each person leads me to the next in some way. Often unexpected, always a pleasure. I have no reason for this to stop. Everyone has a gift of goodness in them, sometimes life has made them forget, but they know the taste when it's put in their mouths."

"I love you," said Oopie as he put the meal out on a couple of chipped enamel plates.

"And me you," said Loïc, taking a mouthful with his right hand. "We're blessed."

18
350 cc

A stray peacock screeched, another dawn broke, bringing tree-filtered light and a host of other bird song to where Loïc was strapping his few possessions onto the luggage rack of the bike. 350cc it proudly displayed on the fuel tank. Although the paint was scratched and faded by the sun it was still a hansom iron horse.

"Use this for the sankhar shell," said Oopie, thrusting his bed cover into Loïc's hand.

"But how will you sleep?"

"I will sleep easy." Said Oopie, "wrap it well, because for sure between here and there you will fall off at least once."

"But you have no other covers Oopie."

"I have my reasons, this way in some small measure I will come with you, north it's much colder. Dual purpose. Packaging and bedding. Two in one, please take."

"Of course, thank you my friend."

A few more knots, a thumb on the de-compression lever, hands clasped, a breath, the engine kicked over, and he was gone. Leaving no regrets behind.

It didn't take long to 'figure out' the bike, the gears, the clutch, the two brakes, the smooth throttle. Loïc found to his delight the easy throaty power of this small engine produced a deep powerful tone. He kept to low speeds until he could change down fast, and slow down without using the brakes. Then on a straight tree-lined avenue going north he opened up the throttle and cruised at 60 mph, the fastest thing on the road, for the next 500 miles.

Days further north it started to rain. Initially it was a cloudburst, the road's uneven surface saved him from skidding as he braked before a bend. He slowed as the hot road became greasy. Water poured off his face, running into his eyes, making it hard to see. At the first village he pulled over and parked outside a small dubha selling rice and vegetables. A couple of men sheltered in the doorway, another scampered past under an umbrella trying to avoid the puddles.

Loïc sat and dripped onto the floor. The owner appeared. Loïc ordered a meal and watched sheets of water run off the roofs across the street. He ate the food and the cook mopped the floor under his seat. Two hours later the rain had calmed but it had settled in. Now the rain was continuous and steady, the sun was obscured and a luminous green light filled the air.

Finding a room on the first floor a few doors down Loïc decided to pass on riding for the rest of the day. He settled in with his few things and the spare can of petrol from the bike rack. The lodging house owner was a little disturbed by having a foreigner on the premises and kept knocking on the door with various items that he felt he should provide. A cracked plastic jug that slowly oozed water onto the bedside table. A glass followed, an extra blanket, any excuse to take another look at Loïc.

The view from the window was of a wall and a tin roof. The toilet was a foetid hole in the floor with a cold tap, but he was out of the rain. It rained way into the evening and when Loïc went to sleep it was still raining. He woke a couple of times in the night. Something was moving round the floor, but as the light switch was by the door he chose to sleep. In the morning he woke early, the same green light glowed at the window; it was still raining, steady and heavy.

He sat on the bed and listened to the clamour on corrugated iron. By mid-morning there was no change. He went down to check the motorbike. As he stepped of the last tread of the stair he stepped into water. The whole of the ground floor was awash. He splashed out into the street, the road was awash. The Bullet still on its stand had sagged to one side as the ground had softened. He pushed it down the street ankle deep in brown water and rested it against a tamarisk tree. He disconnected the battery and took it with him and went to find something to eat at the dubha. It was rice and vegetables, the same as before but less of it.

It continued to rain all day.

That night the two blankets and the straw pallet were

damp and in the darkness something moved round the room, from the door, around the wall and under the bed. When dawn came he woke to an increase in the rain. Looking out of his window was a frustration, he could see nothing but the roof below. He found a small window near the stinking hole. It was shuttered; with some persuasion the catch broke and revealed items of furniture and farming tools floating past. The bike was still next to the tamarisk, now the water was almost over the wheels. On the flat roof of the lodging house he found a plastic covered washing line, it wasn't strong. He doubled it and tied the bike to the tree. By now he was wading in water up to his thighs. The little restaurant had closed its doors, mainly to prevent the seating from floating off but also there was nothing to cook.

Loïc found the landlord continuing to fill the jug of his trapped customer,but now the water was cloudy and tasted of clay. The rain continued to fall with brief intervals, when birds tentatively let loose the odd trill. Then it started again and they stopped. Loïc took to his damp room and sat on the bed. There was nothing else to do but breathe. The rain continued heavy and loud. Occasionally he went to the window to look at the street. After the fourth day the rear view mirror was all that located the bike.

With minor lulls the rain persisted.

His bag was on the bed and he untied the neck of the gunnysack and arranged his worldly possessions around him. The bow and arrows from the Babongo, the remaining sankhar shell wrapped in ijuk and Oopie's bed cover. There was the tree paste, N'zingu had made from the monkey-puzzle tree, as he had come to know it. He now knew it to be an ancient form of pine. He had even used it on Lakshmi. The flies flew after an application of that. He still carried a twist of cloth with ground iboga root in it, but that now seemed far behind, in another land. Apart from a notebook, some matches and a few pirate doubloons there was nothing else save a worn and faded map of India.

Leaving the shell on the bed he replaced everything in the sack. The shell posed a problem. He felt a responsibility was attached to it, a responsibility of safe delivery. To where, he was still unclear, it was his reason for going north. He sat back and listened to the rain.

He sat up and started to breathe.

Loïc persisted with the breathing. At first he realised that he didn't really use his lungs, he just replaced the air in his upper chest without any thought. Once he had started breathing deeply his mind started to still, his situation ceased to bother him, it was just another situation-one with few options and no distractions. The rain continued from a grey sky and he continued to breathe. At first the breath was deep and slow, rising, falling. As he felt the air entering and leaving his body the sensation was round his mouth, the rest of him was quiet. He noticed the thrumming on the roof outside but it became distant and soon filtered out of hearing. The rain paused but soon resumed with a speckle of drops that built into a roar.

Loïc noticed by the end of the fifth day that his attention had reduced to his philtrum. The indentation below the nose, the final feature in the formation of the human face. The dent said to be left on the face of each human, made by the flick of the Angel Lailahs' finger just before birth. A fillip to make the soul forget everything that it knows. The same place we press hard when the epileptic fits and leaves the body, so they can return. Loïc's attention lay in the sensations in this place and nowhere else.

The rain became intermittent but heavy. He paid a visit to the stinking hole. Since he hadn't eaten for four days there was nothing for him to pass. The small window onto the street revealed brown water, a few partly submerged shrubs and no bike. He returned to his damp room, a bloom of mould had developed on the walls. It fell away in a white cascade as he ran his finger across the surface. The rain continued to fall and he returned to his breathing.

Around midnight his nocturnal visitor returned. Loïc had left the light on, but this did not dissuade the rat, for that's what Loïc reluctantly accepted that it was. He had seen many. On board ship he had lived at close quarters with them. He disliked them intensely. He was slow to accept its species because of its size. It was the shape of an overfed terrier. It moved with a confident waddle and patrolled the edge of the room, checking for anything that resembled food. There was nothing, dust and damp do not combine into edible. As it went under his bed, a shudder ran through him, the thought of eating the beast or being eaten by it crossed his mind. Satisfied that there was nothing to scavenge, it left through a hole in the wall by the doorframe. This time his breath was of relief, swiftly followed by one of apprehension. It would return the next night for sure.

The rain was unrelenting, but it did form continuity, a sameness to match his breathing. It was towards the end of dim daylight that his attention shifted from his upper lip to the top of his head. For a moment he lost his balance and nearly fell from the bed. Regaining his breath and composure his attention moved inside his body and filtered down from his head to his neck and shoulders.

Everywhere he found a discomfort or a sensation he sat and breathed and watched it dissolve. Slowly, with deep regular breaths, he scanned down his whole body.

Outside, the squealing sound of corrugated metal and nails being torn out of timber invaded the room The lean-to that had been his sound box, had now been washed away from the side of the building and out into the main flow, accompanied by a barrage of foliage that had collected at the uprights, leaving a silence. He heard it go but stayed sitting and breathing.

By now the force of the water was immense, the whole landscape was under water and surged towards the deeper channel of the small river that ran parallel to the road. Trees were being washed out at their roots and fell across the road causing huge waves to build up behind them until they were shifted into new positions. Smaller trees were drifting past, visible from their roots at one end and their leaves at the other.

Still it rained.

On the seventh day the water level had reached half way up the stairs, the owner was nowhere to be seen and the jugs of cloudy water had long since ceased to arrive.

His breathing now matched the rain, long and

continuous. He found that he had again encountered the grandfather plant. He searched his body for blocks and discomforts but now, just with breath. There was none of the bitterness in his mouth. He forgave his father for being who he was. He searched his body again for blocks and discomfort but now they just dissolved like mist before the sun. A feeling of fluidity coursed through him. A new lightness cleared his mind and his heart.

He loved being himself.

'What a journey.' He heard his voice say.

The rain persisted.

'Yeah what a journey,' his inner voice replied.

That night the lights failed. He was amazed that they had lasted so lon,g since most of the cable poles that he had noticed were eaten thin by termites. He found the stub of a candle and set it in the centre of the floor and despite the dampness of his bed he stayed sitting on it. At the appointed hour the rat patrolled his room. It walked the walls and then sat near the candle and started to wash. Although very large, Loïc noticed that its tail and legs were of normal size. This was a rat with a condition. He was surprised when a wave of compassion for the creature arose in his chest. The rat was obese and couldn't bend its body enough to clean itself. It's dignity as a rat was compromised by its encrusted back end. He found he forgave himself for his revulsion of the species and found the strength to empathise with this creatures suffering. A surge of energy and clarity entered him.

The rat looked at him, not glanced, looked at him and they sat like this for some time, eye to eye, the rat sitting on its haunches by the candle, Loïc sitting cross-legged on the bed. Who broke the gaze first was not clear. Regardless, the rat dropped onto all fours and made for the hole by the door. It turned and checked on the human and then it was gone.

Still it rained.

When Loïc woke the next day the rain was light. He made his way to the stinking hole window. As he looked out onto a sea of water thick with earth, he realised he was standing not far above water level. The stairwell was now a well. He guessed that his bed gave him another day before it too would be submerged. There was only the flat rainswept roof as an option. As he returned to his room something changed. The air was less humid and the noise of falling rain had stopped. The light was different. He was hesitant to believe it but the deluge was over.

By midday people started to emerge on the rooftops, shouting and signalling to each other. Loïc joined in with the camaraderie.

Three days later the waters had receded into the river, which flowed like hot chocolate. The street was littered with debris and valuables. The Enfield stood caked with mud still tied to the tamarisk tree. The rat didn't return to his room. Fortunately, and unusually for India, no one had died. Fortunately, the cook in the small dubha said, because to find dry wood for a funeral pyre would be out of the question.

Loïc stood looking at the Enfield and examined his memory. Had he in some way been untruthful about acquiring this machine from Basco the Goan? He felt not, and he also felt with a few bowls of water it would look all right on the outside at least. He needed clean water to be effective; there was none, just the brown soup that flowed from everywhere to here. There was no clean water and thirst was becoming an issue. Some had had the presence of mind to put catchment pots and pans on the roofs, but he wasn't one of them. Amongst all this brown water people were beginning to dehydrate. Once the sun had gathered some height and heat, a mist started rising from every exposed surface until clouds of vapour hung in the air before being burnt off.

While it hung above the sodden ground partial rainbows appeared, Vertical bands of prismatic colours, chimerical and wraith like. If you blinked they evaporated instantly. It was like a visitation from another dimension, ephemeral and indefinite.

Loïc climbed the muddied stairs to the lodging house rooftop. The flood mark was just below the first floor on most buildings, none were more than two, and of all the bamboo and palm leaf structures, nothing was left save the clogged earth stoves. Possessions lay embedded in the mud, gathered at fixed objects. The bases of trees and telegraph poles alike seemed to magnetise small objects. Amongst the prisms and the debris stooped people with mud up to their knees poked around for their dispossessed valuables.

After the flooding a new set of problems arose. Initially the mud was slurry, but as the sun shone and evaporation rose like steam, so the mud became more viscous. A tractor with a large bucket on the front ploughed down the road in some attempt to clear a path. What it did was to push waves of sticky brown slurry out to either side in a wave, which immediately slid back into the trough it had formed. Two hours later it was back, but by now the mud was thicker and had built up on the wheels so that they would barely turn inside the clogged rear wheel guards. The driver was barely distinguishable and lamely wiped at his smeared goggles in an attempt to see the road.

Loïc watched these events from the roof. As he did so he felt an urgency to help, and as that came to him, his attention was drawn to the far end of the small village. On the outskirts was where the casteless people lived. The ones that Gandhiji had said were no longer 'untouchables' but soon became 'dalits', the same prejudice by another name. The ones that Gandhiji failed, so ingrained are social attitudes. He climbed down the silt slippery stairs into the cloying, knee-deep morass that was ground level. Outside it was even more difficult to move as the sun thickened the mud to a thick paste. Slowly he took a direct line across the road to a large tree that had a short while ago shaded the bamboo and coconut homes of the poor. The buildings had gone and the people had taken to the branches of the banyan tree. From them hung nets full of their domestic life, which although wet, was clean. The families had arranged hammocks under scraps of plastic and were making tea on an old primus stove, balanced on a makeshift platform. These were people who were used to being moved on, being blamed for any ills that befell their neighbours. The scapegoats of a vast and complex society.

As Loïc approached the trunk they called down to him to join them. He scraped some of the mud off his legs and climbed up and sat with them in the branches. At first the conversation was naturally about the mud, the rain and the missing homes. As he sipped his chai his gaze fell on the hanging nets; such a good solution he thought. One was full of tools, a cuttee, two spades, a saw, various hammers and chisels and surprisingly a plasterer's hawk and float. Then it came to him. 'These people I could help.'

"Where does the bamboo grow?"

They pointed out across a brown sea that had been paddy fields to a large stand of the big grass, waving gently in the drying breeze. Loïc asked for a cuttee and they hauled up a net and passed him one.

Although the paddies were full of mud the raised pathways between were still visible. Slippery but walkable. The stand of bamboo was slightly above the worst of the slurry. He chose eight tall mature culms, thick as a good bicep at the base. These he cut, removed the branches and began to shoulder them back to the people's tree. After the first was standing against the trunk, the menfolk joined him.

Without words what he wanted to explain was difficult, but with help of eight branch twigs he showed them the reciprocal frame which was now becoming known to him as the mandala. They were intrigued and when he suggested they build one with the bamboos on the spot of their old houses, they discussed the idea in hushed tones and then agreed.

The tool net was lowered and everyone started to clear a circle of ground near the tree. They cut the first eight feet of the bamboos off the length. Dug a circle of eight holes, erected the lengths and tamped them into the ground. By notching the tops of the uprights they made joints for the roof poles. Loïc took one of the roof poles and stood next to an upright, indicating for others to do the same. One by one they laid them into the centre, forming a circle at the ends. Loïc lowered his in last, threading it under the first, locking them all into place. They fixed where they met with sliced rings of an old inner tube looped together into stretchy ties. Once all the fixings were made, together they lifted the frame onto the uprights. By pegging the tops, more rubber lashings were used to join the roof to the uprights. The excess was cut off with saws and within hours there stood the basic framework of a new building. Hands were shook and Loïc left to cross the village to his room.

He noticed as he went how quickly the mud was hardening, it now had a crust that collapsed when trodden on, and the consistency of the mud below was no longer runny. 'Good material.' He said to himself.

His motorbike stood like a milk chocolate version of itself. When he opened the knurled knob on the toolbox the cover dropped down to reveal the tools encased in thickening silt. He loosened the exhaust bracket by the footrest and detached the whole length of it from the engine block. An air lock had prevented the mud from reaching the new piston. There was hope for the Bullet yet. He cleared the mud from the silencer and soaked it in muddy water and left flushing it out until the next day.

There had been a time when his father had ridden a Solex, it had interested him, a bicycle you didn't have to pedal uphill. That had appealed to him but a mechanic he was not.

He unscrewed the headlight cover and carefully peeled the mud off the reflector, cleaned the bulbs and replaced them. By now the silty water had been pumped out of the village well and although murky it was mostly water. From top to bottom he cleaned the whole bike with a piece of foam mattress attached to a stick and went to his damp bed.

The rat didn't visit the room again. For a rat so fat the pickings were too slim.

The next day his imposed fast was broken with a bowl of soup. The little dubha up the street was up and running. Somehow the owner had salvaged some vegetables from his store shelves and half the village was eagerly lined up with bowls in their hands. It was hot and not too spicy, which suited Loïc. He felt clear and clean.

Back at the Bullet he rodded out the exhaust tube and drained the muddy water from the silencer, then fitted the parts back on the bike. He found the fuel tank needed cleaning so he drained it down and refilled with the spare tank of petrol from the room. Everything else to his inexperienced eye looked good. With the battery re-connected he switched on and kicked it over. Nothing. What was it the 'mistry' in Hospet had done to the bike last? Yes, set the points. He took off the cover, the mud had made its way inside. He cleaned it, and tried again, this time it was good, that familiar thumping exhaust sound was music to his ears.

By sunrise Loïc was out of the door and on his way to put another idea in front of the people up the tree. As he crossed the village he checked the quality of the mud. It was firm right through but still plastic. They had seen him picking his way poking the ground. Standing watching his feet as they sank, mud oozing between his toes. They knew he was up to something, but what?

When he got to the tree a chai was thrust into his hand but he asked for a spade instead; not something that they had, a shovel yes. So he used the shovel to show them his thinking.

Cut the mud into blocks, dry them in the sun and build up the walls between the bamboo supports. They could use the slurry from the deeper puddles where it was still wet, to stick the blocks together. They were on to it straight away, and it happened that the curve of the shovel lent itself to cutting curved blocks for the circular building. The women took the initiative and left with the children to cut palm leaves and plait roofing thatch. The mud blocks they cut were set up along the hot roadside to dry in the sun. When pairs of legs, large and small came down the road with huge piles of palm fronds high on their heads, a buzz of excitement ran through the people and smiles were breaking out on the most sceptical faces.

It took four long days to build. Leaving window holes with bamboo lintels, they tied the woven palm sections onto the roof frame in double layers to keep both sun and rain at bay. On the fifth afternoon the women started to lower their possessions from the tree. The pots were cleaned and a meal prepared. By the time darkness fell they had floored the space with palm fronds and a circle of carpets, back a little from the central fire, laid out the beds and set lamps hanging from the central roof hole. An old black five hole shruti box appeared from one of the nets and as smoke curled up through the roof hole, with smiling faces and voices raised in song they showed their joy and thanks.

When Loïc kicked over the Bullet next morning it fired right away. He had found the knack with the compression valve, which made for a good feeling about motorcycling. Tying his bag onto his rear rack he suddenly found himself surrounded by the tree people wanting to say good-bye and give him food for the journey. They marked the village on his map, telling him to come back. Their gratitude was easy to accept, it was a weightless pleasure. As he pulled onto the mud caked road they jumped up and down shouting his name. He punched the air and rode north.

The flooding had been local. After forty kilometres and a slight rise there was no sign of the brown stickiness that had dominated his recent life. The road was clear and the trees remained rooted in the ground.

The ride north was arduous and a big lesson in full time alertness. By the time he had ridden for five days his body cringed just at the sight of the bike. The numbness that spread from his backside all over the lower part of his body was the only thing that spared him from the reality of the pain in his joints. His hands and arms were bruised and the inside of his right calf smarted from a silencer burn. He needed recovery time and holed up in a small guesthouse with a veranda and a view of the Himalayan foothills. Again he was in hill tribe country, but these were mountain people used to hauling huge slabs of slate onto their roofs to keep out the voluminous rain. They had been independent of external government until recently and were now absurdly proud of being part of India. There was a strong animism in their adopted Hinduism and their culture revolved around the yak, a hugely hairy horned version of the cow, but enormously feisty and a little unpredictable.

Loïc encountered a pair of albino yaks one morning, they were being groomed and fluffed up to appeal to the few backpackers that had started to come into the area in their neverending search for novelty. He found the shaggy pair in the market place at midday having their photographs taken, straddled by nervous foreigners collecting evidence of overseas adventure. The yak owners earned more for a few pictures each day than they could earn by working their small walled fields. A white yak calf was a priceless possession, and bottles of bleach were never talked about.

The sun shone, the sharp highland air was a relief from the dense humidity of the plains, but it cut through what remained of Loïc's shirt, deep into his skin. He needed to adapt if his destination was further north.

Taking the road out of the eastern side of Himachal Pradesh, rising in a zigzag up the mountainsides, the bareness was occasionally broken by a verdant village. These outposts of agriculture were cleverly sun situated and maximised on water collection. Large plane trees indicated water sources and a means of survival. These few highland villages imitated nature and remodelled the landscape to support small communities. These were a rugged and pragmatic people that were used to spending long winters under metres of snow incarcerated in stone buildings with a multitude of biting insects that produced septic swellings and tenacious infestations.

Pajuk was the only man awake when Loïc pulled in and switched off the Enfield. His curiosity about the way things worked was aroused by the sudden lushness of the village. Independently, the two of them walked up the mountain; criss crossing each other's paths until way up under a scree bank they coincided on arrival at a seepage of fresh water. They shook hands and wordlessly met.

Pajuk pointed to the seepage and the plane trees below, by way of explanation. Then waved his arm in a wide arc that encompassed the resulting village. Loïc understood the connection. They walked down either side of the trickle of water until the ground levelled into a shallow lake. At the far end Pajuk removed a hank of grass from the low barrage wall and released the overnight collection into a narrow irrigation channel that led down to the terraced crescent fields of this, the highest of villages. Himalayan peas and a small sweet apple were their cash crops but between grew a range of edible and medicinal plants.

These, Loïc thought, are the Guanches brothers on a

bigger scale.

He rode on. The nights were cold and the few stops were lousy with fleas and offered little in the way of covers. He cut through small towns but he had little reason to stop and explore. As he reached up into Lahaul Spiti an assortment of ancient and crowded vehicles seemed to be converging on a narrow spur, the Pin valley. Loïc fell in with the general flow and after pausing to examine some huge folded rock formations that made the solid mountain look like bakers dough, he followed the narrow rising track arriving at a huge gathering of Tibetan monks and lay people.

Loïc was told the Dalai Lama was coming to give a teaching at this remote Buddhist gompa. The whole regional population had arrived not only to listen to the spiritual teaching, but to trade, meet family and friends and generally have a good time Tibetan style. Loïc was surprised by his ready acceptance of the information that the Dalai Lama was about to arrive. He had never heard of him but his imminent appearance in this remote valley swept through him, bringing to him a feeling of sweet relief.

On either side of the narrow track a whole street of stalls had sprung up, selling everything Tibetan, from yak butter tea to monks' sleeveless vests. Patrolling the road were hawkers with all their goods hanging from sticks. Any flat surface had hastily been converted into a momo or a chai stall. Groups of musicians passed round glasses of 'chang' and sang discordant rounds of tearful songs. Loïc discovered a pair of wolfskin gloves and a thick hooded Chinese army parka and after some spirited haggling bought both for very little. It was as he was checking out his new coat that a small young weatherbeaten woman swathed in a coarse yak hair skin over her long black dress approached him. Draped over her head was a wide felted strip of cloth covered with bright green turquoise stones. Her hair was gathered in whorls over her ears, her eyes a remarkable blue. She was selling coral, red coral. Loïc knew a little about coral, having dived for algae, but red, and up here in the roof of the world?

She assured him in a thickened English.

"Once the Tibetan plateau was a sea, that's how we can

recognise the sankar shell for what it truly is."

Loïc was taken aback by the quick reference to the shank shell but he stayed cool and said nothing. She wasn't trying to sell to him but she was quite clear that he should stay for the three days of the gathering. By nightfall he was bedded down in the back of a clothes stall folded into his new coat with his gunnysack under his head.

At dawn he was sitting on a wall overlooking the compound outside the gompa. Already many families were camped out on mats and bleary-eyed monks were taking their positions in the front rows cradling bowls of hot tsampa tea. An air of calm expectancy was beginning to grow. Within an hour the whole compound was covered with seated souls expectantly focused on the balcony projecting from the gompa front. Large men in suits and dark glasses stood around conspicuously with their arms folded tightly across their chests. The gompa sits twelve miles from the border with Chinese occupied Tibet and there was some anxiety about the safety of the Dalai Lama who was about to arrive by helicopter. Loïc had never seen a helicopter close up and the focus of his attention was on the flat patch of grass with a freshly whitewashed spot in its centre. A knot of westerners waited, standing to the side of the main gompa, with the promise of a simultaneous translation.

A voice at Loïc's shoulder asked if he wanted to join them. He wasn't interested, which intrigued the questioner.

"So why are you here if what his holiness has to say is of no consequence to you?"

"I said nothing of being of no consequence, did I ? That's your assumption. Anyway I am where I find myself to be, for whatever reasons, known or unknown."

"I stand corrected, said the man. He too wore a suit but no sunglasses. He seemed to be curious about Loïc's presence.

"I organise the Dalai Lama's India diary." He announced. "His Indian Secretary, I can organise a seat for you up on the balcony near to his Holiness."

"Thank you, but no thank you, said Loïc. I'm not that interested in what he has to say, I'm more interested in where he's coming from and what he hopes to achieve for his people. As I understand it from the Tibetan people that I have met, he has been outmanoeuvred and politically disappeared by the Chinese since he fled Tibet in 1955."

"This is true, said the secretary, but he has many global achievements to his credit. Statesman, disseminator of the faith, that sort of thing. Yes it true he has almost entirely lost his foothold in Tibet. Politics are a crude cover up for national theft, but what to do if your enemy doesn't even recognise your existence?"

"I guess you have to be smarter than the opposition," said Loïc, wondering where the conversation was going.

" Aren't there other areas that China has occupied that have some autonomy?" He asked of the now seated secretary.

"There are, there's Kartse and Yushu to the north east, they're autonomous provinces. But what's the relevance?"

"Surely they are the ones to make friends with. They are heard by the Chinese, they can speak on behalf of Tibet to the Chinese government. I'm sure they would do it if they could extract oil and minerals from Tibetan soil, isn't that the reason why everything gets done these days?"

"You're right, said the secretary, very interesting. For one so young you seem to understand things very clearly, how come?"

"I understand nothing," Loïc said," there's very little that makes sense to me in this life, nearly everything seems to be in confusion, nothing is what it appears to be and few people come from the heart. That much I do know, but it's all quite intriguing as to how it precariously holds together."

"Well I think your ideas are very interesting and I shall put them in front of his holiness. If you need anything while you are here, I am around somewhere." He said, waving his arm in a wide arc.

"There is one thing." said Loïc." I have a delivery to make and it seems like everyone knows about it but me, can you tell me where to take this sankhar shell ?" He rummaged in his sack. So that it gets into the right hands."

"So it's you," said the secretary. "Yes, you must go further north to Hemis Gompa. You have to cross the

Himalaya and get into Ladakh, the old Kingdom of Guge, that's where the shell must go, Hemis. Druckshen he's your man, he's the abbot of Hemis, he's the re-incarnation of Naropa who is of course the re-incarnation of Milarepa who we sometimes call Mr Murder."

He laughed, Loïc looked blank.

"Oh never mind perhaps you'll find out one day. Hemis, Druckshen, that's all you need to know. Good luck, you'll need it." Then he was gone, absorbed by a bustle of latecomers.

A throbbing helicopter cut down from the sky like a damaged dragonfly and unloaded a god. The expectation level rose a thousandfold. Minutes later the Dalai Lama appeared on the gompa forecourt and mounted a brightly decked out podium and sat, smiling at the assembled purple cloth and yak wool clad crowd.

For three days the Dalai Lama held their attention with teachings in Tibetan. For three days Loïc understood not a word but sat and absorbed the tone of his voice and the ambience of compassion. The one thing Loïc did understand was the Dalai Lama's laugh. He often threw back his head and released a highly infectious chuckle from deep down in his abdomen. A kind and caring laugh that had the whole crowd laughing with him. Even when he had left the podium and the sun was setting the people could not stop smiling.

19

When Death is in the Air

The route from the Pin valley took a long arc northwest. Most of the road was not there, landslides and rivers had seen to that. Often all traces of the road had disappeared and it was easier to ride down the river wash and find a crossing point, then double back on the far side and pick up traces of the old track. At one point, high on a mountainside a landslip had been intermittently closing the way through for a couple of years. An ancient welded bulldozer waited at a pull in, the worn tracks being fitted with an improvised linkage system from an old army tank. All traffic was at a standstill.

A box cable was strung across a huge chasm and people and their wares were being slung across to the other side where others waited and trucks stood with their engines silent. Drivers cooked breakfast on kerosene stoves and rubbed their hands together. The metal box on the cable was big enough to carry six people; progress along the wire was frighteningly slow. When it eventually returned Loïc pushed close to get the measure of it. He estimated that if he unloaded the bike and took off the front wheel the bike would fit.

The Sikh operating the cradle had seen it all before, including a cable break. He'd have to wait. Loïc walked to the cut around the slipping mountainside, that was the road. A crowd of people were pushing a truck full of goods as it attempted to get through from the other side. Their progress through the deep slurry was slow, but they kept moving. There didn't seem to be much in it, either way across was going to be a gamble.

Looking up at the mountain above Loïc could see the process quite clearly. The whole mountainside at this point was a huge bed of shale, bare and unstable. Below the road line lodged a massive scree pile waiting to plunge into a cascading gorge. By continually re-cutting the road into the collapsing mountain an undercut was formed, this was the road, until another slip covered it and resettled.

According to the Sikh, the road had at times been quite stable but the increase in commercial traffic had demanded passing places and a wider road, since then there had been continual slip. This was the only passable point into the next valley; it had become a bottleneck creating even more pressure for a wider road. Three trucks and a bus lay half buried in the scree pile below, a testament to impatience and the risks people were prepared to take to get paid and sell their vegetables.

Loïc watched the slow progress of the pushed truck and the bank above. They were still moving but barely. A group of people carrying suitcases and bags on their heads started out from the far side, knee deep in slurry but hasty in their attempt to cover the two kilometres of sagging mountain. As the truck and its attendant pushers neared the more solid looking section of road a long silent crack snaked across the scree bank above.

For a while nothing moved, and it wasn't until the people pushing the truck started running in front of it to gain more solid ground that anything appeared to be happening. The line of the road, starting from the far side started to disappear. It swept the tiny figures of the walkers away into the mass of stone and mud. The two who had abandoned their baggage were making a run for it as the road disappeared behind them. For a long time they were just ahead of the slip until one tripped and fell. The other kept going but he was tiring, the mud weighing him down and the slide was closing on his back. Then the other side of the arc dislodged and swept the truck aside like an empty carton and mixed it into the scree until it was gone from sight. The single running figure in mid crossing suddenly stopped. He knew what was behind him but now he could see the same in front. As the two ends of the slip enveloped the road either side of him a cry was heard above the low rumble of rock and mud, and he leapt off the road edge into the moving mass. For a long time he stayed upright, treading the slip as if it were water, his arms flailing, shouting ecstatically as he went. Spontaneously the watching and waiting crowds at either end of the slip echoed a roar of support for his attempt to survive. Gradually he fell to one side and disappeared, his blue scarf somehow remaining on the surface marking his descent into the void.

Meanwhile four of the truck's pushers had made it through and were dealing with their terror by clutching each other and shaking under proffered blankets. Loïc stood there in a state of awe.

Awe of the magnitude of nature and the insignificance of human life.

The importance of his being there became acutely clear. He had just seen something that few would witness in their lives. The significance of the individual swept aside with a single brush stroke. The spirit of a single man, the falling man had united all those present. Everyone was falling into death with him. We are not alone. We are all expressions of the same spirit; we are the spiritual expression of life.

The bag on his shoulder noticeably increased in weight.

He turned to the turbaned Sikh who stood nearby, their eyes met.

"Once the beacon force 'dozer has gone through," he said," the slip stays for a while, but never for long so stay right behind it. They start from both ends, two of them so be sure to be on the inside when they meet. Cut past them and go for it. Good luck."

Twice in a few days he had been wished good luck, he didn't believe in luck, but there wasn't much else to believe in at this point.

"Thanks," he said," the inside you say."

Loïc kicked over the Enfield and pulled onto the remaining solid roadside. His heart was in his throat. He thumbed the decompression lever and the engine cut out. It was a lengthy wait while the repaired bulldozer edged its way cautiously into the slip. More scree fell onto the cleared road but largely the mountain had settled into its new position. From either end the grinding machines nudged the loose shale over the edge, it soon settled, only the larger rocks broke free and bounced carelessly at increasing speed down to the casualties and beyond into the gorge.

He sat astride the bike. His mind blank until he heard another engine start up. He glanced back at the waiting crowd. The Sikh waived and Loïc kick started and pulled onto the new narrow slot that drew him forward. He found there was a little solidity if he stayed in the bulldozers herringbone tracks. The central part was soft and at such low speed wanted to consume the heavy bike. He caught up with the bulldozer, which was struggling to flip a large rock over the edge. When it did, the bank slipped into its path and progress stopped as the driver assessed the situation. He glanced back and nodded. Loïc turned to find a truck starting along the track behind him, his way back was all but barred.

N'zingu's voice came to him saying.

'When you find yourself next to death, fly away and look at yourself from above. From there your purpose will shine through your folly.'

Loïc looked up, high above him hung a large, now rare vulture, sitting with outstretched wings on a thermal, surveying human ants in their labours to overcome. For a moment Loïc was again 'in the eye of the bird in the sky'. He saw himself tense, revving the throttle, wanting this time to be over. He also saw that the vultures next meal could easily be waiting below. In truth he was contributing more tension to an already tense situation.

'When all is spoken for, bring something new.' The clicking voice of N'zingu came through.

Loïc slipped the gear lever into neutral and began to sing.

'May the road rise with you
may the sun shine upon your face
may the wind be always at your back
and the rain fall gently on your fields.
Until we meet again, until we meet again
may god hold you in the hollow of the hand.'

Then new words came to him as he sang.

'May the land always feed you
may your children grow up strong and free

and all your worries gently melt away
and love take refuge in your heart.
Until we meet again, until we meet again
may god hold you in the hollow of the hand.'

The bulldozer driver, another turbaned Sikh, looked back at him and smiled.

'May your true self find the reason
for your presence here upon this earth.
And your gifts be well received by all
and your beauty motivate the soul.
Until we meet again, until we meet again
may god hold you in the hollow of the hand.'

Loïc sang on, the bulldozers dug and the driver behind him became more and more impatient.

'May the being in the human
surface now for all to see
resistance soften like wetted clay,
duality succumb and fall away.
Until we meet again, until we meet again
may god hold you in the hollow of the hand.'

As he sang he felt a distinct clarity replace his anxiety. He was only partially aware that he was composing new verses to an Irish song his mother sang to him as a child. He had removed himself from the situation twice over.

The truck driver behind frantically waved him forward. By following Loïc onto the new track the driver had forced the situation. Now traffic could only come across from that end. Both bulldozers would have to exit on the far side. The driver was an old hand and had seized on the situation. If he could get his goods through before his competitors he was prepared to take the risk. He'd gone for an early crossing but he was far from relaxed.

Loïc continued to sing while the driver brought his truck right up behind him almost resting on the bikes mudguard.

'May a true love move between us
for woman and man to be at peace
breathe through the one essential present
so that we can be the ones we came to be.
Until we meet again, until we meet again
May god hold you in the hollow of the hand.'

Then over the noise of the engines Loïc heard the familiar clonking of a neck bell. Above the old snag line of the slip a line of goats picked their way along a narrow but firm path. Two gadis, hands draped over their shouldered sticks, the turned up toes of their shoes following the spore of the flock. Loïc shifted the bike into first gear, it had sunk into the loose surface, but by rocking it and bouncing off the truck bumper behind he pulled free. Using the gears to the maximum he edged forward. The angry driver behind span his wheels trying to get some purchase. By now there was only a short section of mountain to shift and the 'dozer drivers were shouting to each other. Between them they pushed the remaining scree over the edge as Loïc throttled up and cut through the narrow gap left on the mountainside.

As he squeezed through he clipped his knee on the caterpillar track of the second bulldozer and a sharp pain tracked into his thigh, but now was not a time to allow for anything but the far side. With the track clear to his front he changed into second, but it had less power and span the wheel and he dropped back into first and missed it, the bike stopped. He found first and went to pull away but it stalled. Frantically he kicked it over, it fired and then cut out. It wasn't to be, the Enfield was doing its unreliability thing just when it was least needed. Loïc tried again, nothing. The strain slipped into his ears and everything became muted as his blood surged into his head. He swung his leg over the seat and tried pushing, but the heavy bike was immobile in the mud. He felt like he was operating under water, swallowing did not relieve the compression in his ears, but he did hear the whoosh of wings as the vulture landed on the track in front of him. It waddled towards him, its bald neck outstretched, crawking as it came.

Again Loïc kicked the starter crank, it fired and spluttered into life. Carefully he found first gear and pulled towards the oncoming vulture. The bird, enormous at close quarters turned and started hopping in front of the bike. Then it skimmed over a section of track and kept going with its ungainly gait. At the section that the bird had flown the bike sank into a pocket of wetness and cut out, the exhaust choked with mud. As Loïc got off it sank to one side. He couldn't move it. Quickly he untied his gunnysack from the rack, and keeping his eyes on the bird he waded out of the stream that was the origin of the slip. As he ran, pain shot through his left leg. The vulture hopped on ahead, keeping a safe distance but clearly there for him. Small stones began to break loose from above; he ducked their trajectory as they flew across his path. He was over half way from the abandoned bike now when suddenly his knee gave out and he sprawled into the thick grey slurry. The vulture stopped too.

As he lay there looking up the mountain another snag line appeared just below the goat path as a prelude to another major slip.

The vulture had taken to the wing and was now cruising the air to the side of the track. He could hear voices shouting and he knew why, it was his turn. He hauled his body out of the cloying greyness and ran. He struggled to stay upright as he rounded the curve. The vulture was abreast of him and he was sure that it had a hungry look in its eye. He could see people now and parked trucks, their voices were clear and urgent but they didn't seem to get any closer however much he forced his body forwards. The vulture flew closer. He could hear the muffled air passing through its flight feathers. Down he went again, intense pain sucked at him.

'He was up on the crete above his home village, breathless from the climb. He waived to his mother far below as she hung out washing. She seemed to be more concerned about the pegs that the wind whipped off the edges of the bed linen, than his waving.'

'Not like this.' Sprang from his mouth as he dragged his needling leg out of the cloying mountainside. Like this, and he ran.

As he did, his bike, the bulldozers, the trucks and all their drivers slid off the track and plunged down into the depths behind him.

The vulture was a little ahead and he forced himself to catch up as the track way behind him slipped away. First he was peppered with small stones then his legs were swathed in moving mud. Then he seemed to be moving sideways; still the vulture was just ahead, its head craned round fixing him with one beady eye, waiting on the wing for the action. He could see he was a few feet from solid ground but it didn't want to get any closer. He flung himself forward. Outstretched hands appeared to flutter in front of him. With one hand he reached, with the other he still clutched the gunnysack. Something clawed at his back. Then nothing.

Nothing.

Nothing for some time.

When he did have some sensation, it was that of up and down. Up and down and forward. A boat came to mind. It was a gentle supported feeling and he decided that he must be in water. He was certainly cold but not wet. His leg was very painful so he thought he must be alive, but there was no light so he settled for being dead.

Nothing.

A voice with a thick accent announced the date and he realised it was his birthday and that he was now eighteen.

Nothing.

The same thick accent again. This time it was talking about extreme altitude sickness. He felt as though he was being compressed by a pile of mattresses. Which he was.

Nothing.

When he opened his eyes he was looking at the appliqued underside of a Tibetan tent. He thought that the hereafter looked hand made. The smell of yak butter tea drove its way down into his empty stomach and tried to turn it inside out. A round face set with blue eyes peered into his. A hand wiped his fore head, and then again.

Nothing.

The next time he opened his eyes the appliqued clouds had not gone away, nor had the round blue eyed face. Now it was smiling. He felt his own face crack open in reply. A desire to be touched flooded his body. He watched as his hand appeared from beneath the covers and take the cloth from her wiping hand. Gently he put it to one side. He took her hand and pushed it down under the covers to his filling stalk. She took him, held him and with a soft grip heightened his arousal. He had longed for this, longed for this, now it was for real. There was nothing else. He let go and was swept up in the magic of his exhausted body. As he felt himself rush to sweet release she moved her hand and pressed at the root of his sweetness. Waves of pleasure radiated from his groin, through his legs, up into his chest and his heart. For a while he bathed in the whiteness of prostatic pumping. He did not come.

Then nothing

It was still dark, but he knew he was awake. His leg throbbed continuously. It was a sharp but bearable pain. Again he was at first unsure of what reality he was in but the signs were definitely sentient. He poured with sweat and shook uncontrollably. The familiar round smile came to his bedside with a bowl of tsampa gruel for his mouth and tightly stuffed pillows for his back. She held the bowl while he supped and spilt.

Nothing again

His fever had broken and his clothes stank of fear. She persuaded him out of them and took the threadbare items away. There were other sleeping bodies in the tent, which seemed to be a temporary shelter. Bags and baskets stacked next to each slumbering form.

Nothing but troubled dreams, none of which he could remember. The taste of metal was in his mouth.

She was there with a short-sleeved robe, which she put round his shoulders and helped him rise from the thickly covered bed. Supported by her shoulder she led him out to a yak hair tent that seemed to serve as a steam bath. They entered together. She undressed and took his robe. He sat and she unbandaged his damaged knee, it was multi-coloured with bruising but not very swollen. She then wet him down with hot water from the stove then scrubbed him with a pumice stone, her long auburn plaits brushing across his polished skin. Once she had finished she laid him down on a woollen mat and kneaded ginger root steeped in almond oil into his reviving body. She took her time, occasionally pouring water onto the stove to release clouds of searing steam into the small tent. When she was done she lay down next to him. They lay all but touching, feeling the strength of each other's presence. He stiffened.

She stood again and bathed the small space in steam.

She straddled him and lowered herself onto him without using her hands. Their bodies touched in no other place, just the extremes of their arousal. Once she had eaten him deep inside she ceased to move, then she constricted and drew his heat deeper into her. No sound did they make, their blue eyes deep in each other's gaze. Loïc started to move beneath her but her look spoke of stillness. She brought him to his fullness with a subtle swallowing of her softness. She stopped and reached down beneath their joining and pressed against the imminent pumping of his seed with her fingers. Again sweet waves of pleasure coursed through him just beneath the skin, swathing him in an electric glow. She drove the energy up into his heart with light sweeping hand movements up his body, resting at his chest.

Gradually she withdrew until only the tip of him was held inside her wetness. In reply he hardened and curved to meet her teasing. Kneeling over him she took him deep inside to meet her gasp. With her hands on his shoulders and his cupping her small breasts they span through space and time moving with a slow unison of breath. Through groans and tremors to a place of no boundaries they swam. To a place where they were one in the mixture of their flames, bright and unquenchable. He did not come, she made sure his energy was retained. Finally slipped into a soft stillness and she lay down on his sweating body with him still deep inside her.

Like this they briefly slept.

Once more she poured water on the stove clouding the tent with steam. She washed him again where he lay. Palming an arnica oil she worked deep into the tissue around his knee and thigh, then, robed she returned him to his bed and sleep.

Nothing.

Nothing but warmth and energy and goodness when he woke. It was dark. Bodies breathed around him. His nose was very cold.

Of the events of his recent past he could only find fragments. Nothing consecutive. How he had avoided being swept away he would never know. How he had fallen into the hand of a Bon tantrica, for that was who she was, he would never question or forget. How long he had been ill he could only guess at, but he knew his birthday was somehow central to the time. His knee still hurt but it was now a dull healing ache. Otherwise he felt completely energised and alive. The one thing he didn't understand was how could he have moved from death to life so fast and if she was so much to do with that how was it that she barely acknowledged his presence. She had walked past him many times and not once had she glanced his way.

Nothing and everything. The imagined and the real.

He ate, slept and took short walks. There were three distinct tented compounds in the dry riverbed. They all sported a flapping awning out front with plastic chairs and tables. They competed for the all but non-existent trade. The unsurfaced road passed fifty metres away. Otherwise there were mountains stretching for hundreds of miles in all directions. Mountains that fell down while they were being pushed up.

His short walks soon became long. Long but slow. The thinness of the air saw to that. Loïc was fascinated by the interplay of light and eroded rock formations. Along one side of the river, there was a section of a few miles where the riverbank had been eroded by wind and temperature changes wearing away the steep bank into pinnacles that carried flat stones on their tops. These fragments of harder rock protected the softer underlayer from the elements. Sculpting spire after spire in a never repeating pattern of points wearing flat hats. He was intrigued by their source and improbability. In places whole sections of mountain had just crumbled and fallen into immense scree slopes, leaving revealed the plastic rock strata folded and bent into huge looping curves, dough-like kneaded rock.

At times he would be stopped by the grandeur that reduced him to being a mere witness of the continually changing colours of this enormous canvas of mountain. How did a vivid orange boulder in his path become deep violet just by his walking into its shadow? Sometimes a solitary cloud would manifest in its fluffy whiteness against a sky so blue it was hard to look at, and then it would dissolve into curlicue wisps and be gone. This was surely a place of transformation, a fastness where nothing but the essential could survive. Since his fall and his fever something had shifted in his self-view. He was no longer immortal, death had cast its shadow of claim across him. He was now sure of an end to his life. It could scoop him up at any time.

For Loïc there certainly seemed to be nothing fixed about the place or the people. He was unsure of himself. It seemed that what he had once considered to be ordinary was clearly not. Things and people now had fluctuating colours and shape about them. At first he put it down to the altitude, then the fever, then he had to accept that it was himself that had become altered by events. He had been feverish before, as a child. He remembered being convinced that his father had become a goat on one occasion, which had reduced his mother to tears of laughter. He had taken some persuading once his temperature had dropped that all was normal in the household.

This was different, he had been pulled back from the brink, given another chance, taken through a healing that had opened up a whole new world of possibilities. Now there was a delivery to complete.

20
The Kingdom of Guge

It was a cold morning when it did come, everything was covered with a layer of white ice crystals. Unlikely since humidity at this height was almost non-existent. Strangely it was the herald of the short summer, and with it came a team of yak herders and their herds. Briefly the tents were afloat in a sea of shaggy horned beasts while their minders took advantage of the only chai shop for hundreds of miles. They were dressed almost entirely in the reversed skins of their herds, their weathered faces and hands framed by black hair. They had been instructed by their Rimpoche to collect Loïc and take him north to Hemis gompa. They were not interested in waiting and even less interested in Loïc, to them he looked like a liability but they were obliged.

A short conversation with the Bon tantrika over a yak butter tea, a few coins changed hands and he was instructed to walk behind the slowest yak. His leg was almost healed but he was sure that his gunnysack weighed more than ever. As he left, she stepped into his path, put her hands together and bowed. Loïc did likewise and for a moment their foreheads touched and they looked into each other. Loıc realised that there was no emotional attachment there and her gift to him was entirely energetic, again she touched his knee and a smile flickered across her round face as she turned away.

Ahead lay two hundred miles of rough walking and his Ladakhi language was limited to the one word, 'jullay', a greeting. He took the next ten days moment by moment, accepting his fate like a condemned man. On the long trudge into the Kingdom of Guge he decided that he would hand over the shell as soon as possible. Perhaps that way, things would start to lighten up a little. The responsibility for the shell that he had idly plucked from the seabed had grown into a serious weight. It seemed to him the closer it got to its destination the more gravitas surrounded it but he still didn't understand it's significance, would he ever?

The yak drive across the Moore plains was not so much hard as monotonous. The size of everything made for very gradual changes at walking speed. For Loïc this was a blessing, it gave him time to empty his head. He found that the slowest yak and he had about the same rate of progress. They were both a little lame and tended to get gradually left behind each day as they passed across a vast highland plateau ringed by distant mountains. They became insignificant in their surroundings and enjoyed each other's silent company.

On the fifth day out, around midday, the wind picked up, Loïc gratefully zipped up his Chinese parka and walked down wind of the elderly yak. Her hair streamed out in the wind, her body blocking its full force, the rest of the herd and herders mere specks on the horizon.

It was then, out of this vastness, that Sri Pukka Baba first appeared in Loïc's mind, walking a few feet away on the other side of the lame yak. He was dressed in his usual style, nappy and stick. The wind threatened to tear the flapping white cotton from his groin. He did however seem to have made some effort to adjust to his surroundings; on his feet were a pair of large unlaced army boots which he was evidently having great difficulty with, his feet wanting to escape the leather with each step. He appeared to be surrounded by large empty thought bubbles. In one hand he grasped a rolled up comic, which he shook at Loïc. He started shouting but his words were whipped away by the wind.

"I've come to collect one shell, Loweek." appeared briefly in one of the bubbles near his mouth. Loïc shook his head in amazement. Can this really be happening or is he inside my head again?

"Promises, remember, promises are there to be kept." appeared in a speech bubble, before the wind peeled each letter away, scattering them into a non-sense. They kept moving, battened against the wind, the scoured land devoid of attachment.

Loïc looked hard at Sri Pukka Baba. Yes he seemed to be actually there, in all his absurdity, there on this bleak plain with Taglang La soaring up behind him in the distance.

Loïc put his palms together as if to pray then laid his cheek on the back of one hand as if to sleep then felt down his one side as if looking for something. Sri Pukka Baba's face broke into a grin and he threw the comic over the yaks back to Loïc. As it flew it unfurled, then re-rolled and landed in his hand. The wind suddenly powerless, unable to affect its flight. Then he was gone, taking huge bounding strides towards the south. Travelling like a true Lung Gompa man who has untied all the knots that bind him to worldly gravity. Gone to feel down the side of his bed for the hidden sankhar shell, the centrepiece of his ashram to be.

Loïc broke into a laugh that the wind snatched from his lips as he stuffed the cryptic comic into his parka pocket. Again this most eccentric of mystics had shown him the interconnectedness of thought and action. How one follows the other. In so short a time he had mastered Loweek's koan. 'what am I not?' Sri Pukka Baba had become part of everything and had even been transported by his own thought bubbles into the high desert of Zanskar to find the location of his precious shell.

Day after day they weathered the bleak high plateau. Trudging toward the closing peak. Night after night they bedded down between the ranks of odorous sleeping yaks. On the morning of the tenth day they passed over Taglang La, the high pass out of Zanskar and into 'Little Tibet'. The final climb was breathless and sickening. Loïc clung to the thick hair of the old yak's shoulders as his lungs searched the thin air for oxygen. She hauled him up and over the prayer flag strewn crag that led into the next valley. The world of Shangri la, or as some explained it, the blending of Shrinagar and Leh. Either way, the home of the Ladakhi people and the cradle of the Indus River lay before them. A place timeless if not ageless. The rest of the journey was down hill and much harder than crossing the plateau. Loose rock and a bitter wind accompanied them all the way to the door of Hemis Gompa. The yak herders beat on it with their sticks to announce their delivery. They left looking a little shame faced when Loïc was greeted by a lot of bowing and touching of the heart.

His arrival coincided with the end of the annual dance

festival that re- enacted the story of Padmasambhava taking Buddhism into Tibet. The Bon Po, the animistic priesthood of the time, would only agree to the teachings being heard providing they were permitted to perform everything the Buddhists did, but backwards. Whether it was a mantra, a mudra or simply reversing the image of the Buddha. Padmasambhava agreed, seconded them, announcing they would become the protectors of the faith. So it was, on the second attempt Buddhism crossed over the Himalaya to the roof of the world. The four days of dance drama retold the story every year and every year the entranced audience would reel back laughing as the skeletons of impermanence ran across the heads of the crowds. Now those skeleton costumes, terrifying masks and elaborate headpieces were all being carefully folded and wrapped for storage. Yak tails were being lowered from the courtyard poles to be exported for the Santa Claus beard market, and the lime plastering trade in the west. An ancient and enormous tanka painting was being removed from the temple facade and rolled up for the next eleven years. The withered and bony hand of the long dead painter of the tanka was replaced in a reliquary and sealed with wax. Ten snow leopard pelts were carefully carried off to dry storage, long rippling coloured pelmets were being removed from all the balconies and the gompa was preparing to return to normal. Loïc was shown to a small room overlooking the main courtyard. He watched the flurry of activity with interest. After the bleak vastness of the mountains, monastery life seemed very diverting.

Loïc turned away from the shuttered window and put his weighty gunnysack and himself down on the hard pallet bed. The ceiling was made from round timbers with a layer of sticks firmly pressed together above them. He lay there, absently exploring the construction. When he closed his eyes his exhausted body alternately convulsed and relaxed.

'A soft knock on the door of his family home, brings his mother to his side as he tries to open the high catch. Standing there a man wearing a raincoat and a fedora, in his hand a case.

She welcomes him in.

The man takes off his hat and coat, hangs them on the back of the door.

Loic is bathed in a sweet atmosphere. He is a child once again and measures things by a mixture of his senses.

The man enters his room, places the case on his bed and opens it.

It's full, full of blue and gold tins. They all bear a miniature of Nottingham castle on the pale lids. Players Medium Navy Cut Tobacco tins.

They look at each other. The man smiles and opens one of the tins. Inside, pinned to a piece of cardboard is a black and green iridescent beetle. They look at each other and they both smile.

The man kneeling at his side opens tin after tin. Each contains another jewel-like insect.

Entranced and disturbed Loïc understands that the man has collected these insects on his travels.

All the tins become rearranged in the case.

The man closes the case and puts on his hat and coat.

Standing at the open door he puts his hand on Loïc's head and kisses his mother on the lips.

For a long time he and his mother stand bathed in the light coming in the open door.'

When he woke a yellow light filtered into the room. He had woken with coloured dots before his eyes. Coloured dots in other coloured dots. As his eyes adjusted there on the shelf sat an object made of coloured dots. Somehow he knew it was a torma. At first it looked unreal, so he reached out and touched it. It smelt of yak butter, coloured yak butter. A leaf shape stood up from a cone of hardened barley flour. All around the edge of the shape were tiny coloured target shapes of different colours of dyed yak butter, pressed one on the next in diminishing circles. Exquisitely made but at the same time not carrying an air of preciousness. It was, somehow there beside his bed. It felt as though things were getting closer together, he needed some air.

Leaving the small cell he took a dark narrow passage that

led down stone steps to the main courtyard. Taking a path at the back of the high wall of the temple compound he climbed up between the upward tapering houses that formed the small village outside the gompa and kept going until the path ran out at the foot of a crumbling stupa. The cracked plaster was falling away revealing the rough masonry beneath. A feeling of repair came to him. As he stood there, catching his breath, looking at the small house adjacent, a wave of familiarity washed over him.

'This place I have known a long time', came to him.

Loïc pushed at the tired wooden door; silently it opened onto a tiny courtyard, which housed a gnarled peach tree that reached its limbs up to the terrace roof and the leaden sky. Small rooms led off the central tiled space. Fading murals of the Buddha's life peeled from the walls. Leaves persuaded by the wind cringed together in one corner. The stair treads were missing and Loïc climbed the loose masonry. The earth roof tapered out to a promontory sitting on a huge boulder that formed one wall of the building. There at the end a tiny chorten clad in a tatter of prayer flags gathered on a couple of dry branches from the tree below, their printed prayers long since scattered by the elements. Here Loïc sat. There was a strong sense of closure as the sky's mood darkened with heavy grey cloud. He felt he knew the taste of the fruits of this tree, rare in its place and altitude. The tree in the courtyard delivered a sense of secure wealth, and Loïc was reminded of a place in himself, a certainty. The light diminished, the mountain landscape foreshortened by charcoal grey cloud. For an instant the sun pierced a thinning of the cloud and lit the ground with a shaft of light as if it brought fire from the rock itself.

A fragment of his memory stirred into life. Had he lived here once? Had this been his home? A partition, a paper wall slid aside in his mind. He observed his hands as old, blotched and defined by leathered lines. Hadn't these hands at one time made the chorten next to him? A sharp pain ran from his left knee to his hip as he stood and walked across the crumbling roof. He turned to look out over the landscape again. The sound of an unseen stream ran down to join the Indus below.

From here he could see down into the gompa, into a familiar compound where timbers were prepared for construction and repair. The small room where the lime was slaked, the walls spattered white with its boiling over. All was fresh in his mind. He turned away. From here, the last house in the village, he could look down into the upper most terrace of the gompa and into Druckshen's apartment.

How long had it been?

Both an aeon and yesterday.

Synchronicity speaks the language of real time; it is all now. Tears welled up and ran down his weathered cheeks and then he laughed.

Laughed as he always had.

A laugh that parted clouds, leaving places for the light to get in. Laughter and tears giving rise to now.

The two halves of himself, the part that knows and the part that doubting seeks.

For a moment he teetered on the edge of alarm. Then the iboga came to him and reminded him that those two parts dovetail together, the dreamer and the dancer, reminding him that without the parts there is no whole. At that moment something lifted from Loïc. Fell away like a sodden woollen cloak, no longer of his wardrobe. He was free of having identity.

He knew now what needed to be done. Back down the path between the perched stone houses he entered the gompa and climbed to his room. He collected the torma and the shell from his bag and went down to the temple room. He pushed aside the heavy curtain that opened into the deep gloom of the reverberating hall. Lamas clad in crimson robes, shirted in vests of yellow and red sat cross-legged in rows, swaying slightly as they intoned a growling bass mantra. A thick layer of incense smoke hung above their heads disturbed in swirls by novice monks who walked down the rows pouring a tsampa gruel into wooden bowls. Loïc was moved by the nine foot long 'dung chen' horns that belched out a sound that seemed to come out of the ground itself, but when the huge 'rol mo' cymbals clashed and rattled together the sound was reassuringly familiar.

Making his way to the central aisle he stood in front of the golden Buddha, his eyes cast down. Slowly he walked barefoot and knelt, placed the torma with all the other identical tormas, lit a candle from another and embedded it with the many others. Taking the sankar shell from its wrapping of black palm fibres and Oopie's bed cover he brushed it clean with his fingers. It was surprisingly still intact, after all the knocks, falls and miles, it was, as he had found it, half buried in white sand, smooth creamy and perfect. As he placed it at the feet of the Buddha it seemed to at last to become weightless and almost flew from his hands. He looked up into the face of the Buddha. A strange conviction came to him. This is my work, this Buddha I made. He then remembered the lesson and let go of any attachment to its making, put his head to the floor and then retreated to the back wall where he sat absorbing the magic.

Does time reverse or is it just in cycles like everything else? The way a shaft of light moved across the paraphernalia of the faith, told him of time and the nature of movement. The paintings on the walls, the ceiling, the pillars, all told him of the numerous teachings of the Buddha but it was the rapid rattle of the Bon skull drum, 'the damaru' that reminded him of the balance of opposites and the cycle of life and death. Within the darkness of the place the detail was lost to his eye, but not to his re-membering.

There, folded into the angle of the floor and the wall, Loïc felt suddenly wide awake. The kind of awake when danger threatens and life could end. He realised that up to this point he had been blissfully slumbering in an ignorance that was now over. The completion of his task filled him with a feeling that made him sit up, stay alert and pay attention to the moment.

A sadness rose up in him as the evening progressed. The unresolved matter of his departure from his mountain village floated up in front of him. He was certain that there was a half-truth somewhere beneath the skin. He really needed to let go of whatever it was.

Gradually the light reaching in from above diminished, and the huge yak butter brass bowl lamps took over. The incense was renewed. The mantras changed and then droned on generating an atmosphere of charged peace that washed over him like warm milk. He stayed bathed in sound and smell until late into the evening. When he climbed the worn stone steps to his hard pallet and wrapped himself in Oopie's cover, his head was empty and his gunnysack was without weight.

At dawn he was called to Druckshen's apartment. The rising light pierced the carious skyline. He knocked and waited. On the terrace sat an old lama, he arranged his pallet of coloured butter balls around the edge of a bowl of water. Next to him sat a row of leaf shapes sticking out of cones of barley dough. Without pause, consideration or reflection the old man made torma after torma. Each time he finished one it was taken away before there was any time for self-congratulation. Loïc sat and watched the simple beauty of the process, feeling it in his hands and heart. It wasn't until all the tormas had been removed and the old lama had left the terrace that he was called in and a hot yak tea was put in his hands.

He smiled, they smiled.

We are very grateful to you. Much you have suffered, and a lot you have learned in delivering this Sankara shell. Is there something that you need? We may be able to help with. Loïc cradled his tea. He knew this was not just an idle inquiry. This was nothing to do with payment for his troubles; this was a proposal regarding his inner journey.

"Yes, I have a question, I'm told that at one time Issa or shall we call him Jesus was a student at this gompa. Could that be true?

"Many things could be true, but in that case there are records in our possession that tell of one Issa who spent some years here. The timings seem to correspond with the lost years of Issa or Jesus, and we know he was very fond of this part of the world. There is a tomb in Shrinagar at Khanyer Rozabal that is dedicated to Yus Assaf the healer of Kashmir. It is likely that he came back after his 'crucifixion'. Whether aloe and myrrh cured him of his wounds we will never know, but they have all the properties to do so and it is unlikely that such a man with extensive knowledge would die from a flesh wound. Six hours on a cross does not kill you. We believe Issa, Yus and Jesus to be the same person. The inscription on his tomb is in Greek, however the Greeks have been coming through here since before Alexander the Great.

You should remember that for centuries the busy Silk Road came through these parts. It was a major highway; Hemis was far from remote, as it seems now. Before India and China became nations this was the Kingdom of Guge, known as 'the heartland'. Empires have come and gone and now the famous have become obscure.

We live in the shadows, the shadows of the past perhaps, but more especially the rain shadow, there is no rain here, our water has always come from the glaciers. Melting by day, freezing by night, that is what makes life possible in these mountains. The main rivers of Asia may rise here in the Himalaya but it is largely desert. However now the glaciers have all but melted, there is no certainty of what becomes of us next. Life is precarious enough, without revealing that death through crucifixion doesn't happen to a yogic master in six hours."

He raised his right hand with thumb and little finger touching. Druckshen could trace his lineage of reincarnation back over a thousand years; the tone of his voice was not one of idle speculation.

"It's all happening so much faster now, so many souls incarnated. There's so much to be resolved before we can move on."

"Can you tell me about the eight auspicious symbols. Loïc said. What's so important about them?"

"Now is not the time for such a discourse, I have to leave very soon. I am going into retreat for some time and cannot answer your question briefly. The sankhar shell however, symbolises the truth of the Dharma and the voice of the Buddha himself."

Loïc had spent time with the shell pressed to his ear and what he heard was an infinity of heart song laced with despair. Could that be the truth of Dharma?

"I can however recommend two people to you."

Druckshen cut into Loïc's musings. "One is the Oracle at Sabu and the other is Mr Elvis in Leh. Both of these people you will meet. They will help you with your journey. And these, you will need these."

Druckshen handed Loïc a small rolled piece of paper.

"Say them often, let them accumulate inside you"

That was it, a thank you, a vague answer to a question and a couple of names after 'the much suffering' in the delivery, and now a piece of paper. How unimpressive thought Loïc. This must be yet another lesson in acceptance. He settled for being a free agent again, bowed and left the terrace. He climbed down the stairs to his pallet cell to retrieve his bag.

Unrolling the paper, there in long hand, The Three Fierce Mantras.

'ci yong ba shog'; 'whatever has to happen let it.'

'gang Itaar gro ba song'; 'whatever the situation it's fine.'

'ci kyang dgos pa med'; 'I really don't need anything.'

He had to laugh, but it wasn't a laugh that lasted long.

After Hemis, north was his only possible direction. The road east was closed by the Chinese, who now controlled the whole of the Tibetan plateau. To the west lay more snow-capped mountains and the Pakistan border. North led to Leh and the Nubra valley then more mountains and then desert. By going south he would be retracing his steps, which he wasn't prepared to do.

He joined the remaining traders as they hauled their unsold goods back down to the road at Karu. At this point the Indus River was a swift glacial melt full of glittering mica and the bridge was a span of army engineering. A few small food stops, set up for the festival still plied their momos and tea; Loïc paused at one, and ate. The surrounding landscape was grey on grey blue. A few shrubs and small trees grew up inside stacks of used tin cans, goat deterrents. These plants struggled to cast a little green into the mix but were easily overwhelmed by the vast greyness of rock.

Loïc fell in with a group that were taking the Leh road

and walked alongside the new concrete channel that leeted off river water to feed tourist demands in Leh. The glacier that for centuries had daily provided melt water to irrigate the fields and homes of the tiny capital was now so reduced it was unreliable. At points along the way people in twos and threes left the valley bottom road and struck out for settlements high up on the valley sides.

Gradually the sound of metal on metal incongruously arose from the bare rock landscape. A manic hammering filled the air while huge crumbling stupas lined the route. The noise grew as if to compete with their stillness and grandeur. Round the next bend all was explained. Outside a solitary corrugated iron shed two men methodically flattened new sheets of corrugated iron. Beating the ridges flat over a solid sheet of steel. By now they were surely stone deaf. The noise slowly diminished as they walked on, as did the group. Eventually there were just the two of them. Loïc and a blue eyed, perac wearing woman. Those blue eyes that were so remarkable in this sea of brown eyes that were typical of Ladakh.

It was some eight miles outside Leh when she veered off the road and beckoned for him to follow her. Long since Loïc had learned to follow without question, and it was with a sense of relief that he placed his feet in her footsteps. Now that his reason for being in this extraordinary mountain fastness had been left at Hemis Gompa he was without direction and purpose. Somehow this was much more disturbing than all the events that had coloured his path into the mountains.

"Sabu." She pronounced the name with a deep affection. "The Oracle of Sabu."

She spoke the words as if they were the answer to a question.

Loïc nodded his assent.

"Sabu." She pointed up the tiny path. Rocks had been carefully moved to either side making a path, almost imperceptible in the mass of fragments. It was dark when they arrived at the village. Once the sun had dropped behind the nearest ridge night was immediate at this altitude. Within minutes Venus sat in the cup of a crescent moon. Nearby stood a small stupa with the same brass symbol perched at its summit. Loïc felt as though he was in the full stream of some rush of rightness. She showed him to a raised pallet and brought a hot broth and some covers.

His sleep was interrupted by falling insects.

Woken early and urgently by the same blue eyes, she pulled at his sleeve until he was ready to leave, then steered him round the water channels of two fields, through a gate clad in flattened metal and placed him on a rock next to a cow just within a garden compound. Then she disappeared into the house.

Briefly the cow regarded him and then returned to its cud. Loïc felt at home, the sweet smell of chewed grass swept him up into familiarity. The rising sun clipped the flat rooftop, highlighting the stacked faggot roof edge that characterised the region. Slowly the brown painted window surrounds that taper towards the roof became bathed in the early morning glow. Little grew in the stony garden. Chickens scratched hopefully among the rocks. The proud clucking of egg laying erupted next to him. There was no hen, just the cow a few feet away. It eyed him as he became convinced that the sound came from within the beast.

A figure emerged from the house and emptied something out onto the ground at the side of the house. There was something familiar about the way she moved. Perhaps it was the long heavy wool dress and the two tied hair braids that all the women wore, but he felt not. She beckoned him in and ducked inside.

He entered the working kitchen, with raised earth ovens, fired up and heating a large aluminium water container. One of two Ladakhi women ushered him towards the cleared main space of the room, the other worked a goatskin bellows at the base of the firebox. Three robed monks sat along the far wall, one with a heavily bandaged leg, the other two nursed a head and an arm. There was an exchange of nods. A slice of sun slipped through the roof hole and lit a peeling portion of pale blue wall. Loïc sat. Other people arrived and silently found their places on the earth floor.

For some time now Loïc had accepted that he had opened up to a purpose not determined by himself. What he usually chose for himself was quite naturally arrived at but now there was beneath his everyday another agenda at work, driving him in and out of events that were beyond his previous experience, as if to confirm that there were many levels of existence happening simultaneously. Here in this room he felt both at home and out of his depth.

Very soon the room was full of a whole cross section of Himalayan life. Apart from the monks, the floor was taken up by a yak herder, a schoolteacher, three women with their children, a merchant and a crowd of less identifiable Ladakhis and a token foreigner, himself. Everyone sat silently, apart from the occasional groan from the bandaged monk, waiting for Llamo the oracle.

He realised that she had been there all along. It had been her at the door, her at the bellows and her just naturally in the kitchen. The other woman moved a tin trunk to the front of the glass fronted wall cabinet. She then covered it with newspapers and took brass bowls from the cabinet and placed them in a row. Each was filled, one with tsampa, two with rice, and the fourth with water. A butter lamp, a bell, a vajra and a small incense burner were placed alongside the bowls. From the cabinet a headdress was taken and tied around Llamos head. She began to chant as she tied on an apron, then a red scarf around her face. Looking up those blue eyes looked out from below a headdress set with a row of inverted seated Buddhas.

The Oracle had arrived.

She sat rocking and chanting as she passed a knife over a charcoal brazier and a copper tube on top of the trunk. A pungent incense smoked the room. At times she involuntarily quaked as she sprinkled rice into an offering bowl. The other woman poured water into her cupped hands, which she inhaled with her nose while the same chicken noise came out of her. Every few seconds she took water from the brass bowl and sprinkled it into the rice bowl. She made small balls of wet tsampa and stuck them to the rim of the offering bowl. All the components were being mixed together. Each connected to the others.

The rectangle of sunlight had moved to Loïc's face and he sat with eyes closed, bathed in its warmth, listening to the increasing vigour of the mantra. The voice seemed to stumble and shading his eyes he saw that the Oracle of Sabu was fully present. Her blue eyes had rolled up and she trembled all over. She cupped a handful of rice grains, turned and threw them against the glass cabinet, they rattled round the room. The other woman, close by, pulled a frightened child to her feet and put her in front of the possessed Oracle. Opening her shirt the tube was put to her chest. Llamo sucked at the tube and spat into a bowl. Urgency had entered the place and people were pulled forward as the oracle moved amongst the intimidated curists. Occasionally she passed the hot knife across her hissing tongue and blew across the blade onto infected body parts. The monks bandages were pulled off his leg and the blade was passed over the suppurating wound, he flinched and fell back muttering. An old man with a whiskered lined face was shaken out of his long sleeved jacket, revealing his pale bare shoulder. Llamo sucked with the tube all around the bruised scapula. When her assistant let go he fell down, his neighbours covering his nakedness.

Then she was in front of him and his shirt was being pulled open. The tube was over his solar plexus, sucking and skimming his skin. At this distance; within the aura of her aroma he knew her. He felt her strength of purpose. She filled a large emptiness both in him and the room itself. How was it that he encountered her in so many forms all along his mountain way.

Always the blue eyes, never the same person.

Were these women from the same tribe, same family, same strain?

The sucking pulled deep at his insides. Pulled on an ancient pain wrapped deep in the memory of his childhood. He let go and tears leapt to his eyes. Through the blur of aching insides and tears, her blue eyes looked at him from the Pin valley, from the steam bath, the walk from Hemis and now this. She was so very familiar but not at the same time. He fell back. She moved on, urgency was everywhere, as if time was running out of time. Hurriedly the remaining people were put in her path. She intuited their needs, injuries and confusion and breathed healing into their lives. Then she too fell back into the arms of her helper, spent but still chanting her mantra. Everyone seemed to know that it was time to go. Loïc too felt drained but had nowhere to leave for. A hand was placed on his shoulder, telling him to stay sitting.

A metal plate of biscuits was placed on the floor at his feet. The shaft of sun bounced off the spun metal in concentric circles illuminating the whole room. A yak butter tea was nestled into his hand as the kitchen returned to its domesticity. He drank his tea, then she was at his side. The oracle had gone and the grandmother had returned.

She held a small child on her hip; it pulled at her long ear lobes, free of the weight of silver. She smiled.

"Baigdandu," she said, "Nubra valley we have been here long time. Not forever, since 14th century. We came looking for the Christ Tomb from Greece. A long journey a long time ago. Tomb not in Ladakh, Tomb in Kashmir, my people stay in Nubra valley, nice hot spring in Panamik next village. People tired of walking, like Nubra valley, good place to stop and make home. Happy people Ladakhi people. You stay in Ladakh? Good place for you."

He smiled as uncertain as he'd ever been. She handed him a folded piece of paper reached down and touched the heart side of his chest. Again he felt moved to tears as he put his hands together and bowed his head. At that moment he knew that he could put his past behind him, it was now history, it no longer held any power over him. He opened the piece of paper.

"From Druckshen" she said.

There it was again, but now it had transformed from eight timbers resting on each other, into eight hands holding eight wrists in a circle. He turned to speak. She had gone. So the 'instructions' had come from Hemis gompa all the time. The smile stayed on his face, more inner than outer.

Once in Leh, Loïc made for the old town, tucked away under the palace mound. The palace itself, no longer occupied by the queen, stood propped in a state of permanent repair. Here the streets turned into covered corridors, wide enough for yak deliveries and pedestrian access. The doors didn't bear numbers. Loïc chose one and knocked.

A child opened the door. The dark interior ate the little light coming from the street. Loïc asked for Mr Elvis, the child shook his head and pointed further into the interior of the maze.

"Five doors, right side, Mr Elvis."

The fifth door opened to his knock, seeping the smell of coffee into the alleyway.

"Mr Elvis?" seemed a somewhat foolish thing to say, as the door was open by a young man affecting a hairpiece that accurately resembled that of the Elvis of legend. Not being blessed with much facial hair in the high Himalaya, his sideboards were neatly defined by an application of kohl eyeliner, but the hair captured the style worn during the white jumpsuit period.

"C'est moi," the young man said. "Mais sans le Mr."

Loïc sat on the low stool he was offered. A small ceramic charcoal burner sat in a basket in the centre of the floor. It made no difference to the room temperature. It was designed to be carried under the long yak hair smocks worn by the men, which explained why all the men appeared to only have one arm and be simultaneously pregnant in winter. Loïc handed Elvis the piece of paper. He looked at it, turned it over and handed it back he then pulled a Lakshmi Travel card from his pocket and gave it to Loïc.

"Perhaps you are not aware of the situation."

"Situation," mouthed Loïc.

"Yes the situation at the airport. It's a well-known problem at this time of year. Ladakh has become a tourist trap. Many thousands of people come here to see the old way of life and in the process change it for ever. Many of those thousands fly into Leh. The tourist trap is that only half of those that fly in can fly out because the mountain at the end of the runway is too high for a full load. So, we have too many people trapped in this tiny city for too long. That is the situation."

"Are you saying that I'm one of the trapped?"

"Certainly looks like it, what's your name? You have your passport?"

"Loïc is the name. No passport."

"That's another reason for not flying out. No passport no ticket. We're going to have to work on this one. Have some coffee. You speak French, English?"

Loïc's questioner was a modern Ladakhi. One of the ones changed forever. Jeans, T shirt, cowboy boots and shades. His French was good and it had been a long time since Loïc had used his mother tongue. Their conversation was limited to Loïc's identity. He found just listening to the cracked and strangled version of his language brought thoughts of his origin flooding back to him. He knew then that somehow he was heading west, in the direction of that other mountain range half a world away. Elvis was a little bemused by the fact that Loïc had so far managed to cross two oceans, two continents and numerous language changes and had never been asked for any form of identification.

"I've never really considered it before you drew my attention to it, but I suppose I was meant to get here with or without. That's the way things work don't they?"

"Myself, I'm not leaving Ladakh ever. I am just hearing the advice from the government departments. Here there are many permits needed for travel, because we are between, how shall I say, possibly hostile neighbours. Even within the region there are some places we Ladakhis cannot go without a permit. As the Indian government publicly states 'boundaries are neither well defined nor well defended'."

"Tell me of the Nubra valley, is that area open?"

"It changes, at the moment you can get in with a permit, but you can only go as far as the first gompa. If you're thinking of the hot springs at Panamik, you can't get to them."

"And Baigdandu village is that open ?"

"Not that I know of."

Loïc's curiosity was going to have to rest for the time being.

Elvis took some notes, dates, places and parentage. Then

he took him to meet a charming old man who ran a small photographic studio. He took a few portrait shots and then as he processed them Loïc flipped through his albums of Ladakh from the 60s and 70s. He was a Kashmiri from Shrinagar who had arrived at the request of the Royal family to record a marriage and never left. His 'outsiders' viewpoint had captured the remoteness of this mountain kingdom that had in many ways avoided the turmoil of the region by being on the outer reaches of both India and Tibet. His photographs captured things that made the place particular, the yaks, the hats, the Queen, the melting glaciers, the perched gompas, the irrigation systems and the dances both female and monastic. The black and white pictures froze a time rapidly slipping away.

Elvis took two copies of Loïc's mug shot and told him to give him a week and meet at his home.

"You must stay at Shardilals," the old photographer told him. "He's from Shrinagar as well. Married to a Ladakhi girl, runs a guesthouse. The Greenview, just down the hill."

Skebsin was no longer a girl and Mr Shardilal had been in Ladakh for over thirty years as well. They let rooms and served communal meals. The bedding was very compacted and the toilet was a long drop destined for the fields.

During the daylight Loïc explored the city, at night he listened to the tales of Shardilal and his guests. One day, he went through a doorway onto the main bazaar that said State Archive and Repository and found the city jail, one cell with lengths of chain hanging over the barred doorway. It hadn't had an occupant for two years and he had been a visitor drunk on 'chang', a barley beer, and needing a bed for the night. The prison and the city strongbox were in the same compound, the thief and the booty placed as neighbours. Crime was still a low priority in these parts.

Leh bazaar was lined with squat yaks and street trading women wearing long thick dress coats in dark red or black. They wore cutaway velour top hats perched on the backs of their heads and their long plaits tied together at the ends. They sold very small quantities of vegetables evidently fresh from their gardens. Other women wearing the same clothes but with peracs on their heads, bought the vegetables and chatted to each other. These peracs were long leaf shaped felted head pieces that hung down the back and had two black wings that stuck out either side of the head framing the face. The peracs were the vehicles for the family wealth. Covered in nodules of pale blue turquoise and silverwork. They weighed many kilos and were worn with a kind of stoical dignity that spoke of family status. Without exception all footwear, male and female, turned up at the toe.

There was a stationery shop full of cheap Chinese school equipment and dated Indian publications.

Two watch menders competed for the wrists of the small population from opposite sides of the street.

An elderly optician sold both new and second hand glasses to a people that suffered badly from glaucoma.

These were a whiskery race, a full beard was a rarity and a barber was extremely hard to find.

One night there was a new guest at Shardilals. He had evidently stayed before because the compassion was palpable. He was a tall, young German, and had come to collect things he had left behind. Skebsin was pleased that he had found a room in Choglamsar outside Leh.

A new beginning for him in the new village being built.

He had been caught in a vehicle fire two years before and his face and hands were not recognisably human. They were now swirls of melted pain and distorted skin growth. He still had all his senses but the horror he evoked in the people who saw him had driven him out of his homeland in search of mountainous solitude. When he eventually arrived in Ladakh he found a people strangely indifferent to his appearance but very interested in what he had to offer. So he taught them what he knew, another language and alternative technologies. In return they did not judge or pity him. He had found his form of happiness. Loïc helped him move his possessions the next day and realised how attached he was to the way things looked. The man without a face was a caring soul who had been dealt a difficult card but he wasn't going to let that get in his way. He was in service to those around him.

Some days Loïc walked along the valley bottoms and

found that the alluvial plane was a rich store of glacial moraines that, when mixed with yak and human dung and given a trickle of water the Ladakhi farmer, could grow a wide range of food. The land was blessed with a liberal coating of mantras and it was rare not to see someone with a small prayer wheel rotating in one hand while the other counted beads on a mala. The sound of Om Mani Padme Hum, drifted from lips while the same was being carved on stones and built into kilometre long walls carefully placed at important points in the landscape. If the air was thin, the prayers were thick.

Armed only with 'jullay jullay' Loïc blended easily with the people and the situation. He rapidly adapted to customs and etiquette. His smile and open manner put people at their ease immediately. He noticed how that angularity, that metallic compression that he was so aware of had not been present since his brush with death. He was much more in the moment more respectful of life in general.

The roll of paper spelt out three mantras.

The three Fierce Mantras, short and cryptic.

Druckshen spoke good English but he had only said 'say them often'.

While Loïc explored Leh he too was muttering like everyone else. They mumbled 'om mani padme hum.' while he mumbled 'ci yong ba shog'; 'whatever has to happen let it'.

He made his way back into the city one day, mumbling to himself 'ci yong ba shog' as he walked along a cobbled track beside a stream. A hand descended on his shoulder. It was followed by some weight, then an old leathery face stared at his lips as they mumbled the mantra. He then pointed at Loïc's empty hands.

How can they be so empty if you're walking? In these parts everything moves either by donkey or by yak or by hand. If the first two aren't available, then walking in a direction with empty hands either means you're in mourning or you're sick in the head. Loïc was evidently not in mourning but was he sick in the head. What was he muttering?

"Carry these." He thrust six live chickens tied at the legs into Loïc's hands. They lifted their heads and struggled to take flight. Loïc held tight more out of surprise than anything else. He leant in and put his ear to Loïc's lips. Loïc muttered, 'ci yong ba shog.'

"Ah, 'ci yong ba shog', yes, 'whatever has to happen, let it.' This is very powerful mantra, very good, very good.

"Carry these."

The farmer fell in beside him with another six chickens dangling from his hands.

"Come," he said.

They passed neat rows of coppiced willow, the stools ancient and ribbed, the new branches lithe green whips. The willows edged small-grassed fields wrestled over the years from the barren granite mountainside. Some housed huge immovable rocks surrounded by a crop. They were soon at the outskirts of the city, a slight bustle condensed. One large and ancient willow had listed from the stream edge and now leant heavily on a building. One branch the girth of a man slowly collapsing the house roof. The tree narrowed the path making for single file. The plastered wall of the building doubled as an advertising hoarding with peeling letters that read. 'Quick and Cheap Home Insurance' and bore a local phone number. They smiled at each other as they ducked under the trunk, the chickens lulled into submission by movement, dangling with their primary eyelids closed.

There was something other about this farmer. He was dressed Ladakhi style, cut away hat, turned up toes, belted smock, long sleeves but his face was other, maybe more mongoloid. Loïc realised, that Ladakh was on the edge of a whole other world that stretched north and east into a vastness he could not imagine.

The farmer pushed open a wooden street door with his back and stepped over a stop plank into a walled courtyard. On the far side of the bare yard sat a man with a large cockerel, which he preened with a sharpened match. The farmer put down his bird bundle and took Loïc's. He chose two birds to release then grabbed one and perched it on top of the other. The lower one squatted down while the top one balanced, treading the others back. Then he swapped them round, both showing signs of being broody. The man nodded and continued fussing with his cockerel's plumage. Gradually the farmer worked through both bundles, rejecting two hens. At one point he had two piles of four hens balancing on top of each other, treading and purring. Loïc was in stitches. They penned the broody hens at one side of the courtyard and put the cockerel in with them. He strutted about in all his finery while the farmer handed over a large denomination note. The warm pocket change was carefully counted. In this economy, margins of error are slim. He was grateful for the help and took Loïc round the corner to a relative's tea stall.

Later Loïc returned to the old photographer's studio to see if he had any pictures of the Nubra.

"Yes somewhere, but where?" He rifled though some drawers, pausing over memories, until he found a couple of albums of black and white shots stuck in with see-through triangular photo mounts.

'Nubra and the northwest', it said in a neat blue ink script. Dated 1952. Ladakh had been open at that time, before the Chinese invasion, before the arrival of the Indian Army. The high contrast pictures showed small fields of millet and barley growing along a watercourse. A group of monks not wearing flip flops, bare heads and bare feet. Shepherds with slings and huge flocks of goats. A wide valley strewn with flowers. Women picking sea buckthorn fruit. Sand dunes with a pair of Bactrian camels wearing nose ropes. Village people of Baigdandu. House building. Portraits of people suspicious of the camera, with no idea that it could capture images, and spirits. No western clothes, no trucks or buses, another time, he was easily entranced.

Retracing his steps he found the right fifth house sheltering in the palace shadow and rapped on the door. True to form Elvis opened the door with newly painted sideburns, still wet.

"Good, look at this." He took from a drawer an old passport and handed it to Loïc. There he was, retouched, looking younger. The franking on the pages roughly followed the route he had described. The stamps for Cape Verde and Gabon looked like smudges made with a potato cut, and were. Madagascar was spelt wrongly, but the Indian stamp and the photograph stamp looked genuine, embossed and with readable dates. The whole thing looked like it had survived laundering and a minor traffic accident. All in all it was a very unconvincing piece of forgery. The smile on Elvis' face announced that it was his handiwork. Loïc called him an artist, Elvis agreed.

"I haven't found you a plane out. Tickets are fetching very high prices, black market prices very high too. Stiff competition. Very difficult having no money Loïc. This is trying to call in very big favour."

It was then that Loïc told of his plan to go to the Nubra valley.

"This is very good, but to go on in that direction is very hard going, not impossible, but very slow and needing very good contacts and good disguise. There are people here in Leh that come from Nubra and beyond. They say it is a land empty of people except Kirghis shepherds in the summer months. They are the only ones to survive, the rest is taken by the wind and cracked to dust. See who you meet in the next few days and I'll call in different favours."

They shook on that and Loïc slipped the passport into his pocket.

"Hang onto that you might need it yet."

"Oh, I will, I like it already. I'm sure I could get into real trouble if I showed it at a border, but it is art Elvis." They laughed.

"I'm sure, if you go up the Nubra and on, no-one will ever see you again. Not even the yak and the snow leopard live up there, there's nothing. Nothing but rock and ice."

21
Snow Leopard Skin Pillbox Hat

Loïc explored Leh mumbling fierce mantras to himself, and keeping a look out for blue-eyed people. Slightly away from the main bazaar and behind the polo ground he found a place making oil out of orange berries and had to ask what they were.

"Tserma, tserma berries," the workers said and pointed up the mountain. The owner saw him and offered to show him round the small factory. The small orange berries were sea buckthorn berries. He had seen the thorny shrub growing along the watercourses and next to the river. Silvery grey spiky leaves, growing in dense clumps. It made a good barrier around young trees which all struggled to grow beyond the goats' reach before they were stripped of all their leaves. He'd tried eating the berries but they were unpleasant and he had dismissed them as inedible.

"What are they good for?"

"Almost everything." Came the reply. "In this part of the world sea buckthorn must be in the top five multi-property plants. The Chinese say it balances out everything in the body. The yin and the yang of all the organs, and there have certainly been plenty of Chinese people to try it on. Ghengis Khan called the oil one of his three treasures, along with organisation and discipline. He said it made his men strong and agile, important for horsemen. Strong agile and full of stamina. Which of course they needed since they rode across half of the hostile world of their time. He also noticed that it healed their wounds very quickly. It's said that those that didn't heal with sea buckthorn oil he left behind."

"You believe all that do you?"

"Most certainly I do. What's more modern analysis adds many more properties to its list of virtues. But I can see you're not convinced. You need to talk to Norbu next door, he's the expert round here, between us we buy from all the growers in this region, some as far away as Pamir bring their berries to us."

"So there is a way through to Pamir from here?" Loïc tried to sound disinterested.

"There is for a yak caravan, but it takes weeks."

"So Norbu you say, next door, what does he do with these berries?"

"Ask him, if you want to know, turn right out of the door."

Loïc thanked the oil maker and stepped into the street.

A small sign above the next door read, Leh Berry Juice Fortifies the Forces. He pushed it open. A small warehouse stacked to the ceiling with tetra pak cartons saying Leh Berry juice, filled most of the space. In the cramped corner there was a desk of sorts sporting a telephone and a pile of paperwork weighed down with a carton of juice.

"Jullay?" Loïc scanned the remaining space, seeing no one.

"Jullay." Came a sleepy voice from behind the desk. Sounds like a non-native visitor to me. Am I dreaming or is there change in this world?

"Norbu?"

"Yes, at your service. Are you a British officer who has missed Independence?"

"I am neither," said Loïc, "your neighbour said you were the one to talk to about the berry."

"Indeed I am, the berry is the future." He sat up on the bed behind the desk." What I can't tell you, you don't want to know."

Without hesitation, Norbu, as if programmed, launched into his sales pitch.

"We are a drinks company making the most efficacious drink made by man. For man functioning in the most extreme conditions that is. Cold like you have never known. So cold that expectoration is not recommended. We make a drink that doesn't freeze right down to minus degree 22. A drink that stops your toes falling off with frostbite and protects your skin from snow burn. Not only will it give you the vitamins you deserve but it will save your life."

"Stop, stop." cried Loïc. "I haven't even tasted the stuff yet, I imagine it's disgusting."

Norbu was stopped. He reached for the carton on the pile of papers and fumbled for a glass in the desk drawer.

"My apologies, of course you must drink first and listen later, my humblest apologies, drink. "He thrust a full glass of deep red liquid into Loïc's hand. He stood and watched as Loïc's expression changed from sipping apprehension to a smiling slurp.

" Good?" he said.

" Very good," said Loïc, " I'm listening now."

"Did you know that the Russian cosmonauts on the Mir space station use the 'golden berry cream' as a barrier against cosmic radiation?"

"What?"

"Did you know that the same cream was smothered over the radiation burns received at the meltdown of Chernobyl?"

"Huh. This is beginning to sound like some kind of super plant growing here in the mountains."

"It is my friend. Super plant that is well put. I like that. It's not just the berries, it's the leaves, the bark, the roots the whole plant. There's a whole mythology that comes with this plant. I expect he told you about Ghengis next door. Imagine it; he comes in from the north, thousands of men, some on foot, some on camel, some on horse. With him he brings a sumptuous yurt erected on a huge wagon drawn by oxen. A nomad on the move, his palace at the ready. Anyway he's fighting his way across a third of the known world of the time. Doing the terrible things that armies do as they go. Basically in modern thinking, stress after stress, day after day bringing down more of the same on his men year after year. As he overcomes all in his path, his soldiers; wild fearsome creatures, collapse and die. But as he goes, he learns of the 'golden berry.' How it mends wounds and then increases their stamina, making men strong and agile again. They say that Ghengis Khan used two things to keep his men doing his bidding; for they rarely got paid. One was the curative power of the sea buckthorn juice, which dealt with their bodies. The other was Chua Ka which dealt with their fear."

"What's Chua Ka?" said Loïc, thinking of the heavily carved bases of the moving towers in Hampi.

"Chua Ka is otherwise known as 'feathering the skeleton'. It's a way of scraping the fear toxins off the bones with a spatula, a Ka. If you're full of fear you can't fight or do anything else come to that. So by getting his men to scrape the toxic nodules of fear off their bones with shin bone spatulas, he made them fearless and hence fearsome in the next battle. So along with the massage, his discipline and organisation and the golden berry juice, his swarming hordes were tip top."

"Do really believe that massage with a bone and the oil of a berry accounted for the success of the Mogols?"

"I certainly think that without them they wouldn't have passed into history as they have here. There was another great warlord to feed the reputation of the berry, Alexander the Great, heard of him?"

"Of course, everyone has. What was his take on the golden berry?"

"He noticed his horses that were wounded in battle went into the sea buckthorn to heal themselves. They ate it, slept in it and generally rubbed up against it. Then they came out with their coats shinning with health. It was him that gave it the name *Hippophae rhamnoides*, 'shiny horse'. Good credentials don't you think? I could go on but that's enough for now. I'm a big fan of the small berry."

"A little more?" he said holding the carton in the air like some kind of trophy.

"Yes, it's very good. Tell me, your suppliers from Pamir, how often do they come?"

"Oh, not often, once a month in the season if that. Once they have a full load and they've seen to the path repairs they come through."

He checked the wall calendar that pictured the Potala in Lhasa since its Chinese makeover. It looked a little like theme park Asia with the Potala palace timelessly perched above a pastiche of manicured Chinese architecture spread out around an artificial lake.

"They could be here soon, they were last in Leh five

weeks ago. Their berries are longer, they call them Siberian pineapple. It's another variety of the berry. Very good juice though. That's why they risk the journey, we pay good prices for the best berries."

"So they bring their berries by yak do they?" Loïc persisted, exposing his interest in this remote region of the mountains. "How long does it take?"

"Long enough for you not to be interested. Norbu said sharply. Pamir is out of Indian territory and to get there you have to cross over northern Pakistan. Pakistan currently falls into the category of being a hostile neighbour. We never really recovered from partition in these parts. Anyway Pamir is now in Afghanistan, which if you didn't know has a war going on. It always has a war going on for one reason or another, usually foreign interference and misplaced blame, whatever the cause the result is the same, death misery and distrust."

"Yes, I know this from central Africa. Fear becomes so embedded in the everyday that a loving gesture becomes a threat."

"You have been in Africa? You are very young to have done all this travelling."

"Not nearly as young as I once was." Loïc smiled reflectively. Babies in boxes floated through his mind.

"Indeed, that's common ground to us all." They looked at each other and laughed. "What's so interesting about Pamir for you?"

"The mountains have a lot to teach me," said Loïc, and, he paused," I'm looking to get back to Europe that way."

"The mountains will surely teach you a lesson, most likely your last lesson."

"You seem to be afraid of where your best harvest comes from, perhaps you need some of Ghengis' skeleton feathering. Haven't you been to Pamir?"

"I'm a business man not a mountaineer."

"That's what every other Indian says, I'm a business man. Is that it, I'm a businessman and then you die. There's more to life than money. Don't take offence but it's not money that makes the world go round, it's imagination. You must be able to see further than soldiers and berry juice. If what you've told me is right your market is much bigger than soldiers stationed on a glacier getting frozen feet and runny noses. It sounds to me like you're talking about a super food, like acai or goji or even papaya. I'm sure you know about these plants, how they are marketed. I'm sure there's more for you out there than a contract with the Indian army. Anyway whatever your vision is you need to get out more."

"You may well be right there." said Norbu, "but the super food market is half a world away from here. I'll check it out. Oh, when the yak team arrives I'll let you know. Where are you staying?"

"Shardilals, Greenview," said Loïc as he turned to leave. "The berries sound great."

"Try this as my final shot. They alleviate pain, yes! They kill off skin parasites, you know mites that sort of thing. And it is said that it can be used successfully in the treatment of certain types of cancer. Prostate is the one I've heard of. The sea buckthorn is said to regenerate cells faster than the cancerous cells can multiply."

"No wonder Ghengis Khan said it was his third treasure, he was regenerating his troops faster than the enemy could kill them." They laughed as Loïc closed the door behind him.

The white smudged lines of the polo ground snaked away in front of him, leading his eye up to the 'dzong style' palace perched on its eerie rock imitating the Potala before the Chinese synthesis. Once the highest building in the world it stood there, floor after floor of dereliction, mute, devoid of its embroidered regality. Two identical curlicue cumulus clouds hung in the sky as if carefully removed from a temple tanka painting and placed back at their point of origin, northwest, the direction of Pamir. Loïc read them as an omen.

There arose in him in equal parts, excitement at the prospect and a sharp edged fear. He had been surprised when Norbu had started talking about Chua Ka and fears gathering on the surface of the bones. Chua Ka sounded like something he could use. Fear of possible death had become a feature of his imagination. It was a new dimension to his life. It didn't affect his decisions but it did bring to the surface a darker element, the reality of danger that hadn't been present in his consciousness before the hungry look in the vulture's eye. It had been then in the eye of that bird, that he had first seen the true colour of fear; a deep congealing dark red verging on black. Alongside his usual enthusiasm floated a form, a cautious form disconnected from any kind of logic. A form that had tentacles that invaded his confidence. The shadow of doubt had reared its naked neck and spoken the word 'fear'. He gave it little of his time but, like all shadows, it was ever present; wherever he stood it was with him. Watching the motionless clouds hanging in the palace sky, he had a strong feeling that one was shadowing the other.

Two days later a breathless boy arrived at Shardilals. He had a message 'for the one with the blue eyes'.

"The berries have come from Pamir, come quickly, they do not stay, the weather is on the turn."

This was familiar. He put his few things in a backpack the burnt German had given him, said a tearful farewell to Shardilal and Skebsin and followed the small boy across Leh. He made a detour at the palace mound and knocked at No.5. Elvis wasn't surprised when he spoke of his plan to go over the top as he put it.

"Okay, said Elvis, you're going to need those contacts."

He wrote two names on the back of a Lakshmi Travels card.

Torsoon Boi. Big Pamir.

Pandi Bey. Little Pamir.

"You get to Little Pamir first but they're both a long way from here." He thrust a previously drawn map into Loïc's hand. "It's what my father can remember of the route, but there was no road in his day. He says if you meet a glacier you've gone the wrong way. He also said avoid the check points because they won't know what to do with you."

"How long will it take?"

"If you make it at all I'd be surprised, but I won't know anyway. Don't be worrying about time. Yak herders usually loose yaks not men, but you will need to stay alert and out of the wind at night or you won't wake up. Oh, and this, you'll need this."

Elvis thrust a bundle of fur into his hands.

"What is it?" said Loïc dropping it on the floor and stepping back.

"It's a hat, you're going to need a hat."

"Ok it's a hat, but whose hat?"

"It's a hat to stop you freezing."

"Look it's not new, I know about wearing dead men's hats and shoes."

"It's my father's and he's not dead, you've met him, he's known all over these parts, the hat will help."

"I've met him, when?"

"He's your photographer. Your passport, remember?"

They laughed and embraced, kissing each other's cheeks French style, then laughed again.

"Go well," they said simultaneously and laughed again.

Loïc left clutching the papers and a snow leopard skin pillbox hat.

He followed the hurrying boy down to the polo ground. He knew these things to be true. Crossing Zanskar, if it hadn't been for the yaks he wouldn't have made it. Daytime was all right, but the temperature drop at night was extreme. The yaks were okay; they had a naturally matting undercoat. They excreted an oil that triggered the matting. Over the top they had a long shaggy coat that made them look like they're in water when they're in the wind. 'Yes,' he thought 'it's not only the temperature that's ferocious at night, the smell of those yaks under your nose is as well.' Step by step he reminded himself and tried out Druckshen's second fierce mantra.

'gang itar groba song.'
'whatever the situation, it's fine.'

Standing outside the door of Norbu's juice factory were bundles of sacks. Norbu greeted him and introduced him to the Kryghyz berry traders. One spoke a little English and smoked a long stem pipe; the other two stood rotating prayer wheels. They all wore yak skin boots and vacant expressions. There were no yaks but there was a truck.

Norbu put a hand on his shoulder.

"You go with them, they will show you how to get to Pamir."

Loïc looked at the three traders, they seemed as unfriendly as the yak herders. He put on the hat. An eyebrow or two were raised and the pipe smoker, who seemed to be in charge, indicated with his free index finger for him to turn around. Slowly he turned, the three of them looked at the back of his head. Loïc looked to Norbu for a clue. When he came round to facing the pipe holder they were all smiling and nodding. They proffered hands and shook. Loïc never knew that the way he wore the hat was backwards. Inadvertently he had personalised anothers' much loved identity.

"I thought they came by yak," said Loïc.

"Not all the way these days, it's a long way. You'll get yak, but for now jump in. Oh, and take a couple of these."

He thrust a couple of cartons of Leh Berry Juice into Loïc's hands while the traders loaded the empty sacks into the back and climbed in. The driver fired it up with a cloud of black diesel smoke and they were on the move.

The truck took the only road going north. Within two kilometres it was a track, a single track leaving the lushness of the Indus valley and climbing into a world of grey white and blue, where green soon became a memory, a rare gift. Gradually they advanced across vast shale banks, crabbed around severe hairpin bends and then returning at a slightly higher level until the next hairpin. Back and forth until the ridge was eventually reached. Then with the truck perched on the crest with the track little more than the width of the wheels, the driver edged forward with the ground dropping away steeply on either side. Two prayer wheels revolving faster than the truck wheels accompanied by back-to-back murmurings of 'om mani padme hum'. The pipe silent and smokeless and Loïc sitting in the toolbox on top of the cab. They crept north again until they zigzagged down into the next valley making five kilometres advance in every twenty crawled, the driver rarely getting into third gear. Cautiously they picked their way across banks and streambeds, over slips and around boulders.

At times traffic would collect on either side of one of these rocks as bands of small dark Tamil road workers clad in outsized rubber boots and little else recognisable as clothing, cleared the road. Using long metal mining points they levered the massive chunks of crumbling mountain off the road and over the edge. Just before the final nudge a whistle was blown and a red flag raised as if that were sufficient warning. The same was done on the road below then the final heave and the boulder dropped over the edge. Gathering speed as it went, attendant rocks and scree with luck cleared the road and plunged into the canyon below. If not the crew shouldered their spikes and set off down the road to remove it from its new resting place. Where they lived Loïc could not detect. There was no tent to be seen and in this great barrenness everything was conspicuous especially the yellow sign that read 'Go gently on my curves'.

At Pullu there was an army checkpoint. In theory they were entering hostile territory. In military reality it was a disputed zone, both India and China claiming the region. In everyday reality, there was a soldier on duty at the roadside, who recognised everyone who passed through. The berry traders hid Loïc under the sea buckthorn sacks and then stood on him peering over the edge of the truck chatting. Once they were out of earshot they uncovered him laughing at his crumpled appearance. They edged further up into the enormous wasteland of snow-capped crumbling mountains that rise two inches higher every year, which is twice as fast as your fingernails grow.

Miles and mountains, gradually rising; this was the highest driveable road on earth. After some hours they reached the Khardung la at 18,380 feet above sea level they were two-thirds the height of Everest. The marker point was swathed in fluttering coloured cotton prayer flags, g'tuks, bells and carved mani stones. Even in summer time it was strewn with banks of dirty snow pitched against a cobalt blue sky. An incongruous shop and museum with a camouflaged painted roof sat next to a red painted pyramidical roof judiciously painted with a large white Om. Everyone went to touch the mani stones and give thanks and a prayer for the rest of the journey. Loïc followed suit, there was no other guarantee apart from taking the advice of the road signs to heart.

As he climbed the slight slope away from the road a bitter wind froze hard the mucus in his nose. The lack of oxygen in the sharp air made him light headed and brought points of pain to his chest. The slightest effort made breathing difficult. He walked and wished for bigger lungs.

"Always go down before you sleep, said the yakker with the long pipe. This way you don't get sick."

"Thanks for that," said Loïc already beginning to feel queasy.

Along the way there was little to compete with the sheer grandeur and instability of the mountains. Looking across these huge valleys from above, they displayed their shifting majesty. Poured like salt; scree lay between rock formations, cracked and fragmented by severe temperature changes. The colours of a modest pallette brought to its full range by the changing light of day. Occasionally there was a road sign that said nothing of distance, occasionally of height, usually some sobering poetic phrase.

'No hurry daddy, I am waiting'. Loïc hoped it was read as an order. Another announced, 'Caution is cheap, life is not guaranteed'. Yet another, just before an unusually straight section of road read, 'If married divorce speed'.

One of the berry traders travelled in the cab to ensure that the driver's eyes were open at all times. Loïc knew from driving the Enfield on these roads that it only took one mistake and it was probably your last. They kept moving, seeing little traffic from the other direction. When they did, miraculously there seemed to be just enough road to squeeze past. They were held up on two occasions by huge herds of goats that skittered across the road completely out of range of any greenery but within range of a couple of boys swinging slings.

At a particularly weakened hairpin the truck suddenly ground to a halt and dust formed a cloud that drifted forwards obscuring the truck and the road ahead. As it settled there appeared standing resolutely in mid road, a bull yak, backed up by three females in season. He was not pleased about being disturbed, as a flat mating ground, luxury to a yak.

"Dzomo", called one of the yakkers. They watched from the truck as a string of bad jokes kept their toothy grins oiled with laughter.

These dzomo are a cross breed favoured by the locals for their meat and milk. Part yak. part cow, the males are infertile but not the females. They are larger and stronger than yaks and even more cantankerous. The bull yak was huge, the height of a man at the shoulders with a horn splay of the same. The female dzomos were a little skittish but his dominance was formidable. They waited to be serviced by him then he led them off down a small path after pawing the road just to show who was in charge. That was why the yakkers had stayed in the truck. In season the yaks' domestication is very frail and if disturbed they have no qualms about using their horns. They are superbly adapted to the severe conditions of the mountains. Unlike the reindeer which thrive in the cold dry air of the far north by having hollow hairs to form their insulation, the yak and the dzo responding to altitude cold, naturally felt their silky underhair and leave the outer hair long, windblown and aerodynamic. Different solutions determined by the cold wet and the cold dry climates. It is this undercoat that inspired the making of felt which ensures the lives of many highland nomadic peoples. Loïc marvelled at the subtle adaptions that always surrounded him and was very amused when he realised the yaks grunted like pigs instead of lowing like cattle. He hadn't noticed that before. He'd thought they were mute.

The yakkers went on to tell him about their sheep, 'guspan' they call them. They told Loïc that they were like their camels. They had two fatty lumps on their rumps that enabled them to go without water, allowing them to range much further into the mountains searching for the sparse vegetation. At one settlement near Satti a flock of these woolly, lumpy creatures filled the road. His companions looked at them as a Frenchman would salivate over a blue cheese. These fatty fluid lumps have given the nomadic communities a delicacy high in protein with a different taste; a seriously chewy treat.

As they drove on a bank of cloud swept in and ate the sky. Loïc recognised its particular qualities immediately. What had been the roof of the world soon felt like the sea bottom. The loose rock became like sand, the sky like the undersurface of moving water, casting dappled shadows into a shallow ocean. Loïc's whole perception was shaken. It was as if dimensions had switched, the large had become minute in the presence of the enormous. The air had become water-like and the cloud was becoming 'familiar undulatus'. By the time they had reached the Kardung canyon the erosion forms had persuaded him that he was entering a deep-sea trench.

At Satti, sloped between river and mountain, the cloud moved westward and the vista emerged in sharp focus. This truly was another world. A vast flat-bottomed valley with the shifting tendrils of the Shyok River weaving from one side to the other made a permanent roadway impossible. Granite mountains reared up on either side enclosing the corridor. Ribbed by erosion, capped with snow, both sides had spills of cascading scree pouring down in an act of raw majestic slow motion.

The truck stopped at a promontory, the engine cut. At first the silence was enormous, gradually filling with bird, wind and rock song. Loïc climbed down and walked to the edge. The mountain plummeted away into a deep chasm, a crack in the world in one dimension, a mere fissure in wet sand in another. As he sat there these two extremes of reality jostled for position in his perception. He closed his eyes, knowing that this moment would feed him, stay with him. When he opened them again the view rushed toward him as if to fill him to the brim. He breathed deep and slow, relishing the thin air as tears welled up and trickled down his dusty cheeks.

It took some time to boil water at this height and was not possible without the old brass primus stove the driver handed down from the cab.

"This you like?" the old herder sucking on his pipe gestured towards the Nubra.

Loïc put his hand on his heart and they all laughed and

nodded.

"Special place." the old man added, putting his hushed index finger to his lips.

By the time they had descended the twisting ribbon down into the valley it was almost dark. The whole mountain range became blue with the sinking sun, turning the snow peaks to a radiant umber orange. The truck pulled up outside a walled compound. Inside a single story house was hung with a cast iron kettle over the door. Then it was pitch black, tsampa and yak skins.

22
Mergen and Baykt

The night was brief, Loïc was up at the first hint of dawn. A cockerel strained to complete its call. He stepped out of the building and walked. The sun clipped the snow-covered rim of the valley. Bright pink peaks stretched away into the distance. He stopped at a small watercourse, beyond, plants grew in profusion, everything was in flower, a whole palette of points of colour lifted off a middle ground of greens and browns. The growing light intensified the hues as it slid down the valley side. Over all this exquisite stipple lay a fine dusting of snowflakes. Large and clearly formed, unique and six pointed. The delicate effect of the snow peppering the plants was breathtaking. Loïc felt light headed and blessed by the beauty that was unfolding in front of him. He stood, his skin prickled by the chill air, his self swept up on a tidal pull of awe.

Druckshen's third mantra sprang to mind.

'ci kyang dgos pa med'
'I don't need anything whatsoever'

The sweetness of the Nubra was inside him. The jewel of Guge, 'the heartland' as the people called it, was doing its work. Loïc had arrived at an inner calm.

It was then as Loïc was having his serene moment, that two small brown eyed boys burst out of the bushes clutching eggs and scattering snowflakes and flower petals. They hadn't seen him and he noted how different they were from each other. The smaller one, without a second thought leapt over the watercourse, landed badly, recovered a stringy dribble of albumen dangling from his hand. The elder approached a couple of times before putting his faith in fate and threw himself hopefully across. It was once they had both arrived with only one egg broken that they noticed Loïc. They stared frozen, fixed in the present. Surprise quickly relaxed into curiosity, then grew into smiles. They all laughed, and that was how they met, showing their teeth and their laughs. Then they were gone, off on their egg mission. Loïc turned to look at where they had come from. The magic of the rising sun had departed leaving bleached shrubs in an arid soil.

The driver told him he had two options. One was to go north and follow the Shyok River up to the head of the Nubra valley where the hot springs were not far from the face of the glacier that blocked the valley. Or to go with the truck down the Shyok and keep moving. The latter was the berry traders' route. Destination Thang near the Pakistan border, two days drive.

"You have a map?" Loïc asked.

"Map, what is map?"

"Picture of the way." Loïc explored.

"Picture in the head," he tapped his temple as if to produce a copy.

"Show me picture," Loïc offered the driver a scrap of paper and a pencil. He looked blankly at them.

"Show me picture in your head," Loïc pressed.

He shook his finger. 'Not like this.' Then he started to tell the way, tell the pictures of the route, the features of his journeying. From this account Loïc drew his own map. Rivers, valleys, roads that slewed round slides and boulders. Metal bridges; check points, tributaries and mountains. Endless mountains, named mountains, mountains with or without glaciers. Mountains that weren't passable, some that were seasonally passable and a few passes that lead from one range into one more part of the interminable mass of mountains that surrounded everything. In reality there was only one way through, the one that had been discovered millennia ago. That way eventually joined up with the Karakoram highway. South into Pakistan, north into the Mongolian desert.

Loïc showed the driver what he had drawn. His animated face became blank, then he roared with laughter, tapping his head with his fingers and pointing at a crest fallen Loïc.

"You come with truck. At Skardu meet KKH. Go north, after Sost diesel stop. Big sign, 'Last fuel.' You get down. Climb mountain go to Wakkan corridor. Long way, good way for you."

"How far?"

He counted on his fingers mumbling names most of which weren't on Loïc's map.

"Seven maybe eight. Seven days no problem. Seven days no slip. Some times one month. This good time of year. Seven days." They all put their hands together and touched their foreheads, lips and hearts. Then laughter broke out. Seven days was only possible with a jeep and two drivers.

Loïc had been watching the sun. He knew it must be nearing high summer. He had six weeks maybe two months before the first snows. They agreed with his calculation, they also agreed that they could no longer be sure of anything. In the last ten years the glaciers that peppered the area had retreated so fast that there was more flooding than freezing. At one time it was easy to get around in winter by walking on the frozen rivers but now it was rare if the edges froze. The high water levels made travelling by road a hazard. Bridges were the problem; often the footings were washed out by the high waters.

While they talked Loïc considered his options. His objective was to get through and out of the mountains and head for home. He needed to get his priorities in order. His mind drifted to those other mountains of his homeland. They too were only really accessible in the right season. He thought about the regional transhumance; the seasonal taking of the livestock up to the high pastures. A flickering image of Anna Cecille swathed in skirts surprised him, and then, was gone.

Suddenly they were all on their feet. The host taking their cups, shaking their hands. Loïc proffered his as he decided to go with them. It felt right; he was pleased he could change his plans. As he climbed up into the toolbox, the two boys with their eggs boiled, clambered into the back of the truck, flashed him a smile and settled onto the sack pile.

From Satti the road skirted along the valley side, rising only from the water's edge when the scree slips covered the road. The going was easy and the road good. Before Thirit a yellow sign posed the riddle, 'Left is Right'. On a single road it seemed to be merely a clever play on words, until a fork appeared. The right prong going up into the sand desert of the Nubra, the hot springs at Panamik and the ice wall of the retreating glacier. The driver hauled a left, which was the right way to pass through this complex of crumpled rock that filled the landscape from valley bottom to bird's eye view. Loïc saluted his old destination.

They followed the wide Shyok river basin. The polished promontories along its sides spoke of a huge glacier that had run its grinding course millennia before. Now its legacy was shelves of fertility, characterised by the green fingers of poplar trees competing playfully with the vertical rock striations. These sentinels stood over the tiny fields and terraces marking habitation amongst so much rock. A line of yak picked their way across a rock-strewn plain. Strands of the river wove around huge moraine banks seemingly marooned in mid valley. A thin line of water level green gave the promise of a harvest on the far bank.

Bends and more bends before rounding a bluff and a whole new vista opened up. Here the rock had been replaced by sand dunes. A high altitude desert. Not only did it surprise Loïc but also it delighted the boys who had climbed up on top of the cab to join him.

"There, there," the older shouted pointing to the dunes.

Camels, a picnic of camels had congregated. They idly watched the truck as it passed at a distance. They were Bactrian camels, double humped without a drooped hump between them. Evidently they were replenished from the tentacles of the Shyok River. They suck up water between their teeth, filtering 30 gallons in 15 minutes into their back sacks. It seemed so unlikely to find them so high in the mountains but they too have adapted to the temperature swings of 100F in the day to -20F at night. They are better adapted than their mountain surroundings that freeze, crack and crumble all around them.

"Ship of the desert." said the younger boy smiling, pleased with his English phrase.

They exchanged names.

"Mergen," he said pointing to his chest.

"This Baykt," he grabbed the older boys shirt.

"My name is Loïc," he held out his hand.

"Baykt," said Loïc, fumbling with the pronunciation.

"Baykt," repeated Mergen.

They were immediate friends. Loïc to be their hero; the boys Loïc's divided self.

The placid obstinacy of camels slipped from view behind the dunes. Trees fringed the purple valley sides while the road wound its way between crags before dipping into the green mosaic of the Hundar valley. At this point the river basin spreads wide and flat between the mountains that pounce at steep angles directly upwards. This is truly 'the heartland', where man, beast and water have transformed swathes of river valley into havens of production and rugged settlement. They stopped. After yak butter tea and samosas everyone climbed aboard again. The wind had picked up and heads were wrapped with any cloth that was to hand. Sweeping across the valley, a twister rose in a gritty column before dying out on the far side. The river flowed with them as the road showed signs of fraying at the edges. At times the clear water was contained in a channel. At other points it divided and took impetuous detours across the expansive plain, weaving from one side to the other, forcing the road up across precarious steep inclines; a ribbon crimped over a shifting shoulder.

Oil drums and sticks indicated the boundaries of a landing strip soon lost in a splendour of vapour funnelling down the tributaries of the Shyok and into the Nubra. Tranquillity descended with the soft clouds as they shredded on severe snow peaks. For a long time the valley raced ahead with no sign of leaf or stem. The road hugged the left slope having at times to climb up adjacent valleys to bridging points and then hairpin back down to the main valley. Long stretches of daunting insignificance ran mile after mile. After crossing one of the metal bridges the boys pointed down at the ground.

'Kashmir, Kashmir.'

An untended state line slipped beneath the tyres.

At Yagulung the road split, and the driver, following the same road sign 'Left is Right', skirted round three huge rocks, mountains in their own right that straddled and blocked the valley. The road left them mid-valley and steered away from the river, reconnecting kilometres later at the throat of a narrow gully with vertical sides. The road at this point had no option but to be cut from the severe slope of the mountain that formed the left bank. One mistake and the descent would be rapid and final. After an hour of total tension they rounded a huge curve; opposite was a military encampment, bleak and with no sign of movement. Above on a tiny shelf of green, were grasses and fruit trees, apricot and apple. It looked so unlikely, Loïc thought, and at the same time so restful to the eye. After a sweeping bend there were many more. The road was forced to cross the now narrow, deep flow to the other bank, which was immersed in chilling shadow. The three of them climbed down into the truck back whilst the truck took bend after bend. By nightfall they reached the welcome settlement of Turtok. The silhouettes of plane trees swayed on either side of the river as they pulled in at a house with a swinging kettle and stopped with a distinct oil dry clunk.

Beyond Turtok the road was not passable by wheeled vehicles. Two small settlements clung to the slopes, the further was Thang, and it was here that the herders had hobbled their other yaks. They had taken two yaks to Turtok, it was these 'shaggy mats' that they had loaded with empty sacks the next morning. The distant villages either side of the river were the outposts of Kashmiri India. Officially there was no further access along the valley, ahead lay the 'Line of Control', the border of India and Pakistan. Loïc fingered his Elvis passport and felt dubious. In fact there are two paths, one on either side of the river. Wandering animal tracks that pick their way through the terrain, unhurried and underused. The Line is imagined and not even marked by a bored soldier with a year's supply of Leh berry juice. Two engineered metal bridges crossed the river within sight of each other. Technically this was a dead end. In reality the waters continued to flow in their endless search for the lowest point.

At Thang they spent some hours gathering the herd, nose looping them and dealing with hobble burns on their fetlocks. After the sacks were loaded on the bigger yaks, the boys climbed up and they moved out. They made the Frino Bridge by mid afternoon. This was an altogether different way of crossing the river. The structure had been compressed into a twisting gorge; wood cantilevered from stone stacks on both sides and joined with a springy central section. It was a footbridge strong enough for livestock one at a time.

On the far side, the path picked its way around huge naked boulders. Below the torrent sprang in a foaming rage downstream. Loïc admired the ease of the boys on the shoulders of the lead yaks and felt decidedly safer than in the toolbox of the grinding truck. It was good to be back on the ground. For some time they took this ancient path, flanked by rock polished by passing animals and steadying hands, the unimproved Silk Route of legend. This artery of trade had forged new minds and determined great fortunes and it was only the width of a loaded pack animal. There was a charge, a pulse that remained in the twisting between the rocks that Loïc could read; the continuity of human endeavour, a lust that had driven the expansion of opportunity and knowledge.

His musings were brought to an abrupt stop. The path in front had disappeared. Above was a cut out overhang, below was white water. Where the path had been there were wooden pegs hammered into the rock face with nothing between them. Below a plank was wedged between the rocks with a build up of water behind it; otherwise there was no sign of the walkway. Without discussion ropes were uncoiled and Mergen, the smaller of the two boys, was lowered down with another rope to tie to the plank. Dangling over the torrent with both hands free he was swung out to the wedged plank. The water tugged at the trailing rope swinging him downstream. Once he had hooked a foot around it he tied the loose rope end on to it and swung away, skimming the surface and calling to be hauled up. Instead they lowered him, laughing, leaving Mergen scrabbling up the flailing line. Then they brought him up to safety and he beat his fists on the chest of the anchorman, furious at his duplicity.

Loïc felt that in some way this show of callousness was for his benefit. They were watching for his reaction to their sense of humour. These were a people used to living on the edge under harsh conditions. Any opportunity to sharpen the wits of their young helped to ensure survival. There was no malice in their humour. Then everyone was laughing as they got back to the serious work of rebuilding. With the plank back at path level and layed over the protruding pegs, large flat stones were sourced from downstream. These they laid across the plank, over lapping each other, making a crude path across the gap. They stomped across a few times, settling the slabs while the lead yak looked on apprehensively. Smaller stones were hauled in and packed in to take up the slack. Still the yak looked on with head lowered. The baggage was unloaded and manhandled across the now firm but narrow shelf. The lead yak pawed at the ground. The boys crossed tentatively with one hand trailing the rock wall to their right. The lead yak followed behind them and with the leader across, the rest followed. Loïc found it hard to believe that a few hours before there had been no way through and the only option would have been a two-day detour. It was then that he suggested putting a short rope around the plank for the next collapse.

For the next time, he remonstrated.

Next time is in the hands of the great mystery.

Making such provisions was not the way of approaching the future for these people.

With their yaks loaded they pushed on, the path often little more than a gap between boulders and beneath overhanging rock. It took most of the day to squeeze through the narrow gorge and when they finally emerged it was to a widening valley and snow capped mountains once again. By nightfall they reached Frino; the chorten and the prayer flags had given way to the minaret and the muezzine. Hats had changed, Buddhism had been left behind. Loïc felt the acute difference as they walked with the yaks over the next four days. They intentionally camped between settlements, during the day there was little contact with the people they met.

Reception was civil but disinterested, they were off their territory, a tolerated left over from a painful past. This was horse country, yaks were for backward paupers. The road now ran on either side of the river, bridged by serious engineering constructions. The towns of Marcha and Lunkha were tiered mosaics of fields and irrigation channels. Mosques and long narrow polo grounds became dominant structures. Everywhere there was substantial stonework, the fragile and unpredictable mountains had, for a square mile, been cemented into a human order. Poplar and willow hemmed the terraces of barley. The people were well dressed in a thick woollen cloth, sloppy shoes and all the men without exception wore moustaches, which they continually fingered, adjusted and trimmed. These were Kashmiri people in Pakistan occupied territory. Arbitrary borders determined by artillery positions with no reference to natural boundaries.

Gradually the Shyok River grew in volume. Melt tributaries cascaded down into the valley from both sides, swelling the flow and making for tricky crossings through the icy water. Once they had reached Khaplu small rivers had joined the flow, filling the whole riverbed and pushing the road up onto the sloping scree banks that were secured by conifer plantations. This valley that had enabled the passage of peoples and the invasion of Asia, was as dramatic as it was interminably tedious. An unceasing mixture of exquisite beauty and trudging repetition. Around each bend in the river, at each junction of a side valley, the mountains stretched into the distance. The enclosure of the valley bottom gradually became more and more oppressive. Loïc felt trapped in a maze of troughs that threatened to consume him if he dared to leave the river's flow. Had he been able to take to the wing he would have seen that he was right, here the red rock of the Karakoram Range beat up against the white granite of the Himalayas. Had he climbed into the eye of the local bearded vulture, *Gyaeptus barbatus,* and cruised the white crests of these ranges he would have despaired at the impossible vastness of his task.

The yaks preferred to be off the road, which ground their hooves leaving them sore and lame. For Loïc it was better that he drank chai and played Parcheesi at their evening stops, than thinking too much about his situation. He knew movement brought change.

Khaplu was as far as the berry traders were going and once the town was reached, which was spread amongst the typical patchwork of tiny fields, tall trees and stone houses, the small group split up. The yaks and the men continued up the spur of the Hippi valley to their homes. The boys and Loïc were taken to meet the impeccable Mr Dar.

"Call me Rahim." No one ever did.

23
Reaction and Response

Mr Dar is slim, dark and dapper and very decidedly Kashmiri. He is very conscious that he is surrounded by Pathans who he considers to be ruthless and a little uncouth, but as he explains, a childhood in Shrinagar is bound to make a man accustomed to his refinements. Mr Dar is delighted to meet Loïc, sends for some sweetmeats for the boys and positively beams at the prospect of intelligent conversation.

Little does he realise that Loïc too is a mountain peasant. Those however are not these mountains; those are European, that is different, an altogether different quality of peasant.

He laughs; Loïc joins him in this stupid distinction.

"I'm sure you were educated in Paris, Lyon or some other centre of learning."

"I'm sure I was not educated beyond reading," was Loïc's retort.

"My education is that of the encounters along the way, encounters with people such as your good self."

The flattery was perfectly pitched for Mr Dar, who was soon engrossed in Loïc's story and applying his considerable knowledge to the matters at hand.

"In two days I have to go to Skardu with these boys. They start school at the madrassa and I am their mentor. From there the Karakoram Highway goes north, south and there's plenty of traffic both ways. Don't take the bus, we'll find you a reliable trucker. Do you have any money?"

" Little."

"What do you have?"

Loïc emptied his backpack and pockets onto the table. It really was a pathetic collection of valueless odds and ends. The bow and arrows were broken beyond repair. A few twists of paper with their plant contents, his spare clothes and Oopie's cover were rags. His Chinese parka was more stitched than stuffed and the few coins he had were of the wrong currency. The only things that Mr Dar put to one side were the leopard skin hat and the Elvis passport. Turning over a Lakshmi Travel card his face changed to one of re-assurance.

"These people have been arranging your travels I presume?"

"They have arranged nothing but they are always around. Who are they do you know?"

"Yes I know, let's say they are here to help."

"How do they know who I am and where I'm going? They've dogged me since the Coromandel coast."

Mr Dar flipped through the passport. Ignoring the question.

"No visa for Pakistan," he noted," have to fix that."

Loïc was amazed, hadn't he noticed it was a fake?

"There's no visa for Afghanistan either. You can't go anywhere without a visa you should know that, you've travelled far enough."

Loïc showed him the folded hand drawn map, the 'last fuel stop' and the valley leading up to the borderline.

"You can't get into the Wakhan from the KKH. It passes near Sost but there's no road in."

"I'm told," started Loïc.

"Yes, yes," said Dar, "even tanks can't get through that way. I know where you mean. There's a turning circle at the end of the track, then a wall of rock. You have to climb up to the snow line before it levels out. I've checked out that border. It was at one time my job. You can get in but what for? There are only a few Khirgyz guspan breeders who are poor and primitive. Not a good place for a young man like you."

"Poor is how you see them, that's because you value people by their wealth. Isn't that right?"

"To some degree, that's so. Wealth brings power."

"Knowledge is also power; knowledge of how to survive and adapt, which is what your so called primitives do very well. I've seen it over and over. Flexibility, knowhow and imagination, with those you can do anything. With money what can you do? Impress the stupid, buy stuff and get robbed."

"We are very different and I disagree, however it is my place to help you. Since I have the money I shall spend some on you. You need some clothes, two visas and a new hat. Looking down. He added shoes to the list."

"The clothes we can buy here in Khaplu, the visas will take some time. What size are your feet? I may have a spare pair that'll fit. Come let's eat."

Loïc felt judged. It gave him the feeling that he wasn't really being taken seriously, as if his opinions would pass with the passage of time.

"42 European size." He mumbled.

Meanwhile Mr Rahim Dar; benefactor, liberal Muslim, educational pundit and mine owner, recognised an old anger of his own rising to the surface. Resistance to his way of thinking always brought him, after quietly bristling with rage, to a place of doubt. Whenever there was a death at one of his mines, the same doubt about the rightness of his actions descended over him. It was short lived, he was too busy to give it too much attention, but he knew that one day soon it would catch up with him and then everything would have to change.

What was it that he saw in this wild young Frenchman? He knew part of the answer but chose to deny it. He had been here before; young men were always coming to him for help with changing their impoverished lives. Often they were prepared to do anything to avoid scraping a living deep in the isolation of the mountains. The beauty of a place is hard to appreciate when you spend your time just surviving in it.

They entered another room of Dar's house, that looked out over the town, which ran down to the white waters of the river. The bare wooden windows framed its hostility. They ate, the boys on their best behaviour, Loïc uncomfortable but not sure why. The rice, dhal and subji were good but it didn't divert Loïc. He felt ensnared by this kindly man and his unclear intentions.

Bakyt and Mergen appeared clean and smart the next day and climbed into the back of an ancient but immaculate Hindustan Ambassador, the Indian version of the Morris

Oxford Mark 3. Four doors, good suspension, chromium bumpers and a ball on a stick for a gear shift. This was once the official status vehicle of the Subcontinent, a car that spoke volumes about your wealth. Mr Dar climbed into the front with the driver. Loïc, awkward in long shirt and baggy trousers in grey cotton, a thick woollen waistcoat and a spare pair of Dars leather shoes, climbed in with the boys, clutching the pill box hat.

You know the Dalai Lama has asked all the Tibetan people to burn all clothing with animal parts in them?

"Why?"

"Because the Chinese have made a fashion item of them and are killing more rare animals to provide swift sales to the Tibetan nationals.

"This hat was given to me."

"I knew the owner, good man. Not so sure about the son. Boys these days." He glanced into the back of the car and smiled.

Negotiating the road out of Khaplu was easy and very soon the valley opened out. Stands of conifers occupied south facing stretches of the riverside. Goats nibbled in precarious places and the numbers of small horses increased. Quickly conversation ceased as it only can on a car journey, everyone content to be lost in thought as the world slips past. Around Barah Mr Dar pointed out some mining activity high up on the valley sides. Waste piles crowded the road's edge.

"Quartz," he said, "cloudy so not good. Not enough pressure." Then lapsed back into silence.

The boys looked at each other and grinned. Loïc thought about the quartz seams he knew in the Pyrenees and then Anna Cecille. Was she married, did she have children or what?

Just past Kelis the Indus River joined the Shyok, overpowering and flooding the whole valley, which opened out even further. It was now a plain with a large flow. Half an hour later they pulled up at a checkpoint. A soldier with white spats and a beret weighed down by an outsized badge sauntered over to the car. He chatted amiably when he saw Mr Dar, his words passing across the face of the impassive driver.

"Give my regards to the Major." The soldier saluted and released the string. The barrier lifted and the car pulled away.

"New line of control," Mr Dar offered by way of explanation. "Pity Kashmir didn't become a country when it had the chance. Life would be that much simpler."

Loïc had nothing to say and the driver was not expected to give an opinion. The car lapsed back into silence.

The sharp teeth of the mountain started to soften, round out and pale to a yellow tint. Fruiting apple and pear orchards appeared at roadside settlements next to desert dunes. The river was now a stable flow, a deep trench all the way to Skardu. Plantations in the sand jostled with high stone buildings, torrential streams and tidy terraces. This was the regional capital. They passed mosques, hotels, a big polo ground with stone bleachers and a commercial airport. Mr Dar made it clear that he had business to attend to and dropped Loïc and the boys off near the main mosque.

"Give me an hour, I'll pick you up." He thrust paper money into Loïc's hand. "There, get some food into them." He pointed to a small dubbah.

The street was entirely blocked to traffic by a bus. This was not just a bus; this creation was clad with chromium fittings that extended from the wire wheel hubcaps to the ornate railings around the roof rack. Chain pendants and painted mud flaps competed with numerous lights, horns and visors. Picture panels, mirrors and a distinct shine made it the most glamorous object Loïc had seen since the gaudy temples of southern India. If he were going to travel in one of these he would have to wear robes and rings. They edged past examining the detailed painted panels and then found samosas and chai.

Later Dar arrived with the driver. They took the only road out of town, then a valley spur in the direction of Shigar.

"'I'll show you one of my mines."

They drove for some miles and pulled up at a couple of stone huts. Steps cut into the rock led upwards. Loose sand made it dangerous and steps had to be swept to make the climb. Almost vertical, the mountain rose up from the road level a hundred feet. In places a rope was fed through metal eyelets hammered into the rock face. Otherwise there was nothing to hold onto. Near the top the sheer path split. A seam of softer rock a metre thick had been reached. This was one of Dars mines. There was no wheel; no shoring, just hand picks and a very long drop to the road. Here it was that his two workers had gradually indented a horizontal slot in the mountain. Holes and slight recesses edged along the seam making a rabbit run access to the semi-precious stones embedded in the softer rock. Dar showed examples from the diggings - aparite, sphene, morganite and quartz. There was also aquamarine, emerald and tourmaline. Taking one of the workers picks he carefully cut round a beautiful golden topaz extruding from a quartz cluster. Within minutes it was in his bag undamaged. In places single tourmaline spikes protruded from the rock face catching the light. They edged along a shelf to one of the holes. Loïc had long since gone barefoot, Dars shoes, laces tied, dangled from his neck. In the small recess one of the workers was probing around a large conglomerate of morganite by candlelight. It was a slow process; the prize was surprisingly large compared to most of the stones. In the hole it was possible to relax but with the three of them and the candle there was little air.

"Why no safety gear?" Loïc asked fearing the descent on the grainy steps.

"There's little or no profit on this scale, it's more a hobby than a business."

"But at least a rope for getting up and down."

"If I have a rope everyone comes. Everyone thinks it's good money but they are frightened to come up if they know it's not safe. It's security through insecurity." He smiled pleased with his aphorism.

"People die doing this for you?"

"Yes, more would if I fitted a rope."

"These mountains are full of climbers fitting clips and running lines, why don't you learn from them?"

"Listen we've been pulling semi-precious stones out of these seams for centuries, the market's small and the profits minimal. Once princes and kings bought the best, now it's collectors and mystics. There are stones from all over the world crowding the market at super low prices. What to do? Maybe nothing. Just to leave them where they are is one option. Another is to create the market, which is difficult since we have become a political pariah. We had a gem fair in Peshwar for ten years or so but the only people who ever came were other miners, a few military commanders to see if we had found any diamonds yet and the odd minister looking for trinkets to curry sexual favours. There's no international market here, maybe the rich have found other things to spend their money on. It's certainly not coming into Pakistan and Kashmir. So no rope."

"Sounds like you need a major find, Get you back on the map."

"That would be nice. While we're waiting I mount the best pieces in rings and take them down to Jaipur in Rajastan. Like these." He held out his left hand, which glittered with silver and mounted gems even in the gloom of the mineshaft.

They were eating up the oxygen and the candle started to gutter. Crawling to the entrance Loïc looked down the cliff surface. It curved away into the void rapidly. Far below the boys were throwing stones into a stream. Far above a couple of vultures, rare at this altitude, circled on a thermal. His heart was in his throat.

Between the shoes swinging at his neck, the strong sharp breeze and his rising panic, Loïc made his way along the rock shelf to the descent path. Mr Dar pointed up to a second seam but Loïc had lost interest. How to get down was bringing him out in a sweat. He peered cautiously over the edge; the path disappeared into the abyss.

When fear comes it rises like nausea. Organs contract and conspire to send blood to muscles and mind but here there was no place to run to and no enemy to overcome. Instead Loïc's fear fed upon itself. He could hear Mr Dar babbling behind him about stones and collapse but he sounded far away. Loïc was in a bubble and beyond the reach of mortals. His feet were rooted to the spot, his breathing staccato; beads of sweat begun to ooze from his skin like squeezed poison.

The precipice, the void was calling him, beckoning him

forward. Death was talking to him. This life, this existence was about to end. Is life really that random, that absurd? When the end comes is there no order, no director of events, no force, no grace, and no guide?

Mr Dar had stopped talking. Loïc stood trembling in front of him. He looked down and then shook. The heels of Dars shoes knocked together at his throat, his feet would slip and he would die. He would fall through time and space, hit the ground far below be broken and die. His future was crystal clear, clear and short. Fell off a mountain: dead.

Mr Dars hand was on his shoulder, his voice far away asking the stupid question.

" Are you alright?" Why did he ask such a stupid question when clearly there was no answer?

'It's all pointless.' Was running a loop in his head.

"It's all pointless." His shake was becoming a quake. He was quaking from the inside. He was becoming fear itself. He was now its expression. Irrational, starved of sense and on the brink.

"It's all pointless," rushed from below his navel, up through his contracted intestines, swept through his acrid stomach, squeezed through his oesophagus and roared out of his mouth.

"It's all pointless," bellowed down into the valley.

"Ointless, ointless, ointless," bounced back off the walls.

Loïc's mouth twisted into a wry grin. He was right, it was pointless, the mountain said so. He breathed again. The valley didn't seem like so much of a void anymore. It had after all swallowed his voice so at least a part of him was already down there on the valley floor. He peered over the edge, the boys were waving. He managed a feeble hand flutter.

The presence of death nudged him forward onto the steep cut, his path. Mr Dars mouth fell open as his third best pair of shoes flew into space like an amputated bolas, and disappeared. Loïc turned to face the mountain and started down on all fours. Gradually, very gradually, he began the descent. As he went, he thought about what the valley meant to him. For weeks he had travelled the river valley through these mountains. There was no other way, follow the flow; it leads you down, always down. These valleys had a vast emptiness to them, wide and varied, a severe place for plants, people and animals to flourish with such exquisite delicacy and sensitivity. A place of comfort in all this jagged snow capped severity. Not so frightening he thought as he reached up to the section of fixed rope handrail. Turning, he sat gripping the rope. He again peered tentatively over the edge. Again he called out.

"Coming down!" Down, down! His echo yammered back and forth.

The boys shouted something back but he couldn't make it out. The trembling had settled into an occasional shaking but he was very hot and the day wasn't.

He kept climbing, brushing away the windblown grains from each step. Progress was gradual, blind but gradual. He didn't notice and if he had he would have surely stopped. In his attempt to have maximum contact with the surface he backed down a narrow mining shelf that levelled onto the horizontal. When it became flat he knew that he had gone wrong. He stood up to see where he was going. He followed the ledge round a bluff thinking that it may lead down but it was not the case, it tapered out. He was standing on next to nothing, near to nothing and slipping on the collected granules of rock. He realised his mistake. His feet began to slide toward the edge. A massive wave of fear kicked in freezing him to the cliff face. Unable to go forward, unable to step back, a fresh wave swept through him. Not the clear density of fear, this was laced with a sharp zing of panic. The longer he stayed the more he slipped towards the edge. Survival took over. It was now or not at all. He watched as he jumped high enough to switch his foot positions and turn his body, then he was scrabbling back along the path to where it widened and joined the way down. He didn't stop there, not sure of the route down, the adrenalin kept him moving, less cautious, clear and determined to turn the fear of this void into a companion and guide. He realised as his feet touched ground adjacent to the road, how much he had wanted to feel his homeland beneath his feet. He slumped down besides the Hindustan. The boys arrived with his shoes.

"Guspan Loïc, Guspan," they laughed.

He joined them as tears welled. He'd said he'd had something to learn in this mountain fastness; he was certainly finding out about his limitations. Mr Dar climbed down behind him his pockets bulging with stones.

"That better?" he quipped.

Loïc glowered at him; he was beginning to dislike Dars insensitivity. Not everything was hard and harsh.

"I'm almost ready for the next one," he slipped in.

"Don't you have a diamond mine somewhere round here that we can fall down?"

"Come I show you somewhere nice, my house, I'll make you a proper tea."

They climbed back into the car. The driver took them further up the valley to a low stone house overlooking the steep valley and the watercourse that incised it. Mr Dar studied his finds in a bucket of water. The driver and the boys went into a neighbouring house and Loïc sat outside with his confused anger.

It started that evening when Dar asked Loïc what he wanted to do with his life. Questions not unreasonable, questions that asked by anyone else he would have done a good job of answering. But Mr Dar made his queries sound like an interrogation. His dislike of Dar was growing.

By nightfall a heavy mist had covered all surfaces in water droplets and dullness had sucked the lower register of sounds into itself. Loïc could feel himself being drawn into unfamiliar internal territory, alarmed he found his defensive stance crumbling. Dar's questions were now his questions; he was expected to be someone doing something, something in particular that would describe who he was and what he was worth. That's how society organised its hierarchy with degrees of impoverishment overseen by a minority of wealth. How was it that the few had so much?

"You really want to know? "said Dar from behind him.

"Yes I certainly do, you think you know?"

They were at cross-purposes but that matters little when emotions are high. At that point people don't listen to each other anymore.

"I do have a diamond mine some distance from here. Close enough to visit tomorrow if you like."

Loïc was dumb struck. He seemed to be digging himself a pit to fall into. Dar was immune to his frustrations.

For the next two days mist filled the valley, dense, brown and heavy with fluid.

Dar said "mist below, rain above."

Loïc, trapped in the house, resisted being reactive and softened knowing his frustration was only a weakness in his self-expression.

They ate, slept and waited for the weather to change. On the second evening Dar produced a magnifying glass and some stones from his mines and as Loïc looked at them lit by lamplight, Dar started talking about their qualities. At first he was just stating the obvious, the colour, the structure and where he had found them in the mountains but then it changed.

"This one, morganite, is also called pink beryl, is very good for breathing."

"Breathing! How can a stone help you breathe?"

"Try holding it on your throat, see what it does."

Loïc took the small stone and pressed it to his throat, swallowed a couple of times and waited to be disappointed. He stretched his neck and breathed through his nose. He had struggled with the thin mountain air since losing the Enfield. He rolled his head and relaxed, his breaths came easier and deeper.

"It's true, it's easier and my lungs feel bigger, that's amazing! How does it work, auto suggestion?"

"It can't be auto suggestion because it works when people have their eyes closed or are asleep, in my opinion it's a matter of frequency."

"You mean how often you do it."

"Not that kind of frequency, the other kind. Vibrational resonance, its wavelength - what it's putting out? Everything is vibrating at some kind of frequency. Do you experience that?"

Loïc sat and thought about that. Yes everything is giving

off something; colour, smell, shape, movement, yes and frequency, maybe he had to concede.

"Well that frequency changes from thing to thing and stone to stone. Morganites frequency is similar to the heart organ in the body. It's said to have a high frequency, one that inspires spiritual love and compassion but for now you can breathe better, you feel uplifted and that's helping you to oxygenate. When you breathe, you inspire, you open both your lungs and your heart so you naturally feel more at one, more empathy and if you feel you're closer to things, you naturally feel more compassion. All these things are qualities of Morganite. This is what this stone does for the human. It first helps you open the lungs and the rest follows. Magic eh?"

"I never knew stones could do these things."

"Even if you don't know it happens anyway, you just don't know why. These mountains are mostly granite and granite is the natural home of Morganite. Just being in these mountains is uplifting. As for compassion, Buddhist monks thrive on it round here don't they?"

Loïc was warming to this Mr Dar, his patriarchal authority was giving way to the teacher in him.

Outside the mist was clearing; the evening taking on a deep orange hew, chasing the remaining vaporous wisps down to the Indus.

"So if everything has a frequency, we must have a frequency." Suggested Loïc.

"That's what we are, molecules vibrating at various frequencies. You've heard of Max Planck, the grandfather of quantum physics?"

"No, never heard of any of that. What did Max Planck have to say?"

"Well Planck's observation was that all matter originates and exists only because of a force which brings the particles of an atom to a vibration that holds that atom together." He paused to look Loïc in the eye. "We must assume that behind this force there is a conscious intelligent mind. Some would say that was God but Planck called it a 'matrix of matter'. That way it is without personality. I too find it easier not to bring religious ideas into scientific thinking."

"I'm not sure I get that," said Loïc, "everything is vibrating at frequencies that hold them together, is that it?" His hand quivered between them.

"Yes, all matter has different rates of vibration. So wood vibrates at one frequency, water another, stone another and people another. That's how you can tell the difference between them. If they were all vibrating at the same rate everything would look the same.

"Is that right?" Loïc doubted.

Dar continued. "To go a little further, all humans look different from each other because they too vibrate at different frequencies. This you can see but it's not so easy when it comes to stones and trees and water. Everything is matter vibrating to maintain its current form.

To the human every human looks different, to a tree all humans look similar. Because of thought humans create distinctions that trees wouldn't bother with."

"So are you saying that if I consciously change my thoughts that I will create another reality for myself, another form?"

"That's right. Within being human nothing is fixed. Our thoughts condition our expectations of life. Changing your thinking will make differences to your life but not your appearance, well, maybe a little, but you will remain human because you only know human frequencies."

"So you're saying life's a pool of matter waiting for a frequency to give it shape and form?"

"Yes, but humans are always being inhuman to each other, they can't just materialise as humans; they have to be materialistic and become part human. Insatiable and curious, it's their particular frequency I suppose."

"They're not all like that. Most people I meet are very humane, caring and courageous I'd say. Maybe they're the more balanced type that I attract? Mind you saying that, they're usually unusual. So if I understand you right, if I change my thoughts, I change my life."

"Change the frequency of your thoughts and your reality will follow."

The kerosene gone, the wick started to smoke. Dar suggested an early start and they took to their beds, the boys asleep by the fire. Loïc's head span with ideas.

Next day Bakyt and Mergen clean and smart climbed into the back of the ancient Hindustan Ambassador. Mr Dar sat in beside the driver. Loïc awkward in Dar's shoes, with pillbox hat on head, climbed in with the boys. Thick mist had covered the river valley for the last two days and today was the same.

"Mist down rain up." said Dar again.

The driver started the car and pulled out of the walled compound onto the Skardu road. It was going to be a dreary drive, no views no vistas. Leaving Khaplu by the new road was easy going. People walking at the roadside appeared fast out of the gloom. The windscreen was immediately covered with water although it wasn't raining. The driver slowed to a walking pace, the visibility no better. As they dropped down to cross the river it cleared a little but the thick bank of mist swept down the valley overhead. The bridge was closed for repairs, as often happened; driver's were being encouraged along the bank a little way to a shallow fording spot. Other vehicles, including a car, were going through. Mr Dar nodded to the driver. The water was a trickle of melt at this point, running between rounded pebbles. Two years before everyone had to drive through the river to get to the main bridge, it was normal.

Starting to cross they hear a shout but can see no one. Mid stream there's a building roar coming at the driver's closed window. A tumbling ooze of water rocks and mud smacks into the side of the car and sweeps it off its wheels. Suddenly they are moving very fast sideways. The knocking of rocks on the chassis is the first big sound. Then comes the tipping. The boys scramble onto the seats to try and get away from the pounding floor. The engine is roaring now, the panicking driver has his feet hard down on both the brake and the accelerator. The car starts to go. Starts to be pushed up onto its side. The mudslide has a real purchase on it now. They all fall against the drivers side and the car starts to spin. There's a grinding sound and one of the windows bursts inwards. Mud floods in from below. Loïc is lying on top of the boys who are squashed and screaming. Mud is everywhere and its gone dark. Loïc gets a foot on the side of the drivers seat and gets his weight off the boys. He reaches up and finds the window winder and a shaft of gloom illuminates the situation. They've stopped spinning and are now sliding down one side of the flow. Loïc straightens up and out of the window. Outside people are running along the bank. A muffled 'don't damage the car.' comes to Loïc's ears. It's Dar upside down on top of the driver. The car is careering on a smooth course to a deep part of the main river. Things are not looking good. Loïc reaches down and grabs one of the boys hands and hauls him onto the side of the car. The bank is close but everything is moving.

"Jump, jump." Loïc shouts as he gives him as mighty shove. He's in the air a long time. Loïc can see its Baykt in the hands of the gods. He doesn't wait to see a landing; he reaches down for Mergen who's already climbing the backs of the seats. Dar is shouting, but the driver seems to be speechless. With Mergen hauled onto the side of the car it seems they have moved into midstream. The jump is too far to the bank. Downstream two boulders are narrowing the flow, forcing the mudslide through a gap.

"There, there." he points.

They ready themselves. The car slews round, caught. They throw themselves onto one of the huge rocks, Mergen slipping back, Loïc hauling him up onto solid ground. The car momentarily seems wedged in the narrow gap but the build up behind it pushes it through. Dars head appears at the open window, he climbs onto the side of his beloved Hindustan. He's shouting now, the fear in his voice cuts through the cloying mud. Loïc raises himself, and then people are lifting him to his feet. He runs. He's surprised how fast mud can move. The car with Dar balancing on its side doesn't seem to get any closer. Then it hits something solid, jars and Dar is left hanging from the window frame his legs being swept away in the thick grey ooze. Loïc is abreast of him now running along the bank. He's quite close really, he can almost touch Dar.

"Dar, Dar." He shouts. Dar seems to be in a trance. Hanging on for dear life. Loïc bends, grabs a rock and throws it at Dar. It hits him in the back, Dar groans.

"Dar Dar," Loïc shouts," Dar your hand."

Dar strains his head to see.

"Your hand, give me your hand."

Loïc is still running. Dar reaches out. His other arm can't take his weight and the pull of the mudflow. Loïc seizes him and is dragged forward. Dar is still holding the window frame, suspended between them, his legs dangling in the broiling flow.

"Let go, damn you," shouts Loïc.

"Let go you stupid bastard." He's been wanting to say that.

Dar isn't letting go. Loïc can feel his hand slipping through his fingers.

"Let go, let go."

But he can't let go, not of his precious Hindustan. Not now. Not after everything he's been through to get this far.

Loïc still has him. He's still running but he's being pulled in. Then he's gone. Slips from his hand. Slips through his fingers. The car for a while glides downstream. Dar dangling from its side, slurry to his waist. Slowly it rolls over on top of him and sinks roof first and drops down into the main river where it lodges upturned.

The boys are at his sides, clutching him, watching, breathless, speechless, holding on to his hands.

Mergen says. "What's this?"

Loïc opens his hand. In it are Dars three rings from his left hand. The big fat diamond, the emerald and that small morganite that he likes, muddied but glinting in the misted light.

They look back to the car; the mudflow has built up behind it. Slowly it slips to one side and drops into the churning waters of the Indus. Leaving no sign of the driver or Mr Dar.

For a while the three of them walked along the bank, dazed, staring into the flow.

Loïc wonders about his thoughts and feelings about Mr

Dar since he met him. None of them were very positive, in fact there had been times when he had wished he was rid of him, and now this. It had been Dar only hours ago saying 'your thoughts create your reality'.

Could he really have brought this into being? Others, who have watched events unfold, steer the shocked threesome to vehicles and the road back to Skardu.

24
The KKH

By this strange twist Loïc became simultaneously wealthy and responsible. The boys had lost their mentor; were far from family and not placed in a school. Most people in Skardu knew Mr Dar and had heard about his demise but not about the rings.

Loïc tried to make contact with the Leh berry traders but both they and the truck driver had moved on. The boys kept talking about Sost and the seminary. Checking his map showed nothing, but the library in Skardu turned up a map of the area. Sost was on the Karakoram Highway 300 kilometres to the northwest. Overlaying his map on theirs, Sost looked to be in the right direction and by now it was very clear that there was only one way through these mountains for an outsider and that was with the traffic. Yak, truck or bus.

For the next few days they hung around Mr Dar's house, uncertain and still in a state of shock. Loïc busied himself with cooking and mending clothes, unable to make the next move. He noticed how different the boys were from each other and how similar they were to him, the two sides of himself.

The frailer of the two, Baykt seemed unconcerned about his future or the death of Mr Dar, almost philosophical, eating and sleeping as if nothing had happened. While Mergen could not stop talking about the details of watching another person die. He was fascinated and kept asking questions like would Mr Dar's lungs have filled with mud before he stopped breathing. How long would it take for all the paint to be scraped off the car? Where was the driver and why didn't he get out of the window? For Loïc it was another brush with death. Another encounter with the nature of impermanence. He certainly had death as a close companion to his life.

A man from Mr Dar's bank, and it was Mr Dar's bank, arrived. Loïc told him of his plan to deliver the boys to Sost.

The man wanted to know if Loïc had sufficient funds. Loïc as usual had none. Then he showed him the rings from Mr Dar's left hand. He was not suspicious, and if he was he didn't show it. He only asked if Loïc had a use for them.

To be honest he hadn't but he liked the morganite stone.

The manager took the diamond and the topaz, refunding Loïc on the spot. A large bundle of large denomination notes left a briefcase and filled his hands. Suddenly the weight of wealth and responsibility felt good. It placed him, affirmed a new purpose of his journey, and gave meaning to movement; the constant movement of his life. The manager was not there to console. He told Loïc to be at the bus stand at six in the morning and left it at that. As soon the boys and Loïc were out of the way then the real battle for Mr Dar's fortune would begin.

The next four days were cramped, tiring and continuously fraught with the very real possibility of plunging off the road, either into foaming currents or deep ravines. The bus driver chain-smoked and everyone gagged with nausea. The KKH was little more than a rubble track with occasional pull-ins. The word highway had been stretched beyond any correspondence with usability and only related to altitude. It was a wonder of the explosive arts. Huge overhangs featured as normal and very occasionally there were truck stops and chai stalls. The rare sight of an animal was a diversion; otherwise the view was of rock in its many convolutions. The faces of the stoical passengers hardly varied as they jolted along the impact lines of where the Himalayan and the Karakoram ranges meet.

Night stops varied little. At the back of the tiny chai shops there were dilapidated tents stuffed with thick quilts which in turn were stuffed with insects that gorged themselves on the choice customers that filtered through. Occasionally a passenger would climb onto the bus in the morning looking swollen faced after a particularly venomous night. The driver despite his smoked vision never skipped a beat, and if it weren't for the numerous punctures would probably have never stopped. The punctures were the province of the bus boy who, armed with three polished metal levers and a large leather mallet peeled the tyres from their rims with a magical speed. The inner tubes he repaired with knife cut squares from the remains of another tube and a tar-like glue, which he dusted with dirt from the roadside, then foot pumped back up to pressure. The little time this took was miraculous, and the whole bus stood around laying bets on parts of minutes.

By the mid afternoon of the fourth day they pulled up at a small town that straggled along the road. " Sost" the driver called from behind his usual cloud of nicotine and Loïc and the boys thankfully climbed down from the minibus for the last time. For the whole journey tobacco smoke had made Loïc feel sick but never once did he vomit, nor did any of the other passengers.

The seminary was the largest building in the area, set back and above the rest of the rock and earth town. It resembled a place that you might put animals that you no longer cared for, but the director was a kindly old man with a ready smile. He soon eased Loïc's apprehension, telling him he could stay for a couple of days while the boys settled in.

It was during the next two days as Loïc and the boys let go of each other, that he found out the details of the landscape around Sost. To the inexperienced eye the place still seemed to be mired in the never-ending folds of the mountains, but apparently and according to the school caretaker this was not so.

"The corridor is only a two day walk from here. A walk, a climb and then another walk."

"What corridor?"

"Very famous valley, the Wakkan Corridor. Very particular. Politically very important. It is the finger of Afghanistan that kept the Russians out of India. Now it is the back door the Russians used to invade Afghanistan a few years ago. Yes very famous valley. Only way in from these parts. From here you have to go over the Wakhjir pass."

The caretaker dismissed himself and took up a sparse looking besom and busied himself pushing a few leaves around the courtyard as the director walked past.

Loïc tried to digest his good fortune. So the Wakkan

corridor lay only a few days away, his heart raced at the prospect of getting out of the mountains.

N'zingu came to mind.
'The journey is in the detail, not in the destination.'

Next day he climbed the mountain behind the seminary. It was rough loose rock and plantless. At the top he could only see more mountains, mountains in all directions. Still the prospect of the 'corridor' excited him. That evening he ate with the boys who had now made new friends and were much more concerned with the immediate than Loïc's imminent departure. They enjoyed the food, tucked the money Loïc gave them into the folds of their clothes and then were gone after a brief embrace. As he sat drinking a 'namakin chai', pink with salt, he felt the loss of the boys. Since their breaking into his morning reverie clutching eggs they had been his travelling companions. Both as aspects of his younger self and as the bringers of responsibility, they had shown him how his ability to respond was a natural pleasure and not a burden.

The caretaker parked his besom at the door and poured himself a salt tea, took a seat at a respectful distance and lit a cigarette.

"What's in the Wakkan corridor for you young man?"

"The beginning of my return I guess."

"Return to what, where you came from?"

"Yes I'm going back, I've been away long enough."

You may think you can go back, you may even get there, but you will have changed, the place too will have changed, you won't recognise each other. There's only going forward in this life if really alive is what you want.

He pulled on the white tube of black tobacco and spat.

"You'll have to take a gift of change, then you won't return empty handed."

They sat in silence, Loïc sipped, he sucked.

The schools director crossed the far end of the courtyard. Loïc hurried after him and paid the boys fees for the next four years from his fat roll.

"Mr Dar's money."

"Dar's dead you said."

"Yes drowned in the river."

"Shame, there's few men like him in these parts."

"I leave first thing tomorrow." Loïc decided as he spoke.

They shook hands and Loïc rejoined the smoking caretaker.

"Can you tell me the way to the Wakhjir pass?"

He raised an eyebrow and leant on his broom handle.

"North of here, say 10ks, there's a fuel depot, oil drums and hand pumps. There's a sign saying, 'the last fill up until forever' or something like that. Opposite there's a track going up into the mountains, there's no sign, nothing, you go that way. It feels like your going nowhere and you are. First you come to Misgar, ten houses maybe, you stay on that side, don't cross over. Then there's Watwashk a little bigger and finally Mulangi. These people will never have seen anyone like you. They're friendly if a little inbred, so they can be rather odd. You'd better not stop there, you'll probably get offered a girl, they're always looking out for new blood. After Mulangi, which is about 20 kilometres from the road, the track stops and there's a turning circle. That's it. On the high side of the circle there's a goat path that goes up and out of view. That's your way over the pass. I've never been up there but that's the Wakhjir Pass."

Loïc had sketched a map as he spoke. He knew this was going to be a major test of faith for him. He showed it to the caretaker who took it in and then waggled his head from side to side.

Which of course means, yes, no and maybe, if you like.

25

Into the Wakhan

It was warm and clear by the time Loïc turned off the road at the final fuel stop. He had walked the 10 kilometres along the KKH just to find his pace. Little traffic had passed him and he tried clearing his attachment to the boys with Druckshen's third mantra.

Ci kyang dgos pa med.
I don't need anything whatsoever.

He felt he really was leaving.

Misgar was little more than a rearrangement of loose rock from the mountain. There was no sign of cement and the dry stone cube houses were chinked with crumbling yak dung. An old man watched and smoked as Loïc passed. Otherwise little moved.

The track cut along the right bank of a small torrent, clear and ice cold. From Watwashk the valley rose gradually and he reached Mulangi by midday. The people assumed he was heading for the glacier and pointed up saying, '2ks, 2ks.' Loïc kept moving, the track stopped at a tank turning circle after twenty minutes and a collection of stone animal compounds littered the mountainside. He looked around for some sign of the caretaker's goat track, but there was little but rock and more rocks.

'So often,' thought Loic 'I block my own path by imagining how things are; shape colour even atmosphere before I enter the reality. I project to stave off the fear of the unfamiliar. Then when I arrive in the anticipated place I recognise nothing and then despair at the mismatch.

It wasn't till Loïc sat down on a boulder to come to terms with this feature of himself that he noticed the small brown capsules of goat droppings at his feet. Then he started to notice others, they seemed to be everywhere, some of them fresh. He knew them well. One of their childish games had been to cut a branch of hawthorn in spring flower and try and pierce the soft balls onto as many thorns as possible and then present them to the girls as posies. The brown balls and the white flowers looked exotic together but the girls always ran away disgusted.

Then there was a bleat. A bleat out of nowhere. Was this too in his head? Perhaps a bleat from a Pyrenean past. He scanned around nothing moved, this wasn't neck bell country. This was where shepherds used slingshots on the lead goats not just the predators.

When he did see its face, it was the yellow eyes with the horizontal slit iris that caught his attention. The markings and colours of its face were well adapted to the granite and the snow. The goat waited, watching Loïc, waited, watching for Loïc to realise. Then with a shake of its head, wattles flying, it turned and took off up the side of the mountain. Loïc knew the look of a lead goat. He followed.

The col led up between two snow clad peaks. A steep incline with the solitary goat ahead. After an hour or so the ground levelled out and a whole new highland valley spread out before him. In the distance another mountain range. The rocky ground had begun to soften, as he continued it became boggy, thawed tundra. As he stood and stared the goat turned back, tail erect it produced more brown pellets and trotted back knowingly.

For the rest of the day he walked, avoiding the softer ground as best he could. It wasn't easy, the further he entered the valley the more watery it became. At times he was sucked down into the gelid bog up to his knees. By evening he could see a cloud rising from the ground. It didn't behave like smoke and his curiosity drew him closer. It was steam, steam rising from the surface of a large pool caked with pink salt. What more could a weary body ask for? Loïc peeled off his sodden filthy clothes and gradually immersed himself in the hot saline water. As the day closed he soaked, the salt pricking every pore, dissolving the aches from his body as he floated under a canopy of starlight. What he didn't know was that the salt had come from a sea now gone for over 125 million years. A sea that drained away as the impacting Himalayan and Karakoram mountains rose leaving the salt pink and clean. This salt it is remarkable to say, contains 84 of the possible 94 trace elements to be found in human blood. Not only that but the proportions are the same as naturally occur in the water of our bodies, one percent. This correspondence is said to rebalance the energy of the body when taken in small amounts. None of this crossed Loïc's mind as he soaked up the heat and the dehydration. For him it was a dreamy prelude to a night in a blanket and a Chinese army parka, before heading the next day at dawn along the west bank of the infantile Amu Darya River. Known to become the Oxus, which springs from an ice cave a short distance from where Loïc soaked.

Before long he saw a group of conical stone towers with square bases perched on the far riverbank. These were the tombs of Bozai Gumbaz a Kirghiz chief who died in battle on this ignominious river bank some 150 years earlier. The tombs were banked up with rusting rolls of Russian army concertina wire and defunct butterfly bombs. The kind of landmines that children inadvertently pick up and set off.

The Russians had brought 3 million land mines into Afghanistan in their 1979 invasion through this strip of wilderness. One land mine for every family in the country. Even now livestock and shepherds set them off and children no longer marvelled at the staccato flight of coloured wings.

Loïc sized them up from his side of the river, found them on Elvis' map, and moved on downstream. The river was fiercely cold and cut its way through the shallow valley undercutting the banks. It was at a point where the bank had collapsed that Loïc met a young Kirghiz boy watering a small flock of guspan. He was dressed in red, a long sleeved coat decorated with a floral motif, a short black and white beaded waistcoat and a red beaded pillbox hat. His wellington boots were a pale blue and he looked at Loïc in amazement.

"Guspan?" said Loïc.

"Turki goey," said the boy. Giving the regional name of his favourite delicacy. He looked around for some explanation for Loïc's sudden appearance.

"Kirghiz?" said Loïc.

The boy nodded," Kirghiz," he said and patted his chest, pride spilling out as he offered his hand in an adult fashion.

"Jurgal." He announced.

"Loïc." They shook hands.

He was moving his flock and Loïc walked downstream with him; Bright points of tiny flowers peppered the short summer grasses. Before long Jurgal took his flock away from the river's edge and up onto the higher ground of the valley side. There other flocks had converged, the transhumance was about to begin. This was all very familiar to Loïc. Every summer in the Pyrenees the same movement of stock to the high mountain meadows brought the riches of summer into sharp focus. Here he was again, doing the same thing on the other side of the world. Trudging up stony paths to lush highland pastures. Anna Cecille came to mind, a querulous resignation on her face. His desire to talk to her was tearfully strong.

Karchyndy was reached by evening where a small yurt settlement had been erected for the season. Domed yurts the colour of pale gritty snow, their covers ragged at the edges looking like animal skins bleeding into their surroundings.

Jurgal introduced Loïc to Torsoon Boi the leader of the Akbilis. As they met Loïc knew this was a crucial moment in his travels through this remote corridor of wind and ice.

26

Right Place - Right Time

Torsoon Boi sat at the back of his yurt with his knee high boots on. His felt jacket decorated with a column motif, soft, but architectural. Over this was a leather pocketed waistcoat. He wore his light hair short and his clipped moustache marked a subtle line across his dark severe face. He gestured for Loïc to sit next to him. Loïc decided to keep his boots on, a wise move under the circumstances since the women were expected to clean up after the men. He remarked on Loïc's snow leopard hat and Loïc showed him a picture Elvis had given him, of a man in full Tibetan costume smiling at the camera. On his head perched the same pillbox hat. Torsoon Boi touched his heart. This was a deep affection sorely missed. He clasped Loïc's hand and looked deep into his eyes.

A female whale floated through Loïc's mind, again he felt seen into.

A Kirghiz woman came in and poked the small earth hearth and checked the blackened kettle for water. She wore the same flower patterned Chinese brocade as Jurgal but cut into a skirt and long jacket. On her head she wore a high ribbed hat covered with a white headcloth that trailed down her back with one end thrown around her neck. She didn't speak while she mixed barley dough in a white enamel bowl. Torsoon Boi ignored her and Loïc understood that this was a cultural trait as opposed to there being any bad feeling.

Torsoon Boi pulled out a red wooden box. The woman glanced at Loïc then retreated to her bread making. He pulled out a long stemmed pipe and set a tiny brass bowl to its end and charged it with a black sticky substance and lay down against the bed edge. He tilted the bowl at a burning candle and pulled on the stem, a sweet sickly smoke formed a blue layer and the light went from his eyes.

Loïc took in his surroundings. The earth floor was alleviated by the thick carpet on which they sat. The lattice wall was knotted with leather thongs and hung with Chinese carpets. Tied to the tops of the lattice the roof spars rose up in a steep curve and slotted radially into the roof crown, a wide tension band decorated with repeating lozenge shapes, pulled the wall and the roof together. The place mixed poverty and style. The cooking utensils were of polished Indian aluminium or floral print Chinese enamel. Here in this remote place were the fruits of bauxite mining in southern India. The woman made a tea using the same pink salt as caked the hot springs and presented it in a pot with two glasses on a tray bearing the image of a tiered pagoda. Loïc smiled, briefly the corners of her mouth wrinkled then she was away shouting at the red robed children who peered in through the open door.

Torsoon Boi, the glaze of opium in his eyes, offered Loïc the pipe. He refused, and instead sat sipping the pink tea and considered the harsh realities of survival in the winter months. Intense cold winds funnelled down the valley making -40F a common occurrence. Snowfalls blocked the one road for weeks on end and at midday on most days the rock face on the north side, prised by ice, broke free and crashed down the mountainside becoming scree.

The dough began to rise under a cloth next to the stove's meagre heat. Loïc felt solitary in the company of Torsoon Boi and stood to leave. The woman patted the air. Loïc sat again now knowing this was a time to wait. Leaving would be an unwise insult. He kicked off his footwear and got comfortable for the long haul. Travelling had taught him how to wait. How hasty first impressions are just that. How they dominate western social behaviour. Never allowing space, time and silence to feel your way into the situation, using all your senses.

Taking the initiative Loïc pulled Dar's morganite ring from his pocket and slipped it onto his finger. Torsoon Boi registered the movement and the glint of light. Somewhere in the recesses of his stupor a spark fired. He leaned forward and put his forefinger to the outer edge of his eye. Loïc held out his hand. Recall registered on his face as he lost himself in the depth of the mounted stone.

He had in earlier times been free of the 'sticky black' that now plagued so many adult males in the Pamir districts. His mind had been clear, his body an expression of a sharp sinuous strength that reflected his high mountain origin. Now through a miasm of intersected memories he made a link with a truth from his past. He started to speak but the memory was realised in a single tear. As it welled up from his eye duct and began its descent, the interior of the yurt, themselves and the emotion that had evoked the memory were all reflected in the glistening bead.

It was two days before they met again.

In that time Loïc explored the high pasture and decided that this was a place of disappearance. Nothing lasted long before the cold and the winter wind saw to its end. Although the populations of animals and people was few, they were at their limit. The summer pasture was spare and had little hope of increase. The tree cover was threadbare, a few birch and sallow hugged the banks of the Amu Darya. One morning walking this high pasture land Loïc surprised an urial. Timid and rare these mountain deer with long ribbed spiralling horns are sacred to the Akbilis who use them to mark shrines at dangerous places in the landscape. It made eye contact with him and then was gone, leaping from rock to rock with immense bounds.

The only things in profusion here were rock and space.

The few buildings, stone boxes piled high with twigs and the remains of dried yak dung, hugged the ground trying to avoid the winter winds. Now, during this brief summer, the yurts, their truly adaptable homes, moved with the animals to the higher ground. Families by marriage and allegiance gathered at Karchyndy to share gossip and find partners. For the rest of the year the Akbilis people, perhaps only a hundred yurts in total, were spread thinly over a broad swathe of hostile landscape. From all directions they gathered on this high green plateau, creating their spectacle of rounded yurts draped with crude horse rolled felt looking like fairy rings of overnight inkcap mushrooms.

The men strutted around smoking imported cigarettes and discussing animals, weather and women. Most had abandoned their traditional dress and wore synthetic shirts and zip up trousers. Only the hat remained. The Wakhi hat is a rolled up head sack characterised by the tubular details round its hem. It is at least of dual if not multi purpose and here on the plateau competed only with the occasional turban. Loïc still wore his snow leopard pill box and many of the older men, not so much admired it, as recognised it as being that of the Kashmiri photographer. Which in turn brought Loïc some status amongst this traditionally suspicious people.

The women however were much more stoical about outside influences and still wore their traditional clothes to show family rank and wealth. Painstaking embellishments of their clothes using buttons and applique, spoke of status and leisure time. Red was the predominant cloth colour; outstanding in snow, often with a sprinkling of floral high lights embroidered onto the material. Like the children the women wore swathes of white beaded necklaces and their hair in long plaits. The men meanwhile had lost their power to the scissors of modernism. Occasionally Loïc saw a traditionalist, his plaits tied up to cross over his forehead. His dignity intact, while others tried to integrate with the short cut of the flatlanders.

Torsoon Boi laid his hand on Loïc's shoulder. With it came a brief but distinct affectionate squeeze. He said nothing but cracked open a carious smile. Apparently sitting with him in his opiate presence had been the right thing to do and now a reminder to 'always listen to the women', brought alpha monkeys to mind and he too smiled, if a little nervously. Torsoon Boi ran his hand around his shoulders. His acceptance amongst these people of the icy corridor was made clear to those around them.

Since the 1650s the western demand for the numbing effects of the white poppy had continually increased and the ability of supplying from the region had inevitably led to local addicts. It was the scourge of a people who survived by their wits and a constant awareness of their surroundings. The effects of opium weren't needed in an already delicate situation, especially when it was the people's leader who had become the addict.

Torsoon Boi dramatically thrust his hand into the folds of his wrap across jacket and pulled out the same wooden box. He fitted the bowl to the stem and charged it with a ball of sticky opium. All eyes were on him. His addiction was well known but it was never practised in public. For a long moment Loïc thought he was going to be asked to share a pipe to confirm his acceptance. The growing crowd was wary of this display. He offered Loïc the pipe; held up a Zippo lighter emblazoned with a hammer and sickle and span the wheel. Loïc shook his head as the flame roared inside the windshield. Torsoon Boi and Loïc held each other's unblinking gaze.

Loïc knew that it was risky to deny a chief anything but this felt more like a challenge to see whether his resolve would hold. He had learnt that intimidation was a bluff and that more often than not the bullying type was in pain and probably suffering from low self worth. On this occasion none of that reassured him. He held the stare, as it had become.

He had struggled with his dilemma hard and long, Torsoon Boi's decision was being finally sealed. He lifted the pipe and his eyes. Slowly his other hand floated up and also took the pipe. Suddenly with a swift movement, he broke the stem and dashed the parts to the ground, grinding then beneath the heel of his studded felt boot.

A cheer lifted into the thin mid morning air as nomadic hands were put together in appreciation of the rarity of the moment. Everyone knew the horrors of a 'cold turkey', the ravings and cravings as the drug gradually weakened its hold with lack of intake. The sweats, the deathlike chills and the gripping pains they had seen before but a public statement such as this was not to be taken lightly. If so, all power and authority would be gone, relegating Torsoon Boi to a future of disgrace and loss of respect. This loss of face Torsoon Boi was not going to allow. Loïc put a soft hand on his stiffened shoulder. He knew he had been used, he could only hope that it would be for the good.

Torsoon Boi stamped again, this time on the wooden

box, turned and ran towards the line of tethered horses. Immediately all the men turned likewise and sprang onto their mounts and en masse took off at a gallop across the flower-pricked meadow, whooping and throwing their hats in the air. To Loïc these tough riders on their stocky steeds looked like centaurs, man and horse combined, much like the first horse riders must have looked to those that only saw the horse as meat. Apparitions travelling at speed, viewing life from an elevated position. The myth must have travelled as fast as the riders. Half man half beast, combing the land, hunting at will. Arriving with the kill and no exhaustion. Evolving human.

These impressions swept through Loïc as he watched the swarm of riders thunder up the valley towards the limpid crystal waters of Lake Chaqumaqtin, the breeding ground of the mammoth Himalayan mosquito.

Meanwhile the women, knowing the significance of what had just taken place turned their attention to the preparation of food. Some collected the fresh horse dung for drying, others sized up the rumps of the assembled flocks, others poked fire into life beneath cooking pots.

That night before the festivities, Torsoon Boi gave Loïc a felted horse cover and a single rein for a Kyrgyz mare that stood tethered out in the sharp wind. The food was plentiful and the extended family ate together crammed into two connecting yurts. 'Non' a flat bread was spread with 'istach' a yak cheese and passed around as a starter. With it was drunk small bowls of 'kara chai', a milk and rock salt tea. Later there was 'katama', boiled sheep's head stuffed with 'kaimak' a kind of yak cream, mixed in was 'chigri' a mush of wild grass stems and 'piaz' the rare wild onion, the only vitamin C source in the region. The conversation was light and punctuated with laughter. The infants were swaddled and hung on the trellis walls, their cribs removed to accommodate the throng. They watched the evening pass, absorbing their culture from a vertical vantage point.

Once the food was eaten everyone left, knowing this would be a difficult night. The pots, bowls and babies were all removed and Torsoon Boi took to his bed as the cramps started and the spectre of withdrawal loomed large. The next few days and nights would be unpleasant and painful as his body craved its usual fix of opiate. A test of Torsoon Boi's resolve. If he could break with the hold of the poppy then he would be an even greater leader. That night his people prayed for strength. So many of their men had embraced a relationship with the poppy sap and not themselves. If Torsoon Boi could do it then so could they.

Leaving the yurt for the big outside Loïc stood beneath the belly of the moonlit sky sizing up his small horse. The impulse to move on was strong, stronger than the affinity he felt for these mountain people. He ducked back into the yurt, pressed his palms together, bowed and took his bag. The women smiled and did likewise. Torsoon Boi scratched at the writhing of insects beneath his skin.

27
In the Back Door

Outside the slight breeze carried a cutting edge. The clothes that he had been given, he wore them all. The felted saddle he draped over the horse and arranged his possessions to hang either side. His bearings were clear, he led the horse from the moonlit settlement south to the Amu Darya. As they went he talked non-stop to the horse, telling her all sorts of nonsense stories to teach her his voice. It wasn't until the first signs of dawn as they reached a wide expanse of moraine that he mounted her and rode. She was reassured by his tone if not his language and responded meekly to his fumbling attempts at using the single rein and his knees. She complied as he learnt.

They passed through ghostly stands of squat white birch trees, standing stiff and upright to the wind. These were the first plants above ankle height that Loïc had seen in Pamir and their presence gave him the feeling of home. His journey through this massive folded landscape had often felt endless, lost in a maze of extremes. The sight of chattering birch trees reminded him of his mother and all she had taught him about the tree of rebirth. Its uses for rheumatism and arthritis, he had collected the buds and bark with her and pressed out the oil and made liniments. She had cured his father's eczema with a birch sap salve. She always said that the birch was 'rushing mighty with the Holy Spirit' but then she said the holy spirit was in all the curing plants. Along with the sallow and the aspen they were the first to come in behind the retreating ice line. The sallow was a wildfire wood perfect for making a spindle and baseboard for friction fire. It always followed the melt and hugged the streams. As for aspen, this was a chatter tree, its leaves never stopping; even on a stone still day it still whispers 'susurrus, susurrus'. These pioneer trees told Loïc that he was at the edge of change, one climate meeting the extremes of another.

After dawn he pitched up between a birch and the first seepage of a stream. From here it would drop down into the Amu Darya which he was following west, later to become the Panj and soon after the same waters would emerge into mighty Oxus. The sun was well up and the thought of thawing out after the nights chill was too good to pass on. While the horse watered Loïc soaked up the sun lying out on a rock. As the breeze and the sun alternately chilled and warmed him he fell asleep. He woke with a dry mouth and a burning face.

The mare browsed at some distance, the chill of the spring water on his face woke him to the fact that he was alone in this corridor of ice and wind and these brief few hours of warmth and light would soon be over. West and downstream had a bitter urgency to them. The mare was compliant, she too liked company and they moved on down the cracked and crumbling valley until at nightfall they found a grim stone hut at Khan Bibi.

Below Zangok the next day, Loïc again felt relief when he saw stands of willow and poplar along the watercourse. Within an hour he encountered a bridge and relished the feeling that he was getting closer, to what he didn't know, but closer none the less.

The way along the Panj river westwards passed through scattered villages backed up from the river's edge. Apricot trees, heavy with fruit, tempted him from his mount. Small with a rich flesh their taste was exotic after months without sweetness apart from a rare rock sugar chai. He stuffed his pockets and kept moving. He found a herd shelter at Baharaq and was soon in the company of Wakhi farmers, the girls laden with strings of lapis lazuli and the boys standing proud in sky blue wellies. This was a barter economy, the sedentary Wakhi needing meat and animals, the Khirgiz needing grain. A symbiotic interdependence away from the world of war weariness that was the rest of Afghanistan. A day later Loïc reached Sarhad and the beginning of a road.

In Sarhad it was assumed by everyone he met that he was in this remote place to buy lapis. No one believed him when he pointed back up the Wakhan corridor. If he wasn't buying lapis it was agreed that he must be a spy, since there was no other rational explanation. Loïc ignored their speculation and sold his horse to a Tadzhiki trader who had sold barbed wire to the Russians and then been employed to scrap it when they retreated from their unfinished invasion. He was a man that didn't take sides and soon found how to accommodate the needs of both. He was not liked, however he was able to offer a good price. Sarhad had about it a strong feeling of tension. The usual curiosity that Loïc attracted was replaced by suspicion. Although the men folk were still killing time in the few tea stalls their attention was on the street not their parcheesi boards. Guns bulged under clothing and women and children weren't to be seen. Loïc sought out a food hall but no one would share his table. Men stared at him unashamedly as he ate his food too fast and left. It was the same on the street and it was only a matter of time before a tall, armed man stopped him and asked what he was doing in town.

"Selling a horse."

This did nothing to satisfy him as he fingered the safety catch.

"What else?"

"Just passing through."

"No one passes through here unless they want to be killed. I suggest you get your lapis and get out. That way." He pointed south and said "Sar e sang."

Loïc nodded. Perhaps he could get interested in lapis if that would help to explain his presence.

"Sar e sang. Is there a bus?"

"No bus, no bus station." He pointed south as before.

"Sar e sang."

Loïc moved in that direction.

It was clear that out of town was where he needed to be. He was unused to such obvious hostility and selling his horse had been a mistake. He had thought with a road there would be some other kind of transport. He had overlooked that he was emerging from a dead end. No one, as the man with the gun said, comes out of the Wakhan except Kirghiz herders and Wakhi farmers, and he was certainly neither of those. He needed his horse, at least that way he would be on the move.

Out of sight of the gunman he took a side street and doubled back into town and found the horse trader's yard. His horse was where he had left it. Now looking dismal, with head down in the sun, her value had jumped four fold and the Tadzhiki trader showed no sign of guilt. For a change Loïc was not without money thanks to Mr Dar',s death. He paid the inflated price and lifted his felt saddle off the paddock fence. The trader made as if to say something but Loïc cut him short with a clear 'No'. He also took down some tired looking braided harness and rode onto the main street, the stuffing bulging out of his Chinese parka at the elbows. There was no reason to think that the town was going to get anymore pleasant so he took the way west.

On his way out the same men glowered at him from the tea stalls. Loïc noticed that many of them were his age with faces lined by anxiety. He avoided eye contact and rode on. The villages along the way he avoided, the landscape he still marvelled at, even after months in the mountains. Low light on the rock surfaces threw up exquisite colours. The clear azure sky, enormous and achingly pure, formed the backdrop to ochre red and grey rock formations cut through occasionally by rainbow bridges that straddled the water courses along the way.

Loïc's progress was slow. Gradually the valley widened and swung towards the north. A fold in the mountains revealed a slight change in geological impact and pressure. He had arrived at a natural frontier, the landmass formed into less severe slopes and angles.

It wasn't till he reached Ishkashim that he made human contact again. Finding that it was not a good place to sell a tired horse, he accepted a low price just to rest up his saddle sores.

He booked into a small hotel and ate. The food was boiled and full of animal parts that he tried not to identify. From the balcony of his room he watched the main street. Two doors down every ten minutes the owner appeared with a broom and swept the tiny area of cracked concrete outside his shop, conspicuously he didn't look at Loïc. Twice a battered minibus emptied its contents on the corner and drove off. The passengers rapidly dispersed leaving the street empty within seconds. Occasionally a hurried figure would walk to the corner, buy a single cigarette from the vendor and return indoors. Loïc felt that life was on hold and everyone but him knew why. By nightfall the place was silent. By midnight he was sitting bolt upright as distant explosions played out a light show on the wall of his room. For half an hour a bombardment took place then abruptly stopped. The town continued to sleep as if everything was normal.

By contrast the next day was chaotic as a whole new population descended on the town for market day. The street was transformed by country folk selling their week's produce. As he dressed he realised the leopard skin pillbox hat of Elvis' father had served its purpose. He had probably never brought his camera this far. It was time for a new hat. On the street there were a number of hat sellers and he observed the fitting and buying of these tubes of coarse wool. There was not a man who didn't wear one, as there wasn't a man who didn't have a moustache. Choosing a stall and measuring his head with an outstretched hand he matched the spans with a hat, making sure that the hat was a little bigger, he copied the other buyers. Fitting the hat over his elbow and straightening his arm seemed to be the stretching method before putting it on your head. Trying it on first was out of the question; head lice in this region were a major consideration at all times.

With his bag on his shoulder and a spring in his step despite his aching haunches Loïc found that with a 'pakol' on his head people started to ignore him again. It was clear from the number of rock sellers in Ishkashim that Sar e sang was nearby. Large unpolished pieces of azure blue stones were heaped in lockup shops, waiting to be collected by buyers from Faizabad. When they did come they were not armed with bundles of cash, they came with cases of Kalashnikovs. The guns for rocks trade had been established by the Mujahaddin warlords when the Americans had believed that they could furnish them with 'kill power' to get rid of the Russians. Now the place was swamped with weapons, lapis lazuli was much more valuable on the international market.

Gun laundering was the new economics.

28
Lapis Lazuli

It was as Loïc sat eating in a roadside café that he first saw a man wearing a baseball cap. In the context he looked like a cartoon character. Gesticulating and shouting in a drawled English. He was buying stones from one of the old men and making a show of despair about prices.

"Every year more bucks, every year stones more damaged."

Throwing his hands in the air he stormed across the street and into the café, slumped down in the corner ordering a coffee and settling for that god awful stuff you call tea. He was loud and gauche, the archetypal American abroad. Loïc was amused and laughed out loud. He swung round and cast about for the laugh's origin, settling on Loïc's smile.

"What you grinning about ape boy?"

"You must be Chinese if I'm an ape."

"Good god an English speaking Gani."

"You really are as stupid as you look."

"It's a relief to meet someone in this god forsaken place that doesn't want to sell something or shoot me."

"Don't be too sure." Loïc warned raising his chai glass.

Wilbur Carter, came with a large outstretched hand.

They shook and knew this was going to be either friends or foes, nothing in between. Something was going to happen and probably fast. When it was time to leave the café they did it together. Crossing the road to the same rock shop. Loïc went in too, he was mildly interested in stones since meeting Mr Dar but largely he was starved of company and this American looked like some light relief.

When the rock shop owner saw them approaching he got up to close the door but Wilbur put his foot in it, and demurring he let them in. The old man acknowledged Loïc and turned to sit down on his wellworn kilim. Loïc started to handle the stones, amazed at the wide range of colours. The old man watched to see if his interest was genuine or merely passing.

Wilbur's outburst had been one part of his show of bargaining and reducing the price. Both parties had been through this charade many times. The price was being adjusted and the volume of stones likewise. They would reach an agreement but not quite yet. Some of the stones were bigger than a fist, others finger size. It was the colour, not so apparent in the uncut stones, that drew the old man into conversation. He opened a small leather pouch and spread some polished stones out in front of Loïc.

He held up a deep indigo coloured piece.

"Neeli." He passed it to Loïc. It was both deep and soft at the same time.

"Asmani." He said, holding up a more familiar light blue nodule.

Loïc rolled it round his hand enjoying the sky quality.

The third was green and bulbous.

"Suvsi," he said.

All lapis. Same mine. Firgamu, he pointed to them in Loïc's hand,

"Firgamu."

"That's a mine," chipped in Wilbur." Firgamu mine. It's at Sar e sang, it's old. No one knows quite how old but a least seven to eight thousand years. Which is old whatever way you look at it. Anyway stones from there have travelled all over. Pieces of Firgamu lapis have been found in Ur the capital of Mesopotamia. The Egyptians certainly had a soft spot for lapis, they used to grind down the asmani blue and use it for eyeliner. Then there were all those scarab beetles they carved out of the fragments for beads. It was found in Tutankhamen's tomb by a great uncle of mine, it was him that turned me onto it. Anyway there's lapis from Sar e sang, everywhere. What do you want it for?"

"Me, I don't want it for anything, I can think of few things less pleasant than carrying around rocks even if they are beautiful colours."

"It depends on how much money they're making for you. The best ones are very small compared to their value. Good turn over for their weight, they're always good business."

"How come you know all this about lapis?

"It's good to know what you're talking about if you're selling it. Did you know that lapis lazuli has medicinal properties as well as being solid sky?"

"I like that, I'll buy some of that, solid sky."

"In ancient Egypt it was said to cure headaches and there's little that does that. Insomnia and cataracts also get a thumbs-up when treated with ground lapis.

"So what's your story, if you buy it here where do you sell it?"

"The States where else? I take the best stuff to the best markets and the rubble pays for the flights."

"You fly the stuff out of where?"

"Out of here, where else? It would take a lifetime and a spray of bullets any other way. There's an airstrip at Faizabad. Where did you fly into then, not Kabul!"

"I haven't flown for a long time, last flight was in Africa, but it was hardly a plane it was more like a colander."

"Africa!" His eyes narrowed." So how come you're here. Who are you working for?"

"I came in through the Wakhan. I'm not working for anyone."

"No you didn't, no one comes into Gannistan that way, not since the Russians. It's a no go area. Anyway there's nowhere to come from."

"Since you're so informed, when were you last there?"

"Never, everyone knows, not that way."

"Well suit yourself, believe what you like, but remember it's only what you choose to believe.

They fell silent surrounded by chunks of sky.

"Really?" the reality of Loïc registering on Wilbur's face.

"Really," said Loïc and picked up a blue nodule embedded with shards of glittering iron pyrites. "How much?"

The old man stirred and reached for his spectacles. As he perched them on his nose a splatter of gunfire hit the outside wall of the building. A stray shell embedded itself in the interior wall opposite the unglazed window. They hit the floor.

"Tell me later." Wilbur said, as they crawled through piles of stones to the lee of the outer wall. The old man dismissed the gunfire as hotheads and animated his sales pitch a little.

"Those small pieces, two dollar, those big pieces four dollar."

"So nothings sold by weight, just size."

"Size colour and shape."

"What do you get in America for the two dollar size?"

"40 to 60 bucks, it depends."

"Worth your while?"

"Mostly but I don't depend on it, I do other business."

"Something more reliable, huh?"

"Reliable! I don't do reliable, I'm good at dangerous. I do dangerous."

Another rattle of bullets broke the calm. This time they were further away.

"Kids," the old man muttered, clearly familiar with the tension release that comes with letting loose a few rounds. "OK small pieces good price one dollar."

"You think the price drops with the gunfire?" said Loïc.

"The price is a sign of desperation my friend. Only fools like us come to do business in these troubled parts. He had chosen what he wanted, peeled thirty dollars off a roll of notes, and stuffed the stones into a bag."

The old man checked the money and then the street and waved them out. They walked stiffly across the street to the teashop. It was now empty but for the owner who crouched behind a steaming urn and the boy who clutched the empty glass rack under one of the tables.

"Look I'm done here, I have rocks to retrieve from my hotel room and I'm out of here. I could use your help if you want a ride."

"A ride to where?"

"A ride out of this."

"You can't get out of this, you move around and you'll get further in."

"Oh no that's not my way. From here I go up and out."

"Meaning?"

"Meaning I have a plane in Faizabad, we only have to get that far."

"You're on," said Loïc, "let's do it."

The hotel was a few streets away and was fairly easy to reach. A Toyota pickup bulging with bearded armed men crossed the end of the street as they ducked into a doorway. No one noticed as they took an ally at the back of a butchers shop. Fly blown carcasses dangled on hooks. A dog distracted from licking the dripping meat cringed out of their way. They emerged onto another street with a mosque at one end.

"Run." They ran, fast, the dog ran after them barking. Another Toyota ground across the road junction and sprayed bullets at their feet. The dog went down. Through a door and they crouched under the key rack, hearts pumping, seizing their breath. Wilbur plucked a key off the room forty-two hook and they flew up the stairs two at a time. By the time they had dodged across a terrace and up more stairs they were out of breath fumbling with a door lock.

Loïc looked around. Pale blue paint peeled from a collapsing balcony. A few crows argued in a tree. Once they were in the room Loïc could see down into the vast courtyard of a large mosque. Chairs and tentage had been set up at one end in preparation for the amplified address of a visiting radical cleric. Children skirted a large puddle. Tethered horses flicked their tails. The muezzin was silent.

"You going to help or are you just here for the view?"

Wilbur was packing rocks into a tin trunk.

" I could use a hand getting this down."

Loïc checked one of the handles.

"They're far too heavy to carry in a trunk."

Another spatter of automatic fire sent stray bullets into the air. Another pickup cruised along the perimeter wall. Figures in the compound took shelter in the mosque.

"Couldn't we do it in a couple of backpacks?"

Loïc asked, as he took in the situation.

"You want to get this lot onto a plane now?

"Yes, all the signs say now. Perhaps you can't read the signs but it's building and something is about to kick off. I want out of here, and now."

"I guess you've done this before, the trunk I mean. You can't run with a trunk."

"You're right." He left the room.

Loïc reflected on the last hour. Compression had definitely returned with a vengeance, but there was little to suggest that there was more danger than many other situations he'd passed through. The bullets were new. He did seem to have certain cat qualities. Would they last, he mused, as he caught sight of himself in a small wall mirror. Bearded, ragged and weathered summed him up. In the context of north-eastern Afghanistan he looked either like a vagrant or an unarmed militant. Either way, with his new hat he wasn't so conspicuous.

"I've found someone to take us to Faizabad airport but we have to go now." Wilbur was clutching two woven plastic aid sacks.

Between them they emptied the trunk, and stuffed their few possessions in on top of the rocks and staggered down to the hotel lobby. A small battered taxi waited at the roadside. It sagged under the weight and choked its way down the street. At each junction the driver accelerated which made no difference to the speed but produced a black cloud behind them. Gradually they left town and gained the poplar lined road out to the airport. It seemed unlikely that the taxi would make it.

"Was this the best you could find?"

"I took the first, how could I know it was going to be its last trip?"

"Maybe at a glance."

For twenty minutes the taxi coughed and spluttered but it didn't slow. The airport was modern and modest. Razor wire defined its perimeter. A single runway ended abruptly at a bend in the Kokcha River. A fifty five-seater Air Kabul passenger plane sat at the end of the runway. A Dawi tanker truck fed a long black fuel pipe into the port above its wing. A couple of small private Cessnas were tucked in between the control tower and the fuel pump. The rest of the place was bare, flat and devoid of life. Wilbur indicated the Cessnas. The taxi pulled over. He dropped some notes into the front seat and they hauled out the sacks.

"That one, the blue beauty, I need to fill her." Loïc stood and stared. Things were looking up.

Within twenty minutes they were checking in with air control with fuel tanks full. It was a Cessna Skyhawk with two seats taken out, a single folddown bunk and fitted with foam padded stowage boxing down either side of the fuselage. The stowage was already half full of large aquamarine stones. It had been customised for sky pirate use.

"This yours?" Loïc scanned the interior. Climbing gear, parafoil, snowboard and aqualung all stashed away in drop down boxing.

"Yeah." Wilbur was checking to see if the load was balanced by looking at a spirit level built into the floor." She can carry the weight of two sumo wrestlers and that's it. More than that and landing becomes a bit of a hazard."

"How heavy are you?"

"No idea, never thought about it."

When the paddle man waived them out onto the runway they were loaded to their limit. It wasn't hard to see why the conflict in this area was terrestrial, flying opportunities were few. The Air Kabul plane had a flat tyre and the fuel tanker, now empty, was pulling across the tarmac. They hit the gas with a vengeance and Wilbur hauled the small plane up and over the Kokcha River as it wound a torrential course between the steep valley sides. The single engine was well up to the task and they climbed steeply into a sky strewn with cirrus strands of sandbar cloud. Now that Loïc could see this maze of mountains from above he was even more amazed that he had come through.

"You serious?" said Wilbur thumbing his hand over his shoulder.

"You came through that lot on shank's pony?"

"Well yes and no, I did have a Kyrghiz mare for a while but mostly it was bus and truck."

They laughed and Wilbur shook his head." Tell me."

As they flew Loïc relayed the last month to Wilbur from Leh to their meeting. Loïc was detailed and Wilbur was entranced.

"Oh, by the way I have flown before, Africa remember, so if you need a break I'm your man."

"Well to be my man you'd need to freshen up a bit. You smell like a camel herders armpit and look even worse. Check the overhead stowage, there's some fresh clothes and some deck pumps that might fit."

Their bearing was west southwest to avoid Kabul airspace.

Their altitude was over 5000ft.

Visibility, crystal clear.

Ground temperatures in the high 70s.

A light breeze came from the south.

Perfect flying conditions.

Outside the plexiglas cockpit it was numbingly cold and the oxygen was thinning.

"Here take the stick. Hardly recognise you in my kit. Could still use a shave."

Loïc slipped in behind the dual controls. It was good to be back in a metal bird. This one felt like it could go some, he checked it out. Wilbur soon knew he had himself a co-pilot.

29

Al Tar Caves

Loïc relaxed into gazing at the unfolding mountains beneath as the landscape changed. High cliffs surrounded a section of valley grid organised into agricultural pasture and arable crops. Even from this height it was easy to see the cave perforations along their length. At one point two enormous niches cleft from the face housed huge carvings. There seemed to be a lot of activity set back from the sheer rock face.

"Bamiyan," said Wilbur.

As he pointed a cloud of smoke billowed out from one of the niches. Seconds later the plane was jarred by a shock wave.

"Don't drop down," Wilbur warned.

"What's happening?"

"No idea, just raise the altitude, Probably the Taliban destroying a historical relic or two, they keep threatening to get rid of the infidel images. They've tried fighter planes and rocket fire already. There are two massive stone Buddhas in the cliffs down there, and have been for 1500 years. They've probably decided on dynamite this time. God bless Alfred Nobel and his peace prize. It was an early Buddhist community that cultivated this whole valley centuries ago. Buddhas weren't a problem until recently. It used to be a major pilgrimage site and generated some kind of a living for people. Can you see all those small caves, people live in those even now, but there are no visitors anymore, Buddhist pilgrims don't fit the Taliban picture of Islam."

A spray of bullets bounced feebly off one of the plane's wings. Their power spent at the apogee of their flight. Shells paused visibly outside the plane and then dropped back to earth, their purpose leaden.

Loïc peered out of the window as another explosive blast punched shock waves into the air. A huge cloud of rock dust belched out from another part of the cliff face. They flew on not knowing what they had just witnessed from above.

They stayed high, avoiding artillery outposts as best they could, remaining a speck in the sky. Wilbur told Loïc about his other business back in Arizona. Growing medical cannabis he called it. He said it was legal but then went on to tell Loïc that the narcotics police would fly over his land with a defoliant spray while he shot at them with guns. He seemed to be quite used to having bullets for breakfast, and guard dogs barking at the sky.

By evening they were out of Afghani air space flying at 2500ft and hungry for both solid ground and fuel. Loïc handed the controls back to Wilber as an airfield came on line with permission to land. As yet he hadn't made a touch down on his own and he wasn't going to make a mistake right now. They had reached Iran and another possible set of problems.

Mashhad had an international airport some distance outside the ancient city with a concrete spread of high-rise accommodation forming a barrier to the surrounding arid plain. There originally as a pit stop for camel transport on the Silk Road, Mashhad had, due to the poisoning in the 9th century of Ali bin Musa Al Reza, a cousin of the Prophet Mohammed, become the holiest city in Iran. Like most cities it had swelled to its climax long ago and now teetered on the edge of exhausting the immediate environment.

From the airport the city wasn't visible and they stepped down onto the tarmac of a fundamentalist regime. They checked in with air traffic control and then customs. Wilbur was an old hand and knew the procedure; all of his papers were up to date. An officer was detailed to check the plane's cargo and he stood around waiting to accept a fresh pack of American tailor made cigarettes before looking inside the plane and signing forms. Passports were produced for perusal but since they were only refuelling it was a formality. Loïc's rather distressed document produced strange movements in the eyebrows of the tired immigration officer. He flipped through the smudged pages, settling on comparing the photograph with the bearer and stamped it hard. They went in search of fuel.

"Let's have a look at that". Wilbur indicated Loïc's pocket.

"At what?" He feigned.

"Your ID brother, that's what."

He turned the pages slowly, angling the worn document to the light.

"Where's this from? he snorted, you can't call this a passport, it's so obviously a fake it's almost believable."

"Well it's as believable as yours apparently."

It says here you left France over four years ago."

"If that's what it says then it must be right".

"What did you pay for this?"

"Not a lot. Probably less than you paid for yours."

Wilbur studied the stamp over the corner of the mug shot.

"The photo looks quite recent, you haven't aged much in four years."

"Some do, some don't." Loïc held out his hand.

"Damn," muttered Wilbur as he slapped it into his hand.

"It's what you bring with you that's believable. If you're present, then you can usually affect the outcome of events especially if they involve people who are used to thinking along certain lines and we all do. We only need to be right about something or someone once and we think we've got that nailed. In reality it's us that's nailed. Nailed down to a way of thinking. Once that thinking is in place and for most people that's quite young, then things are easy to manipulate. Providing you act outside the box and think laterally."

Wilbur was trying to place himself in this idea.

"I find a small bribe usually does it."

"That's alright so long as you don't have to find bigger and bigger bribes."

"So what's with your passport?"

"That's about being believable. Sure it's a fake, but I'm a long way from home so it's bound to be shabby after four years. The picture looks like me so it's got to be real. So what I do is think about the same thing as when the photo was taken, that gives me the same expression, the rest is just sloppy artwork. All immigration officers take the job to get rich. Some passports have to be genuine, so mine's one."

"Do the thought," Wilbur said, taking the passport. "It's true you've got the same moony expression. What's the thought?"

"A girl."

"A girl! So you are a red bloodied male. Who's the girl."

"There's only one girl, the one the parents disapproved of, the first one."

"That's true, the rest are just learning curves."

They laughed. Wilbur punched Loïc's shoulder in a display of camaraderie. Loïc turned his waist and let it pass.

"Let's fuel up and move on."

While they threw together a quick galley meal from tins and packets. Wilbur told Loïc about the various adaptations he had made to the Skyhawk. The wheel cowls rotated and extended into floats, so landing on water was an option. Some of the stowage had been replaced with spare fuel tanks. Weight had been lost by stripping out all the surplus furniture and niceties. He talked enthusiastically about bizarre landings made and scrapes escaped. He wasn't a point-to-point pilot he used his plane for getting to inaccessible places, picking up fuel as and when he could. He had traded luggage space for range. Suddenly there was a loud frapping on the planes door.

"Passport."

"Passports.?"

Wilbur peered out.

"Not good, forget the cooking."

Two immigration officers stood on the tarmac. Black weatherproof jackets with reflective cuffs and back stripes over their grey cotton pyjama suits.

"Talk to them out of the window," whispered Wilbur.

Sliding the opening panel he smiled out of the window.

"Passport."

"Passport?"

"Passport."

The engine started up, slipped the clutch and moved forward. The two officers jumped aside to avoid the tail plane. They were fumbling to unclip their pistols but their coats were getting in the way. They sped down the runway. Gunfire sounded but nothing hit. It was as they left the ground that they first saw the passenger plane coming into land from the opposite direction.

"That's good," said Wilbur calmly "they won't take that out."

He pulled back the stick and cruised over the plane. The pilot's expression made them laugh as the huge bird slid beneath them. They cleared the runway lights and banked steeply over the city and struck out for neighbouring Iraq.

"Was that really necessary?" Loïc laughed as he pulled on some more clothes and slid into his seat.

"Sorry about that, it's me, unfinished business. Last time I came through they tried to fine me for cargo infringements. I didn't pay the full penalty. They're a bit slow off the mark. It's a black mark on my record. I've got more than a mark now, I've probably got a blot."

"I thought it was my passport."

"No they're not interested in you, you don't look like you're worth a bag of nuts. What they want is something that 'bigs them up' in front of their mates. I'm out of bribes so we'll just have to go 'off piste' for a while. Now we've done a runner they'll put out a general warning."

He brought up a programme on the monitor, punched in some co-ordinates. An illuminated map came up on the screen.

Kirkuk
Fuel Range; 696 miles
Current direction; west-northwest.
Regional time; 11.45
Altitude; 4000 ft.
Alternate landings.

A shortlist of small airfields came up within the fuel range.

"Don't recognise any of these, but we do have the fuel to skip Iraq. We need a small airfield just inside Turkey, definitely won't make Konya without a refill. Take the stick and bring her down some. Less distance lower altitude, but watch out for those mountains."

Loïc took the controls while Wilbur searched for a Kurdish lake.

At midday they flew into cloud a layer. Already they were close to the ground. Wilbur dropped them even further until they were in the cold cloud shadow. It was an expanse of 'asperatus undulatus'. What was it about this cloud? It had a signature for Loïc. Whenever it appeared something new happened. What next? The colours contained within the cloud's depth, blues, greys, reds and brown gave it the flavour of otherworld. Soil particles suspended in water droplets began to coat the windscreen and reduce the visibility.

"Don't use the wipers. Pull the stick." Wilbur barked. "Scratches the screen, do it do it."

They rose steeply, the light aircraft juddering with the effort; they could see nothing but the instrument panel.

"Not too steep, we'll stall."

In the depth of the cloud all the needles swung about erratically. Outside, on the trailing edge of the flaps blue light crackled brazenly. A presence entered the small craft, distinct, palpable. They looked at each other as the dials dimmed and the edges of everything glowed a neon aquamarine, flickering, redefining their body shapes. The smell of ozone gave a headiness to the air, which hissed as if things were about to burst into flame. Then it was gone. The Skyhawk breezed out into full sunlight and Loïc pushed the stick away, levelling them out. Huge undulating waves of cloud billowed below them bringing nausea to Loïc's throat.

"What was that?" said Loïc, a sweet metallic tang in his mouth.

"New to me, not like an electric storm."

"Same sort of thing happens on ships masts," said Loïc. "They call it St Elmo's fire but I've never seen it run all over my body like that. Feels like all my hair's static and there's a singed smell in here."

Wilbur opened a vent and they looked at each other and laughed.

"Plays hell with the planes O rings I bet." Wilbur

groaned.

By late afternoon they had covered 700 miles and the main fuel tank was low. They were still in Iraqi air space and Kirkuk was out of range.

"We'll have to drop her in the desert and that's best done when you can see the surface. We'll put down near here."

He pointed to a large patch of blue green.

" Zazzar Lake, It straddles the Iraqi Turkish border, We'll go for south of the water, it's remote and flattish."

It took two passes before Wilbur was sure about the terrain and the planes condition. He opted for the road, which was straight with no trucks in sight. Pulling off with the steerable nose wheel they left the road, riding over mounds of sand coming to rest near the only feature in the landscape. A large limestone plug pushed up some fifty feet above the surrounding flatness. A table mountain in the dessert, pierced with entrances and welcome shade.

"First things first." Wilbur warned as Loïc jumped down heading for the outcrop.

They refuelled from the tanks built into the luggage compartment, washed off the screens and flap mechanisms. By then the heat was intense and shade was a real necessity. Taking water and little else they headed off for the low cliff raising out of the sand.

The Al Tar caves were clearly a mixture of natural cracks and manmade excavations. The smooth door like apertures penetrated deep into the mass of stone often joining and opening up into large chambers roughly hewn from the soft limestone. Here it was cool and bathed in a breezed shadow. In places there were crude scratchings on the walls and smoke stains on the ceiling. The caves had been a refuge from the desert for centuries. Once their eyes had adjusted it was clear that they still were in use. In niches and cracks various essentials were concealed. Candles, matches a pack of cards, an old newspaper and a corked bottle of oil. Blocks of stone littered the floor, large enough to serve as furniture. An odd blend of the contrived and the natural. They worked their way through an internal maze; huge squared pillars supported the roof and separated areas. Those nearer the exterior seemed to be more domestic, while deeper in the smell and atmosphere became sombre and ceremonial, the acoustics mellow and resonant. There was a distinct odour of pine resin. They explored more with found candles. The whole extrusion was riddled with caves forming enough shade space for hundreds of people. It was nearing sunset as they climbed up well-worn steps to the outcrop roof that looked out over desert.

"Let's stay." They said together and laughed.

As they sat, looking west, the sky spun within layers of orange and pink, they noticed a small group of camels approaching out of the sunset. Wilbur's first reaction was to get back to the plane but he knew it was too risky to try for take-off at dusk.

Loïc patted the air.

"Let's see what happens." Unsettling Wilbur even more.

The plane had been spotted long since and both parties prepared for a meeting. One of the camel riders circled the plane in passing and the group came up to the caves. Loïc had learnt to be forward and open in unpredictable situations. Wilbur was anxious and preparing to run. Loïc pulled him down into a sitting position. He spoke with a calm authority, using the few Arabic greetings that he'd learnt along the way. He offered them water and invited the group to sit with them.

The camel riders were armed but not hostile. Three older men and a group of boys. It soon became clear that the caves were their destination. They had come to put the boys through a rite of passage ceremony. To them the presence of two more males was a good omen, and the plane certainly impressed the boys. They unloaded bundles of firewood, bedding, water and frame drums from the sitting camels and moved into the depths of the caves.

Very quickly they had made fire and brought two glasses of sweet mint tea out to where Loïc and Wilbur were preparing for the night under a sky domed by stars.

"Loïc?" Wilbur questioned," how come you make people feel at ease, myself included. What would you say that was?"

"Probably it's just a self-preservation issue. If you feel good about me I'm more likely to survive. If my laugh makes people smile then they feel more confident, you seem to be.

It's all survival strategy."

"Come on it's more than that and you know it."

"Well what comes to mind is to do with fear. I've known real fear a few times and I've never felt so alive, but most fear is unreal, concocted, misplaced even inherited. Fear my teacher N'zingu told me, is 'what fills the mind when it is not alert' and he says, 'that even a leaf falling from a tree will tell you something, so there's always something to be alert about.' Fear's only use is to keep you alive a little bit longer because you haven't finished yet."

All night the sound of the frame drums seeped out of the depths of the rock and into the desert. At one point Loïc woke and sat beneath the night sky. It felt like an honour to be a gatekeeper for the boys, realising at the same time he was in truth only a little older himself. At some point another tea arrived and a hand was placed on his shoulder. Simple things speak clearly. The old man sat on his haunches breathing in the sky while Loïc sipped the tea. Then he took the glass and Loïc's hand with the other and led him into the maze-like candle lit interior to a large smoked chamber. At first Loïc could see nothing, his eyes streamed with an acrid stinging, the pungent smell of frankincense heavy in the air.

The boys were naked but for loincloths. Their bodies smeared with honey and milk. They shifted their weight from foot to foot in a line across the central space. Blocks of stone and cut stone pillars surrounded them. Tiredness showed on all their faces, tiredness and a resolve not to slip into childish complaint. The cloying sweetness of their mothers no longer a restraint, they stepped in unison with the beat.

Slim bodies, wilfully erect and dignified.

This was their first time away from their homes. As they had left their village, with largely false tears, their mothers had bid farewell to their sons by lying on the ground as the boys stepped over and away from them. Under strict orders not to look back, they had joined the camels and walked into the desert. Three days it had taken to reach Al Tar and now they were being put in front of themselves. They were being reminded of their mission, to leave childish things behind and to prepare to meet 'the golden girl.'

"She," the old man announces, "is the one with two faces. One face looks for law and order, the frontal face, eye to eye. The one that tells you how things must be. The other face, the profile, the wild, moist, dragonish face of desire tells you of your manhood."

The drums, drum it in, the boys shift their weight, they are eager for part of the girl but not ready for the whole reality. The parched stone drips with flickering light.

"This one, the moist one," the leathered mouth spits out.

"This is the one you like, she excites you, but they are one."

She the golden girl comes with both faces.

She is called the woman that looks both ways.

Remember she is both law and legend. She shakes things up, wakes you up to how you feel, sparks your fire, gets you guessing. She's the one who makes you see how good you've been and how wild you need to be."

The boys are paying attention. They have all glimpsed a sister's breast, or had strange feelings about some half met, hidden girl neighbour. They have all watched rutting donkeys with horrified fascination. They half understand who the old man is talking about. In their minds they overlay real women with scary mythical characters from bedtime stories. Confusion and sense jostle and keep jostling as the boys jig from foot to foot. A brass bowl belching fresh incense clouds the boys as it swirls about the snaking line. The drums have increased in number; more men have filtered into the solid chamber from the desert night. The line of boys loosens, they no longer search for the beat of the drum, they are more a group moved by echoes of sound and thought. Flow comes from their cracked and crazed hearts into the mass of their weaving, relaxed and honoured bodies.

The leathered man looks at Loïc, they nod. He knows he must refresh his understanding of 'the golden girl'. Loïc knows that running away all those years ago was just that, running away. The law had said 'no, not like this.' - the taboo, he had been too feeble to confront. He had not chosen to leave. He had been caught up in the slipstream of a world hungry for youthful brilliance. Now he feels differently, now he knows he has a soul and he is not here by chance, his destiny he can find in the movement of his feet. He joins the dance of boymen, smoke smears his body, and he becomes impelled by the insistence of the drum.

The purpose of the dance becomes apparent as Loïc moves with the others. Before they were just a huddle of nervousness. Now drawn out by honeyed words from a leathery mouth. they have started to move into themselves. Gestures, steps and turns have loosened limbs and unlocked feelings. Each boy is throwing down his cloak of guilt, his straps of shame; the stone floor is littered with unseen constraint. They have become moved by their mellowness, their sweetness, by pleasure. They are becoming men. Individuals bleed from the group and move with the fluidity of their dance as if unwatched. One after another in naked patterns they move closer to being who they will become. The boys dance and strut and show who they truly are, unearthing their forgotten boldness, washing away their layers of worthlessness as they are led out into the blistering eye of the rising sun.

Wilbur woke to the emerging drums. Saw Loïc stripped down and moving with the others down the slope to the camels below. He watched, bleary eyed and dream frozen. He shook his head; yes that was Loïc drinking water from a goatskin like a mountain boy. By sun up a train of donkeys tottered into view carrying plastic containers of diesel topped with packs of cheap cigarettes, they passed the aircraft and the Al Tar caves without pause. Loïc and Wilbur cocked their heads towards the Skyhawk, bowed their farewells and steered the primed plane out through the sand hills to the asphalt road.

30
Flesh and Bone

Razazza Lake with its islands spread out beneath them as they took a west-northwest bearing across the invisible border into Turkey with Konya in their sights.

Position 32° 48' 34" North 43° 40' 31" East
Fuel Range 305 kms
Regional Time; 08:12
Altitude; 1000 ft.

Razazza Lake peeled off behind the thrum of the small plane leaving a monochrome featureless swathe of desert below. They flew in silence. By midday Wilbur realised that the fuel situation was becoming critical. Their compass no longer corresponded with the passage of the sun. Instruments were behaving erratically plus they were off course. The whole plane had begun to judder with any change of altitude.

"That'll be the O rings, Wilber mused, trying to keep the craft on an level."

"You mentioned O rings before, what do they do?"

"They seal all the flat plate joints in the superstructure, they cushion where metal meets metal. Now they're all slack, shrunk by that electrical storm."

"What's it mean, the plane feels like an old goose."

"That's about it, an old goose but we'll make it. A landings what we need right now."

"The read out says 38° 46' by 43° 33' that can't be right, that means we've been going north."

They peered out of the windows.

"There's a lake down there, by its shape I recon that's Van Golu, there's a strip at Van."

The plane juddered at different rates as they lost altitude. Once level a kind of flexed rigidity settled in, only to vibrate violently as soon as they dropped down. Wilbur pulled back on the stick enough to tail down and lock the fuselage joints. There was a moment as the wheels touched down, that everything felt very soft and spongy. A bemused confusion amongst the airfield staff greeted them. Why was a private American plane coming into Kurdistan? Flight control was calling it 'an alien craft', American style.

"They're claiming their territory at last, quipped Wilbur. Did you see how all the roads going south are neglected and maintained going every other direction? Severing their ties with the rest of Iraq."

An officious thin-lipped uniform didn't like the unknown language and made that very clear as he examined all the documents.

"Mechanic?" he said for the fourth time. Exploring the pronunciation. Clicking his tongue like a ratchet spanner.

"Yes, mechanic. Yes fuel." Wilbur repeated sourly.

These two were destined to dislike each other.

Loïc, risking the invalidity of his passport, gestured helplessness, with wide-open arms and a laugh; his infectious laugh. A couple of workers standing behind the uniform looked at each other and grinned. The uniform's face remained blank.

Miming, taking objects from his pockets, Loïc started to juggle the invisible. Dropped one, bent, picked it up and continued.

The uniform started looking for the unseen juggling balls.

One of the workers nudged the other and laughed.

Loïc 'bust out a couple of tricks' then replaced the magic balls back in his pocket. Then showed his empty hands.

The two overall clad mechanics, for that's who they were, gave a round of applause as Loïc bowed.

The uniform shifted his weight.

The ice broken, a private smile of amusement surfaced at the corner of the uniform's mouth and then it was gone.

With pen and paper Wilbur detailed their mechanical situation. Neat explanatory drawings flowed onto the page. Attention was turned to the common ground of plane repairs.

Within a couple of days all the affected O-rings had been replaced. The instrument problem had been traced to a damaged fuse box. The customs settled for some bottles of French wine Wilbur had stored in the galley, bottled in Fitou, which squared a circle for Loïc.

'The flock, his father, the ships timbers, the build and Anna Cecille.

He allowed a surge of nauseous longing to surface for the first time since leaving home.'

While the mechanics and Wilbur finished work on the Skyhawk Loïc was permitted to leave the airfield armed with a receipt for his passport. Elvis' artwork was well received in these parts, each new stamp giving the document more authenticity, and Loïc more confidence. He walked along the road into Van, lying along the side of the lake. More like an inland sea the water was deep enough to anchor large steel hull cargo vessels that towered above him from the quay. The town was large and modern; everywhere he looked there were white cats with eyes of different colours. In a teashop he attracted the attention of some burka-clad girls who were buying cakes. They were senior students on their way home from school. They were giggly and earnest, trying out their English phrases on him. They mixed technical jargon with personal enquires.

"I am instructed to establish the place of your origin?" One said.

"Where do you originate from this quarter?"

"Your identity is of a foreign nature?"

There was a lot of elbowing, embarrassment and of course giggling.

"My name is Loïc." He said putting his hand on his heart. This provoked a torrent of names all at once. Burkas pulled under chins. Loïc was surrounded by brown-eyed bronze faces waiting for him to say something else in English, their strong angular features bright with confidence.

A young man, Loïc's age, drawn by the excitement, joined them.

This is my sister, he announced placing his hand on the shoulder of one of the girls, who immediately pulled up her veil. These are her class mates. His tone bore the presumption of stupidity in others.

"I am honoured for you to be in my country." The naive frisson had evaporated and the girls started talking amongst themselves.

"How can you be in Kurdistan?"

"Just passing through." Loïc adopted Wilbur's non-committal tone. Fixing a plane. Your girls have good English."

"These girls are peshmerga." The young man said proudly.

"Peshmerga?"

"Yes, 'those who walk before death.' "

"Meaning?" questioned Loïc.

"Meaning, like me they are educated and trained to die for the formation of Kurdistan. For it to be a recognised independent nation of Kurds. Not Arabs and Kurds, just Kurds."

Loïc had learnt from Wilbur about Saddam Hussain's oppression of the non-Arab peoples in Iraq. How, stateless, they occupied an area reaching over the borders of five counties where they met. Historically a Persian people speaking Qurmangi and Sorani dialects, who have adapted to being occupied, infiltrated and suppressed by Turks, Arabs and Soviets alike. A flexible but stubborn race that has learnt to write their own language in Latin script to deal with the Turks, in Arabic to accommodate Iran and Iraq and the Cyrillic text to fend off the former Soviet Union.

Tapping Loïc's arm the young Kurd demanded his attention.

The girls now listened intently.

"Did you know I was not allowed to speak my own language until a couple of years ago."

Loïc thought about the implications of this.

He went on. "If I was heard whistling a Kurdish tune by the Arabs I would be sent to prison."

Loïc knew a few things about whistling, it was certainly a way of talking a different language, but prison for whistling had never entered his head.

"Yes," his sister said with emotion, "for too long we have not been allowed to be who we are."

Loïc took a deep breath, as he did the dull thud of a nearby explosion pumped through the hot air. Everyone turned to the door. No debris landed, they all ran out into the street.

"Go, go." The girls shouted." Go to your plane. This is not your place."

Loïc knew well enough not to take the direct route back to the airstrip. Instead he went in the opposite direction. It was the wrong way. An Arab girl had just pulled a detonator cord. Her body packed with nuts and bolts, she had just reduced herself and a bus full of Kurdish children to fragments of flesh and bone. The bus lay on its side, injuries were horrendous, dying was happening in front of him. Parts of children still moved. Vehicle sirens converged as people wept and bled. The sight was like no other, Loïc vomited. Red spotted fragments of blue school uniform were strewn confetti like over a slaughterhouse midden. Horror rose from the surface of everything, hanging in the air. Pages from school exercise books shifted listlessly through the mayhem on the breeze. The driver staggered clutching a hole in the back of his head; pedestrians lay crumpled in mid step. Anger was not yet present. People picked up severed limbs with tenderness, as if hoping to match parts. Loss etched into every movement. Loic groaned at the duplicity of God. Others gasped stunned and bleeding amongst the chilling remains of intermingled children.

Loïc was pulled from his horror by the same student shaking him from behind.

"You must get out of here before the police come, this way."

They ran down an alley, past cooped chickens awaiting their own deaths. Past a tap and an overflowing bucket of water, then out onto a parallel street.

"Walk, we must walk, we must look at the sky. We must be looking for the direction of the explosion, like those men. He didn't point. We are moving away from here. We need to look lost, that is normal when these things happen, everyone's hearts are bleeding."

He seemed to have gone inside.

"Come, come this way." Within two minutes they passed through a small square. A water fountain competed with a donkey for highest volume. Everyone was about their daily business. Normality was essential to maintain here, warfare took the form of isolated incidents at the very centre of a people holding firm.

"Come." The tugging helped Loïc from getting swept up in his growing trauma. In a round about way they made it to the lakeside. There was no smoke over Van, the place looked peaceful.

"Go along the lake that way." He said, pointing.

Loïc walked. Images were fixed in his eyes. He feared closing them. The waters of Van Golu were calm as ice and cared nothing for the gushing of arteries and the shredding of life. A series of short blasts, made Loïc start as a large tanker edged from the quay. Loïc forced himself forward along the waterline. Conspicuous, he walked where the swell licked the land. Nothing fitted together inside him anymore. There were no more recognisable seams. Vivid fragments pressed closely together; he walked carrying them firmly wedged inside him.

The small landing strip seemed endless once he reached it and the Skyhawk waited outside the hanger. Wilbur said nothing, just urged him into the immigration officers office to redeem his passport.

"Time to go," he whispered in Loïc's ear. "The receipt?" Loïc searched his pockets and handed it over.

Two policemen were in conversation. His passport was being thumbed through. Questions were being asked, watches looked at. Loïc was being sized up. A report about the bombing was coming through on a handset. Then the tension switched. Loïc had his passport in his hand and it was Wilbur steering him by the elbow out across the flat tarmac. It was Wilbur that pushed him up onto the wing and in through the door. It was Wilbur that buckled both seat belts and ran through the take-off routine. Loïc stared at the white lines of the runway as the indescribable swam before his eyes and then he threw up again. He took on a jaundiced pallor and smiled weakly at Wilbur.

"Here, drink." A water bottle.

Drink. He did.

"Here, drink." A quart of whisky. He did.

Half way across Anatolia Wilbur told Loïc it was time to stop talking. He had insisted that Loïc tell all. Every detail, everything that was in him about the incident. 'We must have it all out now.'

Loïc told all from his graphic imagination, all from his eye for detail, all from his mangled emotions and now Wilbur had said 'it's better out than in.' They flew on in silence. Occasionally Loïc shook. At times he drifted off and shook. Wilbur stayed on course for Konya.

32° 48' 34" North 43° 40' 31" East.

Time passed slowly. At one point, when Loïc seemed to have slept, Wilbur suggested a story.

Loïc said. "No."

"It's about the Blacksheep and the Whitesheep."

"No thanks."

"They lived on the land we're flying over right now."

"Wilbur, really not now."

"They were tribesmen Loïc. Who fought for power over this territory. There was Jihan Shah and Tall Hasan."

"Wilbur, I'll put together something to eat." Not that he felt like eating.

Wilbur settled for the food, passed on the fighting and sat at the stick whistling. Loïc fumbled in the tiny galley thinking about the layers of significance that encase everything. Layers that move from brittle to fluid and serious to trite in moments.

Once the tarmac of Konya airport was beneath the Skyhawk wheels Loïc knew it was time to leave the sky trader to his devices and take to his feet again. Wilbur was more concerned about Loïc's state of mind than losing a good co-pilot. He gave him a list of Konya contacts and a small package. Loïc pulled out his broken bow and Babongo arrows as an exchange. They said goodbye at the glass doors of the airport, shook, embraced and laughed.

"Come to Arizona one day, just ask for Wilbur Carter, distant relative of Howard the Egyptologist, you'll find me." Then he was gone to his Skyhawk.

31
Konya

A row of taxi drivers waited to pounce. Loïc was in no mood for being hassled and produced some Afghan currency. Turning over the worn foreign notes the first driver despaired. Other drivers swarmed round and then walked away clicking their tongues. A young man standing by carrying a briefcase asked Loïc whether he spoke English.

"I do."

"If you like I am going to the city, you can share a taxi with me. I can show you where you can change currency."

"That's kind, Konya is new to me."

They rattled into town. The taxi was upholstered with a red flock fabric. On the radio Oum Karlsom sang at volume eight.

"She's everywhere." Observed Loïc as they all sang, 'ah Habeebee, ah Habeebee' and waggled their heads.

It transpired that the young man was on his way to work in a bank. As they entered Loïc saw a reflection of himself in the glass doors. A scraggly beard under a mop of hair. His clothes were Wilbur's and although smart enough, were at least a size too big. His shoes, stitched together many times by wayside cobblers were ready for the rubbish.

At the international change counter Loïc handed over all the money he possessed. Mostly rupees and a few Afghani notes. A disappointing return in Turkish lira was explained as only being possible because he was a friend of one of the banks' employees. He waived to him as he sat at one of the teller's booths and stepped out into a wall of bright sunlight. Dazed by recent events and being in a city Loïc made his way down a shaded street and found a café. He ordered and they asked him to sit outside, indicating his beard as the reason. He drank a coffee ate a pastry then counted his new notes, knowing nothing of their value he enjoyed their newness.

Across the street, with the door open a small shop

displayed a large cut-throat razor and a pair of scissors in the window. Loïc watched men as they entered and left the shop. After a second coffee Loïc did likewise.

'Needs must' he thought as he entered the small slot of a shop and was shown to an adjustable rexina upholstered barber's chair. Within seconds he was being lathered up and the blade was being honed on a leather strop attached to the wall. With surgical precision his face was skived, soaped again and deep-razored, leaving him smooth uncut and with a moustache that emphasised his smile. Next the barber took a length of cotton from a reel, doubled it, twisted it and opened a loop in one end with his thumb and forefinger. Then trapping rogue hairs in the untwisting cotton he plucked them out by the follicles. A mirror was held behind his head and the result was shown in the mirror in front for the customer's approval. Loïc remembered how he had looked in the bank door and stared at the pale face in front of him. He went to rise and a restraining hand was laid on his shoulder. The barber then began a scalp massage. Taking hanks of his hair and tugging it away from the skull with popping sounds. Once he'd finished his whole head the barber took a flat tin from the mirrored shelf and gave Loïc a light pomade with a rare smear of Dapper Dan, removed the white cloth and brushed the loose hairs from his neck and stood aside.

Loïc eased himself out of the chair half expecting another treatment and gave the barber a note. The barber looked at it and handed it back. He settled for thirteen notes. Loïc realised that once again he was not a rich man. Almost forgetting his bag, he stepped, as many others had before him, out on to the street feeling exposed.

His next step in that narrow street was into a shop that displayed a soiled white shirt on a coat hanger outside. In the depths, past rolls of cloth sat an elderly gentleman behind a hand operated gold scrolled Singer sewing machine. He no longer turned the handle, he was that experienced that he only needed to spin the heavy drive wheel with a quick flick of the wrist. A single bulb hung over the low machine table.

Loïc made out that he was interested in the materials that lined the walls. The old tailor continued working. He glanced up and assumed he had another undecided customer but when he glanced again he realised that this one was different from the average Konyan. This one was from somewhere else, altogether different. A smile spread enormously across his face. Loïc felt pleased to be seen.

"Your language may I ask?"

"French." Loïc said, without even noticing the Arabic spoken by the old man.

"Ah French. Bon. I also am a little French. Un peu de pied noir. On my mother's side. Ici assis, he patted a chair, tea with sugar?" His hand poised over a counter bell.

"Avec."

He hit the bell hard, twice. They laughed and from then on it was only French.

A small boy arrived from the back of the shop.

My grandson, Ishtar. The boy smiled. Offered his hand.

Loïc took it." Loïc."

"Loïc." He repeated.

You're the first person for a long time to say my name correctly. The boy's smile was going to be even bigger than his grandfather's.

He went for the tea.

Over tea with the machine still, these two men were in accord. Sharing incidents and the delights of France like old friends. One from the point of view of a child from the mountains the other view from being an embassy official in his youth. They both revelled in the tongue for a while.

"Pantaloon." Loïc indicated his trousers at a slight pause in their exchange.

"Yes, pantaloon, stand, let's take a look. Not bad shape but they need shortening". He gave Loïc some pull-ups and sat at the machine. Loïc took in the shop as the tailor took up Wilbur's trousers.

After an effusive 'au revoir,' and 'retourne bientot.'

Loïc found the first shoe shop in the street. The owners reluctantly disposed of his very old shoes which would have no doubt met with Mr Dar's disapproval, not once had they been cleaned. Then he stepped into the street in a pair of black plastic sandals which he though were vaguely stylish until he found that most people in the lower income bracket were wearing just the same.

Finding some midday shade was soon a necessity. Walking close to buildings was about to become useless. When he came to an overgrown section of wall with an even more overgrown doorway, Loïc stopped. He sat on the steps in the lush shadows and leant back against the ancient studded door. As he relaxed he realised that the decorative hinges were barely rusted and the door eased open. He entered. Inside was also overgrown. Jasmine and oleander competed all along the wall on the street side. Steps led up and in. Either side metal curlicue balustrades were fitted into the stone steps. At the top the full glory of an abandoned garden grew out of a geometric complexity into a tangled naturalism. A template of Islamic art. On three sides windowless buildings towered, but on the fifth floor of the building opposite the street there was an exception, a window, one with closed shutters and a balcony. Directly below this window was a door at ground level, also closed. Eight tall palms flourished untended, dead fronds hanging ragged and rattling in the slight breeze. The palms, it seemed stood at the points of a mandala water garden. The channels blocked with leaves, the fountain dry, the glazed tiles geometric and cracked. Shaded by the palms, Loïc lay out along a low wall and slept.

His dreams were troubled but he did not wake. His groans were audible and the shutters of the one window were open when he woke. The darkness of the interior ceiling told him nothing, only that what had been closed was now open. He had been observed often, on this occasion he cared little and explored his surroundings in the broken heat.

The garden was arranged with a pavilion at either end, facing east and west. From these it was terraced down in layers of mixed planting flowers, fruiting trees and soft fruit intermingled with ground fruit, all restrained within architectural hedges now out grown and collapsed. Weeds pushed up between the decorative tiles that paved the central fountain from which the clogged irrigation channels spread out. It was as if the day that the gardener had ceased to come to work, the owner had no longer noticed.

As Loïc lay on a raised dais in one of the pavilions that he remembered the package that Wilbur had thrust into his hands. It was in his bag down at the fountain. As he speculated as to its contents he became aware of a movement, a fluttering, not a butterfly, a small light. It trembled on the tiles next to him. At first he pretended to ignore it as if it was not intended for him, but then it played across his clothes. It was then that he reached out his palm and the sun's reflection moved to his hand. Where he moved it followed. For some time an intimate dance took place. Leading, following and losing contact, finding it again and playing. It was when he looked up that he was blinded and prevented from knowing any more. When he looked again the shutters had closed.

The garden had a rhythm of its own. There was a profusion of fruit, many of which Loïc had never tasted before. On the morning of the second day, the fountain began with a trickle and increased to a flow. Channels filled, brittle leaves clattered along the water surface gathering at bends, encouraging Loïc to take notice. As a small child he had played in irrigation ditches, as a man he now ensured that water reached down every channel to each border and tree swale.

Wind had gathered shiny greying leaves in swirled heaps at corners and along paths. Loïc swept them to the outer reaches of the garden with a fringed besom. When he lay in the shade, retreating from the midday heat, the mirrored light again asked him to play. Again the disc of light played across his body, insistent and intimate. Again when it ceased the shutters closed.

Loïc had need of soft contemplation. His belief in humanity had been torn. How could an adult teach children to kill themselves and other children, in the name of anything? He felt skinned, raw and exposed as if his emotions had become physical. He needed the privacy of this garden to busy his hands and calm his heart.

On the third day as he lay, the mirrored light again came to tremble across his reclining form, and for a while the game of move and follow played itself out. Then it disappeared and it its place on the balcony stood a girl in an embroidered dress, bell shaped and porcelain. Loïc stared, believing her to be a phantom, some being from another time, her rich clothes suggesting a past century. Then as if called from inside, she closed the shutters behind her.

By now the garden was taking on some semblance of attendance. He began to feel his vitality return. Directing water, eating fruit and breathing was easing him out his state of shock.

Come the morning of the fourth day there was no mirror, no dance, and no play of light. Shutters stayed closed.

A vapour settled upon the garden. A blanket of evaporation hung in the air. Water droplets gathered on outstretched leaves, drips returning water to the soil. With water, the garden had begun to regenerate itself.

The door opened. She stood there, mirror in hand, diminutive, dark and with intense eyes, her mouth caught open as if on the edge of speech. Entranced, Loïc walked to where she stood, reached out and took her hand. Together they walked, nothing spoken, droplets falling on dry hollow leaves accompanied their path toward the fountain. With little space between them they sat on the splattered surround. She trailed her hand in the water. He sat devouring her naked face, her soft openness. The drips from her fingers formed intersecting rings on the water's surface. Their eyes met and held. Deep and long they travelled through the stories inside each other until sadness and a freshet of tears brought them to the present. Saline beads traced runnels down their cheeks. She caught his tears with her lambent tongue and took them into her mouth and drank his pain. Never had he seen such beauty act with such bravery, draining the images of death from his heart. She held his gaze and waited. When he did start to shake she moved closer and with the lightest of embrace, held him. Once he was calm she took his face in her hands and kissed his eyes. Nothing was spoken, only the occasional 'thwak' of a falling dead leaf, sounded. The surrounding city of Konya remained mute and distant. As shadows started to reach up the windowed wall she became agitated and left him and the garden, passing through the door to reach the shuttered window before it lost the sun.

Loïc, empty and exhausted, watched her back, the door and the shutters remain closed. That night he slept the sleep of a dead man and woke with rheumy eyes. Making his way to the fountain he brushed aside floating leaves and slowly immersed himself in the shallow pool. The water still held the night's chill. He lay with his face only in the air, the cool water penetrating his drained body. Arms outstretched, buoyed by breath, his body floated. Breath by breath he rose and fell, loosening each part of his body in turn, relaxing, completely, drifting between the rotting detritus below and the crisp air above. Even his brow let go, his thoughts becoming incomplete, his monkey mind frustrated by nothing to grasp

'What to say,' Sri Pukka Baba said in Loïc's head.' What am I not?'

Loïc without a thought replied.

'An empty bubble on a page of pictures.'

'Very true, very nice Loweek.'

A smile spread across his polished face, as he rose and fell, liquefied, his body twisting slightly as each lung filled.

Easing himself from the pool, he sat naked absorbing the sun.

The mirror was a conundrum; she was his mirror. She had reflected all his feelings the day before. He glanced up at the window, finding it firmly closed. A fine dust seemed to fill the air. It was time to move on. He collected some fruit and instead of eating he put it carefully into his backpack, discovering Wilbur's package at the same time, the three lapis nodules from the rock shop and a list of contacts in Konya. Also there was Sri Pukka Baba's comic with the bubbles waiting to be filled. Fully dressed, he opened the door onto the street and stepped out, closing it behind him. Small particles of dust were settling everywhere, so that even slow moving animals appeared merged in colour to all horizontal surfaces. A high altitude wind swept overhead, blocking out the sun and leaving in its wake a city the colour of the desert that lay out to the west.

Loïc walked, Oopie's cover draped over his head, gritty air between his teeth. At the first teashop, he entered and closed the door behind him.

Steam rose from his glass of tea, the air continued to drift a fine silt. The owner closed the windows then handed Loïc a newspaper which, between them, they rolled into tight lengths and wedged them into gaps around the door. With wet cloths they wiped the surfaces and, as if this happened often, settled in for a wait,.

The café was half full and the proprietor set to cooking, knowing he had a captive clientele for the time being. In one of the corners sat a table of young foreignersl maps, postcards and a compass lay on the table, amongst cups and plates. They spoke a mixture of languages and gave off an atmosphere of adventure.

"Students," the proprietor said as he put a bowl soup down on Loïc's table. "Going north to Istambul."

"Into Europe?" Loïc asked.

"Ask, ask." He replied.

Loïc supped his soup and considered the lively group from the other side of the café. It was a long time since he had been around a group of his contemporaries. They seemed to be very loud and rather daunting. He found himself being opinionated about their behaviour before even speaking to them. He was surprised and somewhat disappointed with himself.

'No judgement, no projections.' Came to him as he filled in a bubble from Sri Pukka Baba's comic.

The soup was good, spicy and hot. He focused on the bowl and spoon. One of the girls left the table to talk to the proprietor. She smiled as she passed his table. Encouraged he spoke to her as she returned.

;Yes,; they were going to Istanbul. 'Yes,' they were going back into Europe. 'Yes,' they had transport, a camper van." She didn't know, but there might be room for one more. She would have to talk to the others. "Why don't you join us?"

By midday the wind had dropped. The layer of dust

outside was thick and crumbling off the edges of everything. The clear sky emphasised its colour. Any movement stirred up clouds of red powder.

Loïc left the café with the group to check on the VW. There were five of them, two German men, their Dutch and Spanish girlfriends and Leyla who had smiled at him. She seemed to be more reserved, non-European, and Turkish speaking. They agreed that if he paid for the petrol to Istanbul he could ride with them. They were broke and he'd have to sleep outside the van. Loïc explained that first he would have to sell something. Wilbur's stones and addresses were going to be useful after all. Leyla agreed to help and they set off across the city while the others fitted new air filters onto the air-cooled engine.

Between the old centre and the outskirts of Konya lay a vast swathe of neat suburban housing. Planted compounds surrounded large apartment houses that spread across distinct areas bounded by rail and road routes. Multilevel blocks sat in pools of tarmac, linked to coloured plastic play parks and convenience stores; bland soulless zones designed for human storage. It was into one of these areas south of the city that Wilbur's address list led them. Yenibahge was home to seven storey apartment blocks, rows of them. The earth red walls with white outlined doorways and windows were reminiscent of the old style houses, a few of which crumbled at the fringes of this expanding suburbia. On the fourth floor, they knock at a door, 'Stone Trader and Businessman'.

The door stops short of opening. A taut chain glints during introductions. A televised football match demands the man's attention. Not in business mode he smells of drink.

"Just briefly," Leyla insists, "we have a bargain for you."

Bargain is obviously a good choice of words. The door closes, then opens fully. The apartment is well furnished and allows for a view through a sweating metal casement, of a line of pine trees, the high-speed rail link and distant mountains. A balcony houses a row of dead plants, drying underpants and a disinterested cat.

Leyla talks him round to having a look, while Loïc unwraps the stones and the trader silences the shrieking commentator. His initial reticence evaporates as he rotates the stones in his hands. Rather too quickly he asks about price. Loïc has learnt that nothing happens without the formalities of tea and time. He already knows he's going to get a good deal. Between Leyla's charm and Loïc's hard bargaining they leave within the hour with a roll of notes and without 'the piece of solid sky.' It is only when they are well clear of the housing blocks and cutting through Hadimi Park that they look at each other and laugh. Loïc stuffs some notes into Leyla's hand and they race back to meet the others at the café.

The ride to the Bosphorus and Istanbul takes three days. After flying, it was tedious and prone to punctures. After walking it was like gliding through an unrolling film. With the exception of Leyla, his travelling companions seemed to be preoccupied with smoking marijuana and exclaiming in superlatives. When they stopped, which was often, Loïc took off into the nearest slice of landscape and breathed. With these people around him he felt very alone and not for the first time. Previously, be it trudging across a windswept plain or becalmed in mid ocean he had still been alert and absorbed in the details of the present. That openness now lay beneath a layer, a film of self-protection. The aliveness of immortality had become dulled, bleached, leaden even functional. Within these 'post bomb' feelings his aloneness had grown. It's one thing when everyone experiences the same overall trauma; there's a common silence. Being alone with his horror left him feeling cheated, speechless, uninjured, not worthy of pain; when the tongue is numb the body loses its chief ambassador and loneliness is a bitter enemy to befriend.

The Bosphorus was neither river, sea, lake nor canal. This narrow passage between seas was a geographical oddity. Once, in ancient times the northern end of the Bosphorus was blocked by rock and soil leading the Black Sea to the north having a lower sea level than the Sea of Marmara to the south. It is said that an earthquake released the blockage and a deluge of water poured north into the land locked Black Sea engulfing the low lying cities and casting Noah's ark onto Mount Ararat. Whatever the past hides, the passage of the Bosphorus has been wide enough to hold east from west, and narrow enough for a stung cow to clear in a single leap. It is said that when Hera, the wife of Zeus, heard of his affair with Io, she turned Io into that cow, a bous, Then Hera conjured up a horse fly that stung the cow's rump and she leapt clean across, the crossing place-poros, leaving for us all the legacy of 'the crossing place of the stinging cow,' the Bosporus.

They swept across the Bosporus Bridge on a tide of evening traffic, hot noisy, still with the red dust of Konya in crevices and folds. In Ortakoy on the European side they checked the van into a garage to fix a puncture rather than search for a nights parking. The west bank part of the city was a clamour of evening trade, eating and relaxation, the streets full of people and rich cooking smells in the crepuscular light.

Loïc and Leyla chose a river restaurant where an oud player sat in one corner, music dripping from his fretting fingers. The tone was a poignant mix of melancholy and romance. They ate and talked and drank 'lions milk' Turkish style arrack. From the waters below rose the stench of human and industrial effluence. Traders shouted, car horns were incessant and animals bleated before the butcher's knife. The sunset was lurid and layered, the clouds relying on the air's pollution for their glorious variety of colour. They drank more and talked openly about themselves.

She had left her Kurdish mountain village in a truck one day at the age of four with her nine siblings, her parents, a few possessions and had driven to Istanbul never to return. Kurds amongst Turks. For the rest of her life she had been afraid of being found out. Her Turkish, she made sure, was perfect, but everyone knew she was a Kurd for other reasons that were unchangeable. They knew she was an educated Kurd, the dangerous kind, and vilified her despite all her conforming. There is no hiding place from your persecutors she realised and became an articulate radical in her teens, which led to many beatings and much humiliation.

"But," she said, "the hardest thing to swallow was the sneering I got from the Kurdish community, my own people, also ghettoised in Istanbul. They knew my father, they had been his tenants and some were even his creditors, they knew our story and mocked us as a family fallen on hard times, they were merciless."

They drank more arrack and sat closer together.

"My father, she said, once owned five villages."

Evidently a main man in the mountains. Villages means land, villages means land with water, land with water means wealth anywhere.

"He became addicted."

"To what?"

"To chance."

"Chance of what?"

"Chance of winning. He was a gambler, a true gambler, and he was certainly that. A true gambler doesn't know when or even how to stop. He is still a gambler."

"You mean?"

"Yes I mean he lost the lot, he lost five villages."

"That's why we left for Istanbul in the truck that day. He had even gambled our own house away. Even then, when he had nothing he couldn't stop. It's a kind of curse. In the face of all evidence the gambler still thinks he can win. It defies logic, but addiction doesn't recognise logic so he's worse than poor now. He's still got my mother but he's lost me."

"So what now?" asked Loïc.

"Europe, I want to study in England. That's why I'm travelling with these people, they might be able to get me through the border, if I'm lucky," a tone of irony in her voice.

A rain shower cut short their evening but not the feeling of trust.

The next morning started with a quick coffee and then the daylong journey to the Ipsala border and into Greece. Six passports were handed in together on the Turkish side and handed back. The same on the Greek side but only four were handed back. Loïc and Leyla were called out with their bags. They glanced at each other and climbed down. They were led across hot asphalt into a bare interview room and told to sit. A large perspiring man came in and rolled up his sleeves.

"This," he said holding up Leyla's passport. "does not mean you can enter my country. And this, he said holding up the Elvis artwork, is a fake."

He flipped through a few pages, took a school rubber

from his pocket and simply rubbed out the Indian entry stamp. Then he threw them both down on the table and pointed at the Turkish frontier.

"You," he turned on Leyla, "have to pay a fine of 200, now."

"I have no money." Her cultivated Turkish accent irritated him. She was probably better educated than his own children.

"Now or jail."

Loïc was being pushed towards the door. The immigration official needed to get nasty with someone and this girl would do.

"What else have you got?" he leered at her.

The door was about to close. Loïc knew moments never return.

"I have the 200". He shouted.

"Bring him back."

He looked almost disappointed as Loïc peeled off the notes from his lapis sale. Loïc grabbed her hand and the two passports and hurried out and across no man's land to the Turkish side. The Turkish immigration officer was waiting for them. To get back into Turkey it was going to cost them another 200. Loïc handed it over and within twenty minutes they were back where they started, 400 poorer and without transport. The Germans had been told to keep driving and were nowhere to be seen.

That was that, they had been thrown together between east and west. A drudge of intercontinental trucks lined the roadside. They shouldered their bags and walked. Away from the checkpoint a group of drivers were cooking at the roadside. They stopped and talked.

"Yes they could be smuggled through, but not from here. Back in Istanbul was the stowage point."

"No, no they were just drivers."

Very quickly they seemed to know nothing, but one of them did give Loïc a map, just to get rid of them.

"Chios, try Chios," he said as he turned his back on them.

Before dark they were back at the crossroads town of Kesau and signing into a cheap pension as a couple. They sat on a bed with the map spread out between them.

32
The Closing Door

Chios lay anchored in the sea 3ks off the Turkish Anatolian coast but Chios was in Greece. Leyla knew the map of Turkey and its neighbours well. She had spent hours considering ways out but never had Chios been a possibility.

"There is a history of bad press around trying to leave Turkey by sea," she said. "The newspapers have covered a migration racket deliberately. Large sums of money have been taken in exchange for providing migrants with inflatable craft and knives. The instructions given are to slash the boats once in Greek waters and hope to be rescued by the paramilitary Helenic coastguards coming out of Piraeus. The co-ordinates, 37° 56' north by 23° 38' east, have become included in the lyrics of a popular song. Everyone under thirty knows where the nearest port Authority is in Greece."

She explained. "The route is too popular, the Greek Coastguards now watch people drown and then ship their bodies back to their relatives once a deportation tax has been paid. It's very dangerous to go with these crooks, anyway they want the kind of money that we don't have."

"So what do you know about Chios?"

"It's much further south, near Izmir. I don't know Izmir. To get there we either go back into Istanbul or we go south and cross the gulf of Marmara at the Dardanelles."

She slid her finger across the map. This was another long channel joining the Mediterranean to the Marmara Sea, through the Bosporus gap and the Black Sea.

"Can you swim?"

"Yes."

"How far is it, could only be a couple of kilometres, perhaps there's a boat, let's do it."

It was fast becoming apparent to both of them that it was more important that they were together than what they did. The pressure to get out of Turkey had dissolved into smiles and humour. They travelled south and reached the Dardanelles early in May. Next to the Hellespont a group of neoprene clad swimmers congregated at the water's edge at Eceabat. A small motorboat bobbed on the waves. Their arrival had coincided with the annual re-enactment of the swim made by the romantic poet Lord Byron. This group of swarthy aesthetes were the Byron society's active arm preparing for the great bi-centenary swim in memory of their hero, the next day.

They glanced at each other and checked in with the organisers for an acclimatisation swim and were allowed to join the knot of wetsuited swimmers. Introductions were brief and the camaraderie strong. A recitation of a few verses from the lengthy poem Don Juan were delivered at a measured pace and then they were off, leaping into the choppy waters of poetic impulse. If these people were mad they didn't show it, instead everyone struck out with determination. Loïc and Leyla followed suit. The outboard motor started and megaphone directions followed the swimmers for twenty minutes against the current. Then a 'return horn' sounded and they swam back as a huge oil tanker ploughed down the central channel.

"The straits are a notorious channel of water." Stated one of the instructors as they dried off. "Millions of tons of water pound through here every minute. The current from the north is colder and greater and moves at speed in the central channel. The two mile crossing is immediately turned into three as everything is swept southwards. There are warmer counter currents driving up from the Aegean, these are the ones you were in today, but these cling to the banks. The floor of the central channel has been ribbed by the water's force making the flow move in huge undulations. When there's an adverse wind it makes it nearly impossible to swim freestyle without choking on seawater. There are more features to swimming this east west divide, it's home to thousands of jelly fish, most of them harmless and there's lots of flotsam, some rising from the British, French and Turkish wrecks that litter the bottom. Then there are blobs of oil from the numerous oil tankers that plough their way up and down.

For the swim we have the straits free of them for only two hours, and beware in this air temperature expect severe sunburn."

He looked around, most of the swimmers were having at least second thoughts but none showed it. Despite the talk of danger myth exerts a force upon the imagination, driving people to defy their limitations.

"It was Leander of Abydos that started all this swimming. Nightly, so the story goes he swam from Asia to Europe, drawn by a lantern in the window of a Sestos tower. A tower that housed Hero, a priestess and unlikely 'virgin' of a love cult. Each night he swam to the arms of his lover. His was a prowess that Lord Byron in 1810 found irresistible. Being the notorious club footed lothario that he was, it was the swimming of the Hellespont that was the challenge. Undaunted by the fact that Leander died one night when Heros' guiding lantern was extinguished by the wind, Lord Byron and his friend Lt Ebenhead plunged into the water. Byron using breaststroke, to the consternation of the English 'chatterati' back home, crossed in an hour and a half. What they didn't know was that Byron had another side to his story. Unlike the sun-factored and wet-suited swimmers of today, Byron wore only woollen long johns and a grimace. The price he paid, midway, was in the form of a chill, 'ague' was how he described it. His swim was heroic, but it left him exhausted and shaking, and in the keeping of a local fisherman and his wife on the far Asian side. For five days and nights they nursed the fevered Byron until better. Then they provided him with bread, cheese, wine and a few paragraphs for the safe return journey. Byron touched by the selfless generosity of the man, sent Stephano his valet, back with a brace of pistols, fishing nets, a fouling piece and a 15 yard length of silk for the gracious wife, by way of thanks."

"Little for a life you might say."

"Byron's generosity it seems had a peculiar effect. Taking leave of his wife the fisherman took a boat to cross the Hellespont to thank Byron himself. Whether he had other motives, or was carrying the brace of pistols, we will never know as in mid crossing there was a storm and the craft and all aboard were lost. This outcome was not one Byron talked of often as it raised the question of the consequences of one's actions. However he did maintain that, regardless of every one of his achievements in life, swimming the Hellespont was his greatest. Hearing of this death at sea, Byron sent 50 dollars to the fisherman's wife saying he would forever be her friend. Seven years later Byron was again in Canakkale and he went to visit the wife and her son. It is said she didn't recognise him in his lordly dress. As for the son there was no mention of his age."

"That's all I have to tell you." The club secretary said.

"See you tomorrow, good luck."

Tomorrow was soon enough.

Suitably clad, with swim caps, Loïc and Leyla mingled with the international group of open water enthusiasts. There was the smell of thyme on the warm breeze as the shipping channel closed and the race began. They all plunged into the water and struck out for the distant shore. A small flotilla of boats, bearing doctors and stewards followed in their wake. Some were competing with the clock; most were there solely for the challenge. Many wouldn't make it but for now the water was a flurry of arms, legs and enthusiasm.

The warm shore current soon gave way to cold choppy water flowing south. Loïc lost sight of Leyla as his freestyle gave way to a slow breaststroke. He was really unprepared for the strength of the current. At first he thought if he just kept swimming he would arrive, eventually, but the Hellespont was far from being a passive mass of water. It had its moods, and today was turbulence within the strong southerly draw. Even the stronger swimmers were having difficulty staying on course, but Loïc found however hard he swam forwards, he only moved sideways.

After half an hour he was alone and downstream. He could only see the boats, the shore was no closer. Then the current became the colour of cold metal. He found it harder to breathe and he lost all feeling in his hands and feet. The bravado that had driven him, ebbed away, and in its place rose up from the depths a fear; how could he have forgotten the terrible drawing down sensation that deep water had on him. He pushed against it and swam with more determination.

He soon found that fighting the fear was not going to work, fighting water never did. It was then that the cramps started in his legs. However hard he swam, his legs were contracting with pain. He knew 'the distress wave', was his only option. They were next to him very quickly; in these conditions drowning was very likely. They hauled him aboard as he groaned with pain. They wrapped him in foil and took his pulse and blood pressure then rubbed him down. Wherever he put his legs it was the wrong position, everywhere was worse. Intense gripping spasms bit into him. A hot drink was thrust into his hands and someone started massaging his calves. That made it worse but he knew it was the only way. Gradually there were pain-free moments as the muscle contractions became less frequent. They plied him with water, tilting the bottle to his lips.

Where was Leyla, surely she must have drowned? She had said she could swim but this was serious open water. Slowly Loïc came back from his pain, sipped the drinks and took in the situation. There were three other swimmers wrapped in blankets in the boat and the crew were alert for others that were flagging. The real swimmers were far ahead, hauling themselves freestyle through the choppy tidal rip. Coloured skull caps and strong arms amidst a blue grey turbulence. Then he saw a mauve cap, could that be hers? He decided it must be and watched carefully. Definitely female, swimming strongly, keeping pace with a small group behind the leaders. He was impressed, and realised that he wasn't easily impressed. His boat sped off to pick up another swimmer and he lost sight of her. They were over halfway by now and more and more swimmers needed to be rescued by the flotilla of small craft. The current in the midstream was immense and this huge mass of water being forced through a narrow channel, cold meeting warm resulted in turmoil. This was the main reason why east and west had evolved so differently. One strip of water two miles wide had for millennia determined two very singular forms of culture.

Reputedly the same Alexander of Leh berry fame had bridged this divide with a pontoon of boats. Herodotus reported that Xerces had in AD 482 done likewise from the eastern shore when he invaded Greece. Four years it took calculate how to move an army the size of a small city across the Hellespont and invade Greece. After four years of planning he too managed to build planked bridges across boats anchored a few metres apart all the way across and move men, animals, supplies and camp followers across to fight a well-planned battle. An engineering feat that all looked good until a storm broke and swept away their retreat route before returning from their march around the Gulf of Melas.

What was clear was that on a mild day such as this one, the strength of the current beached even a good swimmer a mile or two downstream from where they wanted to be. As Loïc's boat full of rescued swimmers docked at the naval fort near Canakkale, he scanned the other boats for Leyla, she wasn't on the shore, and then he saw a mauve cap being swept along the shoreline. She was tired and struggling to make the last hundred metres to land. A rescue boat was alongside but she waived it away as she battled with the flow.

Loïc ran to where she could see him, and jumped and shouted with his hands in the air. The current was strong but she was making progress despite exhaustion. He thought of leaping in but couldn't take her glory away like that. Instead he kept shouting her name and leaping about abreast of her drift, until way south of the naval base she collapsed on the beach. Race officials arrived and swept her off in a van to check her pulse and blood pressure. She soon recovered and they joined the throng of elated swimmers dousing each other with champagne.

That evening there was a meal in a shore side restaurant, most of the swimmers had never attempted an open water crossing before and were very impressed by Leyla. For that evening at least the Turks ignored her Kurdish origin and she became an international for the first time in her life. Byron's living descendant was one of the swimmers that completed and they spent the evening at the same table. Others from the same group left an open invitation to their yacht moored at

Chios.

"You know Chios?"

"Not yet, they smiled, What's your boat called?"

"Hero of course, we're looking for crew."

"But Hero threw herself from a tower, isn't that bad luck for a boat? said Loïc."

"We're re-defining Heros, the captain has to take the name Leander to get the job. We're keeping the water beneath them not between them."

They all laughed at that, but they were all so tired and drunk that they would have laughed at anything. The evening continued with dislocated banter and laughter until prizes were given, more photographs taken and people stumbled off to their beds.

Leyla and Loïc were back on the road.

They took their time, visited the Ruins of Troy, and slept out where and when it suited them in historic sites along the coast. The constraints of her family life in a small Kurdish community in Istanbul had curbed her availability to boys. Instead she had directed her energy into studying and being the best at everything. Loïc was her first lover, his tenderness made her feel safe. After making love, she shook and cried as he held her. Most of the time they spent together they stayed happily in the present but beneath the surface lay her trapped story. Loïc's recent experiences had presented him with insights into extremes. Indoctrinated violence and deep compassion had both been put in put in front of him in quick succession. He held her while she shook. She was grateful that he said nothing and refused to let her go.

Once they reached Izmir they took the road west through Uda and Cesme to the coast. The island of Chios floated in the clear Aegean just out to sea. Tying their possessions into plastic bags, they trapped air inside and attached a line, then took to the water. Despite the tides turning there was only a slight swell to swim through. They swam together, lazy, floating, playing, the warm water supportive and inviting. They were halfway across and swimming strongly when they first noticed the launch. The island, not exactly a closed community, was Greek, but lay next to Anatolian Turkey at the furthest reaches of modern Greece. It was a place of dry white rocks, laborious terraces, twisted ancient olives and fishing boats. One Aegean island amongst many. There was little to say that it hadn't always been this way. However as with everywhere nothing is as it seems.

The launch was at some distance, unmoving. It looked official but many boats are white. They continued to swim, towing their plastic bubbles. Mostly they focused on each other and the shoreline out to the west.

The thrum of the engine was upon them before they realised. Leaning over the handrail was a tanned man wearing sunglasses and shorts.

"You coming to see me?" he laughed. "You're the couple from the Hellespont, aren't you?" He removed his glasses.

The last time they had met he had been more than a little drunk, exhausted and elated.

"You want a ride?" He lowered a rope ladder and within an hour they were coming in to dock at Sunsail Vounaki Sailing School with freshly caught fish.

"This is not only a place of wealthy yacht owners, sun soakers and botoxed bathers, but also it is famous for a mastic, 'the tears of Chios'. Come to the club."

Once in the nautical bar, it was not the captain, but an old storyteller, a descendant of one of the children of Chios who recounted the experiences of the revolution of 1822 and the terrible massacre of 52,000 people and the depopulation of the island.

The story was one that he had been telling since he was fifteen. Now he told it professionally, without fervour, but keeping the Chian spirit afloat and on this occasion he had decided to tell of Chios former fame and glory.

Loïc and Leyla looked at each other, bought drinks and found seats. If this was the price for getting into Greece then a story sounded good.

"In the south of the island, lies the Apalates region. Arid hot and barren. However not so barren that nothing grows. Here the 'mastic gum', *Pistacia lentiscus*, grows as a low tree with gnarly limbs. A relative of the pistachio, hugging the ground, it casts a welcome shade but is not known for its fruit. In this harshness, its considerable fame is for its sap. For four months, from July to October the ground beneath the tree is cleaned of all leaves and debris and chalk calcite is sprinkled on the soil. Then 'kentos', 5 to 10 inch cuts are made in the lower branches.

From these wounds bleeds the sap, accumulating in 'psito', small piles on the calcium carbonate, which stops the chemical composition of the sap from changing. These clear nodules of hardened sap are collected and more kentos are made every four or five days. For four months these tears of Chios bleed onto the ground and are collected for cleaning over the winter months.

You may wonder why so much trouble is taken over the sap of a tree. The gum tree is one of the many trees that change our lives. Transported by the xylem cells of the clear sweet almond tree these pea sized globular tears have wept onto the sifted and tamped chalk calcite ground for some five thousand years. This bitter, refreshing piney gum has been chewed for curative reasons by countless generations all over the world".

They looked at eachother. Loic indicated the door with his eyes, Leyla nodded and they made for the deck outside the club house. Ranks of sun loungers bearing the melting forms of ageing yacht owners simmered themselves wreathed in the stench of high factor sun cream. Swollen botoxed faces turned in their direction to greet them only to find their youth unfamiliar. Nipped and tucked bodies prevented from their natural decline tottered awkwardly between the palm shack bar and the assisted toilets. There was no escape from the varnished deck except down the steps and onto one of the many sleek white yachts moored in the marina. Despite the obvious priveledge of these people they exuded a vulnerable frailty. Again they glanced at each other and dejectedly returned to the bar and the story teller who seemed to be speaking on behalf of the tourism department. Reluctantly they settled back into the same seats. They had evidently become snared in the Sunsail Vounaki employment system and the only way out was with a job on one of the floating plastic palaces. Resigned to their fate they opted for sitting it out.

The story teller rambled on in the unanimated fashion of a tired performer.

"The Mastic tree made Chios famous for it was only on this small island that it was cultivated.

But fame has a price to pay. That which rises must one day fall. After millennia of prosperity, events conspired and the Turkish rule of Sultan Mahmoud 11, the last great ruler of the Ottoman Dynasty proved to be the undoing of an old world order. Tired of being oppressed by Turkish rule the Greeks were ready in the 1820s to break free. Revolution was in the air and Chios, because of its special 'mastic status' was at first reluctant to join the path to independence, but join they did and as a result paid dearly.

The Sultan ensured that the price was genocide. Five out of every six people were killed by the Ottoman troops in the Chios Massacre. It was a merciless series of events that reached into the ears and hearts of Europeans. The Sultan ordered the deaths of all infants up to three years old, boys and men over twelve and women over forty. Only the prisoners who converted to Islam survived and the Christian population of 17,000 was reduced to 2000. The whole island ran red with blood and the tears of Chios took on a new meaning.

It was the small children that witnessed the deranged massacre. They, it was that spread the words of horror. They went as far as London, Paris and New York to tell their stories to mute audiences in theatres and cinemas. These audiences in turn were moved to tears. This was the first globally reported genocide to depress the world. Seen through the eyes of children, Chios was the harbinger of the next two centuries of killing madness.

Meanwhile the Mayans had moved into the ascendant on the chewing front. The chickle trees of the Yucatan peninsula had captured the restless jaws of the world and the mastic of Chios had to move over for chewing gum. This is why I sit in this bar and tell stories, to keep all the tears of Chios alive."

The bar had filled and emptied by the time the story had

been told. The locals had heard it all before and drank elsewhere. Those present didn't know whether to clap or cry and so they did neither.

"Crew, any crew want work? " a voice boomed out.

Loïc knew the score and recognised the voice. He grabbed Leyla's arm and stepped up to the bar where the captain sat fumbling with a satnav. It had been a long time since the maiden voyage of the Elephanta, but it wasn't difficult to make the right noises for both of them.

"She's a cook." Loïc insisted," No cook no crew. Where are you going?"

"Stromboli, Stromboli island and on."

"Where is Stromboli?"

"Stromboli my young would be crew member, is off Sciliy, nestled in the lee of the Italian boot, seven days or so west of here."

"Sounds good when do we leave?"

"When I know you can do the job."

"Is that your destination?"

"Ajaccio, Corsica, you know it?"

"I know Marseille."

"Ok that's where we're registered, but the owner's Corsican so we'll berth there."

Reassured by Loïc's manner the captain quizzed him on his experience.

"A brig out of Marseille and a old clipper out of the Cape Verde islands a few years ago and I have since crossed the Indian Ocean, but you don't need to know about that."

"I certainly do, but not now, later."

He knew he had a new crewmember with a yarn or two. He looked at Leyla.

"You any good?"

"I'll cook what you like. You tell me what you want and I'll make it."

He liked her directness. "Ok you're both on. Wages on arrival in Ajaccio, check with the bursar for the food budget."

That was it, no formalities, they simply moved into the crew quarters of the crisp clean plastic mod-yacht Hero, captained by aka 'Leander'.

"So this is the Byron boat?"

"That's one way of putting it, but not owned by the Byrons, they just play on it. That's the job, they play we sail. Whatever goes on up there you don't know about. Your job is to look smart, look the other way and get paid so you best get cleaned up and check your uniforms fit."

33
Consequences

Loïc noticed that everyone on board, without exception, was carrying a mobile phone. The passengers appeared to be constantly preoccupied with these devices, contacting and talking to people elsewhere and completely ignoring those that sat right next to them. Coltan was everywhere, in the satnav, the g.p.s., on the captain's wrist, the computers that appeared near every wall seat, the depth sounder, the radar, the game boys and all the sophisticated automatic steerage devices that covered the captains console, all were full of pinhead capacitors relaying signals around the craft and globally via the on board wifi. The struggle would be doing well down there in the Congo, demand was increasing; the death toll must be rising fast.

In the galley the huge microwave oven and the intense strip lighting added to the general hum of electrical frequencies. Surfaces were immaculate, onboard etiquette was defined and the division between client and service made apartheid seem liberal. To Leyla and Loïc the environment was a shock; severe and unforgiving, no blemish would escape. They checked out their narrow berths and resigned themselves to the inevitable constriction, grateful that they weren't compressed into the cargo of a Turkish truck.

After twenty four hours it was clear that Leyla had drawn the short straw, she was at the beck and call of the upper decks, day and night. Main meals were expected to be 'cuisine' and the demand for snacks was continuous. Loïc by contrast was told to stand within view but out of hearing. He was required to look intently at the horizon in an erect manner unless told otherwise. They had become menials. that was their price for entering Europe.

Chios to Stromboli taught Loïc the difference between sea and ocean, and the numbing effects of functioning as a worker with little expected of him. The superior attitudes of the passengers who spoke to him as if he was a lesser being, challenged his ethos of being non-judgemental about people. On board these things became acute as the top deck occupants indulged themselves and intoxicated their egos with cocktails, while he folded napkins and polished railings.

On the evening of the fourth day out of Chios, while Leyla and Loïc were stealing a few minutes in his cabin, a form fell past the porthole and silently dropped into the sea. They were unsure, the blur could have been a person. Taking the shortest route to the stern they peered into the evening swell. Traces of sunlight bounced off cloud edges and dropped into the reflecting sea. A shout, a female voice reached back to them, then died in the teeth of the water's slap and hiss. Loïc loosened the life belt and flung it as hard as the rail would allow. It coiled into the boats wake and sat draughtless on the disturbed surface.

Without thinking he jumped after it, consequence far from his mind. For late in the season the water wasn't cold, but it was the fear of depth that pumped his body into alert. He really hadn't worked this out. Thoughts crowded in vying for his attention, all without exception were laced with the same metallic taste. There were three women on board, two from the top deck, but why?

The life ring was in his hand soon enough, but from water level there was no sign of his reason for jumping. The ring's buoyancy made it hard to swim. With the cord in his teeth he towed it with a breast stroke away from the boats stern. After an initial shout of surprise Leyla ran to the helm to raise the alarm as Loic swam into the diminishing light. When he did reach her she was already exhausted, her face screwed into a ball of panic. He forced the ring under her arms as the question arose, 'what now?' Leyla would have told the captain, it was surely a matter of staying afloat for half an hour while they came back for them.

"What happened?"

"I've no idea," she gasped buoyed by the ring.

"I went to call my friend. I went to the 'hot spot' near the rail." The cell phone still gripped in her hand.

"Next thing I know I'm feeling dizzy, lose my balance

and then I'm in the water. It was all so fast."

"Just hang in there, they'll be back soon.' Loïc said, as much to reassure himself.

The Mediterranean currents at this point in the Ionian basin. converge on the surface from various directions which are then redirected and invigorated by deep water currents which in turn spiral, bifurcate and drive waters of changing temperatures in and out of the Adriatic to the north through the Strait of Otrando. Were it possible to see beneath the surface of the calm sea, extraordinary interlocking ring vortices grow and shed gyres and jets of exquisite smaller energetic eddies which also spin in spirals through other vertical strongly saline elliptical currents. The deep waters of the easterly Levantine basin drive the warmer surface waters towards the coastal land mass and on to the easterly Adriatic entrance off Corfu. Had all this aquatic choreography been seen by the two tiny figures joined by a white floating life ring, it would have been illuminated by myriad tiny coloured plastic particles that now swirl within its majestic formations, disastrously illustrating the invisible with the fragments of the unnecessary. A testament to the unintentional outcome of humanity's addiction to consumer forgetfulness.

The reality they experienced was by comparison the mundane attempt to stay alive while the sea drove and span their life ring on a clockwise course to an unexpected part of the Ionian sea, while their vessel searched the darkness in vain.

By the time dawn showed as a faint glow, they had sung every song they had ever heard even the ones that the words had escaped from. Not only had they been sung, these songs had been repeated, hour after hour. Their repetition had driven a wedge between sleep and exposure, formed an expression for will power and a cradle for the knowledge that neither of them had yet completed their lives. By mid morning they had been spotted and coastguards out of Syracuse hauled them thirsty but undamaged from the sea.

When contact with the Hero was made the next day, Captain Leander was hard pressed to believe the circumstances and reluctant to leave the explanation to Leyla alone. The girl, the daughter of a Greek shipping magnate was still clutching the evidence.

"This," she insisted, "is why; I've felt it before, usually I get headaches and feel weak. It's the microwaves coming off mobiles and computers, all that stuff. I have an intolerance to it. Thanks to this guy I'm still here." Nodding, she looked at Loïc and threw the phone into the sea.

Another cheap death in the Congo, thought Loic. Then it was back to normal, resumed identities and uniforms.

When they reached Stromboli via the Straits of Messina it was night. The island glowed, ribbons of lava hissing into a sea that reeked of sulphur and congeries of light grey pumice balls floated in rasping swirls. The volcano gave off a plume of industrial style smoke and had been doing so for the last two thousand years. They didn't stop, there was nothing to stop for. Once reached Ajaccio harbour was a sweet sight to Loïc and Leyla, who were down the gang plank with their bags and wages as soon as they docked. The electro sensitive girl wanted to reward Loïc asking him for his email address. Loïc laughed, said nothing and shouldered his bag.

Corsica grew wild, wind blown and scented. Jagged outcrops of rock hugged the cave-pitted skyline. The maquis, a dense mixture of low growing thorny plants that made most of the landscape inaccessible protected a place locked in traditions. One of these was the vendetta.

From Ajaccio to Bastia in the north of the island there ran a single track narrow gauge mountain railway, with passing places at remote mountain village stations. They took it and at one station, Casamozza, a nervous young man joined them in their compartment. He nodded and sat blankly watching the passing greenery that brushed along either side of the carriage.

"You're going to Bastia?" He eventually asked.

"Yes and on to Marseille."

The ice broken, he told them that he was on the run from the police and the women of his family who lived near Filatosa, the enigmatic megalithic settlement to the south, famed for swords carved in stone. Nervously he explained. Three generations ago his grandfather had shot his neighbour's donkey for repeatedly grazing his unfenced grass. This had inflamed the neighbour, who, instead of shooting his grandfather's donkey had shot his grandfather. This shot to the leg didn't kill but instead left an embarrassing limp. Now retribution for such a cowardly act required an act of honour. One morning, with gun in hand, his grandfather had limped the short distance to the neighbour's house, rapped on the door and shot dead the young son of the family when he had answered it. This outrageous act triggered the involvement of the 'voceri'. The women of the family gathered around the corpse of the child layed out on the kitchen table. As they washed him and prepared the body they sang. Their voices full of anguish and pain, their words exhorting their men folk to exact revenge. As the priest had quoted from the good book. 'An eye for an eye and a tooth for a tooth'. "Biblical." he said as if that excused everything. Their voices rose in a wailing threnody; the 'voceri' incited their men to meet like with like. To remain men in the eyes of their women, one of them would have to take up a gun. It was for them to decide who would pull the trigger, then run as a fugitive through the impenetrable 'maquis' and hide amongst the caves and forever sleep on a bed of goat droppings with that accursed pistol ready in his hand.

"Now two generations and four deaths later, I am the one who has to kill. All my life I have prayed that my parents would have another son, so that at best I would have a 50:50 chance of not having to kill my neighbour. But it was not to be, I am the one. The cycle is not broken till all are dead. That's why I ride this train."

"Why are you telling us these things?" Loïc asked.

"Because now it is my turn to kill, and this I will not do. I will leave Corsica, my family and my life before I kill a man for a donkey chewing grass."

"But why if you haven't killed would the police want you?"

"Here honour comes before crime. My uncle is the chief inspector in Bastia. If he hears that I am trying to leave he too will lose face unless he stops me and sends me back to pull the trigger. That's the way it is here and has been for too long."

By the time the train had dropped down into Bastia the young man was so nervous, caught between guilty innocence and murderous obligation, that he feared leaving the safety of the train. He stayed sitting in the stationary carriage, clasping and unclasping his hands as if searching the air for some tangible substance to aid his next move. It didn't materialise, and when the train started back over the mountain he was still in his seat. As the growth either side of the track enveloped the reversing engine, they watched fascinated by his inability to escape his fate.

They ran for the Marseilles ferry, slept on the floor between the seats and woke to the smell of dead fish and the sound of police sirens as the city stirred into another precarious day of law and order.

It was time to part company, Leyla on her English quest, Loïc on the last leg of his journey home. As they embraced, the warmth of their intertwined bodies was buffeted by tannoyed announcements and the bass vibration of diesel engines. Then she stepped up onto the Paris train and was gone.

34

Doubt

Marseille, much to Loïc's surprise, was exactly as he remembered it aside from it no longer felt threatening. He now had a clear idea of where he was going as he left the crowded area around the station. It would take some walking to get back to his village but he had decided that it would all be too fast any other way. In addition, there was his trepidation about what he was going back for. How would he be received after all this time? What gift did he bring back from the outside world? His curiosity about Anna Cecille was swathed in an four year long fantacy. The untamed waters of the Carmargue with their vast stands of reeds and herds of wild horses gave him plenty of time to reflect on the uncertainty and excitement he felt.

Breathe. He told himself repeatedly.
Breathe and listen to what has been.

He slept out, making shelters and leaf nests as he encountered different vegetation. The sun high and hot in the day, the earth losing heat early, the off shore wind, almost continuous, driving him into byres and behind rocks as night chilled the air. Walking in the open day, the wind battered him with its rushing urgency to invade the sea. Seized from the land surface, sand, stalks and fragments of salt battered themselves against his face and hands. Reeds and the manes of white horses streamed like waves everywhere he looked. Snatching breaths from the greedy wind he marvelled at the stationary black bulls and the frail pink flamingos, merely ruffled at their feathered edges.

Two days of interminable trudging loosened his accumulated exhaustion. Movement had been his means of survival and surrounded by it now, unable to escape the insistent tearing at his clothes, released him into accepting how wind can enter the body and craze the mind. The mistral, the sirocco, the haramata, the sharki, all rushing from one place to another, unbroken, often seasonally driving the sane to the edge of tolerance and beyond. Loïc was relieved by stillness as he took shelter in the dunes of the upper riverine reaches of the fresh water marshes near Les Saintes Maries de la Mer.

Place of the three Marys, the three Marys that were witness to the empty tomb of Jesus. Perhaps the self same Yuz Asaf that now rests in the Kashmiri tomb on Rosa Bel Yameen street. Perhaps the self same Issa that spent time in Hemis Gompa. Doubt and Faith are forever joined. The Marys were cast adrift in a boat from Alexandria some years later to die at sea, or so the story goes. Sara, black Sara sees them coming in her dream and meets them with sustenance on the beach. Some say she cast her cloak on the waves, others say she walked across the water to bring them to shore. What's more, others claim that she, Sara came with the Magdalene, as a babe in arms, the child of Christ, to the shores of France. Whatever the truth, Les Saintes Maries is an annual place of pilgrimage for the Roma of the world. They come, and the relics of the Maries are lowered into the church nave and the statue of Sara is washed and blessed each year in the sea. The Rroma converge, make music, do business, arrange marriages and spend a little time in a kind of troubled joy.

They were just leaving as Loïc stepped aside from the mistral, The place had an air of debris and departure about it and Loïc stayed on the move westwards up onto the higher ground that had delivered him this way some four years before.

Away from the rushing turmoil of the wetlands Loïc recovered a small portion of his clarity. Like a soldier returning from a war, he carried the marks and scars of his journey, but he would not be able to talk of them. No one incident would summarise what he had become. He would not be able to give an account of himself by relaying events to those who might ask. The retelling of tales from his travels would never portray an atmosphere, never capture the taste of a fear or summon up the texture of a climate. As with a dream an unseen membrane of memory lay just beyond speech.

A hesitation came to him, that of returning. He had gradually become gripped by a nostalgia; an ache that grew the nearer he became to home. As the place grew closer he felt the possibility of his old love was more or less a memory. Ever since walking the other way through this windswept, sand strewn corner of the Mediterranean, he had known returning would be the most difficult thing he could do. Now, here he was and the closer he drew, the memory of his painful leaving grew more vivid. It clung to him like a second irritated skin, that in its dying is slothed off, revealing a tender more vulnerable, unscared layer. Loïc knew that he needed to confront this dilemma before getting any closer to its origin.

As the land began to rise so the saturated ground was reduced to streams and springs. At one of these streams Loïc stopped to drink and think. He sat repeating Druckshen's third fierce mantra.

Ci kyang dgos pa med.
I need nothing whatsoever.

Druckshen's last words had warned Loïc. 'The purpose of using a mantra is not to persuade your self of its content, rather to realise that it is so.'

Loïc sat mumbling, 'ci kyang dgos pa med', gazing into the stream bubbling over a seam of blue grey clay that formed the bed. Fragments of vegetation floated past, water insects busied themselves on the surface, minute shrimps sheltered from the current. He reached in and trailed his hand across the bottom. Blue grey fingertips came up to greet his widening eyes. He scooped out a handful of clay and softened it in his hands, feeling it draw the dirt from his skin. Within minutes he was stripped off and lying in the water working the clay into his back, then smearing more slip over his body. By the time he was questioning what he was doing, the sun was baking the slurry onto his cracking form. It felt good, he liked the way the hardening clay sucked at his skin and pulled at the hair follicles of his body. He became wide-awake and in the moment.

It is so; whatever you need, it is already there, at hand.

Turning, he baked his back in the sun. The whale and the Buddha mingled in the tingling surface of his tactile memory. As the hot clay dried it fell from his cooked skin and left every pore simultaneously cleansed and gritted with a fine dust. Finding a pool downstream he washed himself and lay out in the sun watching the movement of cells on closed red eyelids. Once he'd dressed he stepped out in the direction of St Paul de Fenouillet feeling new and able to face the present with refreshed eyes.

By nightfall a few days later Loïc had reached the Gorge de Galamus. The water level was high for the season and roared through the deep narrow cut. He knew of the hermitage but had never been there. After following the road under jutting cliffs, the small path down into the gorge would have been easy to miss if not for the moonshine leading him down. The night promised to be cold and wet and he made for the shadow of a cave entrance, readying himself for hard surfaces and a restless night.

35
Divination

The day was cooling by the time Anna Cecille reached the town of St. Paul de Fenouillet cradled between two stone outcrops running out to the east. She turned north and made her way up towards the higher ground, the bleached rocks and the rasping trill of cicadas. Gradually the road rose until it twisted its way into the Gorges de Galamus, a sheer slot cut deep through the ridge. The road was narrow and clung to the edge, occasionally creeping under huge overhangs that threatened to break away and block the gorge. Near the crest a small path led down inside of the chasm, this she took, down into the earth itself. After a short walk a large cavern opened out into the wall of the cliff. It reached back into the darkness and smelt of damp and incense.

Beyond was a tiny stone house nestled on a stone shelf. In this house lived the hermit of the Gorges de Galamus, alone except for one cat and one mouse who were the best of friends. It is not a usual friendship, but both cat and mouse preferred to play the game and never finish it. For if the cat ate the mouse there would be no friendship, so the cat pretended, never using teeth or claws and the mouse never ran too far. At night they would curl up together and sleep in front of the hermits fire. The hermit, who after many years of working in the gold mines in the mountains, had become tired of the ways of men and had moved to the gorge and become a solitary, alone with his thoughts about the meaning of life.

Occasionally people would come to him for advice or to read the rune stones that he used for divination.

It was mid afternoon by the time she knocked at his door. Her problem she carried in her hand and her heart. After a short while the door opened and a small man with a mass of curly hair and a beard stood before her. He gestured for her to come into the dark interior. Either side of the fire was a small three-legged stool and after the cat had rubbed itself against her leg she sat down opposite him. For a long time they sat in silence listening to the wood spit in the grate.

"What brings a young woman to the door of an old man?" he eventually said.

She opened her hand and showed him the key.

"This I have held for over four years, not knowing whether the owner will ever return for it, and now I need to know."

"Ah," he said, "is this the key to a door or the key to a heart?"

He weighed it in his hand.

"Both", she said.

"That is more complicated." He said turning it over, for it was of some size.

"I need to know whether it will be collected, for I am likely to leave the area if I don't speak with the owner soon."

A silence descended again.

The cat washed itself.

"We will use the stones," he said reaching up into a niche in the chimney breast.

While he arranged a small table in front of her she looked round the room. From the ceiling hung familiar bunches of dried herbs and flowers. In one corner stood a collection of sticks with carved handles. Animal heads; a bear, a deer, a hawk and others in their unfinished state. As she looked at these sticks she had the feeling that time had stopped, that there was no urgency, no hurry to know the answer to her question anymore. She watched a mouse come under the door, cross the floor and sit next to the cat and start washing its face with its paws. She marvelled at the feeling of love that arose in her heart, love coming from harmony.

"Are you ready?" he asked.

"I'm in no hurry, just being here is helping me to see things differently."

Sitting there they watched the sunlight slip up the side of the gorge wall opposite.

Presently the hermit opened the small pouch and poured out a collection of small stones, each bearing an etched symbol. He turned all face down.

"This," he said, "is one way of answering your question; there are others which you may know, but since you have come to me; I offer this way."

"I am in your hands. For many nights this problem has tormented me, and my answers are always too fearful. I now need to be clear so that I can act."

"We'll consult the ancients then." He said, circling his hand across the table, mixing the stones.

"Choose three, one at a time and turn them face up. But first I want you to sit for a while and consider your question, make sure it is what you want to ask, then silently make your request."

The tiny room stilled, pregnant with the advancing moment. The first she took with eyes closed, her fingers feeling their way towards a choice. She turned it and sat back.

"This," he said, "is reversed, this is Odin, the wise old man, the shaman. But reversed this rune is telling you of an elderly troublemaker. It talks of rumours and untruths that have been spread. Bad advice given in the past. True wisdom will come from an unexpected source. Does this mean anything to you?"

"Yes, this is part of the story."

"Now you need to take another, this one tells you about the present."

Again she closed her eyes and sat with her hands in her lap. Her brow was without lines, her shoulders loose. Her breath spoke of depth and acceptance. Again she reached out, this time into the centre of the stones, picked up the first one and turned it, it was blank. She turned it again as if mistaken, it remained blank.

"This, he said, is the way of Wyrd, the natural way. This rune tells you that the answer to your question is in your hands. If you have the courage and strength to hang on. Powerful forces are working in your favour at this very time and all will work out to your advantage in the end. Can you trust yourself?"

"I can, I will," she said, "I've had a feeling about this question for some time, but recently, yes I have lost my way with it all. It's good to hear that I should stay with my patience. The next one is for the future?"

"Yes, the last is that."

"I'll take my time with this one."

As the house darkened, she ran her fingers through her hair and washed her face with dry hands as if arranging herself before a mirror. He fetched candles and lit one on the mantelpiece. With eyes wide open her now trembling hand reached out over the table. In the distance, way down in the gorge, the faint sound of rushing water mirrored the rising wind that lifted the leaves outside the window.

"This one," she said holding the stone to her chest." This is the one."

She turned it and placed it on the table.

"You have drawn Tyr. Again this speaks of courage on the path, sacrifices made to keep the order of things. However mostly it talks of a passionate love affair, long lasting and with happiness as its outcome. Can this be what you seek?"

"Oh yes, this feels good already, I can't wait."

"Well, you will have to, there is nothing else to do, everything is already in motion. But soon you will be released from waiting."

By the time Anna Cecille closed the door behind her it was darkening. She had nowhere to go, but she needed to be alone with the outcome of the runes. She walked back to the cave and wrapped herself in her cloak. She slept to the sound of drips from above and the torrent below with the key to the 'old ship' gripped firmly in her hand.

36

Everything is Written

Limestone fingers hung, deposited over millennia by the passage of seeping water, fringing the entrance to the shallow cave scooped out by the waters of the Agly river long before the land had names. Loïc entered cautiously, looking to be deep enough inside to avoid the rain that threatened. Thunder shook the sky, amplified by the steep sides of the gorge that dropped vertically below.

A moan and a stirring body froze him.

The sky broke open. Lightning sprang a whiteness brighter than day. A covered figure lay within his reach. In that instant of brilliance he knew. In the clouded moonlight the figure turned and sat, woken by the storm, dazed by dreams. Caught in the next flash from the blackened sky they saw each other clearly.

Silently they reached out, their eager hands bruising the air, his chthonic odour meeting the scent of rosemary that clung to her. The darkened world shrank away from their exquisite intensity. Theirs had been a silent journey and even now there was more touching than words. Intrigued, they explored the adults they had become. She ran her fingertips over his scars and moistened his eyelids with her tongue. As he held her face, her hands became fascinated by the definition of his body. In turn he found soft eagerness fill his hands wherever they passed. She raised herself to meet him and they fell into a torrent of sweet relief. Rain roared from the sky, at the mouth of the cave a sheet of falling water. That night the valley below flooded.

A clear dawn seeped hesitant warmth into the recess where they lay, enfolded. In the clear exuberance of early blue sky they bathed in the foaming waters of the gorge, drying themselves on boulders in the sun. They took the direct cross-country route towards the village. Still neither felt the urge to speak, they touched, smiled and laughed. Mostly they just walked along stony paths through a landscape they knew like their own skin. By evening they emerged on the high 'crete' above the village.

At first, to Loïc it looked like another place. His memory was one of dereliction and ruins invaded by plants and narrow paths. Before him the familiar cadmium orange of pantile roofs had largely been covered by the sheen of passive solar panels. Houses that had been roofless with rotting timbers sheltering saplings were now rebuilt with bedding airing at the windows. White canvas yurts sat in flourishing gardens abundant with soft fruits and vegetables. Re-built stone terraces hid beneath cascades of pumpkins and melons. Orchards hung heavy, ready for harvest. A wind turbine churned in the light breeze. Cattle and horses grazed the hillside. The repaired water channel hugging the mountainside, filled by the stream two kilometres away poured into the old stone troughs. A school was under construction, buckets and blocks being passed hand-to-hand. The place was alive with the sounds of children, tools and water.

It was then as he searched for his own rooftop that he saw the familiar figure of his mother, basket on hip, come into the small garden at the back of their house. As she pegged and plucked at the washing Loïc realised there were none of his father's clothes shifting in the breeze. He turned to look at Anna Cecille.

She nodded." Three years ago."

Loïc waved, his mother stopped and slowly turned her face in his direction, but didn't see them up on the crete. She stayed like that, clothes over one arm, looking up, checking the sky. He turned to see behind him that bank of wave patterns again, surging in from the eastern coastal waters. A massive ceiling of rolling grey shot through with red rays of sunlight. *Asperatus undulatus.*

Then they ran, down the steep path, scattering goats, running over ground so familiar, they barely touched the surface.

It was then that his mother saw them. Her hand shot up to her mouth but from it came no sound. When they embraced, she wept, her head on his chest as if in prayer. Anna Cecille her hand supporting his mother's back, her own radiance laced with compassion. His mother stepped away from him to appraise this long gone son. Mother and woman, side by side, hand in hand, expressions of delight spread across their faces.

"Now that your father is no longer with us, you should know, he was not your father. Anna Cecille is not of your blood."

Loïc's eyes closed as he took in the significance of her words.

"So who was my father ?"

"A stranger came to the bar that day."

"A stranger ?"

"Our paths crossed again, we needed new blood here."

"The stranger with four matches?"

"Yes, four matches and later with a case full of insects."

Cloud swept in and submerged them beneath a canopy that clung imperfectly to the land beneath their feet.

Jack Everett was born in Uttar Pradesh, India. Trained as a sculptor, his work and commissions have taken him to many places. His writing comes out of a curiosity about, and acute observations of people and their adaptation to environments. His chacaraters all have their roots in reality since that is where the extraordinary resides. Verbal histories and experienced geography informs the canvas of his narrative and the dialogue of his distinctive cast. It is from documenting both his work and travels that 'A Case full of Insects' has emerged.

To contact the author.
bamboojack@hotmail.com